Praise for *The Rule of Thirds*

"*The Rule of Thirds* is a stunning novel that travels from the U.S. to Afghanistan and back again. Along the way, we meet fierce photojournalist Annie, the admiral who adores her, and a colorful cadre of confidantes. With masterful prose, Jeannée Sacken pits her protagonists, still freshly grappling with PTSD, against the Taliban and ISIS. The result is heart-pounding action paired with tender storytelling. Beautifully wrought and unputdownable, *The Rule of Thirds* earns 5 heartfelt stars!"

Carol Van Den Hende, award-winning author of *Orchid Blooming* and *Goodbye, Orchid*

"The energy from Jeannée Sacken's *The Rule of Thirds* hits you right in the face from page one as the story follows Annie Hawkins, Pulitzer Prize–winning photojournalist, back to Afghanistan to record the last days before the Taliban takes over. Annie Hawkins is every writer's dream character: tough as nails, badass extraordinaire, riddled with guilt, and filled with love for her daughter and the man she adores. Sacken's words speed through paragraphs and chapters, leaving her readers no choice but to feel the sweat, heat, dust, and dirt as it clings to every part of their bodies as they inhale this book."

Barbara Conrey, *USA Today* bestselling author of *Nowhere Near Goodbye*

"*The Rule of Thirds*, the final book in Jeannée Sacken's powerful Afghanistan trilogy, is a gripping, immersive, vividly rendered story that has everything a reader could want—complex and deeply human characters, a richly drawn story world, and a riveting plot with inner and outer stakes that keep us rooting for Annie Hawkins and the people she loves. Expertly told, *The Rule of Thirds* is a tale of courage, loyalty, determination, and resilience with an ending that's unexpected—and perfect."

Barbara Linn Probst, Sarton Award–winning author of *The Sound Between the Notes* and *The Color of Ice*

"I adore romantic suspense. *The Rule of Thirds*, the last in Jeannée Sacken's Annie Hawkins trilogy, offers another thrilling sojourn into war-torn Afghanistan. While reading (greedily consuming) this much anticipated novel, I appreciated once again the total immersion the author provides. Sacken also paints a realistic picture of how PTSD can impact one's life, career, and family. In this third novel, Annie Hawkins returns to Afghanistan a much less reckless journalist, yet one still willing to risk all for the lives of others. At just about any moment during this read, anything could happen. Careers could be lost, things could blow up, people might die, loved ones could be kidnapped, everything is at stake and the tension is relentless. As with her other novels, *The Rule of Thirds* stands alone, but read all three. It makes the conclusion of this last one so, so satisfying."

Jennifer Trethewey, author of historical romance

Praise for *Double Exposure*
(Book 2 in The Annie Hawkins Series)

This smart, propulsive novel is a thrill, with rich characters full of humor and heart. Sacken knows this world, and she portrays it with a masterful touch of suspense and surprise.

Steven Wright, author of *The Coyotes of Carthage*

Jeannée Sacken follows her excellent debut novel, *Behind the Lens*, with another superbly written story. The protagonist of both books, Annie Hawkins Green, is without a doubt currently my favorite badass woman. She is smart, strong, gutsy, and kind, but at the same time flawed, with emotions (and lingering PTSD) that cause some of her decisions to take her into situations that range from mildly upsetting to life-threateningly dangerous.

Patricia Sands, author of the Love in Provence series

. . . reminiscent of Hosseini's *A Thousand Splendid Suns* . . .

Maggie Smith, author of *Truth and Other Lies*

This high-intensity story with even higher stakes has a female protagonist that is relatable in her struggles, but also a role model in her convictions.

Booklist

Awards for *Double Exposure*

2022 Winner Women's Fiction, Mystery-Suspense, American Writing Awards

Also by Jeannée Sacken

Behind the Lens
Double Exposure

THE RULE
OF THIRDS

JEANNÉE SACKEN

PRESS

www.ten16press.com - Waukesha, WI

The Rule of Thirds
Copyrighted © 2023 Jeannée Sacken
PB ISBN 9781645385608
HC ISBN 9781645385592
EBook ISBN 9781645385615
Library of Congress Control Number: 2023937669
First Edition

The Rule of Thirds
by Jeannée Sacken

For information, please contact:

www.ten16press.com
Waukesha, WI

Cover and chapter image design by Kaeley Dunteman
Editing and interior design by Lauren Blue
Author photo © Agnieszka Tropiło

This is a work of fiction. The characters are both actual and fictitious.
With the exception of verified historical events and persons, all incidents,
descriptions, dialogue, and opinions expressed are the products of the
author's imagination and are not to be construed as real.

For Deb Blair Kamins

and

*for the many journalists and photographers
who gave their lives to the story in Afghanistan*

Arlington, Virginia – August 1, 2021

THE LAST HAND OF the night. Dealer's choice, and Cerelli goes with five-card draw. We ante up. He shuffles, then deals—his motions deft, practiced, economical. The man has clearly played his share of poker. So have I. Being on assignment as a war photographer can involve a lot of downtime, a lot of waiting for action. Card games often fill those empty hours. Over the years and against all odds, I've managed to develop a game face that doesn't give anything away. Not always easy for me, to which Cerelli can attest. He swears he can read me like a book. Unfortunately, that's all too often true. But tonight, I'm determined to give away nothing.

I pick up my cards, fan them open then closed, return them to the table, and think about those two lovely queens and the king who just showed themselves. *Game face!* I remind myself. *Think about something else!*

So, I glance around the table. Senior Chief Sawyer is sitting on my left. Next to him is Nic Parker Lowe, once my nemesis, now a good friend and colleague. Then Cerelli, and finally Chris Cardona, my boss at TNN. Five of us. They're all concentrating on their cards. I go back to Cerelli and study his hands as they shift a couple cards. Large hands, powerful enough to break someone in two, but they make me feel safe. Loved. And they know their way around me even better than they handle a deck of cards. Years ago, in the aftermath of a Taliban ambush near Kandahar, Cerelli saved my life. We met up again, and it's been something of a roller coaster ever since. Our jobs often have us on opposite sides of the world for long stretches. Not to mention that my mothering responsibilities had me living halfway across the country from him. Bottom line: it hasn't always been easy for us to spend as much time together as we'd like. For the last couple years, though, with Mel in college and now job hunting in New York, I've been spending more and more time in northern Virginia.

"Annie?" From the way Cerelli says my name, it's clear he's been trying to get my attention for a while.

I look up to see the muscle at the corner of his right eye pulsing. A definite tell. I'm guessing he's got a good hand.

He allows himself a half grin. "You in?"

That's when I notice the rest of the guys are watching me, too—and trying not to seem obvious about it. They drop their eyes, make a point of studying their cards again. But their concern lingers in the air. They're worried. Not about the cards I might or might not be holding. I'm guessing they're worried about me and what could be going on inside my head.

PTSD. During my last time in Afghanistan, I had a major meltdown. Not surprising given that the Taliban had finally caught up with me.

"Sorry." Looking at the coins and some dollar bills scattered at the center of the table, I try to figure out where the bet stands. Next to me, Sawyer picks up his beer, four fingers splayed down the side of the bottle. Four dollars. He's always had my back. I add a ten. "I'm in. And raise." One of my hard-and-fast rules of the game: if you've got cards, don't limp into the pot.

Sawyer, in the middle of a swig of beer, chokes a bit overdramatically and reluctantly adds his money. This is supposed to be a nickel-and-dime game.

Nic deposits his cards on the table. With a disgusted curl of his upper lip, he reaches for his Boddingtons. "Is this for real, old thing? Or are you just trying to win back what we took off you tonight? Either way, it's too rich for my blood. Count me out."

To my right, Chris is shaking his head. "Seriously, Annie?" He's played with me before and knows when I've got a good hand. He also knows that I'm pretty good at bluffing.

Cerelli eases back in his chair, his eyes not leaving my face. The muscle next to his eye is still quivering. "I'll see you. And raise." Still watching me, he adds a twenty.

I sip my bourbon. Blanton's. Neat. Cerelli keeps a bottle of this precious gold just for me. All the better to seduce me. It works— most of the time.

Cerelli picks up the deck. Three cards to Chris. I discard the top two cards from my stack, eliciting a collective snort from around the table. *Good. Let them think I'm bluffing.* Two to Sawyer. Then I notice Cerelli takes just one. Damn. He does have good cards. And I happen to know that he looks on poker as a blood sport. Apparently, the rest of the guys know it, too. Chris folds.

I take a look at my new cards and momentarily let down my guard. Two more lovely ladies. Four of a kind. Completely on its own, my eyebrow crooks. I match Cerelli's bet and raise him another twenty.

"I'm out." Sawyer tosses his cards onto the table, then pushes back his chair, crossing his arms over his massive chest. Out of the line of fire.

Cerelli doesn't even look at his new card. He just watches me. Intently. Considering. I feel myself swimming into his warm brown eyes. Which is probably exactly what he wants. All the easier for me to slip up. I stop swimming and concentrate on that muscle next to his eye. He's going to match my bet, I can tell that much. Is he going to raise again? What the hell does he have? Another twenty lands in the pot. Then another.

Sawyer shoves his chair a few inches away from the table. Nic looks toward the kitchen, probably debating another Boddingtons, then sits back. It's clear he senses that the main event is about to begin, and he doesn't want to miss it.

Digging deep, I match Cerelli and hope he calls soon. It's been a long night of mostly mediocre cards, and I'm tapped out. But I'm not about to walk away. Not with this hand.

"Call." The man really can read me like a book.

"You first."

He quirks his eyebrow then grins as he lays out three kings. Two aces.

"Well played." Still holding my cards, I smile sweetly.

He raises the other eyebrow. He knows disingenuous when he sees it.

I slowly turn over my four lovelies. And one lonely king.

He lifts his nearly empty glass of scotch in salute. "*Touché.*"

"I warned you she can be cutthroat." This from Chris.

"Cutthroat?" Sawyer laughs as he stands—and heads for the kitchen. "She's downright scary."

"Scary? Bit of an understatement, wouldn't you say?" Nic

pushes himself to his feet, briefly rests a hand on my shoulder, then follows Sawyer into the kitchen.

Cerelli nods to the guys then rests his eyes back on me. He doesn't look away. Neither do I.

Eventually, I become aware of Chris still in the room, clearing his throat repeatedly. "Before you two ignite, we need to talk."

I turn in my chair and face my boss. Somehow managing to find my voice, I say, "Talk? About what?" Even though I know exactly what we have to talk about: Afghanistan.

The place that triggers my hallucinations. My last time in-country, after I managed to escape the Taliban, I was in bad enough shape both physically and mentally that I was well and truly scared. A medical leave from my job followed, and I got some help. My therapist warned me pretty decidedly to stay away from Kabul, Wad Qol, from all of Afghanistan. In fact, he strongly suggested I find another line of work. I didn't listen to him, and six months later, I went back to work with my boss's promise not to send me to the place of my nightmares. What's amazing is that I can go to any other crazy dangerous place—Yemen, Nigeria, Sudan, even Syria—and most of the time, I'm able to keep the monsters at bay. Therapy continues—when I'm not on assignment. Still, a big part of my heart lives in Afghanistan, and I want to go back. Before the Taliban take over and I won't be able to. A real conundrum.

"We're sending Nic's crew to Afghanistan to cover the coalition forces' withdrawal. I wanted you to hear it from me first."

Nic's crew. Which also happens to be my crew. I've been expecting some talk about this assignment. But does he have to bring it up in front of everyone? I think about that for all of three seconds and realize this is exactly the time and place to discuss it. Cerelli. Sawyer. Nic. The three men who do their utmost to protect me. And I'm willing to bet that they've already talked about this. All of them. Whatever *this* is. And Chris wants them in the room because he's worried about how I'll take what he's going to say.

"Okay, Chris. You've got my attention."

"How's therapy going?" Both Chris and Cerelli know I had a tune-up with my therapist this afternoon. Nothing new, except when I asked him to sign a release allowing me to go back to Afghanistan for just this eventuality, he declined. Strenuously. *It's too risky, Annie. Sometimes the kinds of intense hallucinations you've experienced lead to a psychotic break, and sometimes we can't bring you back.*

What can I say to Chris? And Cerelli? "It goes."

"Any progress?" Which is his way of asking if my doc signed the release for me to go to Afghanistan.

I shrug. In other words, no.

Chris steeples his fingers. "I need you in Kabul."

"When?"

"A couple weeks. Maybe sooner."

My shoulders sag. "That could be tough."

"Why is that?"

I lean forward, knowing full well that what I say in the next few minutes could alter my career—in a big way. "Because my therapist doesn't *want* me back in Afghanistan. Even though I haven't had an episode in years."

"So, why's he jamming you up?"

I pick up my glass. "Because he's a complete and total asshole."

Chris looks at me, then at Cerelli, then back at me, and shakes his head. "To be honest, I don't disagree with you. I've heard the same thing from another journalist."

"You *what?*" My crystal glass clunks onto the table, a little harder than I intended. "Then why the hell am I wasting my time with this guy? He wants me to get some nice, *safe* job." I glance at Cerelli first, hoping I don't see even the slightest spark in his eyes showing that he agrees with the shrink. We've argued about this over the years. *He's military, Annie—all the way. He's not trying to keep you out of war zones. Hell, he's signed off on you going to some of the most dangerous places on the planet.* But Cerelli's got his poker face on. So does Chris. I take a minute to calm down, then look Chris in the eye. "So, what happened to the other journalist? You going to give me a name?"

"No names. Let's just say she moved on to another line of work."

"Fuck. Another woman. Don't you see what's happening here?" I push my empty glass toward Cerelli and nod at the bottle of bourbon. He pours me a double. Then a double of scotch for himself and another for Chris, who takes it gratefully and downs a mouthful.

The drinking buys us a minute of silence and calm. Finally, Chris wades in. "Look, I'm over a barrel. I need a crew in Kabul. That includes a photographer. I need *you* in Kabul. With Nic."

The A-team.

I open my mouth to tell him to grow a pair, but he palms the air between us. "I've got a . . . confession to make." His glance at Cerelli tells me he's part of this, too.

From the corner of my eye, I see Cerelli shift in his chair. He doesn't look thrilled, but he nods. I cradle my glass in both hands. "You mind telling me what's going on?"

Cerelli reaches for the bottle of scotch and holds it up to Chris. "Would this help?"

Chris nods. "Thanks." Another sip, then he leans back in his chair and takes off his glasses, all the better to massage the bridge of his nose. Not a good sign. "That medical leave paperwork you gave me a few years ago?"

"Five years ago."

Chris clenches his hands on the table. "That long, huh? Well, I guess time sort of got away from me. Seems that it's still sitting in my desk drawer. I . . . uh . . . never filed it with HR."

"Excuse me?"

He looks up. "It was the only way I could keep you working. On the payroll. If I'd given it to HR, I couldn't have sent you anywhere. There's no way they would've believed your 'episodes' stayed in Afghanistan. You would've been out on disability. Pronto. And with the cure rate for PTSD being what it is, you probably never would've worked again. Anywhere."

"But I took medical leave. Months of it."

He focuses on his glass of scotch, turning it gently on the table. "I submitted it as vacation. Then personal time off."

All I can do is stare at my boss. I honestly have no idea what to say. He definitely saved my career, but what if something had happened? What if I'd really needed that disability?

Hold on! says my inner voice. *You always knew the problem was limited to Afghanistan. There were never any nightmares, any hallucinations anywhere else. Well, not many, at any rate. Cerelli knew it, too. And so did Chris. The man has done you a huge favor.*

"Who else knows about this?" Stupid question. At least Cerelli has the good grace to look contrite.

"They're in this room." Chris shifts his gaze to a point over my shoulder where I'm guessing Nic and Sawyer are now standing.

And sure enough, a moment later, Nic sits down next to me. "Here's how we worked it. I told HR that I'd only take the job at TNN if you were on my team. I also told them that I wanted out of Afghanistan. I needed a change. New assignments."

"But you're the best in the business—"

"Same goes."

I let Nic's words rocket around my brain for a few seconds, and then the pieces fall into place. Five years of traveling from hotspot to hotspot with Nic. Anywhere and everywhere, except Afghanistan. This has been Nic's way of paying me back for his stupid-ass hazing stunt fifteen years ago. Dumping me out in the Afghan desert, miles away from base, in the worst sandstorm of the season. He could've cost me my life. The aftermath could've ended my career. It did result in the interrogation from hell at the hands of Cerelli and some horrific accusations that I was collaborating with the Taliban. But I never reported the hazing, never told on Nic and his buddies, and saved their butts as well as their careers. Not out of any loyalty to them but because I knew all too well that in the old boys' club, a squealing woman didn't stand a chance. The guys would've made my life hell until I quit.

"Thanks," I say to Nic. "I owe you."

Nic covers my hand with his. "And I you."

Chris gulps down the rest of his scotch. "So, what do you think? About this assignment, I mean. Afghanistan? Is it a possibility?"

Afghanistan. Where a large piece of my heart lies buried. But it's also the home of my demons, not to mention Cerelli's fears for me. Yes. No. This could absolutely be the highlight of my career. But damn those demons. I look to Cerelli, but I can't read him. Picking up one of my cards, I fold down the corner. Back and forth I work it until it weakens, frays, tears. Turning it over, I see I've just mangled the Queen of Hearts. "Thanks, Chris. I . . . uh . . ." I shake my head. What the hell am I doing? The man is throwing me a lifeline to save my career.

Say yes! Now!

Chris pushes back from the table and stands. "Think about it, will you? Call me tomorrow. Or Sunday at the latest."

By some unspoken code, Sawyer and Nic join Chris at the front door. I see them out. "Thanks, Chris, Nic. For going to bat for me. For—"

Each man smiles—a little sadly, it seems. It's Chris who speaks. "No need. You've gotten me through some tough times. I'll do whatever I can for you. You know that."

I FIND CERELLI SITTING on the edge of the bed taking off his prosthetic leg. "You might want to move back a little," he cautions, carefully rolling down the sock. "I'm about to take off the sleeve." How well I know that after a long day, the sleeve will be full of sweat—a messy business to get off.

"Let me help."

"You sure?"

"It's easier if I do it." Besides which, no matter the mess, I'd do this every hour of the day for him. He lost his leg to save my life. Something he swears isn't true. *Let's get this straight. This isn't your fault. It's on the fucking Taliban.* But would he even have been in Afghanistan in a firefight with the Taliban if it weren't for me? Who knows? What I do know: I'm here, but Finn Cerelli's leg isn't.

He eases himself farther back on the bed while I kneel in front of him and start the unrolling. Very sweaty tonight. Soon enough, the front of my T-shirt is soaked. But the job isn't done yet. The sleeve needs washing so the stink doesn't set in. I push myself to my feet, ready to head to the bathroom, but he grabs my hand. "Leave it. I'll wash it in the morning."

"Sorry. I don't want to smell it. Give me one minute." A quick rinse in the bathroom sink, and I'm back.

He pulls me down onto the bed. We roll onto our sides, facing each other. "Talk to me. What are you thinking?"

"That I should have said yes."

He smiles, but it doesn't reach all the way to his eyes. "So, why didn't you?"

I rake my fingers through my hair. "It's complicated."

"I'm a good listener." He trails his index finger down the side of my face, sweeping back a few errant hairs.

I look away. "I should've jumped at the chance to go back to Afghanistan. The Taliban will be in power soon. This could well be my last visit. Forever."

"All true. But something tells me you think there could be a downside."

"You know there is. If I have another PTSD meltdown, it could well be my last time anywhere."

"Meaning?"

"Five years ago, when I was in the hospital. When Awalmir came to Seema's room?" Oh, God. Just saying their names brings it all back. My best friend Darya—murdered by Awalmir, a Taliban militant, in front of the girls' school she directed. Leaving the scene, he took her daughter, seventeen-year-old Seema, with him. Some six months later, I found Seema near death, her infatuation with Awalmir long since turned to fear. Rescuing her all but killed me, except miracle of miracles, we both survived.

"Trust me. I remember."

"The thing is . . . I . . . uh . . . didn't know if he was really there or if I was hallucinating. As in psychotic break. What if something like that happens again?"

"Sweetheart." He pulls me into his arms. "He was most definitely there. But let's cut to the chase: you haven't had any problems since."

I take a deep breath. "Correct." Well, except for one time in the doctor's office about a year ago, but I didn't tell Cerelli about it then and I'm not going to say anything now.

From the way he tightens his hold, I'm sure he knows I'm not telling him everything. But for once, he doesn't push me. He also doesn't ask about Nic's little speech tonight even though I know he wants to. Instead, he kisses the side of my head. "Could we talk about this later?"

"Sure. Any reason?"

"There's something else we need to talk about."

"There is?"

"That last hand you played tonight." He unbuttons my jeans and tries to lower them over my hips. They don't go very far.

I sit up, then push myself to my knees to help him. "Yeah?"

"You took a lot of money off me."

I smile. "Those four lovely queens and I *won* a lot of money."

"I think you ought to let me try to win it back."

I pull my T-shirt over my head. "Any specific game you have in mind?"

"Dealer's choice."

2

SUNLIGHT STREAMS INTO THE bedroom, but the fog in my brain tells me it's still way too early to get out of bed. Likely I had too much bourbon last night. I burrow deeper under the duvet for just a few more minutes of blessed sleep, but it's not to be. Trying to remember where I am this morning, I run my hand across the silky expanse. Not in Milwaukee. Only one person I know has sheets with this high a thread count. Cerelli. The condo in Arlington. I reach for him, but his side is empty. Kicking back the cover in disappointment, I sit up.

"Good. You're awake." He's standing in the doorway. Unfortunately, he's already dressed. In khakis.

I look pointedly at his uniform. "Isn't it Saturday?"

"Sorry about this. They called me in for a meeting. I shouldn't be long." He runs his fingers through his military short hair that's a bit longer than the last time I was here. But it's not nearly as long and shaggy as the first time I met him. Fifteen years ago, when he was running a spec op in southwest Afghanistan, he and his team had permission from the Navy to wear scruffy hair and beards to pass as Afghans. Now, though, he's all military.

"Do me a favor?"

He raises an eyebrow.

"Don't cut your hair."

"The Navy may have something to say about that."

"Hello! You're an admiral, part of command central. You make the rules." I climb out of bed and ease my way across the room, taking in his appreciation of my naked body. Would that I could entice him back into bed, but I know all too well that when the Navy calls, Cerelli goes forth. Still, it never hurts to try. "Nice stars." I trace the silver pins on his collar, then shift my attention to his chest. My fingers come to rest atop the SEAL trident. "My favorite."

He grins. "It's not gonna work. I really do have to go in."

Not yet willing to abandon my mission, I wrap my arms around his neck. "I haven't even begun to try—"

His arms circle my waist. "Sweetheart, you don't have to try. You should know that by now." A quick kiss, then his hands are on mine, removing them from his neck. The next thing I know, he's scrounged a T-shirt from his dresser and pulled it over my head. "I've only got a couple minutes before I have to leave. Coffee?"

I pull the T-shirt into place so that it's covering my ass. "Please."

He takes my hand and leads me into the kitchen. Liberating two mugs from the dishwasher, he fills them both, tops one with soy milk, and hands it to me. Still too hot to drink, I breathe in the tantalizing aroma, letting it clear away some of my brain fog. Cerelli downs a mouthful.

"You give any more thought to your next assignment? Whether you'll take it or not?" He steers clear of actually naming the assignment: Afghanistan.

"Exactly when would I have done that?"

He smiles. I'm guessing that he's thinking back to his final hand of dealer's choice last night. The game between the two of us that took several hours to complete. The game I would've been happy to keep playing. "Good point. But afterward . . ."

"I was tired. I slept. You should try it sometime." How the man can function on zero sleep is beyond me. I take a tentative sip of coffee, willing the caffeine into my bloodstream.

"You're not sleeping now."

I peer at him over the rim of my mug. His brown eyes hold me firmly in place, but he's giving nothing away. He's waiting to hear what *I* want to do: go to Afghanistan or continue to stay away. But I don't know what I want. What I do know is that we've come a long way over the years. There was a time when he ordered me not to go—"Too dangerous," he said more than once. He was right, of course. It was crazy dangerous for me to go to Afghanistan where the Taliban had declared *nyaw aw badal* on both of us. Justice and revenge for the U.S. military having bombed a small village. And for me having shot and killed the militant who was about to kill us.

I take another sip of coffee, then shake my head. "I don't know." My eyes are still locked on his. "What do you—"

He holds up his hand. "This is your call. Five and a half years ago, I promised not to tell you what to do. That's a promise I'm taking seriously." He pauses for a long moment, as if he's trying to decide whether or not to say the rest of what's on his mind. "Besides which, you'd have me for breakfast if I told you to stay out of Afghanistan. My therapist would, too."

"Your what?" My voice is barely above a whisper. I hold my mug with two hands to keep from dropping it. "Since when are you back to seeing . . . wait! Sorry. This is none of my business."

"Actually, it *is* your business. You're the reason I'm back in therapy."

Me? Oh, God no. I set my mug on the counter. Something tells me I shouldn't be holding any heavy objects with hot liquid when he tells me this next part. My thoughts rush back to the days and weeks after Cerelli lost his lower leg. He wasn't exactly a happy camper. In fact, he was absolutely miserable. He was also angry—with me—assuming I was hanging around simply because I felt guilty. Which I did. That I felt sorry for him. Yeah, that was true, too. And worst of all, that he was my pity fuck. Which definitely wasn't the case. We worked it out—obviously. And Cerelli definitely got his head back on straight, partly because the brass insisted he see a shrink—a requirement for staying in the Navy.

He clears his throat, and as much as I want to look away, I don't. "Sweetheart, it's not what you're thinking. It's not *you* so much as my feelings about you."

This isn't getting any better, but I try to roll with it. "Dr. Solberg, right?"

"Yeah. He's been around a while, but he's still one of the Navy's best."

"Cerelli . . ."

"Your last couple assignments—Yemen, Syria—I had intelligence coming across my desk that ISIS was making a comeback—exactly where you were. Which was the last place on earth I wanted you to be." His voice cracks. "And I couldn't do a damn thing about it. Talking it out helps."

Determined not to interrupt again, I gnaw my lower lip.

He exhales sharply. "It's hard work—therapy. You know that. A lot of deep digging—digging into parts of me I don't want to think about, much less acknowledge." The gruffness in his voice tells me how terribly hard it was. And from the sound of it, still is.

"I didn't know," I whisper.

"I didn't tell you."

My heart is close to breaking. Cerelli is the most wonderful man I've ever known. What the hell have I done to him? I take a step toward him, but he holds up his hands.

"I kept thinking about the last time you were in Wad Qol . . . that morning . . . the fucking Taliban taking you . . . me hearing it over the phone. Too far away to save you. Not having a clue where they took you, what they were doing to you, if I'd ever see you again. I—it nearly killed me." He wipes his eyes. "Clearly, I'm still working on this. Where you're concerned, I'm finding it impossible to compartmentalize."

I take another step, and this time he opens his arms and gathers me to his chest. I'm holding on tight and undoubtedly making a wrinkled mess of his perfectly ironed khaki shirt. "I'm sorry." I do *not* want to be the woman who fucks up this man.

He holds me tighter. "There's nothing for you to be sorry about. This is my problem."

I smile through my tears and press my hand against his ribboned chest. "I meant I'm sorry about messing up your shirt, but I love you for telling me."

"I've looked worse, believe me." He glances at his watch. "Sorry, I really do have to go. You free for lunch?"

"Absolutely. When and where?"

"Courthouse Kebab?"

"Excellent choice."

"Noon. I'll swing by and pick you up."

"That's totally out of your way. I'll get an Uber." I rise up on my toes and bring my lips to his, fully intending a sweet, gentle, see-you-in-a-few-hours kiss. But that's not how it turns out. The man really knows how to kiss. And who am I to deny him?

"Later," he says when he finally pulls back. Then, "You really don't have any idea what you do to me."

AFTER CERELLI LEAVES, I scrounge up a yogurt and do my best to forget about him seeing his shrink. Again. Because of me. Because of the work I do, the places I go, the risks I take. Damn. He's afraid of losing me.

Afraid. I almost gag on my yogurt. Cerelli isn't afraid of anything or anyone. Yet he's afraid of what could happen to me. And those fears are completely reasonable, especially since he's already witnessed me come way too close to dying two, no three, times. Not to mention that he's a SEAL. He knows all too well what happens in war zones. He's seen way too many people die in pretty horrific ways—things most people couldn't even imagine. So yeah, he knows exactly what could happen to me. And I seriously don't like what that's doing to him.

So, what do I do? Go with Nic and my crew to Afghanistan to cover an amazingly important story? This is a story any and every journalist wants on her resumé. But I'd bet that while I'm there, Cerelli will worry about me, wish he'd convinced me not to go, and then do double duty with his therapist, digging deeper into his feelings. Years ago, I made it clear that he couldn't tell me what I can and can't do with my life. Unlike my ex-husband, Todd, who never could wrap his head around that and, in the end, couldn't deal with the dangerous places my job took me, Cerelli's kept his promise. But at what frigging cost?

What if I don't go? I could talk to Chris about joining another crew and start going to less dangerous places. Let the man I love have more peace of mind, let him worry less, free him up from all that messy mucking about.

Or should I pick door number three? Travel a lot less, spend more time stateside, and make a home with Cerelli. We could actually live together—like most couples do. What a concept.

I stir my cup of yogurt faster and faster until it liquefies, then froths—more milk than yogurt. Staying home. It's an option. But I'd just be repeating the same mistakes I made with Todd, which left me miserable and nearly destroyed my soul. Deadly for me. And in the end, that wouldn't make things any better for Cerelli. In fact, me staying home might have the opposite effect and drive us apart.

Yogurt still in hand, I walk to the wall of glass in the living room and look out over Washington, D.C. shimmering in the July heat. In the distance, through the haze, I can see the Washington Monument on the Mall. The Capitol rotunda. The White House. So much power.

And my job is to document what happens when powers around the world clash. To reveal the sometimes corrupt and nasty truth behind the power, the effects of the conflicts on civilians, women and men, boys and girls. Could I walk away from that? My chest tightens. No, that's the last thing I could do.

So, what the hell do I do?

No closer to a decision, I touch my forehead to the glass, cool despite the near one hundred degrees outside.

I LEAN AGAINST THE marble tile wall of the mega-sized walk-in shower, big enough for a wheelchair, and let the warm water embrace me. I try my best to push out of my mind unnerving images of Cerelli opening the door to a U.S. Navy chaplain in service dress blues there to tell him I'm dead. Will I be caught in crossfire? Blown up by an IED left over from years ago? Beheaded? Does it really matter? I'll be dead. The chaplain stays front and center in my imagination. A chaplain? No. Given Cerelli's rank, they'd send another admiral. Like that would make it any easier.

For a moment, my thoughts wander to my daughter. Oh jeez. Nothing, absolutely nothing, would make it easier for Mel either.

I reach for the shampoo and, eyes closed, lather up my hair, digging my nails down to the scalp and working the suds. Okay, I'll admit it. No matter the danger, I want to go to Afghanistan. I want to be with my crew, doing what each of us is meant to do. What each of us does so well. I turn around under the shower and rinse my hair.

Eyes open, I catch sight of the shower chair pushed into the back corner, an arm crutch propped in the other corner. My heart clenches. I take a deep breath to force myself not to cry. Cerelli would kill me if he knew I was getting weepy over his chair—a constant reminder of his amputated leg. Most of the time, I can handle it, but sometimes—like now—the chair gets the better of me, reminding me of how frigging close I came to losing him.

Get a grip! All this guilt isn't going to change a thing.

Except it does change things. He saved my life. And not for me to go back and lose it to the very same assholes that took his leg.

Grabbing my razor, I plant my right foot on the seat of the chair and soap up my leg. I force myself to think about Cerelli and me, tonight, to anticipate his appreciation. Not that he's ever complained when confronted with my unshaved limbs. But I can just imagine his grin when he runs his hands up my silky-smooth legs.

The other leg. I'm one swipe away from being done when I feel the burn on the back of my ankle and watch the pebbled shower floor turn red with blood.

3

THE MOMENT I STEP INSIDE Courthouse Kebab, mouth-watering aromas of roast lamb and eggplant, chicken *kofta* and *nân* engulf me. I look around, taking in the stained-glass lanterns hanging over each table, and not three seconds later, I'm aware of Cerelli. Even seated at the opposite end of the restaurant, in a private corner far from other diners, he's like a force of nature, drawing me to him. I watch his eyes light up when he sees me. It must be the dress. I hardly ever wear them, but a couple months ago when I took Mel shopping to buy some decent job-interviewing clothes, she found this dress. A navy ikat- print linen sundress. For me. She's always trying to clean up my act. It's exactly the kind of dress I'd wear, low neckline and all, except I don't wear dresses. But under threat of doing something that would really piss me off, she convinced me to try it on. *Trust me, Mom. He'll love you in this. You can thank me later.* Now, if she'd only find a job.

I strut my way across the restaurant, my silky bare legs sweeping past each other. From the look on Cerelli's face, it's clear Mel was right. Again. His appreciative smile goes all the way to his eyes. When it comes to my love life, Mel is almost always right. I smile back, anticipating the rest of the afternoon—post-lunch.

My eyes drift to his right. One of the most beautiful women I've ever seen is sitting next to him. Her khaki uniform has Navy written all over it. A few more steps, and I notice the gold oak leaf on her collar. Lt. Commander. In that moment, something clicks. Cerelli told me he has a new assistant. A woman.

I walk toward the table, and with each step, my sandal strap catches on the Band-Aid plastered across the back of my gouged ankle. Cerelli meets me halfway. "Love the dress," he whispers.

I nod toward the woman. "So much for our hot date."

"I thought you two should meet."

"Why?" I shake my head. Definitely not the best idea he's ever had. My next words: "She had to be gorgeous?" The almost plaintive tone in my voice makes me cringe. I am not jealous. I refuse to be jealous.

He crooks his half grin that normally would leave me weak in the knees, but I manage not to succumb. "She's a great aide-de-camp. But definitely not my type."

The sound I make in response is something akin to a snort. "Since when aren't you attracted to stunningly beautiful?"

He swallows a laugh and puts his hand at the small of my back, all the better to steer me around the empty tables toward the beautiful woman. She's standing by the time we get to the table. Smiling warmly, she clasps my hand in both of hers. "Annie. Hi. So glad to meet you. I'm Sam Harris. And I'm a huge fan."

Not what I was expecting. "Excuse me?" I'm not quite sure what to say. Is this why Cerelli thinks we should meet? So she can fan-girl me? Does he think my ego needs this boost?

Cerelli keeps his hand on my back, exerting just the slightest bit of pressure. Sweet, and I appreciate the gesture, but I wish we were both sitting down so I could unobtrusively kick him under the table. I'm seriously not into date sharing.

As if he's reading my mind, which he often does, he pulls out the chair across from Sam. I sit, and he pushes the chair forward. Another nice gesture, but always a bit awkward as I shuffle the chair into the right position. And decide to forego kicking him. Sam seats herself with Cerelli in between us.

She leans forward. "I love your work. The best war photography since Dickey Chapelle's."

I wait a couple moments for her to say something more, but she doesn't. Dickey Chapelle was known for being in the trenches with the Marines. And they revered her. Pretty much the opposite of what I do, so I'm a little confused by the comparison. "She was one of the greats, that's for sure. And a lot braver than me. I try to stay behind the battle lines, but she was always right there in the middle of the action. Which, of course, is how she got killed."

"Yeah. She paid the ultimate price. But it's your images of civilians, especially the kids, that inspire me. You really have a way of getting them to open up. And I'm not just talking about your picture of Malalai."

She means the image I captured years ago of a feisty ten-year-old Afghan village girl. In a Taliban village, as it happened. The photograph ended up on the cover of *Time*. It also won me the Pulitzer. But my taking that shot likely cost Malalai her life, not to mention that Murphy and Lopez, my intrepid military escorts, were gunned down in the firefight that followed. In the fifteen years since, I've done my best to keep everything that happened that day buried as deep as I can. But someone always seems to remember my picture, and then the horrific memories come roaring back.

Right now, I'm determined to steer this conversation away from my ghosts.

Smiling almost shyly, Sam herself comes to my rescue. "So, anyway, I love photography, and I fiddle around a bit. Nothing like you, of course, but I just got a new camera—a Canon. I was ... uh ... kind of hoping you might be willing to give me a few pointers . . ." She picks up her cloth napkin and starts to unfurl it. "I've been after the admiral to introduce us."

"Pointers?" I hear myself say the word, but I'm actually focused on the telltale lighter band of skin on the fourth finger of her left hand where a ring used to be. My heart sinks. Oh, great. Not only is she beautiful, she's single. Then, before I can stop myself, I start wondering if Cerelli's been talking to her about me. No, I'm not wondering. She wouldn't be here otherwise. What intimate details of our life has he been sharing with Sam?

She catches me looking and grins, a little ruefully it seems. "Last winter, my wife put in for a transfer to the Pacific fleet. Not necessarily my choice, but it was time. Certainly for her. I haven't exactly been the easiest person to live with."

Wife? "I'm sorry." I keep my eyes on Sam but am back to thinking about kicking Cerelli under the table. "This is kind of weird, don't you think?"

She tilts her head to the side and studies me, clearly not understanding what I mean. "Weird? You mean because I'm a lesbian? Believe me, the admiral knows. It's not always easy being gay in the military, but he's one of the good guys and absolutely doesn't ask and doesn't tell."

"Except maybe about me. I'm getting the feeling that you two have been talking about me. That's what I meant by kind of weird. Maybe not for you, but it sure feels that way to me."

"Ah. You think . . ." she says—again with that rueful smile.

Cerelli picks up his empty water glass and nods toward one of the waiters. "You know, I'm right here. I can hear what you're saying."

"Okay, so tell me." I train my eyes on him. "Why are we really here? The three of us?"

The waiter chooses that moment to appear for our orders. I pick up my menu and quickly narrow down what I want to eat. Chicken *kofta* with a side of *borani banjân*. Cerelli and Sam both go for the lamb kebab platter.

Once the waiter heads to the kitchen, I'm back to looking at Cerelli. "You were about to enlighten me?"

Cerelli shrugs. "Sam happened to be at the meeting this morning, and I thought it would be a good idea for the two of you to meet. So—"

Sam smiles. "It's true. I really did want to meet you. Like I said, I'm probably your biggest fan. And I'm serious about wanting some pointers . . ." So, the new aide-de-camp already feels free to interrupt the admiral. I thought that role was reserved for his commanding officer. Maybe the president. And for me.

"Sorry. I don't understand." I'm back to looking at Cerelli. "Why did you want me to meet Sam? And I'm guessing it's not for 'pointers.'" I'm working to keep my voice low and sweet. *Don't try fobbing off something about talking photography with your assistant.* My eyes are flashing, and the man knows exactly what that means.

Cerelli raises an eyebrow. *I wouldn't dare.*

I narrow my eyes. *Good. Maybe I'll let you live.*

He crooks that delicious half grin. *I'm counting on it.* Then, his hand finds mine resting on my lap. The briefest touch, warm and reassuring. Maybe a little high schoolish, but trust him to know exactly what I need to calm down. And I do trust him. Well, at least most of the time.

"You going to share?" My voice is maybe a little sharper than it should be. Then, I almost bless the waiter who delivers our food—huge, honking platters of food—in record time. We immediately start eating—a welcome break. The *kofta* is reasonably authentic, but not nearly as good as what I used to eat in Afghanistan. Then I take a bite of the *borani banjân*. Oh, God. I nearly moan, but catch myself. I notice Cerelli's watching me, probably waiting for an invitation to help himself. He finally gives up and spears a piece of eggplant. I look up to see Sam pressing her lips together. With as much purpose as I can muster, I take a piece of his lamb and invite her to think the worst of me. Oh, this lamb is good! Way better than my *kofta*.

"We have this thing about eggplant. Please, you've got to try it." I offer her my plate.

She hesitates. "No thanks. Eggplant really isn't—"

"Yeah, I know, but you've never had eggplant like this. Seriously, I think this could alter your relationship with the universe. Or at least with this particular member of the nightshade family."

"You sound like my mother. Don't get me wrong, you're a lot cooler than my mother, but . . . okay." She forks a tiny piece and pops it into her mouth. I'm expecting her to swallow the piece whole without chewing, but instead she savors the morsel, a smile lighting up her face, her hand almost instantly above her head, signaling the waiter. "What is this?" she asks, pointing to my plate. "Eggplant something. I must have a side order, please."

"How about a full order," says Cerelli. "For the table."

"Of course." Smiling, the waiter offers a slight bow, then turns on his heel and heads to the kitchen.

I'm back to scrutinizing my tablemates, trying to figure out this conspiracy they've got going. "Now, is one of you ready to tell me why I'm really here?" I figure enough time has passed to get us back to the purpose of this cozy meeting.

Sam laughs. "Is she always like this? Like a pit bull with a bone?"

Cerelli concentrates on chewing his lamb. "Pretty much."

"Okay, then." Sam eyes my eggplant. I edge my plate closer to her. "So, I thought I could say something about having followed your work, seeing your website, wanting to meet you. All of which is true, by the way."

I inch my plate back but not before Cerelli scoops up the last two slices of eggplant. "I don't have a website."

"That's what Admiral Cerelli said. But, well, you should. I really did just buy a camera and honestly need all the help I can get. And I actually *did* look up your work. It's wonderful. But you know that. Of course, you do. You won a Pulitzer."

Cerelli stops eating. I can feel his eyes resting on me.

"I . . . uh . . . don't talk about that."

Sam is watching me, too. Much more intently than I like. Sizing me up.

The three of us sit uncomfortably in the awkward silence. I'm waiting for Sam to ask *why* I don't talk about having gotten the prize every journalist covets. A logical question. But she doesn't.

The waiter returns and clears a spot in the center of the table for the platter of eggplant swimming in tomato garlic yogurt sauce. "*Borani banjân*," he says, whipping the cloth away from the edge of the hot dish with a flourish. His bow from the waist adds a final touch of class, and then he heads back to the kitchen.

When I look up, Sam is back to watching me. The concern in her eyes is all the confirmation I need that Cerelli has, indeed, talked to her about me. I know that look all too well. I see it on my shrink's face at every appointment—like he's worried I could fall off my chair and shatter into a million pieces. Not likely. "And something tells me this brings us to the real reason you two wanted me at this lunch."

"Sweetheart—"

I hold up my hand to stop him.

But he one-ups me by twining his fingers through mine and bringing my hand down to the tabletop. "When we talked last night, you seemed to be having a tough time deciding about this next assignment. Whether or not to go. I know you're worried about the PTSD—"

"Yeah, well, that's not exactly new."

"I thought it might help to talk to Sam."

"Why is that?" I glance at Sam, who's looking way too earnest.

"Because," says Sam, her voice low, but firm, "I'm dealing with it, too. Three tours in Iraq. One in Afghanistan. Then it got bad enough that I couldn't deal without being stateside. Without a shrink and some serious treatment." She looks down at her plate. "That's actually the reason why my wife left me. She couldn't cope with it—with me. PTSD can be really hard on the people who love us." Raising her eyes to me, she whispers, "You're lucky."

Pushing my plate away, I stare at the stained paper placemat in front of me, not sure what to think, what to say. I'm not at all sure I want to talk about my PTSD with anyone not in my very small inner circle. But Cerelli has invited someone else into that select group. The last time he told someone—my best friend Darya and her husband Tariq, as it happens—I had a major meltdown. That was six years ago while I was staying with them and teaching at Darya's school. After that, he promised to let me be the one who told. And I trusted him not to tell anyone else.

Hold on! my annoyingly astute inner voice interrupts. *Could be the man loves you. Could be he's trying to help. What's he supposed to do? He's respecting your demand not to tell you what you can and can't do, but he can't stop worrying about you. Especially when you yourself are worried about going to Afghanistan and running headlong into another bout of PTSD. And you're not just worried, you're frigging terrified. You know what happened at the hospital in Anabah when Awalmir came for Seema, when he was about to blast your head off your shoulders. You didn't know whether he was really there or not. Listen to the woman. She might be able to help.*

"Yeah, I'm lucky." I bring my hand down on Cerelli's. A quick glance at him and I see the muscle next to his eye twitching. Okay, he's aware that I'm not happy. I shift my focus to Sam. "So, do you have any 'pointers' on dealing with PTSD?" My inner voice is back. *No need to be so snarky!*

Sam purses her lips, clearly deciding how to respond. "Why don't we back up a bit? While I eat more of my new favorite food, you can bring me up to speed on your PTSD." She spoons some eggplant onto her plate.

I stare at the platter, not sure what to do, how to feel, wishing Cerelli had tried talking to me instead of running to Sam.

"What do you want to know?"

Sam swallows a mouthful. "Tell me the therapies your doctor used."

"You mean the drugs?" Next to me, Cerelli stiffens. Probably because this is the first time he's hearing about drugs. I glance sideways and, sure enough, the muscle at the corner of his eye is twitching again. Good. I take it that means he's on my side in this battle of narcotics.

"That's an accepted course of treatment," Sam says between bites. "It's what my therapist did for me. What did yours prescribe?"

"Zoloft."

"Mine, too. It worked pretty well for me. And?"

I shake my head. "It knocked me out . . . absolutely *flattened* me."

She forks another piece of eggplant. "That's what it's supposed to do."

"I can't be flat. I've got to have an edge. Otherwise I can't work. Hell, when I picked up a camera, I couldn't do a thing with it. I couldn't *see* anything."

"So, what did you do?"

"I took it for a month or two then quit."

She grins. "Ah. I can just imagine what your shrink said."

"Said?" I snort. "He yelled that *he* knows what he's doing, and if I don't trust him, he'll just cut me loose. And since I needed him to sign off that I'm okay—well, I thought I did anyway—being cut loose would've been career-ending. We negotiated, and he put me on Prozac."

"Was that any better?"

I shake my head. "Just as bad. Flattened, blunted. Like I said, I need that edge. I can't function as a photographer without it. Not to mention that if I don't have an edge in a conflict zone, it could be a death sentence. Hell, you know that better than I do. That sixth sense is sometimes all we've got to keep us safe out there." Next to me, Cerelli shifts on his chair.

"Did this guy try EMDR?"

"Is that another drug?"

She smiles. "Sorry, sorry. Eye movement desensitization and reprocessing."

"Oh, yeah. He *subjected* me to that."

Sam leans in, her forearms resting on the table. "I take it that didn't work too well for you?"

"No, it didn't."

Sam looks curious. "Interesting. It worked really well for me. But it's not a one-off. My therapist put me through the paces for months."

I pick my fork up from my plate and turn it over in my hand. Then I look squarely at Sam. "It. Didn't. Work."

Cerelli stops eating. Something tells me he's going to want a fuller accounting. Later.

Sam ignores the icy tone in my voice and continues in digging mode. "Did your guy offer an explanation?"

"Oh, yeah. He made it very clear that his method is sound, that *I'm* the problem." My voice cracks. I force myself to breathe deep, to regain control.

"May I ask whether you've had any episodes since you've been back stateside?" Sam's voice is just above a whisper, even though no one is close enough to hear.

I'm not about to admit to the hallucinating meltdown I had in my shrink's office. Not to her. Not to Cerelli. But I've taken too long weighing my answer. Across the table, Sam looks thoughtful. The muscle next to Cerelli's eye is full-out spasming.

The three of us sit in silence until the waiter returns to check on us. "The *borani banjân*, it is all right?"

Sam looks up and smiles brightly. "It's delicious. Could you please pack up what's left? Three separate containers. This will make the perfect dinner."

A moment later, the waiter is back with his tray. He loads up our dishes for a return trip to the kitchen.

Once he's out of listening range, Sam turns back to me. I can just imagine what she'll say to Cerelli the next time it's just the two of them: *She's in deep. Run. Don't walk. Get away from her before she drowns you both in her mess of a life.*

But she doesn't say that at all. "Look, stories like this really piss me off. I've been through a couple therapists because the first ones . . . well, let's just say we weren't a good fit. The only 'pointer' I can offer is for you to find someone to work with who understands what you're dealing with. Not everyone reacts to PTSD the same way. Not every therapy works. You absolutely need someone who realizes that, who sees you as an individual, who *gets* you. My therapist gets me. She's the best."

"She's a Navy doc?"

Sam nods, then presses her lips together and studies me thoughtfully. "You know, if you two were married, I'd bet Admiral Cerelli could get you set up with her . . ."

"We're not. Married, I mean." And not for want of proposing on Cerelli's part. Out of the corner of my eye, I watch the man cross his arms—a study in phenomenal patience.

Sam stands next to her chair and helps herself to one of the aluminum boxes the waiter brings by our table. "Oh, one more thing, and this has nothing to do with the Navy. I just started massage therapy."

"Massage? Does that really do anything for PTSD?"

"For me, it does. Actually, it's gaining a lot of traction as a treatment. Carol, my therapist, does myofascial release. She works on the pain points associated with my PTSD until she gets them to . . . well . . . relax. Anyway, it's taken a while, but I'm dealing with my triggers a lot better." She pulls a business card out of her pocket. "Interested?"

Quite a coincidence that Sam just happens to have her therapist's card. "I'll think about it."

"Give her a call." Placing the card on top of the two remaining aluminum containers, she turns down Cerelli's offer of a ride home and heads toward the door. But not before smiling conspiratorially at him, as if the two of them had arranged all this in advance.

4

"I DIDN'T SET SAM UP to say that. I had no idea she'd play the marriage card." Sounding sincere, but also maybe a little wishful, Cerelli follows me into the condo.

Hands clenched into fists and digging into my hips, I whirl around to face him. "I'm not upset that she brought it up. Although, to be honest, it's none of her goddamned business."

"Then what has you so upset?" He takes one of my fists and gently unfurls my fingers.

"The fact that you've obviously talked to her about me. My PTSD."

"Guilty. You're right. I shouldn't have."

"Then why did you?"

"Chalk it up to trying to help."

"Yeah, well, some things are strictly between us."

"You mean like getting married."

"Exactly. Why are you talking to her about that?"

He kisses the palm of my hand. "Sorry to disappoint, but I haven't talked to her about your turning down three of my proposals."

I cringe. "Really? That many?"

"It might be more than three."

"You must be a saint."

He takes my other hand and straightens the fingers. "Not a saint. Just willing to wait. As long as you say yes eventually."

"Yes."

"Yes?"

"I'll say it. Eventually. I promise."

"Just not now?" He raises an eyebrow.

"Things are a little . . . chaotic . . . right now. I'm trying to decide what to do about Afghanistan."

"Let me get this straight." He's still holding my hand and looking for all the world like he's about to go down on one knee. "You're seriously turning me down again? For the fourth time? Or maybe it's the fifth. Hell, it could be the fiftieth."

I pull back my hand. "This doesn't count as a proposal."

"What would? I need all the help I can get." He sounds serious, but his eyes are laughing.

I plant my hands flat against his chest and push. "Jeez, Cerelli, I don't know. A romantic dinner. Roses. Me wearing a gorgeous dress. You in your dress whites. I have complete confidence that you'll come up with the perfect moment."

He gathers me against his chest. "With the exception of today, you don't wear dresses."

"Don't be so literal. But speaking of dresses, mine is officially done in." I pull the wrinkled, sodden cloth away from my chest. Even linen can't stand up to the steamy heat and humidity in this part of the country. "Let me change into something drier."

"Don't! Please." Cerelli runs his index finger along the inside of the low neckline. "I have plans for this dress."

"Really. What kind of plans?"

After a brief detour into the kitchen to pour himself a scotch and me a bourbon, he leads me to the deep leather sofa facing the bank of floor-to-ceiling windows with the view of D.C. I've come to love. At the moment, though, it's hazy from the midafternoon heat, but come night, it will dazzle with a thousand mesmerizing points of light. Sinking back against the pillows, I drape my legs over Cerelli's. I'm determined he's going to have to iron his khakis before he wears them again.

He glides a hand up my silky leg. "Talk to me about EMDR."

How to kill the moment. I lean away from him. "The eye movement thing?"

"Eye movement desensitization and reprocessing. You told Sam it didn't work for you. I'd say you were pretty decisive. I'm wondering what happened."

I knew he'd pick up on that. But this is the last thing I want to talk about. Now or ever. I take ten seconds, or maybe thirty, looking out the window at the lights that haven't yet come on. Finally, I say, "Is this another one of your interrogations?"

I can feel him wince. "I don't interrogate you."

I can't help laughing. "Have you forgotten about that week on the *Bataan*? I think you called it a debriefing. I, on the other hand, remember it as something akin to hell."

"*Touché*. But, I should point out, I had two Marines dead in a Taliban ambush, and I had to figure out how you were involved. Also, that was fifteen years ago."

"What about at the hospital in Anabah?"

He leans his forehead against my cheek. "Six years ago, and that was hardly an interrogation. As you well know."

He's right. That time, his questioning was about as gentle as humanly possible. I'd just escaped from the Taliban only to be leveled by a massive infection. Not to mention a miscarriage.

"Are you going to talk to Sam about this?" There's way too much snark in my voice. Cerelli doesn't deserve that. But knowing that he's been talking about me to his aide-de-camp makes me squirm.

"No. And I take exception to that question." He strokes my leg again, more slowly, pushing my hemline above my knees. Way above my knees. "To set the record straight, I didn't talk to Sam about *you*. She told me about her PTSD when she came to work for me. She's pretty open about it. At our meeting this morning, your name came up."

"Point taken. There's a world—no, an ocean—of difference between your telling and her asking."

He raises his glass. "Much appreciated. Talk to me?"

Damn. He never gives up. "Do you have any idea what this eye movement thing entails? The therapist's index and middle fingers move back and forth, kind of hypnotically, and you have to follow with your eyes but not your head."

"I do."

That stops me. Cerelli knows a lot about everything, but how the hell does he know this? Unless . . . "You've done this, haven't you?"

"I have. And before you ask, yes, it worked for me." His voice is quiet, measured. There's not a shred of judgment or criticism. "But Dr. Solberg knew what he was doing, and it definitely wasn't a one-off. It was a hell of a lot of work, and not always very pleasant."

"Not very pleasant." Now I sound absolutely bitter. "My experience didn't come close to *not very pleasant*."

"Tell me what happened." He clasps my left hand in his. Tethering me.

I take a long swallow of bourbon, then put the heavy crystal glass on the coffee table. If I'm going to tell this story, it would probably be best for me not to hold any potential weapons.

He sets down his glass, too, lining it up next to mine. "That bad?"

"Oh, yeah."

"I'm listening."

Do I really want to tell him this? Burden him with more of my PTSD baggage? No, I do not. I'm about to shake my head, retreat into my bourbon, when I surprise myself by saying, "Do you remember that day in the Hindu Kush six years ago, after the firefight? I was tearing up my *burqa* to make you a tourniquet. And all of a sudden, there was Ghazan. *Not* dead. In fact, very much alive. And our guys were off tending to the wounded." My voice sounds odd, pitched way too high and very strained.

"I remember."

Steady! Just tell him.

"He was trying to decide which of us to kill first. You or me. He moved that gun back and forth, from me to you to me to you." I point the first two fingers of my free hand toward our glasses, directing it from one to the other and back again. "Back and forth. Back and forth. All I could think was that he'd force you to watch while he shot me first. Or maybe he'd do you first to make me suffer."

I keep waiting for him to press his finger against my lips to stop me from talking. Or to put his arm around my shoulders, to hold me closer—to comfort me. But he doesn't do any of those things. He just lets me talk.

"I had the Sig, but it was jammed in my waistband all the way on the other side. I kept reaching for it, but I couldn't get it. So, I kept talking, asking about Seema, where she was, hoping to stall him. But I was so scared he'd figure out what I was doing, that he'd shoot me. And you. Then, when I finally got my hand on the gun, I couldn't remember if the frigging safety was on or off."

He tightens his grip on my hand. So powerful and warm, making sure I stay in the here and now, keeping me from floating back to the craggy mountains in the northeast of Afghanistan. Or is he holding himself together? Maybe both.

I take a deep breath. "And then, that doctor, with his frigging fingers moving back and forth, just like Ghazan's gun. I told him to stop. But he wouldn't. I told him about Ghazan and the gun and your leg and Darya and Malalai, Lopez and Murphy. But he wouldn't fucking stop. He kept waving his fingers back and forth. Over and over and over. Until—" My voice cracks.

Cerelli's arms encircle me, drawing me against his chest. "Until?"

"I was back there. In the mountains. You were bleeding out. Ghazan was taunting us. Ready to kill us both. Right there. In his office. I lost it. Completely and totally lost it."

"Sweetheart."

"And all that did was convince him that I really do need drugs. For the rest of my life. And that I've got to be out of the field permanently. Such a fucking asshole."

He brushes my hair off my face and gently chucks me under the chin so I look up at him.

"You know what really got to me?" My voice sears the air between us. "He had the balls to say, *What was a photographer doing in a firefight with the Taliban?* After all that, he didn't even believe me."

"Or . . ."

"Or what?"

"Maybe he did believe you. Maybe he was wondering who the hell was insane enough to get you caught in a firefight."

I stare at him. "No. This wasn't your fault. I refuse to let you own this."

He tightens his hold on my hands. "How are you feeling now? I mean right now—telling me this?"

"Do you believe me?"

"Oh, yeah. I was there in those mountains, remember?"

"Kinda hard to forget. I'm angry."

"Angry is good. That means you're with me, you're not having a flashback. You can talk about what happened without hallucinating. It means you're getting some distance. Baby steps, but it's progress. If it makes you feel any better, I'm angry, too."

I try to smile, but it's more of a grimace. "You gonna kill my therapist? Ex-therapist."

He leans forward to collect our drinks and hands me mine. "The thought has crossed my mind. But no worries. I want to spend my life with you, not in prison."

I clink my glass against his. "I love you."

"Good to know. Now, about this dress?" Again, he hooks his finger just inside the neckline.

"What about it?"

"I like it. You should wear dresses more often. Would you mind taking it off?"

IT'S DUSK WHEN I wake up. And just as expected, a few of the D.C. lights are twinkling in the distance. My head on his shoulder, I can feel Cerelli breathing evenly, his chest rising and falling in a smooth rhythm. Maybe he's even asleep—a rarity. I take care not to move. If he's sleeping, I don't want to wake him. Staring at the lights on the horizon, I let my thoughts drift across the Pacific to Doha, then to Afghanistan, stopping in Kabul. I need to make a decision about going and call Chris in the morning.

"What are you going to do?" It's just a whisper, the words barely reaching my ear, but it startles me.

"How did you know I was awake?"

He wraps his arms around me, warm against the cool of the A/C. "I didn't. But I can hope. You're thinking about Afghanistan. Whether or not to go." The wistful tone in his voice warms my heart. His hands trailing down my back make me want to stay with him, right here, forever.

I pillow my head against his chest. "I haven't decided yet. First, I need to figure out what to do about you."

"Meaning?" His hands linger at my waist.

I don't really want to explain myself, so I take a deep breath and try to muffle my words against his chest. "How you'll deal with me being over there."

His hands reverse course, slowly climbing my back. "Take me out of the equation. You need to make this decision for yourself. I won't give you an ultimatum. Todd already played that card. You don't need to go through that again."

"But this morning you said—"

"Forget what I said this morning. I was out of line." His hands stop on my shoulders. "I'm here for you, whatever you decide. Nothing's going to change how I feel about you."

"Cerelli. Thanks, but this isn't helping."

"Tell me what will help you make the decision." His eyes soften, inviting me in. He lifts my chin and lowers his lips to mine.

I block his kiss with my hand and start to push myself to my feet. "You know what could help? Whaddaya say we heat up the leftovers from lunch."

His hands are back on my waist, pulling me down. "Later."

I don't stand a chance.

5

FOR ONCE, I WAKE UP before Cerelli, but only just. By the time I sit up in bed, he's rolled onto his side to face me.

"Decision time." He mouths the words.

I groan. "Don't remind me."

He laughs. "Sweetheart, it's a good thing you're not in the Navy."

"What's that supposed to mean?"

"Decisiveness. A key requirement for any officer. Figure out your course of action and commit to it. You don't like to make decisions."

I shove his shoulder hard enough that he rolls laughing onto his back. "That's just not true. I make decisions all the time."

He raises an eyebrow.

"Yeah, well, maybe not always the best decisions." I pause to watch him try—and fail—to swallow his laughter. "But this decision? Damn it, I want to go. It's just—"

The pounding at the front door stops me. But at least I don't mistake the knocking for gunfire and dive to the floor. A major improvement.

Cerelli's already out of bed, scrambling to pull on jeans and a T-shirt. Then, he's up, balancing on one leg as he straps his stump onto his iWALK. Despite being a leg down, the man hasn't lost a step. He's already out of the bedroom and halfway to the front door, and I'm still scrounging for something to wear. Finally locating a pair of questionably clean black leggings and my new favorite *The Only Easy Day Was Yesterday* T-shirt, I pull myself together and head toward the voices in the kitchen.

Where I discover Cerelli deep in conversation with my twenty-two-year-old daughter, Mel, while they time the coffee steeping in the French press. I do a double take. Mel's sporting her own leggings, a tie-dyed *Embrace Your Story* T-shirt, and long, red hair. I take a second look. The last time I saw her during our clothes shopping trip, her hair was brown—her natural color—and she was adamant about keeping it that way. *Sooo much better for job interviews.* Now, she bears an uncanny resemblance to . . . me. Which shouldn't surprise me. I mean I did give birth to her. But for the last two decades, I thought she looked like her father, my ex, Todd. Now, I see that she doesn't look anything like him. If someone isn't looking too closely, they could fairly easily mistake her for me.

"Mom!"

"Your hair!" I pull her into my arms and hug her tight.

She dances out of my embrace and runs her fingers through her hair. "You like?"

I'm not quite sure what to say and am grateful that Cerelli rescues me. "My favorite color."

Mel manages an impossible smile that's both beatific and self-satisfied before taking a mug of coffee from Cerelli.

"So saturated and . . . natural-looking," I blurt out by way of recovery. "Wait. What are you doing here?"

"Oh! You know." She smiles coyly. "The admiral and I were just talking. He was telling me how much he loves your new dress. The dress I talked you into buying." Her eyes flash the rest of her message: *You're welcome.*

Maybe she's got a point, although Cerelli and I don't seem to need any help in the love life department.

I turn toward the man himself for my own cup of coffee and catch the fleeting smile playing across his lips. He's clearly remembering the ruin he made of that dress.

I let the coffee cool all of ten seconds, then take a long drink, trying to turbo-charge caffeine into my veins. "I meant, what are you doing here? As in, it's kind of early for you to be out of bed on a Sunday, much less visiting us. And what are you doing in Virginia anyway? Last I heard, you were in New York."

That's when I notice that even though Mel's leaning against the counter, doing her best to look casual, she's far from relaxed. In fact, she's literally vibrating. And it's not the caffeine. One glance at Cerelli confirms he's noticed it, too. Oh, God, please let it not be drugs. Six years ago, I caught her smoking dope, but she ended up getting rid of both the marijuana and the boyfriend who got it for her. Since then, she's been pretty vocal about staying clean and strictly organically vegan. I take another look: she's drinking coffee. With milk—cow, not soy. Not so vegan.

"Well . . ." She combs her fingers through her hair, but she can't hide her excitement. "Actually, I've been in D.C. since Thursday."

"Thursday?"

Don't go there! My inner voice is quick to jump in and save me from myself. *Do not say anything about Mel having been in town for four days and that she's just now letting you know!*

"OMG! You'll never guess what happened. This is so epic!"

She's definitely vibrating, not to mention rocking from one booted foot to the other. She's even wearing leather. So much for PETA.

"Tell us." This is from Cerelli, who doesn't seem to mind in the least that Thursday was four days ago.

Mel looks a little disappointed, like she was hoping we'd guess. And fail, of course, which would build the reveal up to maximum effect. But she gets over it quickly enough. "Well, you know I've been applying for jobs since January."

Cerelli and I smile our enthusiasm.

She wisely sets her mug of coffee on the counter. Obviously, she takes after me in more ways than looks. "And I had a few interviews, but nothing came through. Then, early last week, I got a call to come to D.C. for a job interview!"

"And?" I'm starting to vibrate, too.

"I got the job! I interviewed on Friday, and they called last night. Me! They hired me!" There's nothing in the least professional in her shrieks.

Trust Cerelli to ask the pertinent question. "What's the company?"

"Oh, God! You'll never believe this! Al Shabakat."

Somehow, I manage to keep smiling, but I've definitely stopped vibrating. And I say exactly the wrong thing. "Did you say Al Shabakat?"

"I know! One of the best, most prestigious, most admired cable news organizations on the planet. More watched than even TNN. Isn't it great?" She takes a time-out from squealing to launch a *tour jeté* across the kitchen, barely missing Cerelli and me.

I open my mouth, but no words come out.

Cerelli, though, manages to speak. "Impressive." But his voice is missing the congratulations I'm sure Mel is expecting. He shoots me a look that says he's as perplexed as I am. Mel's adjectives may be a little over-the-top, but Al Shabakat does have a presence and a mostly great reputation around the world. So, why on earth would they hire Mel? Okay, so she was a reporter for *Ripples*, her high school newspaper back in the day, and wrote an article that went viral online and on-air and also nearly cost me my life. And she wrote a couple terrific investigative articles for her college paper. But Al Shabakat has been raiding other news organizations— TNN, Fox, MSNBC—and not hiring recent college grads.

"What's the job?" Cerelli again, being an attentive almost-stepdad. The muscle at the corner of his eye looks like it could start pulsing any minute. As he well remembers, Al Shabakat and one of their story-at-all-costs reporters tried to destroy my career. Mel was never privy to all the dirty details, but she knew enough.

Mel's sparkle fades just a bit as she picks up her mug and slurps some coffee. Like she needs more caffeine. "Well, I'll be starting near the bottom. Of course." She looks at me over the rim. "Even though I'm your daughter." Then shifts her gaze to Cerelli. "And your almost-stepdaughter."

Cerelli remains admirably stoic, although the muscle next to his eye is now pulsing. I'm not nearly as admirable. I take the bait. "You used Cerelli's name? My name? To get a job at Al Shabakat?" I'm not yelling. Not exactly. But I'm definitely sputtering.

Mel rolls her eyes. "Yeah. Of course. You always said you'd do whatever you could to help. Besides, everyone plays every card they can. It's what you have to do to get a job these days. So, when the producer put my name together with how much I look like you . . ." She flips some hair behind her shoulder. ". . . that was my cue, and I took it."

Before I can gather my thoughts, Cerelli quietly asks again, "What's the job?"

She's back to smiling, all the way to her eyes. "I'll be the assistant to the producer. And the crew."

In other words, a gofer. Wait. She said *the* producer, meaning there's an assignment.

Cerelli beats me to the question again. "Where's the assignment?"

"Wait till you hear. It's killer." She chugs more coffee, delaying her announcement, all the better to ratchet up the suspense of the moment.

"Well?" I'm not real thrilled about the suspense.

"Afghanistan! To cover the withdrawal of the coalition forces." She's back to vibrating for a moment, only to turn suddenly wistful. "If only Auntie Dar and Uncle Tariq were still there."

"No." My voice is way too curt, too loud, too everything.

"Jeez, Mom, chill." Mel is quick to respond. "I'm not an idiot. I know they're not there."

Cerelli's almost imperceptible shake of the head warns me to ease up. Back off. Take it slow. Sometimes I think he knows Mel better than I do. I'm fully aware how Mel will react if I play the mom card. Nevertheless, that's exactly what I do. "I wasn't talking about Darya and Tariq."

"Then what?"

"When I said no, I meant you're not going to Afghanistan." I'm trying really hard to control my voice, keeping it low and measured and reasoned, but even I have to admit that I sound angry. And what the hell, I *am* angry. Very angry. Not to mention terrified. Who the hell would send a twenty-two-year-old with no journalistic experience— at least no professional experience—to Afghanistan? Especially now. God only knows what's going to happen when the coalition forces leave. Check that. Practically everyone except the White House knows exactly what's going to happen. The Taliban are going to ride a wave of white pickups, motorcycles, and camo-painted Humvees into Kabul and every other city across the country and take over. No matter the agreements they have with the current government, not to mention the U.S., there's no way they're going to power share. My guess: when the Taliban get close to Kabul, President Ashraf Ghani's going to be on the first flight out. Actually, I'm pretty sure that the Taliban are already in Kabul. They've likely infiltrated every level of government—from elected leaders on down to the police and agents at the airport. There's not a doubt in my mind.

Mel stares at me in something close to disbelief. "What did you say?"

"You're not going to Afghanistan. It's too dangerous." I almost cringe as the words dart between us. I can hear the echo of Cerelli saying the same thing to me more than once over the years—until I made it clear that I'd leave him if he ever said it again. But this is different. Mel has absolutely no experience in Afghanistan or any place else. Surely, a semester in Paris her junior year doesn't count. Not for the kind of international savvy she'd need to run errands for a producer of foreign news stories in Kabul. Why the hell did they hire her?

"Mom?"

"Look, sweetie. You don't have any experience in the field. Much less in Afghanistan. You don't know your way around Kabul, and you don't speak any Dari. Besides, no one knows what's going to happen when the coalition forces leave. You could get caught up in God knows what." Okay, I admit, I'm far from calm. My voice is getting louder, and I'm throwing every single one of her weaknesses at her. Not fair, but I seriously don't want her in danger.

She, on the other hand, seems totally in control and even manages to take a sip of coffee. "Are you going?"

"I might. I haven't decided yet. But we're not talking about me. This is about you."

"So, it's too dangerous for me but not for you."

"I've had years of experience."

"Whatever." She pauses a moment, then aims for my jugular. "How old were you when you first went into a war zone?"

I count back, then hesitate. "Twenty-three." My voice is barely above a whisper.

"How exactly do you think I'm supposed to get experience?"

"Not by going to Afghanistan. Not now. Not when the Taliban are about to retake control. ISIS is there, too. Like I said, it's too dangerous." I'm trying for a reasoned tone, but I can hear my voice getting shriller.

Mel stands stock-still for a count of something close to twenty. Then, she carefully, too carefully, sets her mug on the kitchen counter. Turning to me, she slams the palm of her hand into the space between us. "Let's get this straight. I didn't come here to get your permission to take this job. Or for your advice. Or for anything else. I've already signed the contract, and they're working on my visa as we speak. I'm *telling* you that I'm going. Whether you approve or not"—she diffidently shrugs one shoulder—"it's not my problem."

I don't back down. "You have absolutely no idea—"

Again, the palm in the air. "Just because you couldn't hack it over there—"

"Excuse me?"

"Oh, the people at Al Shabakat told me all about your PTSD and you trying to shoot one of their journalists. You are—"

"Mel!" Cerelli crosses his arms and narrows his eyes. He only says the one syllable but in a tone of voice I've never heard before.

She looks at him. Then at me. Her face is flushed in anger, but her eyes are tearing. "You just have to ruin everything, don't you! When I was growing up, it was always about you. You and your career. You were never home. Ever. I was stuck living with *them* when all I wanted was my mother. But you just couldn't bring yourself to sacrifice your precious job. And now, you're trying to . . . to . . . well, fuck you!"

"Mel." Cerelli again. Only this time, I recognize the tone in his voice. I've heard it often enough—each time he's had to talk me in off the ledge.

She whirls on him, arm extended, index finger at the ready in full lecture mode. "No! You, I thought I could trust. In the middle of all her craziness, I thought you'd be normal and rational and . . . and . . . well, fuck you, too." With a stomp of her boot for good measure, she spins on her stacked heel and storms out of the kitchen.

The front door slams shut with enough anger to shake me to my core. I bend at the waist, feeling the full force of her sucker punch. Then, my knees wobble, and I sink to the floor where I stare at the black crescent my daughter's boot heel has marked on the hardwood. A few moments later, Cerelli has me on my feet and heading toward the living room. I collapse onto the sofa, unable to make out the D.C. skyline through the haze. Or maybe it's my tears that are obscuring the view.

"Drink this." He presses a glass into my hands.

I look at him quizzically. "It's too early for bourbon."

"Drink it. Then we'll talk."

Two swallows. I relish the smooth burn. The ache doesn't subside, but the numbness does. Now, though, I'm left staring at the mess I've made not only of my life, but Mel's. Cerelli's arm around my shoulders is seriously the only thing keeping me from going off the deep end.

We talk. That is, I talk, and he listens. He's so good at listening.

Hours later, I realize he really has talked me in off the ledge. Not to mention salvaged my ego and my sense of self as a mother. I've admitted that Mel was right: I did sacrifice my role as her mother—for weeks and months on end—to pursue my career. To save myself. Although she didn't acknowledge that as a big part of the equation. Nor did she mention my guilt at being away from her, guilt that followed me nearly every moment of every day on every assignment. Both of which I've confessed to her in the past.

"I'm sure she'll remember all of that one day," says Cerelli, unbuckling his iWALK and liberating his stump. "Maybe not today."

"You think?"

"Sweetheart, she's a good person. And she loves you. She came here to share her triumph, and we shot her down. We didn't give her what she wanted, and she's lashing out."

"You're right. She *is* a good person. I just don't like being on the receiving end of her fury."

"I take it you were never like that at her age?"

Good of him not to mention the eruptions of fury I've launched at him on occasion over the years. "Perish the thought."

"Must come from Todd." He chuckles.

"Absolutely." But I'm not able to laugh about it. "I'm still angry with Al Shabakat. What the hell are they thinking?"

"Al Shabakat isn't doing her any favors. They're setting her up to fail in a potentially volatile and extremely dangerous situation."

"I'm pretty sure I've heard you say some of that before—and not about Mel."

He lays his arm across my shoulders. "There's a huge difference. You've had a lot of foreign experience, you know your way around Afghanistan, and you're reasonably fluent in Dari. Mel's spent a couple months in France—"

"Don't forget the spring breaks in the Caribbean."

His fingers on my cheek, he gently turns my head so we're looking into each other's eyes. "Do you think we've got any hope of changing her mind?" His voice is so calm and . . . rational, but the worry in his eyes has me flustered.

"I wish, but I kind of doubt it. She seemed pretty resolute when she left."

"What if I get in touch with Al Shabakat?"

How well I know Cerelli's ability to work the back channels to get results. I shake my head. "I don't know. If we get them to pull her from the assignment and she finds out . . . No. Besides, maybe we're selling Mel short. She's smart and savvy. And who knows what she said in the interview. She may've been a total rock star."

Cerelli tightens his hold. "True. She must've been convincing for them to hire her. Al Shabakat is a first-rate, respected orga- nization . . . most of the time. The last thing they want to do is set themselves up for trouble. Even if she did mention our names, there's no way they'd have hired her if she wasn't up to the job."

Snuggling against him, my head pillowed on his shoulder, I drape my legs over his. "Can you reach my phone? I'm ready to call Chris."

"Decision made?"

I nod. "I'm going to Afghanistan."

"Of course you are." He kisses the side of my head.

I just wish he didn't sound so resigned.

6

IT'S MIDAFTERNOON WHEN I decide to call Bonita, my good friend and the tenant of my two-family house in Bay View, Wisconsin—a quirky, slightly edgy town that's part of Milwaukee. For the last six years, Bonita's also been Mel's substitute 'mother' when I'm not around. Before that, my ex, Todd, and Catherine Elizabeth—Mel's stepmother—had charge of her. A relationship that went sideways during my last assignment in Afghanistan. Lucky for me, Bonita and Mel have a mutual adoration society, so it all worked out. And, as I've learned over the years, Mel often tells Bonita things she'd never share with me.

"Took you long enough." Bonita's gravelly voice sounds more than a little miffed. With me.

"So, you know."

"Of course I know. I can tell you our Mel is hurt. Very hurt. What were you thinking?"

Sometimes, Bonita loses sight of the fact that Mel may not

know everything about life and the world. That maybe, acting on what she wants to do—like going to Afghanistan as part of a news crew—isn't necessarily a well-thought-out plan.

"I'm thinking that Mel has no frigging idea what she's getting into. And she's going to a crazy dangerous part of the world as a first assignment."

"And where was your first assignment, missy?"

"Sears. Taking Christmas portraits of little kids with Santa. Something else I wouldn't recommend."

"You know very well that's not what I'm asking. Where was your first out-of-country assignment?"

Oh, hell. Sometimes I wish I hadn't told Bonita so much about my past. "Bosnia," I mumble.

"And exactly how prepared were you for that? Pretty green as I remember."

"But I knew about the business," I protest.

"And which network did you work for then? Or was it a newspaper?"

"Cut the crap, Bonita. We both know I was a stringer. Working freelance and hoping to hell that the AP or UPI or someone would pick up my images. But at least I was with other photogs and journalists. Far behind the lines."

"Our Mel will be, too."

Somewhere close by Bonita, the lab we share—coincidentally named Finn—barks hello. His voice is getting hoarser in his old age. In fact, he's sounding an awful lot like Bonita. Still, he knows it's me on the other end of the phone. Or that's what I like to tell myself. But the truth is he loves everyone and is always gregarious.

"Give Finn a kiss for me?" I picture her planting a kiss on his graying muzzle.

"Might be good if you came for a visit and kissed him yourself. Before he forgets who you are."

"You think that could happen?"

She takes a minute to pet Finn's head and probably bestow a few kisses. "Nah. But he misses you. It's been a few months."

"*Mea culpa.* And I won't be able to get home before I take off again."

Finn's bark of disapproval is loud and sustained.

"Where're you going? Wait. By any chance, could it be Afghanistan? No, as I recall, you swore you'd never go back."

"Your sarcasm isn't working on me, Bonita." I wait a beat. "How'd you know?"

She laughs. "Pretty obvious, don't you think? There's no way you'd let Mel go without following along to check up on her."

"That's what you think I'm doing? Well, I'll have you know I've got an assignment. With TNN. For real."

"Why now?" She sounds taken aback. "You haven't been there in years. And we both know why."

"Because it's the end of Afghanistan. Because I have to go."

"You take good care of Mel while you're there."

"I'll do my best."

A farewell bark from Finn ends the call.

7

I GIVE MEL TWO DAYS to cool off, then I call her. Typical Mel, she doesn't answer. I text, then wait the requisite twenty-four hours. Again, no response. So, either she's still furious and punishing me or . . . or what? Could she have already left for Afghanistan? More likely, she went home to Milwaukee for a couple days to pack and see her father and stepmother. That doesn't feel right, though. Todd and Catherine Elizabeth would demand to know where she's going, and there's no way they'd sign off on her going to a war zone. Knowing them, they'd lock her away in a tower.

Ten more texts, and it occurs to me to check in with my boss. Chris Cardona would know better than anyone how to ferret information about Mel's whereabouts out of Al Shabakat. Well, Cerelli could, too, and probably a lot faster, but I don't want to bring the weight of the U.S. military down on the news media. Or my daughter. That would have repercussions I can't begin to fathom.

This is a big ask and best done in person. Besides which, I need to pick up my passport with the Afghanistan visa and my other travel docs, so I catch the Metrorail into D.C., then hoof it over to the TNN offices.

My comrade-in-arms Kevin isn't in his usual place, guarding our boss's office. In fact, there's no evidence that he's even in today. No sooner do I knock on Chris's door than it swings open, bringing me face-to-face with the man himself.

"Annie. Please tell me you're not backing out of going to Afghanistan." Chris actually sounds worried.

"No way." I laugh. "Like I told you the other day, I'm definitely in. I'm just here to pick up my travel docs."

He waves me in, past the long conference table and video screen that once featured prominently in me almost losing my job. Sitting down behind his desk, he pulls a large manila envelope from the top drawer. "Kevin took the day off, but he said everything's in here." He hands it to me to check over.

I scan the docs and check that the visa is glued into my passport. "Trust Kevin to keep my life running smoothly. You know, if he ever resigns, I'm going, too."

"As will I." Chris leans back in his chair. "What else is on your mind?"

"What do you mean?"

"Give me a break. Why else would you be here? I could have messengered those docs to you."

I drop onto the chair opposite his and sigh. It gets downright annoying that the men in my life can read my every thought. I give him an update on Mel. Or, more to the point, the total lack of information I've accumulated on her. "She's not answering my calls, my texts. I've got no idea where she is—if she's even still in the country."

"Let's see what I can find out." Chris picks up his cell and flips quickly through his contacts. Phone to his ear, he pushes himself to his feet and strolls to the opposite end of his office. "Dave."

This is interesting. I'm pretty sure Chris is talking to his counterpart at Al Shabakat. What I do know for a fact is that these two men don't see eye to eye. Chris has told me more than once that he can't stand the guy, but they are most definitely talking—about Mel. Although I hear her name, I can't make out more than that— and not for want of trying.

Three minutes later, Chris is back behind his desk, pulling open his bottom drawer. Where he keeps his stash of scotch. He sets two glasses on the desktop and pours us each a double. Damn. This isn't going to be news I want to hear. We each pick up a glass. I sip. He downs his. "Mel Hawkins Green flew out yesterday with a few of the other crew members. They should be in Doha about now. Then on to Kabul later today or tomorrow."

I set my glass on the desk with enough force to splash out the remains of my drink.

Chris ignores the spill, instead opening the bottle and topping off both our glasses. "If it makes you feel any better, Dave promised to have the producer keep a close eye on her."

"She's a frigging gofer." We both know that means Mel is there to run errands whenever and wherever needed. No one's going to babysit her. No one's going to care that she's never been to Kabul, that she doesn't speak Dari or Pashto, that she often acts before thinking. They're only going to care that she does what she's ordered to do. I take another sip, then sink back into the chair. "I hate having to depend on an Al Shabakat producer to keep Mel safe."

"Sorry to be so blunt, but why the hell did they hire her?"

"Honestly, I don't have a clue. She's not going to know the first thing about getting things done in Kabul, and that's just going to piss off the crew." I pause for a moment, stare into the amber liquid in my glass, and try to sort my way through Al Shabakat's bizarre hiring decision. "You don't think they could still be sore about what happened six years ago, do you?"

Chris steeples his fingers and presses them against his lips. Finally, he shakes his head. "I could be wrong, but I don't think this has anything to do with what went down between you and Piera McNeil, about Al Shabakat having to take it on the chin and admit they were at fault. I doubt HR knew anything about that. Could be Mel stretched the truth about her experience? Could be she used your name? Could be she nailed the interview."

"All highly plausible." I ignore the rest of my drink. "But this just feels . . . sleazy."

"It does. And I don't like it, but I'm betting it's on the up-and-up. I'll ask around."

"Thanks."

We sit in companionable silence for a few more minutes until finally, I stand, ready to bear the brutal heat and humidity that is D.C. in July.

Chris walks me to the door. "Let me also find out where her crew is staying in Kabul. I'll be in touch."

THANKS TO A BREAKDOWN on the Metrorail, I get home a lot later than expected. As I ride up in the elevator, thoroughly wilted from having spent an hour plus in a stalled, un-airconditioned train, I pray Cerelli has thought to send out for pizza. Or better yet, crisp, chilled salads. I absolutely do not feel like cooking dinner. I can't imagine he'll want to either—not after a long day doing whatever he does at the Pentagon.

I key the lock, push open the door, and immediately hear voices. Cerelli and another man. No. The last thing I want this evening is company. I listen to the other voice. Familiar. But not Sawyer, not Nic. Then I recognize it. Todd. My ex-husband. Mel's father. One guess as to why he's here. I stand quietly, not even breathing, hoping against hope that they haven't heard me come in.

"Annie? Come join us. Todd's here." Do I detect a plea for help in Cerelli's voice?

I shut the door and make my way across the foyer to the living room. At the far end, Todd and Cerelli have kicked back with beers at the dining table. To all appearances, they're having a friendly conversation. Which stops me dead in my tracks. Todd, friendly toward Cerelli?

"Hey. Be with you guys in a minute." A bit light-headed and possibly dehydrated, I head to the kitchen where I pour myself a tall glass of water. And drink it. Then pour another. Something tells me to save the bourbon for later. If Todd and Cerelli are actually getting along, I'm going to need my wits about me.

Cerelli quirks an eyebrow when I deposit my glass on the table. Todd doesn't notice anything amiss, quite possibly because he's got something else on his mind. Something big. Our daughter.

He doesn't pull any punches. No sooner have I sat down than Todd begins his assault. "You mind telling me what you were thinking getting Mel a job at Al Shabakat?"

"Excuse me?"

He closes his hand around the bottle of Boddingtons. I vaguely wonder what Nic would say about Todd drinking his ale.

"Our daughter called, all excited, and said you got her a job. She sure couldn't have gotten a news job without your help. She was a dance major. Who the hell would hire her onto a crew to go to Afghanistan?"

Who indeed? I lean back in my chair. "You're probably not going to believe me, but I had absolutely nothing to do with getting her this job. Or any job. The first we heard about it was Sunday—three days ago—when she showed up and announced it."

"So, she lied." Todd curls up the corner of his mouth—a poor imitation of Cerelli's endearing half grin. "That's what Finn said. I just wanted to hear it from you."

"Now you have—from both of us." Why would she lie about this? Did she think telling Todd and Catherine Elizabeth that I arranged for her job would make it more acceptable? Or maybe that they'd blow up at me instead of her? I take a long drink of water, my thoughts shifting to the oddity in this room. Finn? Todd? Two old buddies just shooting the breeze. The only thing they've got in common is me, as in they've both slept with me.

Todd takes a long pull of his beer. "She on her way to Afghanistan now? Or what?"

I nod. "The one thing I was able to confirm this afternoon."

"So, what're you going to do about it?" His voice is definitely getting tighter, angrier.

I run my index finger around the rim of my glass, then set it on the table. "*Do* about it?" I nod toward Cerelli. "What we tried to do was talk her out of going."

"You can't *talk* to Mel. Do you really know so little about your daughter? She's headstrong. The only way to handle her is to cut something off—her allowance, her car. Oh, I forgot. You don't think that's fair, do you."

"She's twenty-two, Todd. An adult. Cutting off her 'allowance' isn't going to accomplish anything."

"It is if that's what's paying her rent."

"News to me," I say mostly to myself.

"What?"

I wave my hand through the air. "Nothing." Cerelli edges my water glass out of range of my flailing arm. "Look, I spent the last couple days trying to reach Mel, but she wasn't taking my calls or answering my texts. So today, I went to TNN and was able to find out that she and a few members of her crew are already en route to Afghanistan."

To my right, Cerelli offers a curt nod. Clearly, he's been expecting this news. Or maybe he also made this discovery today.

Todd, though, gives loud voice to his frustration. "That's it? You're just letting her go? To fucking Afghanistan? In case you two haven't noticed, it's a goddamn war zone. And it's gonna get a whole lot worse with those Taliban running around beheading people."

I fold my hands in my lap, willing myself to be the sane, rational person in this conversation. But I'm still having a hard time comprehending that Todd is even sitting at the table in Cerelli's condo. "Why are you here?"

"What kind of answer is that? I'm talking about the Taliban, and you want to know why I'm here?"

"Why didn't you call?"

"Why didn't I call? Because Catherine Elizabeth and I thought it best that I come in person to find Mel and take her back to Milwaukee."

"And how did that work out?" I bite my tongue as soon as the words are out of my mouth. My snark is just going to piss him off more.

Instead, he seems defeated, his head sinking against his splayed fingers. For a moment. Then, he's firing on all cylinders again. "Why don't we go back to my question? What are you two going to do to get her back?"

Get her back. Is that what Todd wanted to do with me when I went on assignment to Afghanistan and other crazy dangerous places? I was only a year older than Mel when I first started heading out. Soon after, Todd and I got married. And a couple years after that, there was Mel, though we called her Emmy then. I took some time off, but soon I was itching to get back to work. And I was a stringer—out there on my own, sending in images to the AP. No crew to protect me.

Protection. Half the time, I needed protection from other journalists. Male journalists who were intent on hazing the newbie female photographer. Particularly when I was embedded with the coalition forces in Afghanistan. Which leaves me questioning how secure any woman is out in the field. The ultimate irony: Nic Parker Lowe, once the worst of my hazers, has turned out to be one of my most devoted protectors.

TNN didn't hire me until after the Taliban ambush, after my image of Malalai hit the cover of *Time*, after I won the Pulitzer. That's when I finally was part of a team. I sneak a quick glance at Cerelli. Did he ever think of hauling me home? He sure tried to stop me from going to Afghanistan.

Wait just a minute! My inner voice reminds me. *He didn't want you running around on your own. He was fine with you going on a TNN assignment. Well, maybe not fine, but he didn't try to stop you.*

"Annie? You planning to answer?" Todd has ratcheted up his frustration.

"I'm going to Afghanistan—"

"*You!*" He practically spits the word across the table. "What the hell are you going to be able to do?" He nods toward Cerelli. "Why aren't you gearing up to go? You're the one who could actually do something. Rescue her. The military does that—rescues civilians stuck in wars. Get her back here. Send her to Milwaukee. Catherine Elizabeth and I will take it from there."

Before I can launch my own salvo back at Todd, Cerelli speaks up, quietly but firmly. "The military has been known to rescue civilians." How well he knows that. He's rescued me often enough—the first time being after the Taliban ambush. Although I've never quite figured out if I was the priority or if their primary mission was retrieving Lopez's and Murphy's bodies and blowing up the Humvee. I guess it doesn't matter, but since then, I've landed him numerous times in the middle of the insanity also known as my life. Which for all the world sometimes seems like another ambush. "However, Mel went to Afghanistan of her own accord. And technically, Afghanistan isn't a war zone."

"Bullshit!"

Cerelli gently palms the air between them. "That's not to say it isn't a dangerous place. But, as Annie pointed out, Mel's an adult. There's not a lot I can do unless she asks for help and wants to leave."

"Double bullshit! You could damn well go in there and haul her out. She's just a kid. She's probably already realized she made a mistake. She's probably scared out of her mind and can't get out on her own."

"She's with her crew," I say. "And they do know their way around Kabul. They're not going to let her run around on her own." Which really is bullshit. That's exactly what they're going to do and what her job calls for. But that's the last thing he needs to know. "And I can assure you from personal experience, if she's terrified and flipping out, her producer is going to put her on the first plane home. She'd be putting them at risk, and that's the last thing anyone wants."

Todd slaps his hands flat on the table and pushes himself to his feet. "She's there because of you. Because she's desperate to impress you, to get your approval." He points at me first, then at Cerelli. "If anything happens to my daughter, it's on the two of you."

"Todd—"

"You heard me. This is your fault. All of it." He rounds the table and is only two paces from me when Cerelli's hand stops him.

"Back up." Cerelli's voice is as lethal as the Ontario MK 3 knife he carried when he was in the field.

"Easy, man." Raising both hands to shoulder height in a show of surrender, Todd slowly turns ninety degrees to face Cerelli. But he doesn't back away from me. "I'm not gonna hit her. I'd never hurt her. I lo—"

"Good. Glad to hear it. Now, step away."

Neither man moves an inch. Barely able to breathe, I stare back and forth from one to the other. They're both big men and very fit. But Cerelli is top dog here. He may be a leg down, but he could take Todd one-handed. And I'm pretty sure Todd has realized that. Then, I smell it. Fusty, iron-sharp, and acrid. Fear. Todd reeks of it. He's terrified, probably unable to move, and desperate for a way to save face and get the hell out of Dodge. I'm trying to figure out how to give him that when Cerelli pulls his hand back to his side.

Todd slowly relaxes, although the telltale odor is still oozing from his pores. As he lowers his hands, I see the tremor—slight, but definitely there.

I can't think of a thing to say, except to tell him to leave.

Cerelli, though, clasps Todd's still-trembling hand. "Thanks for stopping by. It's good that we're all on the same page as far as Mel is concerned. We'll keep you posted. Annie's got your number."

8

A FEW DAYS LATER, my gear is packed and lined up next to the front door, and I'm about to get an Uber to take me to the airport. Cerelli takes the cell phone out of my hand. "I'll drive you to Dulles."

I note his perfectly pressed khakis, the knife pleat in his slacks, and wave him away. "That'd be crazy. You need to get to the office, and a trip to Dulles is the opposite direction. You'll be hours behind."

He keeps my phone. "Not crazy. And I don't care how long it takes. I want to see you off."

I smile my confusion. "Why this trip? I always Uber to the airport. In all these years, you've never once driven me."

"Humor me. Please."

"What's going on?"

"Maybe I want to make sure you get there in one piece."

"Ah. You want to make sure I *get* there. As in, you've got some other woman lined up?" I tease. Not that I believe it for a second.

"Sweetheart, jealousy does not become you." He brushes his lips against mine.

And that's all it takes.

NOW WE'RE LATE. AND 495 is a disaster, alternating between masses of cars careening across lanes in front of us at ninety miles per hour, then sudden stoppages that leave us stalled for fifteen minutes at a time. His left hand on the steering wheel, Cerelli drives the Subaru with ease. And apparently with little fear. Me? I'd be white-knuckling the wheel and exhausting myself from the concentration of making sure no one crashes into me. As it is, I'm gripping the passenger handle, anxious about making my flight.

We finally pull into the parking lot.

"I thought you'd just drop me off."

Cerelli offers the half grin I love. "I'll help you carry your gear."

"If you'd dropped me off, I could've gotten a cart."

He raises an eyebrow.

"Sorry. I'd love to have you lug my stuff. Thank you."

Loaded down with my Pelican case of cameras, lenses, and laptop, plus my duffel, Cerelli leads me across the parking lot, into the terminal, and to the Qatar check-in counter. Nonstop to Doha. Where I'll meet up with Nic.

"An upgrade?" the handsome agent asks, eyeing me appreciatively. Or so I like to think.

I smile my gratitude. And maybe even bat my eyelashes. "That would be lovely." Thirteen hours in business class is far better than the close quarters I'd have to endure in coach. Not to mention the welcome glass of champagne and having access to the lounge here and in Doha.

Cerelli walks me to the TSA checkpoint. I get in line, but he reaches for my hand and pulls me to him. A farewell kiss, I'm sure.

Brushing my hair back, he traces the small crescent moon I had tattooed in my hairline six years ago. Hidden from everyone except the two of us. A memento that speaks volumes to me and clearly means a lot to him as well. Leaning close, he whispers in that voice no one but I can hear:

> *The merest sliver of a crescent moon shining tonight*
> *May you blind no other lover but me with your naked light.*

9

Kabul, Afghanistan – August 11, 2021

HAMID KARZAI INTERNATIONAL Airport is strangely quiet. Not at all what I was expecting. I thought for sure there'd be noisy and chaotic lines of people desperate to flee the country, especially considering that many towns and cities to the north and west have already fallen under Taliban control and many of their residents have fled to Kabul. Plus, we're seeing film on cable news networks of the Taliban driving their flotilla of white pickups and motorcycles toward Kabul. They're rumored to be within seventy kilometers. And even though the Ashraf Ghani government is still talking about power sharing, no one else believes that'll happen. In fact, word is that First Lady Rula Ghani has already left the country, even if no one is willing to go on record to confirm that.

But here at the airport, there aren't any long lines. No frenzy. No obvious fear. The people departing on planes to Doha and Europe and the U.S. are calm and orderly and polite as they check their mountains of luggage. And dutifully wear masks.

Nic and I breeze through Immigration, where the agent barely looks at our visas and doesn't even glance at our COVID test results. Foreign correspondents are the only people entering the country, and there aren't very many of us. Just a few crews scattered around the large hall. We head to the Foreign Registration desk, once an all-important step that most of us made sure not to skip, lest the Ministry of the Interior send the police to haul us in. But the desk is now vacant with no evidence of anyone coming to work anytime soon.

We continue on to Baggage Claim, where I retrieve my case of camera gear and my duffel. Nic's duffel takes forever to show up, and when it does, the lock has been snapped off and the zipper left partially open. He takes a quick inventory of the contents. Shirts, jeans, underwear—half his clothes are missing. But looking around, we see no officials interested in helping. And all the luggage carts have gone missing.

Nic shoulders his pack. "We're lucky it wasn't your cameras. I'll see what I can pick up on Chicken Street."

An obviously bored Customs official yawns as he waves us through, not interested in checking any paperwork, and we find ourselves in the Arrivals hall, looking for our fixer Ajmal. It's been a few years since either Nic or I have seen our wiry, clean-shaven friend, and unless he's drastically changed his appearance, I'm not seeing him now. Then, Nic raises his hand in salute and walks more quickly. Across the room, a long-haired and bearded Sawyer, clad in a *shalwar kameez*, stands next to the exit.

"What's going on?" I ask as I trail behind. "Where's Ajmal?"

"Don't know, old thing. Guess we'll find out."

Stepping forward, Sawyer relieves me of both my duffel and the Pelican case. "You got everything?" He reaches to grab my pack, but I bat his hand away.

"Except for half of Nic's clothing, we're good to go."

Sawyer shoots a sharp look at Nic. "Anything else missing?"

"Nothing that can't be replaced." Nic shrugs, then keeps walking.

Something tells me these two are talking in some kind of code known only to them. What could Nic be bringing in-country that has Sawyer antsy? It couldn't be a gun or ammo. There's no way either of us would risk that.

We pick up our pace and start across the parking lot to the Humvee with tinted windows. Armored, I assume. Looking around, I don't see anything different about the exterior of the airport. Except that there are many fewer vehicles in the lot and only one taxi hoping to pick up a fare. Afghan soldiers, heavily armed, are out in force, patrolling the building as well as the perimeter. To protect the airport from invading Taliban? Far from making me feel secure, they're adding to my sense of doom, especially since many of them are taking long, hard looks at me. Which leads me to wonder if some of them might just happen to be undercover Taliban.

I make sure to stay close to Sawyer. "Am I glad to see you!"

"Don't get used to me." Sawyer grins, although his good humor doesn't go all the way to his eyes. "I'm just here to pick you up and pass along a few gifts. After that, I'll be in the wind." I can only imagine what he'll be doing—the operations he'll be shutting down, the equipment he'll be destroying, and the papers he'll be shredding, not to mention the people he'll be trying to get out of the country.

At the Humvee, he stows our luggage in the rear, then unlocks the doors, directing both Nic and me to the back seat. Climbing in, I look up to see Ajmal—six years older, still as wiry as ever, and no longer clean-shaven. But there's no hiding his warm smile. When I think of Ajmal, this is exactly what I see in my mind's eye: his joy, his hospitality, and his love of Afghanistan.

I return his smile. "Ajmal. *Assalâmu alaykum*. It's wonderful to see you. I was worried when you weren't in the Arrivals hall."

"*Wa 'alaykum assalâm.*" He nods, then reaches past me to shake Nic's hand. "To see you and Nic again, the pleasure, it is mine." He doesn't say what I'm sure we're all thinking: *One last time, I am able to welcome you to my country.*

"Ajmal and I agreed it'd be best for him to stay in the vehicle while I went inside to get you," says Sawyer, sliding behind the steering wheel and firmly shutting his door. "From what I can tell, there are Taliban all around us—undercover in the Afghan army. And everywhere else in Kabul—the police, the government, universities. The less he's seen with coalition military forces, the better." He keys the ignition, and we head out of the lot toward the highway.

"It's that bad?" Nic sounds worried.

"It's actually quiet. For now." Sawyer looks over his shoulder at me. "But things are gonna get bad—even though the government leaders are behaving like a flock of ostriches with their heads up their asses. They're still convinced the Taliban are going to share power." He snorts in disbelief.

"Herd," says Nic.

Sawyer peers into the rearview mirror, confusion clouding his eyes. "Pardon?"

"A group of ostriches is called a herd."

"Good to know. Learned that at Cambridge, did you?"

Nic doesn't explain and gives me a sidelong glance to warn me away from saying anything about his living in South Africa with his zoologist husband. Six years ago, he trusted me with the fact that he's gay. Cerelli and Sawyer and Chris all figured it out a while back, but until Nic comes out to them, they're all sworn to secrecy.

I lean forward. "Ajmal, will you be okay with us? Nic and I aren't military, but the Taliban sure aren't fond of Western media or either one of us. Especially me." I'm betting they never canceled the vow of *nyaw aw badal* that tribal leaders swore against Sawyer, Cerelli, and me back in 2006. And again in 2015.

Ajmal smiles away my concern. "You are not to worry. *Inshallah*, all will be well."

Does he seriously believe that? Or is he just trying to make me feel better? I catch Sawyer's glance at me in the rearview mirror. A definite eyeroll. Well, at least I know where he stands.

We make it across Kabul in amazing time. Once we exit the highway and are cruising along mostly empty city streets, I see a few people on sidewalks, walking home from work or stopping in food stores. We're just about to my favorite mosque with its exquisitely tiled façade when the *mu'adhdhin* calls the *adhan* for *salat al-'Asr*. In the past, I would've seen hundreds of men hurrying along sidewalks to this large mosque for late-afternoon prayers, but not today. Just a few men, walking fast—and it seems to me furtively—to prayer. I'm guessing many people must be holed up in their homes, afraid that the Taliban are already in the city and hoping to wait out the fighting soon to come. The dread and fear are palpable, turning the air acrid and weighing down on the roof of the Humvee.

I take advantage of the lull in our conversation to check my texts. A few lines from Cerelli. I let him know we've arrived safely and are heading to the TNN apartment. The same in response to Chris's text. But there's nothing from Mel. It's been more than a week since she stormed out of the condo, and not a word. We've had blowups before, but we've always resolved them. Evidently, not this time.

Sweetie, I'm in Kabul with TNN. I'm so, so sorry for everything I said. Can I please see you?

My text is pretty close to a full grovel. Damn, I hope it works.

Another ten minutes and Sawyer pulls up in front of the six-story building where TNN has an apartment for its correspondents. Sandwiched into a row of similar buildings, it's pretty nondescript, which I've always thought was a good thing. Modern enough with poured concrete slab walls and windows offering limited views. Out front, the ten-foot-high wall topped with barbed wire catches my eye. So do the two guards, AK-47s slung over their shoulders, standing in front of the wrought iron gate. They're clean-shaven, but that doesn't mean they're not Taliban.

"Hold up!" Sawyer evidently has a few more instructions to impart.

I pause, my hand on the door handle.

He pulls a metal lockbox out from under his seat. "For you, Annie. As I recall, you know how to handle a Sig Saur." He gives me the gun that caused no end of trouble in the past. Some packets of ammo come next, followed by my trusted sat phone.

"A sat phone? I've got my cell, and the plan is for us to stay in Kabul." Where reception is fairly reliable.

"Plans can change," says Sawyer gruffly. "Not to scare you, but no one knows what's going to happen. Cell towers—hell, the entire grid—could go down. The admiral said to give you the sat. He'll feel better knowing you've got it. So will I."

Stuffing everything into my pack, I let my thoughts linger on

Cerelli. Bottom line: he'd rest easier if I weren't here at all. But if he feels better knowing I have the ability to defend myself, then I'm all for it. From the look Sawyer gives me, I get the feeling he'll be talking to Cerelli later. Hard to believe there once was a time when I fought against these two guys teaching me how to shoot. Now, I'm actually relieved to have the gun.

Glancing first at Nic, then at Ajmal, he asks, "Either of you gents want a Sig? I've got plenty."

Nic looks thoughtful for a few moments, then shakes his head and climbs out of the vehicle. Ajmal, though, accepts one and slips it in his waistband before joining Nic at the gate in the wall.

"One more thing, Annie." Sawyer hands over a loosely wrapped package. "And believe me, I know this is the last thing you want, but as always, the admiral wants to keep you as safe as possible. You may find you really do need a *burqa* in the next few days."

I take the package, which seems thicker than just one *burqa*. "Anything else in here?" Maybe a second one that I could somehow get to Mel? I seriously doubt her crew has thought to outfit her with one. And even though she won't want it any more than I do, Cerelli and Sawyer are right that *burqas* could keep both of us safe. Especially in the face of the Taliban.

"He thought you might be more amenable to wearing an *abaya*. You know, not covering your face could make it easier to take pictures."

Right. Like I want to wear either one. But I absolutely do want Cerelli resting as comfortably as possible. So, I say, "He's right." There, let Sawyer report that back to him. With any luck, he won't worry to distraction or run back to his shrink to talk about his feelings for me. Or talk to Sam Harris.

He grins. "Now I'm worried." His grin slides off his face.

"Look, I won't be around much from here on out, but my number's programmed on that sat phone. Number two. Right after Finn's. Things could get dicey. Hell, things will get dicey. It's not just the Taliban we're dealing with. We've got solid intel that ISIS is here, too, hoping to take advantage of the chaos that's about to erupt. There's no love lost between those two groups, and ISIS would like nothing better than to step into the void and take over."

"Thanks for the warning."

"One more thing."

"Yeah?"

"This is between you and me. When're you going to marry Finn and put him out of his misery?"

All I can do is stare back at Sawyer. Cerelli's miserable? Seriously? Well, sure, he's proposed a few times, but I've kind of thought we've been doing okay the way things are. Finally, I muster some words. "He's been talking to you about this, has he?"

Sawyer shakes his head and has the decency to look abashed. "Not on your life. He'd have my head if he knew I said anything."

"Then why did you?"

"The man means a lot to me. I don't like seeing him suffer."

He's suffering? "What can I say? One day we'll get it together."

Sawyer studies me for a long ten seconds, then offers a clipped nod. "You mean a lot to me, too. Look, you need me, you call, and I'll do what I can."

BY THE TIME I MAKE it inside the sixth-floor apartment, the four men in the crew have taken up positions on the two sofas that overwhelm the small front lounge. Sensing that our producer,

Sadim, isn't thrilled to see me as part of the crew, I sink onto the floor pillow at the far end of the room. Totally out of sight. Maybe it's intentional on their part. Maybe not. But from here, I can fully appreciate the cramped room as well as the tiny kitchenette with its two-burner hot plate and the dorm-room fridge. Down the narrow, dark hall, as I well remember, are two claustrophobic bedrooms, each with a pair of cots that aren't quite wide enough to be called twins.

On previous assignments, only the foreign correspondents stayed here, so it didn't feel quite so cramped. But this time around, Sadim and the videographer Azizullah both think it's better—and safer—for them to bunk here. Ajmal, too. Although they all live in Kabul, they're understandably reluctant to go home at night, running the risk of encountering Taliban in the streets and, even worse, possibly endangering their families. Their daily interaction with Nic and me will be noticed and could easily bring unwanted attention to their wives and kids. The Taliban have been known to punish the innocent for the deeds of husbands and fathers, brothers and uncles. God only knows what ISIS could do. Besides which, we'll likely be putting in long days and nights. There won't be much time for the Afghan guys to run home anyway.

We negotiate for sleeping arrangements, and I end up the loser, stuck sleeping on one of the too-short sofas.

One bathroom. Normally this wouldn't be a problem, but with this many people, things could get tricky. Sadim announces the morning schedule for the bathroom, each of us getting five minutes. I get the last spot, which could be good if the guys don't take their full time. Or run through all the hot water. It could also be a nightmare. I'm hoping no one gets the runs—a real possibility if this becomes a war zone, water gets scarce, and dysentery hits.

We're each responsible for our own meals, but after a moment's thought, Ajmal voices his objection. "This plan, it is not good."

Sadim looks ready to knock our fixer sideways. It's clear he doesn't want to be challenged, but a few seconds later, he relents. "Go ahead. What is your idea?"

"The food, it will become hard to obtain. The prices are already very high. I think I will be in charge of the meals."

Ajmal is volunteering to do women's work? A look of astonishment crosses the other Afghans' faces.

I come to Ajmal's rescue as quickly as possible. Being the only woman on this crew, I definitely don't want to get stuck cooking for the guys. "I think that's brilliant. Do you want us to ante up money now?"

He flashes me one of his famous smiles. "Yes." He nods. "Thank you. Money now, that is a good idea." In the past, when we've struck similar arrangements, we collected receipts and TNN reimbursed our fixer later, sometimes months later. But I'm betting Ajmal realizes that could be next to impossible. I can't imagine how we'll get payments into the country once the Taliban take over. Besides, he'll need as much money as he can get for his family to survive in the coming days and weeks. We each hand over a hundred bucks. I'm pretty sure this is only the beginning. Food is going to get scarce, and when it does, prices are going to skyrocket.

On the plane coming in, Nic and I both thought we'd spend our first day in Kabul reconnoitering the city, and that's exactly what Sadim has planned—for later in the day. "First thing tomorrow morning, we will interview the minister of the interior—General Mirzakwal. I am also working on a meeting with Mullah Abdul Ghani Baradar—maybe for the next day."

"A great start!" Nic sounds pleased. "I've always wanted to interview the Taliban leader."

Sadim tips his head in appreciation, but he isn't looking at Nic. He's directing his gaze downward—directly at me.

My heart sinking, I know what he's about to say. *Dress modestly and cover your hair.* This isn't the first time he's pulled the alpha male card. I lock eyes with him, determined not to give in to more than a headscarf.

"I think you will not be part of these interviews, Annie. You being there, that could make the general uncomfortable. We want him at ease so that he will speak the truth. Not the pap he has been spouting to other networks. Mullah Baradar, though, he will definitely refuse for you to be there."

This I wasn't expecting. "Sorry." I keep my voice steady. "That's not going to cut it. TNN sent me to get photo—"

Out of the corner of my eye, I see Nic lift his chin and cross his arms. "Not on. If Annie has to stay back, so do I."

Sadim also crosses his arms and shifts to talk this out with Nic. The body language is telling. Clearly, he's more comfortable dealing with men, which has me baffled. I've worked with Sadim in the past, and other than covering my hair, there was never a problem. What's changed? "Azizullah can take some still images."

Next to him, looking surprised, Aziz stiffens. "I am a videographer." From anyone else, this would sound arrogant as hell, but he's being savvy. Instead of actually refusing, he's left the rest of his sentence unsaid for Sadim to fill in the blanks. Which allows Sadim to save face and retreat.

But he doesn't. At least not right away.

Testosterone quickly overwhelms the room, so potent I can see the fog of it and smell it. The room was overcrowded before but is fast becoming intolerable. Too many egos. Too many men. And far too hot. I notice the A/C unit in the window next to me isn't on. Looking to Ajmal, I tilt my head in question. He responds with a quick slice of the hand. Damn. Nothing to cool down the room. And no A/C will make for miserable nights. To make matters worse, there's no way to open the windows; they're fixed in place. No hinges, no handles, no hardware of any kind.

Finally, Sadim responds. To Nic, not to me. "She will wear the *burqa*."

I answer for myself. "I'll wear an *abaya*." No way am I going to have a hatched screen blocking my view.

More testosterone wafts through the room.

Sadim looks pissed, but he doesn't actually say no to my offered compromise. "The *burqa*. You will have it with you. In case it is necessary."

I dip my head in agreement, noticing for the first time how dingy the white walls have gotten. This place was pristine the last time I was here. The grime and grease could be the result of years of use and no upkeep. But the smears of black and specks of reddish-brown that look disconcertingly like blood are a whole other story.

10

IT'S GOING ON 10:00, long after we've eaten the *kabuli pulao* and crisp *salaateh Afghani* Ajmal brought in for dinner. The sky is now inky dark and heavy with the lingering heat. Given our early wake-up call tomorrow, the guys have all retreated to the bedrooms, leaving me alone in the lounge. From the sounds of the syncopated snores alternating from one side of the hall to the other, it's clear they're all asleep. Damn, they're loud! I actually debate sneaking back and easing their doors closed but quickly decide against it. With this heat, they'll either suffocate or drown in their sweat.

Still, I need to sleep or I'll be dead on my feet tomorrow, giving Sadim the excuse he wants to leave me behind. I've just decided to call Cerelli when Nasrat Parsa begins to sing one of his romantic songs, which tells me this is the same sat phone I used back in 2015. It also tells me the man himself is calling. Unless, of course, it's Sawyer reporting that things have gotten horribly worse sooner than expected. Digging the phone out of my pack, I press the call button and whisper, "Hey."

"Hey, yourself. Can you talk?" Cerelli's voice. Exactly what I need to hear.

"Walk with me outside. The TNN apartment is tiny, and the guys have all gone to bed." I check my *Double Exposure* T-shirt and baggy pants to make sure I'm decent, pull on my *keffiyeh*, collect my flashlight, and head toward the door.

"I've been in that apartment. It's not that bad."

Why am I surprised? Of course Cerelli's been in the apartment. "It's cramped when five people are camping out here."

"Yeah, I should've figured the Afghan members of your crew would want to stay there. A lot safer for all of you. Tell me you're not sharing a room with anyone. Or, if you are, please say it's Nic."

I stand in front of the elevator for a full minute, but it isn't answering my call. Probably down for the night, so I pick my way carefully down the dark concrete stairs. "Lucky me, I drew the short straw and got the sofa in the lounge."

Cerelli makes a noise akin to a growl. "I don't like it. You're exposed out there. If someone breaks in . . ."

"No one's going to break in. There are two armed guards out front."

"The guys in the apartment have easy access to you." He sounds seriously bothered.

"Come on, they're good guys. I trust them. Mostly. Although Sadim's been kind of strange since we got here." I step onto a partly crumbled concrete stair, and my foot slips out from under me. "Shit!" Dropping the flashlight, I manage to grab hold of the handrail and sit down hard on the step. My flashlight clunks its way stair by stair down to the landing, the sound echoing eerily around me.

"You all right?"

"I'm fine. I just slipped. And lost my flashlight. Wait! The universe is with me. I can see it shining down there." Descending carefully to the landing, I retrieve my light and continue slowly down to the dimly lit reception area. Unstaffed. A good place to talk with no one listening in. I try the front glass door. Locked, just as Sadim said it would be—as of 9:00 p.m. I can get out, but no one—including me—can get back in without a key. Glancing out at the gate, I trust that's locked, too. I really am feeling fine. No prickling at the back of my neck. No sense of being watched, stalked. I'm good.

"About Sadim?" Leave it to Cerelli. He never gives up.

"It's probably nothing, but the man obviously doesn't want me here. Much less going out with the crew on interviews. It's one excuse after another. The rest of the guys finally backed me up, saying if I don't go, they don't either."

"You think he could be trying to protect you?"

I laugh. "If he is, it's not going over well. I'm here to do a job, and everyone knows it."

"Be aware."

"Promise."

"Sweetheart, as much as I like talking to you, I've got a reason for calling."

"Tell me."

"I found out where Mel is staying with the Al Shabakat crew. You have something to write this down?"

"I've got nothing. Let me check out the lobby." A minute later, I've still got nothing. "Just tell me the address."

"You know as well as I do that Kabuli's don't know street names. So, my guy didn't give me an address as much as directions."

"Go for it. I'll do my best to remember."

He dictates some fairly basic directions with landmarks that I know. I repeat everything back to him and shine the flashlight on my watch: 10:30. Late. But is it too late to see if I can rouse anyone at the Al Shabakat apartment?

As if he can read my mind from seven thousand miles away, he says, "Promise me you're not going over there tonight."

I take all of five seconds to answer, but evidently, that's five seconds too many.

"Annie. I'm not telling you what to do, but God Almighty, you'll kill me if I find out you're wandering around Kabul in the middle of the night."

I lean my forehead against the glass door. "It's not the middle of the night, and I wouldn't be wandering." That's when I realize I don't see the armed guards. The entire time I've been standing here, neither of them has walked in front of the gate or anywhere that I can see. I scan the narrow courtyard in front of the building and see no shadows lurking, just a hammock slung between two trees, but it's twisted inside out. No one's sleeping there. Which means if I were to go looking for Mel tonight, there'd be no way for me to get back in. So, where the hell are the guards? Sadim didn't say anything about them disappearing come nightfall.

"Annie? You still there?"

"Yeah. Sorry. I was just . . . look, I promise I'm not going anywhere tonight. I'll wait till tomorrow." That should make him happy.

"Good. Thank you." Cerelli sounds relieved. "And promise me you'll get one of the guys to go with you."

"Cerelli . . ." My voice rises.

"Hey, you can't fault me for trying."

"Yeah, well." He's right, though—I probably should have someone with me. We'll see.

"Now, tell me what's bothering you."

The last thing I should do is tell him about the missing guards. He's already way too worried as it is. "I'm tired is all."

He exhales. A sure sign he doesn't believe me. "Come home to me. Please. Don't make me load you into a body bag."

"No worries, my love." I do my best to laugh, but it comes out sounding pretty wobbly. "A body bag is absolutely not in the plans."

"You have plans?" His voice is warm again, wrapping around me, almost making me forget the missing guards.

"I do."

"Tell me." The smile in his voice has my heart singing.

"Soon enough, Admiral, soon enough."

11

August 12, 2021

BY 5:00 A.M., WITH THE guys still snoring and the sky starting to lighten, I give up trying to sleep. My T-shirt and baggy pants are drenched with sweat. Digging a fresh *shalwar kameez* and clean underwear out of my duffel, I make my way to the bathroom. Ready to step in the shower, I remember the groaning hot water pipe from years ago and decide it's far too early to wake up the household and possibly the people in the apartments below. Besides which, Sadim will likely lash into me for not adhering to the rota he set up and will definitely put down his foot about my planned walk over to Mel's apartment. I settle for brushing my teeth and splashing some cold water on my face. Good enough.

Dressed for the day, I shoulder my pack and let myself out the apartment door. That's when I remember Cerelli's attempt to make me promise not to go alone to the Al Shabakat apartment. Should I wake one of the guys? No way. If someone were already awake, that'd be one thing. But as I well know, sleep comes at a premium on these assignments. No one will be happy if I deprive him of even a minute.

One look at the elevator tells me it's still not operational, so again I make my way slowly and carefully down flight after flight of stairs. I'm mentally reviewing the directions Cerelli gave me last night, making sure I know where to go, when I hear a stairwell door whisper shut above me. A few footsteps. Then nothing.

"*Salâm!* Hello!" I call. No answer. Strange, but my fear factor is on zero, so I'm pretty sure I'm okay. Another ten seconds then I hurry down the rest of the stairs.

I heave a sigh of relief when I reach the lobby. Pushing my way through the front door, I immediately notice an armed guard peering at me through the wrought iron bars of the gate. A moment later, a second guard joins him, then opens the gate. They're back!

"Good morning, madam."

"*Assalâmu alaykum*," I say, pausing a moment to chat, hoping that whoever was following me shows himself. But no one opens the door to the building. No one crosses the courtyard. All is well.

The guard responds with a smile. "*Wa 'alaykum assalâm*." Then, in Dari, he adds, "You will be careful, please."

"*Balê*." I nod. Yeah, I'll most definitely be careful. Anything else and Cerelli would kill me.

Following my street a few blocks, I come to the small mosque Cerelli specifically told me to check out. *It's my favorite mosque anywhere in the Middle East. I think you'll see why.* I do. Not nearly as grand as others in Kabul or Islamabad or even Saudi, this quiet mosque speaks to me in a personal way. I linger a few minutes to admire the intricately patterned mosaic tilework—so many gorgeous blues and royal purples. And the gold plating of the minaret shimmers in the early morning light.

Slipping my camera with the wide-angle lens from my pack, I line up a shot. Not quite what I wanted to capture. No cars are coming, so I step into the street. I'm almost to the middle of the road when I see the deep rose of sunrise appear to the left of the mosque, making the aqua tiles absolutely dazzle. My fingers tingle as I press the shutter, and I know I've captured its peaceful beauty. My heart soars as I imagine Cerelli's appreciation of this pic. Then, a sense of impending dread congeals in my chest as I realize he may never see this mosque in person again.

Time to move on. I'm out this early for a reason—to find Mel. And talk to her, make sure she's okay. Do whatever it takes to get our relationship back on track.

At the corner, I take a right. Six more blocks to my favorite bakery—already open and selling *nân*. I linger for a few moments in front of the window, breathing in the intoxicating aroma and remembering the fabulously delicious pastries and cookies I've bought here over the years. But none of them are on display. From what I can see, except for stacks of flatbread, the inside shelves are bare. Still, as my stomach reminds me, this is definitely worth a stop on my way back.

I continue walking, anticipating how wonderful that round of warm bread is going to taste. Before I know it, I'm at the park. Spanning several city blocks, it's so green and cool with all that shade—a perfect place to rest when the day heats up. But this early in the morning, I don't see a soul here. Check that, I see white tents in the distance. And a few narrow columns of smoke—probably from cook fires. I know people from outlying towns and villages have been fleeing ahead of the Taliban. Could this be where some of them are camping out? How long before it becomes a full-blown displaced persons camp? I'm kind of surprised the police are allowing it. Then again, the police probably have a lot else going on.

Wait! What did Cerelli say about the park? I put my memory on rewind. *If you come to the park, you've gone too far.* I backtrack a block, and, trusting that he said *a block too far,* I make a left. And there's the Turkish Embassy, just like he said—its red flag with the white crescent and star waving atop the flagpole, armed soldiers at their posts just inside the gates. *Two blocks past the embassy, you'll come to . . . then right across the street . . .* What? I'll come to what? Damn! What did he say?

Two blocks past the embassy, I come to a wrought iron gate set in a ten-foot-high protective wall. *Al Shabakat* is etched in Dari and English on the shiny brass plaque. As luck would have it, I'm just in time to see the guards unlocking the gate for a man in Western clothes who's hurrying out of the building. Clanging the gate shut behind him, he turns to look at me. Just like five years ago, his black eye patch takes me aback.

He cracks a broad smile. "Annie Hawkins. I didn't expect to find you loitering outside my building."

"Josh. It's been a while."

"Crikey, last time I saw you was in Doha."

I nod. "I was on my way home from Yemen. You were trying to get in."

"Eh, spent weeks in Saudi, but never did make it in. As I recollect, you weren't very helpful with advice on how to get over the border."

I shrug. "Some of us get in. Some don't."

"Kudos to your team. You put together a great documentary. Your photos were ace, by the way. Won some more awards, I hear."

"Thanks. Still working for Al Shabakat, I see."

He grins. "I've come up in the world. Chief foreign correspondent."

"Congratulations." And he hasn't changed a bit. Still those rugged good looks that once, years ago, might have tempted me. A few crinkles around his eyes, but if anything, he looks even younger. "So, I hear you're working with my daughter."

For a split second, he looks like an emu caught in the headlights, eyes wide, mouth agape. But I'll hand it to him, he recovers fast. "Your daughter?"

"I think she's your gofer."

"Mel Green is your daughter? I never would've guessed. She must look like her father."

"I'd have thought the red hair would be a dead giveaway." Even if it is out of a bottle. I tilt my head toward the gate. "Could you let me in?"

"What? Why?" His voice climbs an octave.

"I'd like to see her. My daughter."

He runs a hand through his still-blond, attractively shaggy hair. I'm pretty sure his hand is trembling. "Can't now. I'm already late. And . . . Mel left a while ago. That girl never sleeps. You know how it is. We're all keeping nineteen-hour days."

"Damn," I mutter under my breath. "Look, what would be a good time to catch her?"

His shrug is overly dramatic. "Jeez, Annie." Again, he rakes his hand through his hair. This time, I'm positive I see the tremor. "I don't know what to tell you. We're running nonstop. Maybe later this evening. But honestly, I can't promise anything." He leans forward to shake my hand, then thinks better of it and bumps my elbow. A last-minute bit of social distancing from a man who isn't masked-up and looks like he hasn't worn one in months. If ever.

"Tell you what—I'll let her know you came round. Maybe she could text you."

The perfect out, and what can I say? I seriously doubt Mel's going to text me—unless her producer or Josh orders her to. "Sure. Okay. Thanks."

At exactly that moment, as if it were planned, a black Humvee with tinted windows pulls up to the curb next to him. "My ride. See ya!" He raises his hand in farewell and practically bolts to the car.

The door is open for barely a handful of seconds, but that's long enough for me to see two other people in the back seat. Is one of them Mel? It's dark inside, and they're both looking away from me, so it's impossible to say. The Humvee speeds away, cutting right in front of a white pickup, which sets off a cacophony of honking horns. I shield my eyes against the morning sun and watch the rear brake lights of Josh's vehicle blink on as another car runs the intersection directly in front of them.

Why so fast? Maybe they've got an important interview lined up. I glance at my watch: 7:10. Unlikely at this time of the morning. Or maybe he wanted to get away from me. Which could also explain the tremor—something I've never noticed before. Not early onset of Parkinson's. Nerves.

I start my long walk back to the TNN apartment, thinking all the while about Josh. The man's been a foreign correspondent for decades—often in war zones. It could be he was telling the truth, that he really was running late. Except the Josh I remember from our embed with the coalition forces at Forward Operating Base Masum Ghar was as laid back as they come.

Masum Ghar. The main thing I remember was the hazing I endured at the hands of some of the male journalists—Josh and Nic were two of the perpetrators. Oh, fuck. I stop walking. Hazing.

Could Josh actually be doing something to Mel? My heart pounds as I imagine the possibilities. Dumping her somewhere in Kabul. Or even worse, outside the city, far from any village.

Except, as Josh made clear years later when we met up in Doha, he wasn't the instigator. Nic was. And even though Josh went along with it, he later apologized. As I remember, he sure seemed sincere. Not to mention a little scared when I reamed him out, swearing I'd have his balls if he ever hazed another female journalist. Would he dare do something like that again? No, that just doesn't feel right. He promised, and for some reason, I believe him.

I'd feel so much better if Mel would just shoot me word that she's okay and doing well at her job. Is that too much to ask? I pull out my cell to see if maybe she's texted, but find nothing. Which could be her typical letting days go by without responding. Or she could still be royally pissed and giving me the silent treatment. I slip my phone back into my pants pocket. There's nothing for it but to get back to my own crew, do my job today, then try her again tonight. Arguments with my daughter have always done me in, left me twisting in the wind. But I can't let my speculation affect my job performance. Besides, even if she's a fish out of water, Mel is most definitely smart and savvy and can figure out what she's got to do.

Back to walking, I detour into the bakery where the only item on offer really is *nân*. I'm guessing that no one's in the mood to bake or buy pastries. Only the basics. I dread thinking how long it will be before this store returns to creating my favorite buttery *kulcheh chaarmaghzi* and decadent fried *khetayee*, sweet *roat* and cream rolls. For now, I buy a *nân-e-roghani* and, relishing the warm yeasty aroma and the pillowy texture, start back to my apartment and my own crew.

I've gone only half a block when the hairs on the back of my neck start to prickle, then stand on end. Someone's following me. Damn! It's been so long since I've had to deal with this that I actually let myself believe it wouldn't be an issue. I try to shut it down. *Look!* I tell myself. There are other people on the sidewalk, out and about, going to work, running errands. All normal, regular people. Chances are they're not Taliban, not ISIS.

My neck's still prickling.

Who am I kidding? Any one of these men could be Taliban. Any one of them might remember me, remember that there's an oath of *nyaw aw badal* sworn against me.

My heart sinks. I shouldn't have left the apartment without letting someone know. More to the point: like Cerelli said, I shouldn't have gone out on my own. If I'd been in Yemen or Nigeria, Syria or Iraq, even Pakistan, I would've asked someone to go with me. Nic. Our fixer. A male someone is always the best bet. What am I trying to prove by doing this alone? God, I hope Mel isn't running around the city without an escort. Of course she is. That's exactly what a gofer does.

I walk faster, then faster still until I'm jogging. My military-issue boots slap against the sidewalk, and the pounding of my heart fills my ears. But I'm pretty sure I can hear the slapping of someone else's shoes—leather sandals—behind me. Someone's *chasing* me?

Clutching what's left of my bread, I run through the heat billowing off sidewalks that are now strangely empty of people. Where did everyone go? I push myself to run faster, but with each stride, my pack slams against my lower back. The tunic of my *shalwar kameez* is wet, clinging to me in all the wrong places. Please don't let any Taliban see me looking like this. Even though I'm not Afghan, I can just imagine a whip unfurling and coming down hard across my back—punishment for indecency.

Finally, I round the corner onto my street. Up ahead I see three men standing in the middle of the sidewalk. The two guards seem to be sticking close to the gate. When I get closer, I recognize my crew. Even though I'm still half a block away, I can see that Nic and Azizullah are grinning about something. Sadim, though, looks frigging furious.

I slow to a walk for the last thirty paces. "Good morning." Nearly breathless, I gasp out the words. Bending at the waist, I struggle to gulp air into my lungs. Then allow myself a quick glance over my shoulder and see Ajmal half a block back running toward us. Was he the person chasing me?

"Where have you been?" Sadim is way too close to an explosion. "We needed to leave at seven."

"Sorry about that. I didn't know. Last night you said eight o'clock, so I figured I had enough time." Checking my watch, I confirm that it's now 7:45, plenty of time before the agreed-upon departure.

Sadim takes a deep breath, clearly trying to get a handle on his anger. "I received a call from Mirzakwal's office early this morning, changing our appointment time. But you left without telling anyone."

"You could've texted me." I pull out my cell and hold it up to make my point.

"I think when you check your messages, you will find that I did." He's even angrier now, his voice getting louder with each word.

I pull up my messages, and there it is. Sadim wanting to know where the fuck I am. Telling me to get back to the apartment ASAP. Absolutely my fault. "Sorry. It won't happen again."

He's not ready to forgive. "Now we are *very late*." He emphasizes the last two words. To punish me, I'm sure.

I make a snap decision and decide there's nothing to be gained by trying to explain. Or responding at all.

Then, breathing hard, Ajmal stops beside me. I take note of the underarm sweat stains on his dampened tunic—which is probably exactly the way I look. Except he won't be going in to photograph the minister of the interior. I drop my eyes to his well-worn leather sandals, which would produce the sound I heard behind me. I exhale my relief. It was Ajmal following me. Why on earth? Was he at the bakery to buy breakfast? Or maybe Sadim sent him out to look for me?

"Ajmal." Sadim's voice is low, his words curt. "The vehicle, please."

And Ajmal is off running again, this time to the locked parking area around the corner.

Sadim takes a step closer to me. "Again, I ask you, where did you go?" He lowers his eyes to my chest, and I know he's taking stock of my now inappropriate clothing.

I stand my ground. "No big deal. It was a personal errand. I'm sorry I held everyone up."

Eyes back on mine, Sadim sneers, "I have heard about your 'personal errands.'" He raises his index finger in lecture mode. "I tell you here and now, it is far too dangerous in Kabul or anywhere else in Afghanistan for you to go wandering off without telling me or Ajmal where you are going. I cannot protect you if I do not know. From now on, one of us will go with you. Do you understand?"

Again, I feel the hair on the back of my neck bristling, and this time it's not out of fear that someone's following me. I'm mad at Sadim's new paternalistic attitude but don't have a clue what I can say without pissing him off even more and quite possibly putting my job in jeopardy. A sidelong look at Nic reveals an eye roll and his lips pressed tightly together. Clear indications that he doesn't think I should say anything. That's when I notice for the first time that he's carting my Pelican case. Thoughtful of him.

Back to Sadim. I'm not about to work this entire assignment with him creating new rules and constantly throwing up barriers. Knowing it will irritate him even more, I've got to say what's on my mind and get our parameters clear. "Sadim, I appreciate your concern for my well-being. I really do." I take a deep breath. "But let's be clear: it's not your job to protect me. Your 'protection' is going to hem me in and make it impossible for me to do my job."

Now standing just behind Sadim, Nic covers his eyes with his hand. Azizullah curls his upper lip.

Okay, so that was probably a little too forceful. But I had to say it. Even Cerelli would agree with me. Or maybe not. Being that he's worried to the point of distraction, I have the sinking feeling Cerelli might well agree with Sadim.

Sadim crosses his arms. His scowl deepens.

I brace myself.

Then, Ajmal rounds the corner with our Humvee, pulls up next to us, and Sadim does the unthinkable. He doesn't say a word. Instead, he uncrosses his arms and climbs into the front seat of the vehicle. All of which leaves me looking like the idiot I suppose I am. Except, I remind myself, I was trying to track down Mel.

Aziz loads his video gear into the back of the Humvee and continues around to the far side of the vehicle. Nic stows my camera case, then slides into the middle seat. Smart man. Since we'll be thigh to thigh, it's infinitely better for me to sit next to him.

I'm about to join him when Sadim catches my eye. "Put on the *abaya*," he says softly, for my ears only.

Desperate to disagree, if only because it's going to be far too hot today to be enveloped in an extra layer, I don't. Mainly because he's right. Thoroughly wet, my tunic is not only clinging to my breasts, it's bordering on transparent and is completely indecent. There's no way I could be part of an interview or photograph anyone, especially an Afghan man, looking like this. I'm sure I surprise every last man in the Humvee when I nod, then dig the black *abaya* out of my pack, and, in full view of the now-crowded sidewalk, drape it over my head. To emphasize my new compliance, I rewrap my *keffiyeh* over the *abaya* head covering, then climb into the back seat next to Nic, my pack contritely on my lap.

Despite the A/C that is most definitely working, I don't have to wait long to begin suffering from the heat.

Nic leans close. "You could've played that better."

"Tell me about it." My cheeks flame from having inconvenienced everyone, not to mention having been reprimanded like a naughty little girl.

WE DON'T HAVE FAR to go. Ajmal drives us along the streets I just walked, past the Turkish Embassy, to the presidential palace—what the locals call the Arg. Stopping at the guard station, Sadim apologizes for our lateness and explains that we have an appointment with the minister of the interior. It takes a few minutes for the guard to check his clipboard and then to call ahead to the palace. He returns with a smile.

"Follow the main drive and pull up to the door. The guards there will direct you." Something he would say to any visitors on any day. There's no sense of foreboding, that we could be some of the last visitors he welcomes.

Ajmal proceeds slowly, letting us take in the grandeur of the palace where the cabinet ministers meet with President Ashraf Ghani. This is also where Ghani and before him Hamid Karzai have welcomed world leaders. As we bump over the brick pavement, I study the double rows of green and red and black Afghan flags with the white crest of a *masjid* unfurling in the breeze. For how many more days will those flags fly before they're hauled down for the last time and the Taliban raise their plain white flags with the black *shahada*?

When we stop in front of the simple entrance, Sadim exits the Humvee to talk with the guards. Nic nudges me to climb out, and we walk to the curve of the driveway.

"We've got a couple minutes while they sort things. Enough time for you to bring me up to speed."

"Nic, just leave it."

"What's going on? You didn't just wander off."

I start to walk away, then stop. What's it going to hurt for Nic to know? It might actually help to have a second pair of eyes on the lookout for Mel. So, I tell him—the abbreviated version, leaving out the part about her not speaking to me.

He stares at me, aghast. "Let me get this straight. She's here in Kabul, *now*, and this is her first assignment?"

"Exactly. Now you see why I'm concerned and trying to check on her."

"Bloody hell. If she were my daughter, I'd be flipping crazy." He starts pacing, which has the effect of making me feel even more anxious.

"Well, I'd sure like to see her, make sure she's okay."

"You said she's with Al Shabakat?"

I nod.

"At least their crews know their way around. You happen to know who she's with?"

"Josh Forbes. He's the only one I know."

Nic pales.

"What?"

"Sorry. I'm probably overreacting. More than likely, everything is fine. In fact, word is he's reformed."

I nearly gag. "I think you better tell me."

"There's no good way to say this. Josh is notorious. At least he was two decades ago. Didn't he ever put the moves on you?"

"No. The only moves he put on me was when you three hazed me. I might add that he put the blame for that little incident squarely on you."

"Typical." He looks away for a moment, then back at me. "Annie, I was just as guilty for that as the other blokes but definitely not the instigator. And . . . you know I'm sorry. But Josh? I'll be honest. I wouldn't want my daughter working with him, reformed or not."

Fuck. I tighten my hands into fists. Not hazing. Sexual predation. My own daughter. Oh, Mel! Are you okay? If he's hurting you . . . I think back to the tremor in Josh's hand. No wonder. Well, if he's preying on Mel, I won't keep quiet. Like I told him in the Oryx Lounge at the Doha airport: *Don't do it again. To anyone. Next time, I won't stay quiet.* And I won't.

"Come on, old thing. In all likelihood, Mel's fine. You're well known, and you've got connections. Josh would be an idiot to go after your daughter, and he's no idiot."

He's right. Not only do I have TNN behind me—unlike when the guys hazed me back in '06—I've got Cerelli. "Thanks. That helps."

"For now, we've got a job to do. And there's Sadim waving us into the building." As we walk toward the front door, he quietly asks, "So, what's our plan?"

I like that he said 'our.' Something tells me I'll need help from all the males I can rally. "He wasn't very forthcoming about when she might be around, but I'm planning to go back to their apartment this evening."

He puts a reassuring hand on my shoulder. "I'm going with you."

12

BUT FIRST, WE'VE GOT to interview the minister of the interior. If we aren't too late. As I reach the entrance, a grinning Ajmal hurries over and hands me my case of camera gear, then offers a thumbs-up. I'm not totally sure what that's about. Azizullah is ahead of us, already hauling his video equipment past the two guards in their olive dress khakis who are holding open the plate glass doors—modest for the front of a palace.

Once Nic and I are inside, a smiling Sadim leans in close. "Another change of plans."

Nic purses his lips. "No interview then?"

"An interview we most definitely have. An exclusive. General Mirzakwal has invited us to accompany him to inspect some checkpoints outside the city." Sadim hurries us along. "He's waiting behind the palace."

The general's aide-de-camp escorts us the length of the wide corridor. On each side, doors open and close as increasingly frantic government and military officials rush from room to room, meeting

to meeting. At the end of the corridor, two guards step forward and
in unison pull open the doors.

Pausing at the top of the staircase, I stare in astonishment
at the convoy of military vehicles stretched out in front of me. I
stop counting at forty. And hundreds of soldiers and police. Quite
obviously, the general can't risk leaving the palace without almost
a battalion of firepower protecting him. Another sure sign the
Taliban are closing in on the city.

And there, at the bottom of the stairs, is the general himself,
looking exactly the same as in the film clips I've seen. Dark hair
slicked back. Heavy mustache brushing his upper lip. Jaw in serious
need of a shave. I take note of his navy-blue uniform—completely
unadorned. No insignia to give away his rank. As if that would
keep any Taliban from recognizing him immediately.

The general steps forward to greet us in Dari. Well, me, actually.
"Ms. Hawkins, we meet again. It has been too many years." The
man has quite the swagger, and today, he's turning all that charm
on me.

I'm truly at a loss. He clearly thinks we've met before, and I
literally don't have any recollection of him. Not a clue.

"Perhaps you do not remember me. When we met at Dalan Sang,
you were busy saving the lives of Ahmad Shah Massoud's son and
grandson. I remember you very well. You are a courageous woman."

Dalan Sang. That horrible day when the Taliban blew up the
checkpoint, killing scores of people. It took a while before Sawyer
and some Afghan troops could helicopter in. But I don't remember
the general being there. "I'm so sorry," I say in Dari, my voice suddenly a bit wobbly. "That day . . . I . . ." On the pavement in front of
me, a hole starts to open. Small, but it's there. Threatening to get
bigger and to suck me down into it.

No! I can't let that happen. Absolutely no PTSD moments allowed.

I tighten my right hand into a fist and straighten my spine. Forcing my eyes up, away from the hole, I take a deep breath. Then another. "To be honest . . . I remember a colonel being in charge that day."

He nods. "Yes, you are correct. I was promoted to general shortly after. Finally, I am able to thank you for your help to the Afghan people that day."

I smile sadly. "Dr. Ghafoor and I did what we could." Sneaking another look at the pavement, I see that the hole is shrinking quickly. Until it's no longer there.

A glance at Sadim tells me he's thrilled with this turn of events. I have no doubt that he's figuring out how he can use the general's obvious fondness for me to our advantage.

"Please." The general leads us back to the armored Humvee where Aziz is waiting. Turning to me, he sweeps his hand toward the back door. "You will ride in my vehicle."

"With pleasure." That should make both the general and Sadim happy.

Nic is right at my shoulder, whispering in my ear. "My Dari's pretty rusty. Never was great in the first place. So, what was all that about?"

I'd forgotten how rudimentary Nic's Dari is. Was he able to follow any of what the general and I were talking about? If not, how the hell is he going to interview the man?

Before I can answer Nic, Sadim slips in front of me, blocking the rear passenger door to the Humvee. "General, sir. If we could please have Nic Parker Lowe and the translator with you in this vehicle?" A quick look at me, then a nod toward the vehicle behind tells me where he wants me to sit.

The general makes a show of looking around at his entourage, ostensibly in search of his translator. After just a few seconds, his aide-de-camp steps forward and clears his throat for attention. "It is with great regret I inform you that the translator must stay at the palace."

"I think there is not a problem." The general lines me up in his sights. "Perhaps, Ms. Hawkins, you could translate for Mr. Parker Lowe and me?"

Seriously?

Nic shoots me a glance. Oh yeah, he understood what the general just said. A quick shake of the head confirms he's thinking exactly what I am. For me to translate would be way out-of-bounds. Not to mention that it would keep me from doing my job. On second thought, maybe that's exactly what Mirzakwal wants. No photographs.

"Sir," I say as firmly as possible. "I'm not a professional translator."

The general smiles coyly. "Ah, but my dear lady. There is no one else. By all accounts, your Dari is flawless. You will do a superb translation. I trust you completely."

Oh, great. He trusts me. How do I tell him that he shouldn't? Glancing toward Sadim, I see he's no longer smiling. He's in a terrible quandary. So am I. If I make a mistake, the least little mistake, miss a word, translate incorrectly, I could put us all in serious jeopardy. Then I get it, and I see from the expression in Sadim's eyes that he gets it, too. This is the general's way of ensuring deniability.

"Sir." Sadim looks ready to salute. "With all due respect, I suggest that I would be the best person to translate for you."

"Yes." I nod. Of all of us, Sadim is the most fluent in both Dari and English. Not to mention that he's the only person not holding a camera.

The general shakes his head. "No, I must insist. *If* there is to be an interview, it will be Ms. Hawkins who translates." His emphasis on the 'if' belies his smile.

Sadim does his best not to scowl. My translation could undermine the entire interview. But not doing the interview at all—that's something he doesn't want to contemplate. This is most definitely a major scoop that could get him a visa to work in the U.S. when Afghanistan falls to the Taliban. His future's at stake here, and we all know it. I'd like to think that Sadim would stand fast to the ethics of journalism. That he wouldn't cave, especially for personal gain. Then again, I've got a U.S. passport that will get me out of this country and back into the States. He doesn't have that luxury. Nor do his wife and children.

He takes a breath and lets it out slowly, then offers one clipped nod. "All right then. Annie, you will translate. But I will sit in the front seat." To make sure there are no errors. He doesn't need to say it. And to be honest, I want him there.

But we can all count. With Aziz and his shoulder-mounted camera up front filming, there won't be room for another person. Much to Nic's dismay and my annoyance, the aide-de-camp directs Sadim to another car farther back in the convoy.

The general gently takes my Pelican case and hands it to the driver to stow in the trunk. I hold tightly on to my pack. Then, hoping for the best, I gather the front of the *abaya* in my hand, lifting it so I can climb into the Humvee and slide across the back seat. Mic'd up, the general helps himself to the seat next to me, then Nic joins us. Aziz settles in the front passenger seat and finishes the sound check. Finally, with his camera focused on Nic and the general, we're ready to roll.

The long caravan of vehicles slowly pulls out onto the street, bringing all traffic to a halt. Pedestrians on the sidewalk stop to gawk, undoubtedly wondering if the president is on the move. Or possibly fleeing the country. I'd love to reassure them that the president is in the palace along with all his ministers and other government officials, but I can't because I'm pretty sure that any day now, the leaders really will disappear.

As if he can read my mind, Nic asks his first question. "Many people are watching this convoy. What do you imagine they're thinking?"

I repeat the question in Dari just as it occurs to me that the last time I spoke to the general back in 2015 at Dalan Sang, he answered me—and Sawyer—in English. Not that he said much. But what he did say was flawless.

The general takes the question in stride. "They are grateful their government is taking action. They know that as long as the army and the police are out in force, the Taliban will stay away from Kabul."

I nearly gape. Seriously? He believes this? Or maybe he's just doing his best to keep the Afghan people calm. I catch Nic looking at me expectantly and quickly translate the answer. *Don't listen to what the man says, just translate his words!*

Nic's follow-up question comes fast. "You're not worried that they think the president could be fleeing the country? Maybe—"

"Absolutely not. The president will never leave. I will not leave. None of the ministers will leave. We will all stay for the sake of our country."

Nic still isn't done. "What about when the Taliban enter Kabul?"

"No! The Taliban will never come into the city."

There's no way the general can avoid seeing the disbelief

that spreads across Nic's face. "Sir, the Taliban are only seventy kilometers from the gates of Kabul."

Still the general is upbeat and calm, his hands resting open on his thighs. No fists. No pounding. No raised voice. "We have their assurance. We ask them to sit down with us. With love. Definitely with love. Together, we will make a coalition government that will be good for everyone. For all Afghans."

That's when I realize he's leaning against me. Shoulder to shoulder, thigh to thigh, we couldn't be any closer unless I were sitting in his lap. I can't risk embarrassing him by asking him to move over, and there's no room for me to squirm away. I'm already wedged in solidly between this muscle of a man and the steel door.

In the front seat, Aziz pauses the video. "General, sir," he says in Dari, possibly to make sure the man understands. Then he gestures with his left hand for the general to move closer to Nic.

I lean forward to see a full eight inches between the two men.

The general opens his mouth, clearly ready to protest.

But Aziz doesn't give him the chance. "Sorry, sir. It is such close quarters, and I need to have both you and Nic in the frame, otherwise I have to pan back and forth. I don't want the viewers feeling like they're watching a tennis match. And we don't need Annie on screen anyway."

"Yes. I think this will make for a better film." Shifting away from me, the general eases closer to Nic.

I'm ready to laugh at his too-obvious attempt to take credit for the seating rearrangement. Although maybe he's just trying to save face. A quick glance at Aziz and I hope he can pick up on my gratitude from my smile. He offers the barest of nods and gets back to filming.

An hour later, the general calls a halt to Nic's questions. "We are here. The first checkpoint that I want to inspect." He leans forward to peer out the window. Maybe he's expecting to see hordes of grateful Afghans? Or, maybe not, but he's certainly expecting to see the soldiers who've been assigned to this station. But the checkpoint is completely empty. Just a small hut with a crossing gate blocking the road. Unguarded. Ready for any Taliban to cross the line into the city.

We wait in the Humvee for the rest of the convoy to arrive. After the soldiers scour the area and find no one and nothing suspicious, we climb out, my Lowepro draped over my shoulder.

Nic asks the question we're all wondering: Why has the post been abandoned?

The general is quiet at first, probably thinking through what he wants to say that will be optimistic but also believable. We wait patiently. I take the opportunity to capture some images of the hut that has the feel of being long empty. It's obviously been days, if not longer, since anyone has guarded this post. Whenever they left, the men took their supplies with them. There's absolutely nothing here—not a chair, not a bowl, not a bullet casing, not even a crust of bread. I trust my photos show that. Then, I take some photographs of the man himself, thoughtfully examining the gate and the empty building. Clearly puzzled at this turn of events, he smooths down his thick, dark mustache and rubs his beardless chin, refusing to be angry.

Finally, he turns toward the video camera. "The soldiers, they were unsure about their orders. No one came to relieve them." He waves over a group of ten young soldiers and barks out orders to stand guard. "Now that the men know there are reinforcements to help them, they will return."

This time, it's Nic who nearly gapes in surprise at such self-delusion. But he somehow manages to rein himself in by asking more questions. "When? When will they return? And what about these reinforcements? How long will they remain?" In other words, what's to prevent the current group of soldiers from abandoning this post as soon as the convoy is out of sight?

"Soon." The general nods with a confidence I seriously doubt the new guards share. "As soon as they see these men are here. Then they will come back. Our soldiers and our police are completely loyal to their government. They will do whatever they can for their country. They will never hide from their duty. They will never support the Taliban."

Nic doesn't follow up with another question. What could he possibly ask in response? He just lets the general's words rest in the air, or, more accurately, on the ground, until they dissipate into more dust.

A minute later, the general's aide-de-camp rounds up everyone and directs us to our vehicles. I hang back, scanning the horizon, searching for any hint the Taliban could be out there, watching us. And I do see something. In the distance. It looks like a cloud of dust. Is a sandstorm brewing out there?

By the time I get to the Humvee, Nic and the general are already ensconced in the back seat. I start to climb in, but momentarily forgetting that I'm wearing an *abaya*, tangle my feet in the fabric and trip into the general's open arms. My camera bounces off his upper thigh, dangerously close to his crotch. Oh, that must have hurt.

"Sorry," I mumble, trying to push myself up and away.

Other than a momentary grimace of pain, he doesn't react. And he's enough of a gentleman to avoid copping a feel as he helps me right myself. "You are all right?" His concern sounds genuine.

"I'm fine. Really." My face burning with embarrassment, I do what I can to unobtrusively remove his hands from my rib cage.

Instead, he takes my fall as reason enough to sit close by me again. Too close.

Nic sinks into his corner, laughing silently.

Aziz quietly captures it all on video. Until Nic signals that he's ready to start up the interview again. "Sir?" Aziz keeps rolling. "If you could move into the shot, please?"

The general freezes in place. It seems he's finally realized that his hands are actually on me. A clear violation of the Afghan rules of propriety. The very strict rules. Afghan men do not touch women to whom they aren't related. Full stop. Not that the Taliban always obey this code of ethics, but the man next to me does. He might undress me with his eyes, which I think he's done at least once this morning, but he doesn't touch.

Whispering an apology in Dari, he moves closer to Nic. Much closer.

And we're off to the next checkpoint.

Along the way, Nic peppers the general with questions—a welcome distraction for all of us. In between translations, I take advantage of my newfound space to capture a series of images of the two men sharing the back seat with me. Not the greatest compositions, but wedged in as I am by the door and Aziz's camera, I'm forced to work with what I've got. I go back to basics and, relying on the rule of thirds, superimpose an imaginary tic-tac-toe grid over the image. How many times did photography profs tell me to line up the key elements of my shots at the cross-hatch points of this grid pattern for maximum emphasis? With the general occupying the right third and Nic the left, I let the blur of landscape and the occasional civilian outside the speeding vehicle tell the story of our urgency as we rush to the next checkpoint. After the third shot, I sense the tingling in my fingers. I take a quick look at the LCD screen and like what I see. Despite the general's optimistic words, anxiety is etched in the lines around his mouth and worry clouds his eyes.

The sudden silence reminds me that Nic is waiting for me to translate what the general just said. Even though I only half heard him, it's more of the same, and both men seem satisfied with my translation. Obviously, the general really does speak English. And Nic probably knows a lot more Dari than he's letting on.

It takes almost an hour to get to the second checkpoint, where it's even drier and dustier than at the previous stop. And hotter. We're closing in on noon, and the sun is glaring white overhead, heating up the day well into the nineties. A few minutes outside the Humvee and I'm sweltering under my black *abaya*. Sweat is streaming down my back and pooling between my breasts. How the hell do Afghan women endure this every single day?

Maybe Nic sees me fanning myself because his next questions focus on the lot of women under Taliban rule. Will they have to return to wearing the *burqa*? Will they be forced to give up all the advances they gained under the current government? Will they be barred from getting an education? From working outside the house? From running for elected office?

After each question, the general repeats that the Afghan government will protect the rights of women—even in the new coalition with the Taliban that is coming soon. In September, he insists. After the Western military forces withdraw.

Nic presses him, pointing out yet again that caravans of white pickups and motorcycles and camo-painted Humvees are bringing armed Taliban militants ever closer to Kabul. His eyes conveying his disbelief at the assurances being spouted to the camera, Nic swings his arm wide to encompass the emptiness around us. "Where are the armed forces to stop the Taliban?"

Glaring directly into the video camera, the general lifts his chin in a show of defiance. "The Taliban commanders, they have assured us that they will not enter the city. They will stop at the gates."

"Why?" asks Nic. "Why should they stop?"

"They have given their word." Arms still crossed, it's clear the general is determined to play his part until the very end.

I very nearly roll my eyes as I translate his words. Seriously? The Afghan government actually believes anything the Taliban commanders say? Or is this all for show? Oh, hell! This interview isn't a scoop for Sadim and TNN at all. Nic and the rest of us are simply facilitating the last propaganda efforts of a dying government.

Nic, though, is in total control. "Sir? Do you believe them?"

Instead of answering, the general motions to his aide-de-camp to leave another group of soldiers to guard the post. I watch as the young men march forward and take up their positions. But no matter how hard they try to look determined and fierce, the aura of dejection is hard to miss.

Everyone heads toward their respective vehicles. This time, Aziz joins me as I stop to study the horizon. There's no wind, just the barest hint of a breeze, and yet the cloud of dust is bigger now, spanning a greater distance. I pull out my big lens and am able to make out some white pickups and motorcycles. The Taliban? Closing in on Kabul? Somehow, I don't think so.

Aziz starts filming.

Then Nic is standing in front of the camera, positioned to the side so the focus is on the horizon. "Refugees moving in from the countryside, leaving most of their worldly goods behind them. Many with only the clothes they're wearing, they are making their way to Kabul where they hope to find safety ahead of the Taliban who have been taking control of every village and city in their path with little to no resistance."

I check the screen on the back of my camera to see what I've got. An expanse of land, flat and dry, continuing until it meets the sky where swirls of brown dust rise. My images hardly tell the story. Maybe I'll be able to see something more when I upload the pics onto my laptop.

One more checkpoint to go, which I'm sure will hold no surprises. All of us know that there will be no one there. Even the general knows.

I'm wilting in the heat. Nic and Aziz are also sweating heavily. The general, though, doesn't seem at all bothered by the high temperatures. The driver conjures up bottles of water, which help a bit. Although I'm having a tough time concentrating, Nic is in his element, not letting up in his questions, prodding constantly. But the general is a good match. He's got an answer for everything, even though much of what he says doesn't ring true.

We're just pulling up to the third checkpoint, deserted, as we expected, when Nic poses a question I would never have predicted. "Sir, are you afraid of what's going to happen?"

The general rears back. Ah, Nic has finally caught him off guard. Not to be undone, the general regroups first with a dismissive laugh, then with a certain indignation. "I am a soldier. A soldier is never frightened." He plucks at the navy-blue sleeve of his fatigues. "This. You see this uniform? When I wear this uniform, I am not afraid, but I am ready for death."

I scrupulously repeat back in Dari what he just said and am

equally careful with my translation into English for Nic. Of all the things the general has said, this is the most telling, the most revealing. And probably what the man himself, or more likely his aide-de-camp, will say I got wrong when they spin the interview after it airs tonight. But when I finish, he nods in satisfaction. From the corner of my eye, I see that Aziz got it all on film.

No matter all the general's bluster to the contrary, there will most definitely be a lot to fear in the coming days.

13

WE MAKE GOOD TIME HEADING back into the city until we meet up with the caravans coming in from the countryside. The roads are clogged with pickups and motorcycles, wagons and people on foot—everyone coated in dust. It's slow going. The general explains, "People are coming from all over the country. From other cities." Just what Nic said earlier in front of the camera. The general continues, "They seek safety, and they know that we will protect them from the Taliban."

"Where will they go?" asks Nic.

"These people, many of them have families in Kabul who will take them in." The general's voice oozes confidence and compassion.

Far from envisioning these people in the ritzy apartment where *Hama* Bibi and Uncle Omar used to live, or even the much less glitzy place where our crew is bunking, I see them crowding into the ramshackle squatters' shacks on the slopes of Chindawul Hill in the Hazara section of Kabul. The place I visited some years ago had one room with way too many people crammed inside, sleeping on a couple of old bedbug-ridden mattresses with a curtain hung down the middle of the room for privacy. No services except electricity, and that was intermittent. They told me that the shacks in the steepest and cheapest sections farther up the hill didn't even have that. The girls had to fetch water from the foot of the hill, hauling it up a nearly vertical staircase in big plastic jerry cans. There was a single gas burner and a pot that turned out one meal a day. Crowding more people into Chindawul is hardly a long-term solution. And where will they get food? I think back to the tents I saw in the park early this morning. Kabul is careening toward being one giant displaced persons camp. The perfect breeding ground for yet more COVID and probably typhoid and dysentery.

With the general's approval, I lower my window and photograph the crowds around us, looking for an image that will tell their story—their fear, their flight. In the front seat, Azizullah is doing the same. I finally happen upon a bedraggled family, the mother and some of the younger children in a wooden cart being pulled by a mule, the father clasping the rope around the animal's neck. Next to him, holding onto his vest, his daughter. Covered in dirt and clearly exhausted, she's probably about eight. Her long, dark hair hasn't been washed or combed in far too long. It's her white patent-leather party shoes that capture my attention. No longer shiny, they're exactly what she shouldn't be wearing for this long trek from home. But I'm betting these are her favorite shoes, and she means to keep them with her. My fingers tingling, I capture the image, knowing it will be on the TNN website in a few hours.

Either the general loses patience or his aide-de-camp decides he can't risk his boss's life. The Humvees at the front of the convoy surge forward, sirens blaring, pushing aside the vehicles and people who don't move out of the way fast enough. Aziz and I do our best to document the men and women and children now sprawled on the pavement. I'll be submitting these images, too, for the website. They finally clear a path through the crowds, and then we're speeding with purpose to the presidential palace.

"An emergency?" Nic asks, his eyebrow raised to emphasize his disbelief.

The general glowers. "Of course! I am needed to help protect the city."

BY THE TIME WE MAKE it back to the apartment, the sun is ready to sink behind the Hindu Kush Mountains. Soon the dust hovering in the sky above the city will shimmer in shades of orange and pink and red. I can only hope that as night falls, the temperatures will, too. The apartment is a furnace, and as we discovered last night, the air conditioner only churns hot air.

Ajmal presents us with a feast. A crisp and refreshing *salaateh afghani* and my favorite of all kebab variations—a perfectly spiced and aromatic *kebabeh degee morph*. Then, there's *borani banjân* and, of course, *nân*. It's while I'm savoring my second bite of eggplant that I realize where he bought this food. At first, I thought maybe he prevailed on his wife to cook. Remembering some of the meals I've eaten at their home has me salivating. But no. The food is from *Khosha* restaurant. Fatima's husband, Sami, prepared this meal. Which answers the question I haven't yet asked Cerelli—whether his former lover and her husband have fled Kabul for somewhere safer. I'd hoped they had. Given that Fatima worked as an operative for Cerelli, she'll be in great peril when the Taliban take control. So will Sami. I would've thought they'd have been high on Sawyer's list to evacuate out of Afghanistan. She once mentioned to me that she'd grown up in Iran. But I can't imagine they'd want to move there. So, where would they go? The U.S.? My heart skips a beat at the thought of them moving to northern Virginia. Even though Cerelli has assured me repeatedly that there's no longer anything between him and Fatima, I'd just as soon not have her living close by. She's nice enough, but I seriously don't want to spend time with the woman. Okay, so maybe I'm just a bit jealous. And as Cerelli discovered: I don't do jealousy well.

We eat voraciously, taking second and third helpings until there's nothing left. The look on Ajmal's face makes me wonder if this food was intended to last for several meals. Given the invasion that's coming, we probably need to eat more sparingly.

When we've all finished, Sadim catches my eye and starts to pass me his plate. I narrow my eyes and give a slight shake of the head. No way am I taking on the role of an Afghan woman—cleaning up after these men. Ajmal quickly comes to my rescue and collects the dishes, carrying them out to the galley kitchen where he promptly sets to washing. Which doesn't seem fair either. Meanwhile, Aziz and I get to work. He retreats to the room he's sharing with Nic to edit a bit before he uploads his video. I hunker down in a corner of the lounge with my laptop to select my best images to send first to D.C. and then batch the rest afterward—just in case our editor finds something else she can use.

Stretching out the kinks in my back, I pack up the laptop and my camera gear—all set for tomorrow.

Nic glances up from his notes. "You ready?"

Sadim looks up quizzically.

"Seriously? You still want to go?" I hope he can hear the

gratitude in my voice. It's been a long day, and the last thing he should be doing is venturing out into the night with me.

"Out? Where?" Sadim sounds seriously displeased. I almost expect him to veto our plans.

I take a couple seconds to formulate a convincing reply, but Nic answers for me. "We won't be long. Just over to the Al Shabakat apartment. Annie's daughter is working with their crew. Her first job out of university. We have some concerns about what's going on and want to make sure she's all right."

Nic pitched the situation well. A lot better than I would've. But I don't know quite how well until the clatter of dishes in the kitchen suddenly stops. Ajmal comes to stand in the doorway, his lips pressed tightly together.

Then I see Aziz standing in the hall, arms folded over his chest. "That's Josh Forbes' crew, isn't it?" He's on full alert.

Sadim offers one curt nod. "It is."

I roll my mental recording of what Nic said, trying to pinpoint the signal that's all too clear to the other three men. "That's where I went this morning. I managed to see Josh, but he insisted that Mel was already out running errands."

"At seven in the morning?" Ajmal scoffs.

"You think she was in the apartment?" This from Aziz.

I shrug. "I don't know. He wouldn't let me in. Said she's always on the go but thought I might be able to catch up with her this evening."

"I will drive." Ajmal pulls the keys from his pocket.

Sadim checks to make sure he has the keys to the building and our apartment.

The four men head out the door, then wait for me in front of the elevator.

"Is it working yet?" I ask hopefully.

"Intermittently." Nic shakes his head in disgust. "For a couple hours in the middle of the day. When no one's here."

We clamber down the stairs—another furnace that has me sweating by the time we reach the lobby.

Ajmal drives the nearly empty, dark streets straight to the Al Shabakat apartment. No hesitations. No wrong turns. Of course he knows where he's going. He followed me this morning. When he pulls up next to the wrought iron gate marking the entrance to the building, we don't move. Instead, we eye the heavily armed guards.

"How should we do this?" There's a wariness in Nic's voice that takes me by surprise, almost as if he realizes this may not be quite as easy as he initially thought. What? He thought we'd just march in, grab Mel, and take off?

"Leave it to me." Sadim sounds confident.

"And me." I've never heard Aziz sound so gleeful.

We watch the two men approach the guards, who don't seem at all surprised to see them. Ajmal explains, "Sadim and Aziz, they used to work for Al Shabakat."

After a great deal of back-slapping and bear-hugging, Sadim waves the rest of us forward. Ajmal decides to stay with the car, but Nic and I practically jog to the gate. The guards seem happy to see us, too. They let us in, then lock the gate. "Party time!" one of them calls after us. Oh, yeah. There was a time in the not-too-distant past when Kabul was quite the party town. Especially for foreign journalists. Afghanistan may be a Muslim country, but the liquor definitely flowed. Big-time.

I turn to look back at them, and that's when I notice the bottles of beer tucked just inside the thick concrete wall. "Smart thinking," I murmur to Aziz. Not only did those beers get us in, they could make for a much easier getaway. "You guys know where we're going?"

"Oh, yes." Nic sounds definite. "We've all spent quite a few evenings on the eighth floor."

MY GUYS STAND DOWN the hall, out of sight, as I knock on the door. Then knock again. And again. A solid sixty seconds later, Josh finally opens the door. He presents quite the picture. Jeans slung low on his hips—no belt. A *Try Me* T-shirt stretched taut across his chest. He cradles a bottle of Victoria Bitter between his index and middle fingers. The smug grin on his face conveys a certain victory. Only his bare toes curling into the richly colored Afghan carpet betray any nerves. He takes a long, slow pull on his beer. And that's when I smell the sex on him. Unmistakable.

My stomach roils, and I know that vomiting is a distinct possibility. God almighty, I hope Mel hasn't fallen for his swagger.

"Well, Annie Hawkins Green." He takes another pull on his beer. "Oh, wait. Got that wrong, didn't I? You're Annie Hawkins now. You dropped the Green."

"Josh." I cross my arms.

"Steady on, old thing." Does Nic actually whisper that from a few feet away? Or am I imagining it? Whatever, am I glad to have these guys with me.

"I must say, Annie. You're the last person I expected to see tonight." Another pull of VB. Another whiff of sex.

"Really? And why is that? You did suggest I stop by this evening to see my daughter."

"Did I? Well, once again, you just missed her."

"At this time of night? I find that hard to believe."

"Believe what you want. But she's not here. Out running errands."

"Well, excuse me." I move to the side and crook my hip against the doorjamb. "But I don't believe you."

Nic steps into the doorway next to me. "It's odd that the guards didn't mention Mel going out. In fact, they said no one from this apartment has left since you got back late this afternoon."

Josh isn't backing down. "Talked to the guards, did you? They probably didn't see her. Mel took the car and went out through the garage."

Nic takes a step into the apartment, leaving room for Azizullah to take his place next to me. "Up to your old party games." Aziz's nostrils flare.

Josh's eyes widen for just a moment. "No games. The girl's not here."

I walk over and stand next to Nic. From here, I've got a good view of the lounge. Unbelievable glitz. It reminds me of *Hama* Bibi and Uncle Omar's luxe apartment. White leather furniture with marble floors and pricy rugs. And the lovely hum of A/C. This is the coolest I've been in the last thirty-six hours. Why the hell is Al Shabakat shelling out like this for their crew? I guess the better question is why couldn't TNN get us better digs? Something without squashed insect bodies decorating the walls? Or maybe a working elevator and air conditioner?

"You say Annie's daughter isn't here?" Sadim moves into the doorway. "Then you won't mind if we check the bedrooms?"

Josh shifts so he's standing in front of a closed door. Presumably the bedroom in question. "Sadim. Good to see you, man. It's been a while. Sorry she had to drag you into this." He reaches out to shake

Sadim's hand. But Sadim, bless him, simply stares as if he's being offered a dead fish.

I step forward. "Josh, let's cut the crap, shall we? You know why we're here. Let me just see Mel, then we'll leave."

Josh literally sneers. "Annie, you always were a stubborn bitch. Like I told you, Mel isn't here."

"Then where is she?" Sadim sounds like he's running out of patience.

"God almighty, you people. She's out. I don't know where the hell she is."

My stomach keeps on roiling. "Shouldn't you?"

"Not my job."

"I disagree." Nic's voice hits the danger zone. "She's a young girl. Only twenty-two. She doesn't know Kabul. Who knows what could happen to her? And you let her go out. Alone?"

"Fuck you, Nic. When did you become such an old lady?" Then, he turns on me. "There was a time, Annie, when you were able to fight your own battles. That was when? Back when you were hopping from bed to bed? Now that you're shagging the old man" —he nods at Nic—"he's gotta take care of everything for you?"

Nic has just taken a step toward Josh when the door behind him flies open. And there is Mel, hair rumpled, cheeks flushed, T-shirt on inside out. At least she's pulled on a pair of jeans.

Behind her, I can just make out a double bed, the sheets most definitely mussed.

"What are you doing here?" She actually looks confused. As if I'm the last person she expected—or wanted—to see tonight. Evidently, Josh didn't mention that I stopped by this morning. Nor did he tell her I'd probably be stopping by this evening. Then again, maybe he did.

I scramble. "I . . . uh . . . just want to make sure you're okay."

"I'm fine. Obviously." To emphasize her point, she raises her hands and arms and strikes a dramatic pose.

I try to smile. "Good. That's good."

She narrows her eyes and takes half a minute to study me. "So, you going to tell me why you're really here?"

"I really am just checking on you. In case you haven't noticed, it's dangerous here and getting more dangerous by the day."

She takes a moment to think about that. "Your point being?"

"Honestly? I know you don't want to hear this, but I think you should consider going home."

"Excuse me? You want me to give up my job? Because *you* think it's dangerous? Why exactly would I do that? So *you'll* feel better?" Her voice is most definitely getting sharper.

Enough dancing around the bull elephant in musth in the room. "Sweetie, do you think maybe we could talk privately?" I look toward the bedroom—truly the last place I want to talk with Mel, but I've got to get her away from Josh. Not to mention that my three guys are also pretty intimidating.

"Privately?" She shakes her head. "What are you talking about? I don't have anything I need to discuss with you in private."

I look pointedly at Josh. And Mel knows instantly what I want to talk to her about.

Zero to ten, her eyes are blazing. "How dare you!" She practically spits out the words. "I knew that's why you're really here. Not because it's 'too dangerous.'" She makes air quotes around the last two words.

"Mel, please—" I reach out a hand.

"No, Mom. I already told you that I'm fine. Everyone on this crew will tell you I'm doing a good job. But you're obsessed with who I'm sleeping with."

Josh stiffens noticeably. Despite his initial swagger, he wasn't expecting such a direct confirmation of what he's been doing in bed. With my daughter.

"And you know what? That's got nothing to do with you."

I try again. "Mel—"

"No! Just get out of my business and stay out!" She takes a step closer to Josh, nearly pressing her body against his back and gently rubbing a hand on his shoulder.

Which feels like a kick in my gut. I backtrack. "Look, I just wanted to make sure you're okay."

Her face is flushed with anger. "Well, you've got your answer. Now, just stop interfering."

"I'm not . . ." Am I? But I've got a good reason: I'm trying to keep her from getting hurt. Except she sees it as interfering, undermining. What can I say? Especially when I hear the echo of me saying the same thing to Grammy when she caught me in bed with Todd one college break. *Stop interfering!*

I take a step back and say the only thing I can think of. "Okay. I'm glad your job is working out." Tears are burning the back of my eyes. Acid is climbing up my throat. Any minute, I'm going to burst into tears or throw up. Much as I'd like to hurl in Josh's smug face, that's not going to help matters. I've got to get out of this frigging apartment. Holding up my hands in surrender, I head out the door, then down the hall to the elevator.

My guys don't follow me right away. I can hear the deep rumble of more words being exchanged but can't make out what anyone's saying. When the apartment door slams shut and the three men join me, I reach out to press the down button.

"Annie, you are all right?" Aziz sounds concerned.

I shrug and step into the elevator. "That could've gone better."

God, I wish I were alone. All I wanted was to see Mel, and if things weren't going well, to get her the hell out of Josh's clutches. In a way that would let her save face and not lose her job. Instead . . . oh, God, instead . . . I've totally screwed up my relationship with her. Then for the guys to have witnessed Mel's furious outburst, not to mention the sexuality she all but threw in my face. And my inability to do more than tear up. What the hell kind of mother am I?

We reach the lobby and are out the front door when my cell phone vibrates against my thigh. Way too much of a coincidence. I've got a sinking feeling I know exactly who's texting me. "Just a sec." I pull out my phone, swipe it on, and read Mel's text aloud to the guys.

Don't think I won't tell the admiral about you cheating on him with Nic Parker Lowe.

14

NIC LOOKS AWAY, HIS LIPS pursed, his eyes pained. Then, bowing his head, he climbs into the Humvee. Sadim and Aziz follow until I'm the only one left on the sidewalk.

I should go back in. Try to see Mel. Try to explain. Just suck it up and tell her I'm sorry for interfering. Do whatever I've got to, including grovel. But short of knocking down the door, how exactly can I apologize? All these years of leaving her behind so I could pursue my dreams, and this is what it's come to: me telling my daughter that her own dreams are out-of-bounds. Even if those dreams involve someone whose behavior seems damn close to predatory. Not to mention her being in a dangerous country that's getting more and more dangerous every day.

Sadim's window rolls down. "Annie?"

"Yeah." I climb into the back seat next to Aziz. Nic's on the far side.

Ajmal pulls away from the curb, driving us past the embassies, their lights ablaze. Something tells me it's all hands on deck—

probably shredding documents they don't want the Taliban gaining access to once the diplomats evacuate.

No one says a word. I mean, really, what's there to say?

But then, Nic clears his throat. I expect him to ask how I'm doing. I don't expect him to say: "I'm not sleeping with Annie. Never have, although years ago, the thought did cross my mind. More than once."

"Nic." My voice carries an audible warning. *Don't! Don't let my daughter's threat force you to say what I'm pretty sure you're about to say.*

He ignores me. "I . . . uh . . . probably should have said something long ago. Too frightened, I guess. Silly, really. Look, what I'm trying to say is that I'm gay. Before anyone says anything, I've been in a committed relationship for years."

I listen to the hum of the tires beneath us and wait for someone to say something. Anything. Next to me, in front of me, I can feel the tension—three Afghan men struggling to come to terms with Nic's announcement, trying to figure out what they can possibly say.

Finally, Aziz claps Nic on the shoulder. "No worries, my friend."

Sadim turns around to look into the back seat. "It is not a problem for us. But I do not think you should talk about it here in Kabul. Not with the Taliban about to enter the city. They have tortured and killed gay men."

I swallow hard as I remember the Taliban pushing gays off tall buildings. Surely they wouldn't do something like that to a renowned foreign journalist? Then again, the Taliban have vowed *nyaw aw badal* against Cerelli and Sawyer and me. They don't exactly abide by international law.

Much to my surprise, Ajmal says nothing. Eyes riveted on the road ahead, he just keeps driving.

15

"I GOT SOME INTERESTING texts from Mel this afternoon."
The laugh in Cerelli's voice reminds me why I love him. The fact
that he doesn't for one minute think I'm cheating on him confirms
his trust, and that feels good. Although I'm sure he's not thrilled
that I spend most of my life with an all-male crew.

"Oh, I bet you did." Wearing my super lightweight *The Only
Good Day Was Yesterday* T-shirt and leggings that reach just below
my knees, I hunker down in the hall outside the TNN apartment,
where it's marginally cooler than inside. I hope to God no one
from the other apartments on this floor comes out to investigate
who's talking this late at night. My clothing definitely won't pass
the dress code. Leaning back against the cinder block wall, I tell
him all about my failed morning visit to the Al Shabakat building.
"I saw Josh on the sidewalk out front, and he insisted Mel had
already left for the day."

"Josh Forbes?" Cerelli's voice is tight.

"The same."

"Damn. I had no idea he was their new chief foreign correspondent."

I look cross-eyed at the sat phone. How could I not have known this about Josh? "The rest of the TNN crew had the same reaction. They say he's a player. Which was news to me."

"Believe me, he's made quite a name for himself, even with some women in the military. Word is he also found his way into bed with Azizullah's wife. Now ex-wife. Your videographer."

"Seriously?"

"Oh, yeah."

"Well, the guys—including Azizullah—insisted on going with me when I went back tonight. But if what you say is true, Aziz was awfully cool about it."

"They thought he'd hit on you?" Again, Cerelli is laughing.

"What? Like that's not possible?"

"Sweetheart, it's all too possible. But I think you struck a chord with your team when you told them about Mel. So, tell me what happened. I take it you confronted Josh?"

"Indeed. It was quite the show of denial he put on. Then Mel put in an appearance. Hell hath no fury and all that."

"Not exactly how that adage goes, but I get your point. She's royally pissed."

"Oh, yeah. Anyway, it was pretty clear we'd interrupted them *in flagrante*, and she let loose. On me." My voice cracks.

"Her texts did sound pretty angry. So, what's next?"

"I honestly don't know. It's pretty obvious that she doesn't want to see me or talk to me."

"Give her time. She'll get over this. Eventually."

"You really think so?"

"She's a good person, sweetheart. She thinks you're trying to undermine her, and she's lashing out."

I notice he says "you're trying," as in me—not both of us. Then I remember that he and Mel have their own relationship which doesn't always include me. I consider that for just a moment before I ask, "You've had other texts from her?"

"I have."

"Sorry, sorry, I shouldn't have asked. That's between the two of you. But could you at least tell me if you think she's okay?"

"She's okay. If she weren't, I'd have told you. Immediately. Although I'm not at all happy about how she's treating you or that she's in bed with Josh. If he were in the Navy, I'd have him up on charges yesterday."

She's okay. "Thanks. That's really all I need to know. For now." I'm glad, I really am, that Mel confides in her almost-stepfather. And I absolutely respect that he keeps her confidences. Like Bonita does. But oh, how I wish she'd confide in me—the way she used to. Then, cradling the phone, I add, "I could sure use you here in Kabul as an intermediary. It's not only Mel I miss. I miss you."

"Just say the word." His voice wraps around me like a warm comforter.

Very warm. Which, to be honest, I don't need. But I really do want him here. I'd be able to deal with my daughter's rejection so much better with Cerelli here to get around Mel's anger and Josh's defenses. "Somehow, though, I don't think the Navy is going to post an admiral to Kabul. Especially now." I sigh.

"So, tell me why Mel fired off a text about you and Nic having an affair. I will say she sounded like she was sorry to have to tell me but thought I should know." He's back to laughing, but there's a certain confusion in his question. No, check that. Cerelli's almost never confused. Curiosity might be a better description.

"I'm sure Josh told her about Nic and me."

"But there is no Nic and you. He's gay."

"Well, until tonight, very few people knew that. And clearly, neither Mel nor Josh do."

"Meaning?"

"Josh made some comments about Nic and me while we were in his apartment. Then, after we left, I got a pretty in-your-face text from Mel saying she'd be telling you about how I'm cheating with Nic."

"And?"

"I was with the guys when the text came through, so I read it aloud. Nic apparently decided he had to clear the air, so he came out to the guys."

"That took balls. Although announcing you're gay in Kabul may not be the best plan."

"Which is exactly what Sadim told him. None of the guys seemed upset or even surprised." I pause and replay the car ride. "Although Ajmal didn't say a word, which was kind of strange."

"Do me a favor? Keep an eye on Ajmal. I'd hate for anything to happen to Nic." Cerelli sounds serious.

"Come on. Ajmal? He's a wonderful guy."

"Annie, in wartime, people change. When they need cash, food. If Ajmal gets picked up for working with foreigners, especially U.S. citizens, there's no telling what he'd do to save himself. Not that I think he would. Just be aware."

Shit. And no one could blame him. Even if he were to give up Nic—or me—to save his wife and kids.

"Back to Mel. What are you going to do?"

I look toward the elevator, at doors that haven't opened since I've been here. "Honestly? I don't know. It's pretty clear she's sleeping with Josh."

"Under duress?"

"Maybe. Maybe not. Who knows what he's said to her, promised her. No matter what either one of them says, it's clear he's taking advantage of her. But she was adamant about me staying out of her business."

"You want me to have Sawyer—"

"No." Best shut down this idea before it goes any further. "Much as I appreciate the offer of having Sawyer beat the shit out of Josh and then whisk Mel away out of his sleazy claws, I think it's a no-go. I'd lose her for good."

"So, then . . ."

I comb my fingers through my damp and matted hair, hoping against hope that a brilliant plan seeps out of my follicles. Nothing. "I hate to say it, but for now I think I've just got to let it play out. As long as she's with her crew, she's safe—in a manner of speaking—and that's really all that matters. I'll do what I can to keep tabs on her. But she really is just about the same age I was on my first foray into the world of photojournalism. And, well . . ."

"You telling me you had to deal with crap like this?"

"Endlessly. In fact, it was probably worse when I was her age. But . . ." I'm not at all sure I want to finish what I was about to say.

"You care to elaborate?" He sounds a bit wary—almost as if he's not sure he wants me to continue.

"I don't know, Cerelli. When I was twenty-three and out in the field for the first time, plenty of guys came on to me. But, well, it just didn't feel quite as predatory as what I'm getting from Josh. And I sure didn't sleep my way to my current job. Who knows?

Maybe I'm reading it all wrong. Or maybe I'm not remembering all that accurately."

"I have no doubt that you're reading this situation right. And remembering your own experiences accurately. Mel's playing with fire. I hate to say it, but Josh is a legend, and not in a good way." He sounds frustrated, like an almost-stepfather who wants to solve the problem and save Mel from the wolf and from herself but knows he has to respect my wishes. "Just a sec."

He muffles the line for a count of ten and then is back on. "Sorry, sweetheart. I've just been called upstairs. You okay for now?"

"I'm fine." I wave my farewell. "Go do your admiral thing."

"You be careful."

"Always."

"I'll call you when I can." Cerelli has a wonderful way of making me feel that he's fully engaged even when I know he's already heading out the door to his meeting or whatever he's off to do.

"Love you," I call into my cell, but I say the words to a dead line.

16

August 13, 2021

IT'S DARK OUT WHEN Sadim wakes me up. "Ten minutes. Then we are on the road."

I wipe the sweat off my face. I've just managed to fall asleep in the sauna that passes for an apartment. "Ten minutes?" When we're on assignment, stories often break suddenly, so I'm used to getting little advance notice. But seriously? Pushing myself off the sofa, I grab my *shalwar kameez* and clean underwear, then take a step toward the bathroom.

"There is no time for showering!" Sadim calls to all of us. "Put on your clothes and let's go! Ajmal, you will meet us in front with the vehicle."

Fuck! No shower. Again. Also not unusual when we're in-country. I should've showered last night, but there's nothing to be done now. I forego changing my clothes and pull my tunic and baggy pants on over my T-shirt and leggings, then comb my fingers through my greasy, grimy hair. Socks and lug-soled boots on, I shoulder my pack, pick up the camera case, and I'm ready. Kind of.

Sadim herds us out the door and into the stairwell. We're clomping down flight after flight when Nic calls out, "Where to?" As in, what's this apparently top-secret story that has us on the road under cover of darkness?

"I will tell you when we are in the Humvee." Sadim's code for not letting any prying ears in on where we're going.

Ajmal didn't race out of the apartment much before we did, but somehow he's managed to get the car out front and waiting for us. I can't begin to imagine how he does it. Azizullah and I stow our gear in the trunk, then climb into the back seat on opposite sides of Nic. My Lowepro on my lap, I steal a sideways glance at my purported ex-lover to see him grinning like a kid on Christmas morning. And jiggling his legs as if he can feel this is something big.

"Come on, Sadim. Out with it!" Nic can barely contain himself. Which is new for him. He used to be steady-on and patient. Very British.

Sadim clues us in while Ajmal drives west through the city. "We are going outside Kabul to a village. Ajmal has a contact who called an hour ago to say the Taliban are not yet there. But they will be soon. This morning. With luck, we will film them arriving."

I'm usually pretty calm en route to a story like this. But today it's the Taliban show, which definitely has the potential to go sideways and take me with it. Still, it's an important story, one I'm committed to covering. And I'm okay. No cold chills charging up my spine. No prickles on the back of my neck. So far.

Nic, though, rubs his hands together with glee. The man does love reporting on an invasion. No matter the possible danger.

Definitely a notch up from running around with the general yesterday and filming not much of anything.

"Annie, you must wear the *abaya*. It will be safer for all of us."

"Done." I'm not about to argue the point.

"Ajmal, you and I will share translating for Nic. If he needs it."

Ajmal responds with a clipped nod as he turns off onto the highway heading southwest—in the direction of Kandahar, although there's no way we're going that far. But I see his hands tighten on the steering wheel, a clear sign that he's not happy. Does this have to do with Nic's coming out last night? I take a deep and anxious breath, then let it out slowly. Cerelli could be right; I'll need to keep an eye on him.

We've been on the road for well over an hour. Behind us, the sky dazzles in rose and apricot and gold. Any minute, the sun will crest the horizon, announcing the day. Another hot one. And dry. More dust and a lot more sweat.

Another half hour and a few turns, and the macadam road starts to disintegrate. Ajmal slows the Humvee, but even so, we're jouncing over potholes. Bigger and bigger swaths of the road are gone, replaced by dirt and drifting sand.

"How much longer, Ajmal?" Far from complaining, it's clear that Nic just wants to have it. This is what the man lives for.

Again, Ajmal's hands tighten on the steering wheel. He doesn't answer. Although I think his hands are saying plenty.

"You do know where you're going?" This from Azizullah, who's sounding like he's also ready to be wherever we're going.

Another twenty minutes, another few turns, and we pull up to a large village, the yellow mud-brick houses looking solid and in good repair. Nothing at all like the run-down village of Khakwali from so many years ago—where the Taliban ambushed my military escort and me. Where they killed ten-year-old Malalai as she was trying to warn me to get the hell out of the village. Even though this place is different, the hair on the back of my neck is starting to prickle. I'm on guard lest a girl that looks like Malalai triggers a PTSD attack.

Although it's still fairly early, the villagers are out and about. We park on the far side of a building that looks like it could be a school. Smart of Ajmal to find a place for the Humvee that can't be seen from the road. A posse of kids, boys and girls, clad in *shalwar kameezes*, surround us as we climb out of the vehicle. Thanks to my *abaya*, they pretty much ignore me, although a few take a second look. As the only obvious Westerner, it's Nic who gets most of their attention. A few of the younger ones reach for his hand and chatter in what sounds like Pashto. No wonder Sadim volunteered himself and Ajmal to translate. I'd be worthless. Instead, I do what I do best: take photographs of civilians. This is what life is like in the run-up to the Taliban retaking control of the country. I wonder if the kids have any idea what's about to happen. Or if their parents do.

Quite soon, the parents and grandparents wander over to see what's going on, why we've descended on them. They're obviously not used to being the center of media attention, and from what I gather, no other Western, or even Afghan, media crews have visited.

Everyone is more than happy to let me photograph them, especially the kids. And they're like kids everywhere—giggling, goofing off, putting each other in headlocks. Which makes them laugh even harder. I can barely keep up with them.

After a while, the children's antics soften up the older kids and adults. Some of the *burqa*-clad teenage girls, wearing—of all things—fancy high-heeled shoes dulled with dust, wrap their arms around each other's waists and look toward me. For a moment, I wonder if they somehow knew we were coming and that's why they're wearing their best shoes. But no, these are likely their only shoes. People out here in these countryside villages can't afford more than one pair. A *burqa* rides up just a bit, revealing a pair of red high heels and dusty bare ankles. No stockings. No socks. Looking through their woven eyepieces, I can make out merry, crinkled eyes but know that the camera won't capture that. The *burqas* are doing their job.

Eventually, a few men, smiling behind their scraggly beards, stand in a group next to the back wall of the school. Like their kids, they grin and chuckle and offer me a thumbs-up. For today, for this moment, all is right with their world. They're making the most of this photo op. Do they realize that later tonight some of their smiles will be on television and websites around the world?

I take a moment to scope out Aziz, who's busy filming Nic deep in conversation with the gray-haired and bearded headman, his white *taquiyah* neatly in place. A few of the other men, clad in brown *pakols*, hover nearby, nodding in agreement. For his part, Nic looks serious and attentive, friendly and absolutely focused— the expression that's kept him on television and in viewers' homes for decades. Sadim is still translating. Where's Ajmal? Isn't he going to share the interpreting work?

It takes me a few minutes to locate him squatting in front of a house across the way with a man who looks enough like him to be a brother. Or maybe a cousin. So, his contact is a family connection. I hope his inside information is accurate, not just a come-on to get the village some media coverage.

I'm back to taking pictures of the teenage girls, when I hear it. A noise I know well. The faint roar of motorcycles. One by one, the adults look in the direction of the road. Then, the teens stop posing. Finally, the kids hush. Glancing over at Nic, I see that both he and Sadim have shifted focus. So has the headman, whose worry is visible in his troubled eyes and his tightly pressed lips.

The headman and his entourage lead the way out to the road. Nic and Sadim are right with them. So are the men and boys along with Aziz, who's filming it all. I follow behind with the women and girls.

There, in the not-too-far distance, is a caravan of vehicles, progressing slowly but, as far as I'm concerned, way too fast. The motorcycles in front each carry a pole with a white flag emblazoned with the black *shahada* in the center fluttering in the light breeze. The flag of the Islamic Emirate of Afghanistan. As I well know, the white stands for the Taliban's self-claimed purity of faith and government. In black, their actual declaration of faith. Seeing them arrive like this, two heavily armed men on each cycle, many more in the white pickups, turns my heart cold. At least I see them coming, unlike years ago in Khakwali, when the Taliban stayed hidden in houses until they suddenly opened fire. One of the teenage girls I've just been photographing reaches for my hand and holds on tight. I can feel her trembling. She's clearly terrified.

I'm doing my best to stay in control. I've got a job to do, which means tamping down my fear of what could happen here in the next few minutes. But the hair bristling on the back of my neck reveals how I really feel.

The militants draw closer, raising their clenched fists and cheering.

I return to the Humvee behind the school, still out of sight of the Taliban who will soon be pulling into the village. Stashing my good camera into my Lowepro, I stuff it as best as I can under

Sadim's front seat. Then I haul my camera case out from the back and find my least valuable camera. Pretty much a point-and-shoot when I set it on auto. I also grab an old SD card from a previous assignment in Afghanistan. Just in case. Looping the strap around my neck, I return to the crowd of villagers standing in front of the school.

The Taliban are parking their motorcycles. And, I notice, women and girls and younger boys are slipping quietly away, retreating into their houses. Probably the best thing they can do. But I stand firm and, firing off shot after shot, inch my way through the crowd of men until I'm close to Sadim and Aziz and Nic. And the headman.

Out here, away from the shade of the school, not a tree in sight, it's hotter than yesterday—even though it's only midmorning. Or maybe it's that I've got an additional layer of clothing on under my *abaya*.

Nic catches my eye. *You okay?*

I offer a quick smile then get back to documenting the capture of the village.

The first militants off their cycles stride forward, quickly moving toward the houses and deeper into the village. When the first of the pickups pulls to a stop, the man who climbs out of the front passenger seat ambles over to our group. He nods to the village headman but eyes Sadim and the rest of us warily. I assume he won't acknowledge me, but he most definitely takes me in his gaze. When first the headman and then Sadim explain our presence, he doesn't seem at all fazed. In fact, to my surprise, he actually welcomes our presence and Aziz's filming.

"We want the world to see how just and fair we are. We do not harm the Afghan people. We welcome them to join us in forming a new government that is faithful to Allah and the teachings of the Qur'an," he says first in Pashto, then in Dari.

I start to translate for Nic, but he shakes his head and whispers, "Got it." A moment later, "Might be better if they don't know how rudimentary my Dari is. Or how fluent you are."

He's absolutely right. I just need to make sure I'm always nearby—in case.

Several other Taliban leaders join the group, and the rest of their conversation with the village men and Sadim is in Pashto. I try to figure out what they're saying, but my Pashto is as basic as Nic's Dari. Instead, I concentrate on photographing the deliberations going on just a few feet in front of me.

Until I hear the screams. Girls' screams. And women's. Some of the females of the village are being led at gunpoint to the open area where we're standing.

"Na! Na!" The screams are getting louder.

The militants corral the group in front of us then form a circle around them. I count them. Ten terrified women and girls. I look at their shoes. Red and black and brown. The three teenagers I photographed earlier are out there, huddling together, their shoulders heaving.

The militant in charge of this operation shouts at them to be quiet. And to form a line.

They huddle more tightly together, clutching each other.

When he holds up his automatic rifle and points it at one of the women, they stop resisting. And form a line.

The leader signals ten Taliban militants, who immediately obey orders and eagerly run to form a line. Most of them look younger, but there are a few older, graying men as well.

Fuck! This is a marriage market. They've rounded up all the

single women and girls they could find and are going to give them
to the militants. Probably for valor in action or some such drivel.

But first, the Taliban in charge turns on Azizullah and, pointing his gun at the shoulder-mounted camera, orders him to stop
filming. Aziz looks at Sadim, who quietly nods. Furious, he makes
a great show of turning off his camera, but conveniently leaves it in
place on his shoulder.

It's up to me.

I inch my way behind Aziz and, using him and the SONY as
a screen, fire off snap after snap. Far from composing my shots or
worrying about metering under this glaring white sun, I just get
what I can. Fingers crossed that I get something usable. But it is
what it is. With any luck, the techs in D.C. will be able to salvage
something.

When the last of the women and girls have been awarded to
the waiting militants, one of the Taliban leaders notices me. "*Na!*"
he yells.

Quickly I push my shoulder against Aziz's back and, huddling
over my camera, flip it open and pull out the SD card. Then load
in the old card and close the camera. The work of two seconds. As
my camera dangles loosely around my neck, I slip my hand and
the card under the *abaya*, under my tunic and T-shirt and into my
bra. A trick I used successfully once before, years ago, when Cerelli
thought I was a Taliban collaborator and interrogated me aboard
the USS *Bataan*. He never found the card I'd secreted in my bra,
and I choose to believe these guys won't either.

I back away from Aziz and wait for the militant to grab my
camera.

He doesn't disappoint. First, he points his gun at me. His
message is clear: *Open the camera and give me the SD card.*

I do exactly that, praying that he doesn't suspect I've got the real card hidden elsewhere. Then, to complete my charade, I make a scene, begging him not to destroy the camera.

Of course, he does. With a sneer, he hurls the camera to the ground, pounding it over and over with the stock of his gun, then the heel of his boot.

What a waste.

Amazingly, the militant seemingly in charge of the entire operation takes it on himself to apologize to Sadim for the damage. Sadim plays his part, accepting the apology and apparently saying something along the lines of "she should have known better." At least that's what I'm able to make out from his words and scowling expression. The two men have apparently reached an agreement, and we're waved off. Free to return to Kabul to spread the word of how fairly the Taliban treated us.

IT'S NOT UNTIL WE'RE back at the apartment in Kabul and Ajmal leaves to scrounge up dinner that the rest of the guys ask if I got anything. I smile and whip out the SD cards. "Let's see!" I haul out my laptop, boot it up, and plug in my card reader.

I'm not expecting much, so I'm surprised when some potentially usable shots pop up in the gallery of thumbnails. Clicking on one to bring it up to full size, I hear a gasp of appreciation behind me. Nic? "I'm just looking to see if there's anything worth uploading to D.C."

"This image is." Nic's voice. He's talking about the girls in their *burqas*, each of them holding up a bit of cloth to show off their shoes.

"I missed that when I captured the image. I just saw the one girl's shoes."

I move on to the next shot, then the next. "Some good stuff. But the real question is whether I got anything at the marriage market." I change out SD cards and upload the next batch.

The first few images leave me quashed. "Not looking good." But I keep going until I pull up an image of the three teenage girls clutching each other, their fancy shoes on display and their terror evident despite their *burqas*.

"Yes!" Nic loves the image.

"Definitely." Sadim is also hovering over my shoulder.

Aziz wanders over and joins the guys behind me. "This is it."

"Sorry they shut you down, Aziz." What a lousy break for him. If they hadn't, we'd be sitting here celebrating his work. He's that great of a videographer.

He shrugs. "It was not meant to be. Maybe tomorrow."

"Nic." Sadim motions him away from my laptop. "Let us write the story and call it in. Annie, can you upload those shots to D.C.?"

"Sure thing." But instead, I pull up the next shot and smile. Still standing behind me, Aziz practically purrs. One of the militants, an older man with a grizzled beard, has grabbed the girl with the bold red high heels and is twisting her arm as he leers at her. He could almost be licking his lips in anticipation—the image is that graphic. Looking down at her feet, one heel snapped off a shoe, I can see she's dug in, trying desperately to prevent the inevitable. Even though my heart is breaking, I know this shot will end up on the news tonight as well as on the TNN website. I have the feeling it could also show up on the covers of a few national magazines. "Sadim. Nic. This is the shot. It tells the whole frigging story."

Nic and Sadim are back, peering over my shoulder.

"It needs some work, of course." I'm tempted to do it myself, but Sadim and Aziz are quick to stop me. We all know that the D.C. folks insist they be the ones to make any edits. Something about their computers being color-calibrated to the printers and the media.

"Stop being so modest. This is nothing short of brilliant."

"This girl," says Azizullah quietly, mournfully, "she knows her life is over."

17

AFTER DINNER, I UPLOAD my images. Nic and Aziz and Sadim finish their video of the day's story, which soon is also on its way to TNN. Then, we kick back in the lounge and, over bottles of illicit, black-market beer, toss around ideas for tomorrow. Settling on a follow-up to today's marriage market, Sadim and Ajmal start working their phones, calling every possible connection, calling in every favor.

A little after 9:30, Sadim holds up his hand. The room goes quiet as we listen to him say repeatedly, "I understand." Then, there's a pause, a very long pause during which he glances at me, then turns away. "I'll get back to you in a few minutes." This he says in Pashto.

"So?" I'm the first to ask after Sadim ends his call.

"We have an interview first thing tomorrow morning with Sirajuddin Haqqani. If we want it." He grins. But he's also tapping his cell with his index finger, a sign I've picked up over the years that something's bothering him.

Not a follow-up to the marriage market. But damn! An interview with the man everyone in this part of the world knows simply as Siraj? Talk about a coup!

Lounging on the sofa, Nic sits up straight and slowly claps his hands. "Well done. How the hell did you land him?"

Aziz looks up from his cell phone. "I heard that the Taliban just named him minister of the interior. Somewhat of a dark horse considering how reclusive he is, spending most of his time in the North-West Frontier of Pakistan."

Sadim nods enthusiastically. "I heard the same thing. He's also deputy head of the Taliban. And we beat out Al Shabakat for this interview."

"Brilliant! I always like outmaneuvering them," Nic gloats. "I've got to hand it to you, Sadim. I didn't think he gave interviews. He never has before."

"And he's certainly never been filmed." This from Aziz, who's clearly excited about being the first to get Siraj on video.

I'm back on Aziz's mention of Pakistan. Why is that bothering me? Any number of Taliban have spent time there over the last two decades, but something is just out of mind, demanding that I remember, that I put the pieces of the puzzle together. It's eluding me, though. At least for the moment.

I turn my thoughts to wondering how the guys got all this intel. They must be looped into a network I know nothing about. Scanning the room, I come to Ajmal. His lips are pressed tightly together, and his brow is deeply furrowed. He catches me looking at him and shakes his head. He doesn't like this.

"Then we're on for tomorrow?" I ask to a room that goes suddenly silent.

Sadim rests his forearms across his thighs and dangles his

hands between his knees. He looks up at Nic, then Aziz, then Ajmal. But not at me.

"Sadim?" Nic's voice is tempered.

"It seems that we have Annie to thank for landing us this exclusive interview."

Now all four men are looking at me.

"Sorry?" I don't have a clue what he's talking about.

"You're the reason Siraj agreed to TNN's interview request. Siraj himself has asked that you be part of the team. Just you, Nic, and Aziz."

I shake my head. "Wait, what about you and Ajmal?"

"Just the three of you."

"This doesn't make any sense. The only reason for me to be there is to photograph him, and he's never allowed anyone else to take a single picture. I'm also having a hard time believing he'll allow Aziz to film him."

"I do not like it." Ajmal leans back against the wall, his displeasure washing across his face.

"I'll admit that it's very peculiar." Nic clasps his hands behind his neck. "It would make a lot more sense if they'd okayed Sadim. But let's be honest: this is the story of a lifetime. The reason we're all here."

Nic's right. Every journalist in Kabul would give his right nut for this interview. But why ask for Aziz and me to be part of the team? I retreat to 2015 when the Taliban 'asked' that I be part of the TNN crew they approved to spend thirty-six hours in Chimtal District, one of their strongholds. A secret assignment, it would've been quite the exclusive then, too—every bit as much as this will be now.

I glance up to see Nic studying me. He was part of that interview team—before it got canceled. I've never told him all the details of what happened, but I'm sure he's figured it out—that I was recuperating in Anabah Hospital after having been kidnapped by the Taliban. Now that I'm thinking about it, I wonder if there was more to that cancellation than even I know. Could Cerelli have gotten to Chris, told him about the Pashtun declaration of *nyaw aw badal* sworn against me? Justice and revenge. They blamed me for the bombing of Khakwali Village back in 2006—retaliation for their killing of two U.S. Marines. Who the hell knows? But it's been a long time since all that happened. And maybe that price on my head never went farther than Omar Mohaqiq, who's been dead for years. Darya's "Uncle" Omar—married to her *Hama Bibi*—who spent a great deal of time in Pakistan. And there it is: Pakistan. Maybe Omar wasn't the person who ordered Darya's killing. Maybe he didn't call for my death either. Maybe the orders came from higher up.

Could they seriously be taking another run at me? I let that thought spin for a minute and finally decide it's just too far-fetched. Like Nic said the other day: I'm part of the TNN team. I've got an international reputation. The Taliban is working hard right now to convince the world to recognize them as the new and legitimate government of Afghanistan. To take them seriously. To deal with them. To staff their embassies. To loan them money. The last thing they'd do is jeopardize any of that by killing me.

Sadim keeps his eyes on me, as if it's just the two of us in the room. "I told them I'd call them back. How do you want to handle this?"

I nod my appreciation that he, too, recognizes how strange this is, how potentially dangerous. Not just for me, but for Nic and Aziz, too. Then there's Cerelli. I can't begin to imagine how he'd react to this. Not true. I know exactly how he'd react, and it wouldn't be a pretty picture. Knowing Chris Cardona as well as I do, I'm pretty sure he'd never approve this. Or would he? This story is huge. The pictures and video will be epic. This is the story every journalist wants to cover. Print media will be begging for the images. Not to mention that it'll be a definite ratings boost for the network.

Across the room, Ajmal is staring at me. He's getting more upset by the minute. Aziz doesn't look thrilled either, although he clearly wants to go—to be the first to film Siraj. Hell, I want to be the one to photograph him. I want it so bad, I can taste it.

I look at Nic, who puts up his hands. "Don't ask me, old thing. This is your call. I'm fine either way." Liar. He so wouldn't like it if I said no.

I seriously doubt they'd do anything stupid, but I won't go in empty-handed. A loaded Sig Saur in the waistband of my *shalwar kameez*. Ajmal could probably come up with a knife or switchblade for me. Keeping my voice steady, my eyes on Sadim, I nod. "I'm in. Let's do it."

Before I can change my mind, Sadim is back on the phone.

Ajmal catches my eye, then tilts his head toward the kitchen. I follow his lead. Arms crossed, he scowls his displeasure. "This I do not like. I know the Haqqani network. They are bad people. They have helped Al Qaeda. And . . ." He looks like he might say something else, but the moment passes.

I let out the breath I've been holding. "Look, they're not going to do anything to us. At least not during the interview. Nic, Aziz, and I will be together. There's no way they'll go after all three of us. Plus, I really do think the Taliban is trying to . . . you know . . . show a kinder, gentler side to the world. I'll be fine." I really hope my bravado isn't misplaced, especially now that I'm remembering the FBI's ten-million-dollar bounty on Siraj for a long list of bombings and the resulting casualties.

He scoffs. "Please, you will carry this with you." He really does sound worried. In short order, he hands me exactly what I was hoping for: an Ontario MK 3—the knife favored by U.S. Navy SEALs when they're in the field.

My eyes widen. "Thank you. You going to tell me where you got this?"

He shakes his head. "That I cannot say."

However grateful I am to have this knife, something's not adding up. Where did Ajmal get a SEALs knife? Could he possibly be one more of the operatives that Sawyer—and Cerelli—have been running for years in this part of the world? Now I'm really confused. Cerelli told me to keep an eye on him. So, is he one of the good guys or not? Is he plotting to give up Nic to the Taliban for being gay? Or am I just imagining things?

"Are you going to tell Sawyer? About . . . tomorrow?"

He shrugs. "That is my decision."

Fuck. If Ajmal reports it to Sawyer, I know Sawyer will absolutely tell Cerelli. And what will Cerelli do? Will he call me and order me not to go? Probably not order. But he might beg. Not something I want to think about. Then again, he knows full well that this is the kind of risk I often take. And not just in Afghanistan.

WE'RE ALL UP TILL after midnight, planning our strategy for the interview. The questions Nic wants to ask—he insists on hitting Siraj where it hurts: questions about women. We also come up with some semblance of a plan for what to do if things go sideways. Or if it just feels like it could. I don't tell anyone that I'll be carrying. Although I'll take a camera with me, I highly doubt Siraj or his handlers will allow me to use it. It's more likely that I'll have to sit idly by, my hands in my lap—ready to whip the Sig out of my waistband. Will I have enough time to get the safety off and shoot?

Finally, the guys retire to their rooms, and I turn off the lights and stretch out on the sofa. We're under orders to be ready to roll at 6:00 a.m. I should be letting myself relax enough so I can fall asleep. Usually when I'm on the road, I can fall asleep on a dime. That hasn't been happening on this trip.

Besides the heat pressing down on me, I just can't stop worrying about Mel and whatever power Josh is holding over her to share his bed. I have no doubt that she thinks she's a willing participant, that she's doing what she thinks every woman does to get ahead. Knowing Mel, she may even be proud of herself. I hear her response: *It's just sex, Mom. No biggie!* That's where you're wrong, sweetie. Even if your generation doesn't attach quite the same meaning to sex, one day I hope you'll see that it's important.

What exactly has Josh promised Mel? Probably something vague like helping her advance her career, putting in a good word at Al Shabakat. Maybe he's even told her that this is what she's got to do if she wants to make it in the business.

I heard it all myself. And back in my day, it probably was true—at least for some of us. But now? There are still some men, like Josh, who plow their way through new female hires like they did in the old days. But there's rarely a promotion at the end of the assignment. Just the realization that she's been played. Wait until Mel finds out the truth. If she'd just let me talk with her, if she'd only listen, I could save her from the hurt I feel certain is heading her way. This new side of Mel is hard for me to get my head around—and it's driving me crazy. I shift my position, struggling to find a dry portion of sheet and idly wondering if this is what Catherine Elizabeth and Todd have been dealing with over the years.

August 14, 2021

WE'RE OUT THE DOOR and in the Humvee by 6:00 a.m. A very tense Ajmal clutches the steering wheel while Sadim relays the driving directions he's getting via texts. Where to turn and even the speed limit. Whoever's on the other end of the cell is leaving nothing to chance.

Nic, Azizullah, and I crush into the back seat. Aziz has got his camera out and ready to start filming. From the look on his face, though, he clearly thinks he won't even be turning the camera on.

I've stowed my camera case in the back with every intention of leaving it exactly where it is. Another of my less valuable camera setups is in my Lowepro, where it's probably going to stay. Like Aziz, I have little to no confidence that I'll be taking any pictures. As for the sat phone and more ammo: I debated keeping them hidden at the very bottom of my pack, but ended up leaving them in the apartment. The *burqa*, too. I figure if the Taliban saw that, they might well think I'm a spy. The loaded Sig is already in the waistband of my baggy pants. The knife in its sheath is strapped to my calf. I shifted my passport, credit cards, and money from the leather portfolio I usually carry in my pack into a pouch hanging around my neck under my long tunic. Scratchy but tolerable. Concealing it all, the black *abaya*, which for once in my life I'm very happy to be wearing.

Fifteen minutes into the drive and I'm doing my best not to listen to Sadim's constant recitation of directions, his commands to Ajmal to slow down or speed up. Nic's ironic commentary, usually entertaining, is falling flat.

Another half hour and I'm still trying to get into the zone, as my high school and college cross-country coaches used to advise me. I'm almost there, but part of me is still focused on this endless ride. We're basically driving in a giant circle. Another part of me is focused on Cerelli—no way I can ever tell him about this gig. And Mel—I hope to hell she doesn't find herself caught up in something like this.

Ajmal glances in the rearview mirror, his eyes meeting mine for just a moment before he focuses on the vehicle behind us. "This is not good. They are right behind us, I am certain. That Humvee has been tailing us since we left the apartment. There is another car a few blocks ahead of us. Why are they making us drive like this?"

Nic turns to look. Subtle.

"They want to make sure no one from the government is following us," says Sadim, still calling out directions as they pop up on his cell.

"They're telling you that?" Aziz asks.

"They are." Sadim turns, ostensibly looking at Aziz, but really doing what he can to peer out the back. "I'm guessing someone has binoculars."

"I'm guessing someone put a tracking device on our Humvee."

Nic chuckles. For some reason I can't fathom, both Sadim and Aziz find this amusing.

One final check on the Sig and the knife—they're both in place and easy enough to reach.

"Slow down!" Sadim is back to giving directions. Then, "Stop!" Ajmal quite literally slams on the brakes, causing the Humvee to skid sideways just a bit. I seriously hope this isn't a metaphor for how this interview with Siraj will go.

I look out the window and see that we're in front of the Pakistani Embassy. Of course we are. I should've figured out that they're sheltering Siraj and his henchmen. After all, they let bin Laden live in Abbottabad, so why not help Sirajuddin Haqqani and his network?

The entrance gates are just ahead, but there's no one around. Not even any guards. Have they been warned off? Ahead, the street is empty, except for the lead car that's now stopped directly in front of us, our bumpers almost touching. The car behind us pulls right up to our rear bumper. And suddenly, the embassy gates swing open, and yet another Humvee, this one with very darkly tinted windows, speeds out. Tires squealing into a hard left, the driver pulls up and stops alongside our Humvee.

Before I can catch my breath, armed, heavily bearded men dressed in military camo fatigues and turbans are out of their vehicles and surrounding ours. They open the rear doors and motion us out with what look like AKM assault rifles. A quick pat-down of Nic and Aziz, and they're ushered into the waiting Humvee. They study me for all of ten seconds, their eyes slithering from my face down the *abaya* to my booted feet. Then one of the men gestures for me to hand over my Lowepro. He turns away, rummages inside for a few moments, then signals all clear. I breathe a sigh of relief but wonder why someone didn't do at least a cursory pat-down.

Two seconds later, I'm climbing into the back seat next to Nic. Like he did when he interviewed the general, Aziz is sitting in the front passenger seat. This time, though, he's wedged hard against the door by the same guard who searched my pack, now with an automatic in hand. An almost inaudible click, and I know he's taken the safety off. And next to him is the driver.

All this happens in less than a minute.

Then we're rolling again.

So far, we're still alive. Exactly how long will that be the case? Which is most definitely a thought I need to tamp down as far as I can so I can get on with my job. I pull out my camera with a 17-55 mm lens, offering it up to the guard to examine. He seems surprised at first, but takes it. Opening first the card slot, then the battery compartment, he nods. He starts to hand the camera back to me, but stops to take off the lens and check out the inner workings. I hold my breath: *please let him not stick a finger in there or spit.* God only knows he could scratch the mirror or short out a sensor. He keeps his fingers to himself and, after a five-second glance, screws the lens back onto the body.

The guard turns toward me and with a nod and a smile places the camera in my waiting hands. A smile? That surprises me. I notice, though, that his back is to the driver and Siraj. Aziz is busy checking sound levels. That smile is for me alone.

It takes me a moment to realize that the slight man slumped in the corner, his black hair partly covered with a tan woolen blanket, his dark brown eyes locked on mine, is actually Sirajuddin Haqqani, wanted around the world for having sheltered Al Qaeda and for the 2008 bombing in Kabul that killed at least six people. A ruthless murderer, this is the man who in the next day or two will become the Taliban's first deputy head of state and quite possibly also the minister of the interior. This man is what the Taliban is all about: murder and terror.

We study each other for a full minute. I'm positive he knows about the vow of vengeance declared on me—how could he not?—and that's got me twitchy as hell. But I'm determined to be strong, not to let him see the fear that's gripping my heart and roiling my gut.

Nic pulls his cell out of his shirt pocket, powers it up, then holds it up for both Siraj and the guard to see. Neither one seems in the least interested in examining it. He pushes the record button, then stops and utters the question we scripted last night. "Annie? You'll interpret?"

"Sorry, Nic. My Pashto is limited." Also scripted.

My friendly guard turns partway around, this time facing Siraj. "I will interpret." His English is perfect. Better than perfect. He's got a decided Cambridge accent, which causes Nic to grin.

"You lucked out, old thing."

It occurs to me that the Taliban are incredibly savvy in how they're handling this interview. Going with TNN, instead of Al Shabakat. Bringing their own interpreter, who was clearly educated at one of the premier universities in the West. They're doing everything they can to appeal to Western governments and civilians. Maybe also to Afghan citizens, who'll be sure to tune in when this film airs. For the next few hours, this slick marketing ploy rests in the lap of Siraj. Can he pull it off?

I get to work photographing the man who has stayed as far away from cameras and television as he possibly could over the last decade. Hell, he's avoided even being seen in public for years. The first image and my fingers are already tingling. If I live through it, this could be a really great morning.

Nic records himself giving a not-so-brief introduction of

Siraj, summarizing some of his more infamous activities over the last few years. Then he launches into the questions he and Sadim sketched out last night. "In the past, the Taliban were known to have sheltered Al Qaeda and specifically Osama bin Laden. What will be your government's policy about terrorists going forward?"

Both Aziz and I listen intently to the translation. I pick up enough words to decide that the guard has interpreted the question reasonably accurately. Aziz gives Nic and me a discrete thumbs-up. Thank God one of us is fluent in Pashto.

Siraj is on stage now. I capture an image as he lets the blanket slide back off his head. Hunkering down, I snap off more shots as he sits up straighter and somehow manages to appear like a much larger man. An amazing transformation. Holding up one hand, slightly cupped, he doesn't dance around the question. "Our land will not be used as a threat to anyone. To any other nation."

"What about Al Qaeda? The Taliban has a long history with them."

"Let me be very clear. Al Qaeda has no presence in Afghanistan."

"Even Ayman al-Zawahiri? He's been known to visit Pakistan and Afghanistan." Nic is like a pit bull with a bone. I want to cheer him on, but he's got to be careful not to antagonize the man.

"Al-Zawahiri? No. He is not welcome here. We will be focused on the Afghan people, making sure they have food and education. Everything they need."

Oh, badly done, Siraj. You've just opened the door for questions the West really wants answers to. Nic strikes. "Education? Will girls also be able to go to school? Will women be allowed to attend university?"

Surely he's been expecting this question. But Siraj pauses, the slightest confusion in his eyes, a bit of a furrow across his brow, which I trust I've captured. The pause continues a beat too long before he crosses his hands gently in his lap—the very image of reasonable and thoughtful. I take the shot. "For the answer to this question, we will need to consult the *Qur'an* and the teachings of the Prophet Muhammad himself, may peace be upon him."

I nearly roll my eyes. Why do the Taliban need to consult the *Qur'an*? Shouldn't they already know what it says? But at least he didn't come right out and respond like the religion teacher at the boys' school in Wad Qol did every time he saw me. *Bah! Education for girls! You ruin them for their husbands! You pervert the word of Allah!* But to say that the Taliban will have to consult the *Qur'an*? Give me a break! I know what the *Qur'an* says. At least according to my Islamic Studies professor way back when I was in college: *The same command for education and learning applies to women just as it does to men. As do all of Allah's commands because women and men are considered equal in Islam, but each different with their own strengths.* And let's not forget that the Prophet Muhammad himself taught women—his own wives. What can the Taliban possibly find in the *Qur'an* to go against Muhammad? But as I well know, the Taliban are all about life according to their perverted interpretation of the *Qur'an*. I also know that the last thing they want is women questioning their hold on power. And the best way to guarantee that: bar them from getting an education.

But Nic doesn't follow up with any of these questions. Is he going soft? Instead, he stays with the woman theme but shifts to work and jobs outside the house. Much as I want to hear how Siraj puts a rosy glow on his answer, I tune him out. And Nic. I concentrate on capturing images.

Leaning down and slightly forward, careful to stay clear of Aziz's camera, I study the man's *shalwar kameez*, a pristine ecru—a far cry from the military uniforms his men are wearing. All designed, I think, to present to the Afghans and the world a new, gentler, and kinder Taliban. Although Siraj is in his forties, his hair and beard aren't grizzled like so many of the militants who've put in years in the field. He has wrinkles around his mouth and eyes, but his skin is whiter than that of a fighter who's spent decades under the sun. And he doesn't shout, doesn't lift his index finger and lecture, doesn't proselytize. Someone has coached him well. And here we are, giving him a platform.

Nic and Siraj continue talking.

We keep driving around and around Kabul. I assume there are well-armed guards in vehicles behind and in front of us, probably many more than the two Humvees I noted earlier. There's no way the Taliban are going to let one of their top leaders out and about without a lot of protection, especially in this city that's still ruled by the enemy. But I've stopped paying attention.

I've also stopped worrying about the fact that I'm in a vehicle with people who very probably want to see me dead. That is, until several motorcycles zoom past us. The roar is deafening. Then, a series of loud noises. Gunshots? Our vehicle bucks, and my head thunks hard against something.

Just that quickly, my chest tightens. I can't breathe.

Where the hell am I?

Think!

Afghanistan. I know that much. The Panjshir Valley? Wad Qol? No, that doesn't feel right. I struggle against myself to surface.

The Taliban. I'm with the Taliban.

Oh, God, no! They've got me.

They're taking me back to that hellhole of a house up in the mountains.

Will Seema still be there? Or is she dead? No! Seema's back in Boston. Awalmir is dead. Seema killed him. In the hospital.

Then where am I now?

I can't think.

"Annie?"

"Cerelli?" No, that's not his voice.

Strong hands help me back onto the seat. Still not totally sure where I am, I wriggle away, wedging myself next to the door. Where I'm safer.

"Hey, old thing. Are you okay?"

Nic? What's Nic doing here? "I . . . I . . ."

"Quite a hit you took on your head. There was a pothole. You slammed your head on the roof, then collided with Aziz's camera on the way down."

I look around. A Humvee. I'm in a Humvee. With my TNN crew. And Sirajuddin Haqqani, one of the leaders of the Taliban.

I take a deep breath, then exhale, doing my best to let go of the ghosts that are spinning around in my brain. We're interviewing the deputy head of the Taliban.

From the front seat, the guard is watching me closely. "Madam? You are all right? Do you need to go to the hospital?" He seems genuinely concerned—not like he's trying to kill me.

Next to him, Aziz looks miserable. "Sorry. I—"

"Aziz, I'm fine. Just a little bump." I'd like to put my hand on his, to reassure him that I'm okay. But touching him would morally compromise both of us. Instead, I touch my forehead. *Yow!* There really is a bump, and it's definitely going to hurt more very soon.

Then, to the Cambridge-English–speaking guard, "Thank you, but no hospital is necessary. I was just a little dazed for a moment." *Not to mention terrified you were about to kill me.* "I'm good now."

I'd really like to tell him that I've been through much worse at the hands of his comrades. Best to let them all think I rattled my brains on the roof of the car and Aziz's camera. I seriously don't want anyone, not even my guys, knowing I briefly entered PTSD territory. Thank God I was able to fight my way out of it.

Even so, chances are high I'll likely have another moment on this trip. Please let it not be anytime soon.

HOURS LATER, WE PULL UP and stop in front of the Pakistani Embassy again. Climbing out of the Humvee, Nic and Aziz and I watch as Siraj's caravan departs at a slow and steady pace, trying to blend in with the rest of the Saturday late-morning traffic, which is way sparser than usual.

"I was sure he'd go back inside the embassy," I say mostly to myself.

"He will. Eventually." Nic laughs. "They just don't want us or anyone else to see it. Not so soon after letting us out."

Aziz walks over to the wall in front of the embassy, out of the path of oncoming pedestrians and out of the sun's glare. "That is exactly what they are doing. They do not want us filming them retreating inside the embassy. The Pakistanis don't want that either." He sets the Sony on the sidewalk. "Or perhaps they are going to a different safe house. That would not surprise me."

"You mean a house run by Al Qaeda?" I roll my eyes.

Nic guffaws. "What was all that crap about? We know al-Zawahiri and other powers-that-be in Al Qaeda are in and out of Kabul all the time."

"What we saw today is the Taliban trying to convince us that they've changed. Talk about a marketing campaign!" And I, for one, want to see how these guys are going to work that into the video footage and Nic's accompanying story.

Nic and I amble over to Aziz and into the narrow ribbon of shade, a few degrees cooler—at least for people not wearing an *abaya*. A sigh escapes me as I lean back against the wall.

"You really all right?"

I wave away his very well-intentioned concern. "I told you before. I'm fine."

"Hardly. Well, you weren't earlier. I saw your eyes. Aziz did, too. You were bloody terrified." He looks like he wants to say more, a lot more, but instead he just lifts a very dubious eyebrow.

"Annie, I am very sorry. I've never hit anyone with my cam—"

Put the man out of his misery, once and for all. My inner voice is determined. I palm the air. "Guys, I'm fine." I touch the bump and wince. "It's just tender. And Aziz, let's get this straight. You didn't hit me. I fell against your camera. After I slammed against the roof of the car."

Nic shakes his head. He obviously doesn't believe me.

Aziz looks away for a moment, then back at me. "You get anything? Before you hit my camera?"

"Oh, yeah." Up ahead, I see our Humvee, Sadim in the front seat and Ajmal at the wheel, pulling slowly to the curb. Thank God they finally received permission to pick us up—half an hour after we were dropped off. Pushing myself away from the wall, I add, "Let's just hope my pics convey the new Taliban with its kinder and gentler leader who is full of compassion, especially for women and girls."

19

THE BATHROOM ROTA IS for mornings, but I'm not waiting—even though a cold shower isn't my favorite. Still, it's wet and sluicing off days of sweat and grime. My treat to myself after getting my images uploaded to D.C. I don't usually hear back from the photo editor, but tonight I did. The entire department was amazed by today's shots. *He hasn't been seen in years! How did you get these shots?*

I'm still asking myself the same thing. An interview is one thing. But why did they let us film and photograph him? And why did they specifically insist I be the photog? And let me live to tell about it?

I lather up my hair, scratching my fingers against my scalp, determined to have clean hair for the first time since I've been here. Rinse, condition, rinse again. I'm just about to end my shower when the first hints of warm water run down my back. Seriously? It took all this time to get up here from the boiler? Great, just great. The guys will be happy though. They'll get to enjoy nice, warm showers.

Shivering, I towel off and comb out my hair. No point in subjecting myself to the heat from a hair dryer—even if the one in the apartment were still working. Just sitting in the lounge will dry my hair soon enough.

"So much for your ten minutes in the bathroom." Nic grins as I open the door. Farther down the hall, Aziz and Sadim are standing in their doorways, towels slung over their shoulders.

"What's fifteen minutes? I haven't seen the inside of the shower since we got here." I lean forward to speak to all three of the guys. "And you should thank me. My shower was cold, but I got the warm water flowing for the rest of you." I swing my wet curls in Nic's direction and head toward the lounge. Empty. So, the guys have finished up. And it's not quite midnight. Hallelujah! I can give myself another treat. Digging the sat phone out of my duffel, I tap Cerelli's number: #1.

"HEY."

"Sweetheart. You caught me at a good time." Cerelli's voice is loud and clear, almost as if he's in the room with me. How I wish. "Tell me everything."

"Well, what I can," I tease.

"I take it you're engaged in secret activities that would seriously upset me? Secret until, of course, they're broadcast on TNN later today?" Even though he's playing along with my tease, I detect the undercurrent of worry.

"Not so secret." I hate lying to him, but there's no way I'm going to tell him about today. He'd be more than worried. And probably with good reason.

"Start with Mel. Anything good to report? Or is she still refusing to talk?"

I count back two days. Has it really been that long since we last talked? "I haven't heard a thing." Then I remember that Mel has a relationship with her almost-stepfather that definitely doesn't include me. "Please tell me she's talked to you?"

"Wish I could."

Which doesn't exactly answer my question. But it's a good reminder that if she did confide in Cerelli, he's keeping her confidence. Although he'd absolutely tell me if there were something I need to know.

"Worried?" His voice is full of worry. I'm betting it's equal parts for Mel and for me.

"Yeah. Even though I've been there—well, not in bed with Josh Forbes or anyone else to secure a promotion—I know there are some things that happen in this business that you've just got to get through. As her mother, though, I want to ram my fist in that asshole's face. Or better yet, take a pair of scissors to his *cojones.*"

"Feel better?" He laughs. Sympathetically, of course.

"Oddly enough, I do."

"From what I'm seeing on the television and TNN's website, you've been busy."

Oh, God, could they already be running today's footage on air? No, the guys just uploaded that video. D.C. hasn't had it long enough to edit, much less run it. I do my best to keep my response vague. "I just go where the assignment takes me."

"Yeah, that's what I was afraid you'd say. But the photos you got of the girls are first-rate. Really moving."

Oh, good. He's talking about yesterday's assignment. I heave a sigh of relief. He doesn't know about what happened today. Yet.

And honestly, I'd rather not be anywhere within calling range when he does find out about today. Let Sam calm him down—before he lets loose on me. "It was actually a pretty upsetting moment. I was photographing the girls having fun, showing off their fancy shoes, when the Taliban arrived to take over the village."

Cerelli makes a noise akin to a growl. I can picture him ramming his fingers through his no-longer-so-short military hair.

"You know this is what I do."

"I know. But that doesn't mean I have to be thrilled that the love of my life is present when those thugs take over a village."

"Yeah, well."

"That picture looks like the Taliban were helping themselves to the spoils of war." He's not asking.

"That's exactly what was happening. Although they were quick to put a spin on it. They insisted the single women wanted to marry the conquering heroes. Or maybe it was the liberators?"

"It's a brilliant image, Annie."

I know he means it, although I can hear how much it's costing him to say the words. He seriously doesn't want me here. And how fair is it that I'm torturing him like this? "Thanks." I keep my voice to a whisper.

"Any chance that *Time* or maybe the *Washington Post* will pick it up?"

And that question tells me that deep down he truly understands why I'm here. "I haven't heard anything from the print media, but they'd probably go through TNN."

"Are they also going through TNN for the pictures you got of Sirajuddin Haqqani today?" He's whispering, too. But his voice is tight.

How the hell could he possibly know about today? It's only been a few hours since I uploaded the images, but enough time for the editor to let me know that everyone at TNN is going wild. Which means word is leaking out. Someone's clued him in. Probably my boss. Or maybe Ajmal actually did report in to Sawyer. Which means Cerelli could've been sitting on this since this morning. Maybe even last night. I pluck my already damp T-shirt away from my chest, lifting it up to let some air underneath. But it's way too hot in the lounge for me to cool off.

I decide to stick with answering his question. No more. "Not that I've heard."

"Annie." I hear his voice crack.

Oh, please. Don't go all Todd on me, saying that this is killing you. He doesn't. "Tell me about it?" His voice is quiet and steady.

I decide to skip the PTSD moment. "It was an overt attempt at marketing the new Taliban. You know, kinder, gentler. A younger, more moderate generation moving into leadership. Total bullshit."

"That commentary didn't make it into the clip I saw." He chuckles, but there's still an undercurrent of worry. "And before you ask, no, TNN hasn't aired it yet. Just a teaser for an upcoming special report."

"I'm sure TNN isn't including my opinion. They want to make sure we can continue getting access to the Taliban. At least for a while."

"To be honest, I'm surprised Sadim agreed for you to go. I'm even more surprised you went."

Before I'm able to think through the ramifications, I admit, "If I didn't go, there wouldn't have been an interview." As soon as the words are out of my mouth, I close my eyes. Shit, did I really just say that?

"You mind explaining what you just said?"

"Actually, I'd rather not."

"I'm sure. But please tell me anyway."

"You won't be happy." Do I seriously think saying this is going to make him back down?

"I know that." How could the man be laughing?

"Look, Sadim's contact with the Taliban insisted I be part of the crew. Otherwise, no interview. Sadim and the others, all of us, thought it could've been a setup. Ajmal even took me aside and pretty much begged me not to go."

"Good man."

I drop my voice even lower. "I thought you told me to keep an eye on him."

"I did. Regarding Nic. Not you."

"Why?" I'm totally confused.

"Annie, I'd rather not go there right now."

"Oh, let's." I'm tired of him always determining what we talk about, what I can or can't know.

He pauses, obviously trying to parse out what he can tell me. "This is just between us. It goes no further."

"Absolutely."

"You've heard of the *bacha bazi*?"

"You mean the dancing boys?" Because Pashtun girls aren't allowed to dance in public, underage boys dance for Pashtun men. Word is it's usually more than just dancing. A lot more. "Please, no. Tell me they didn't . . ."

"It's predation, but a little more complicated. At least sometimes. After his parents died in a Soviet bombing attack in the eighties, Ajmal lived with his uncle near Kandahar. The family was poor. They needed the money Ajmal could bring in, dancing and—"

"Oh, God. Cerelli . . ."

"Yeah, I know."

"Wait, how exactly do you know this?"

"That's the part I can't tell you."

I start to protest but then remember last night in the kitchen when Ajmal gave me the MK 3. I don't need to ask. He really is an operative for Cerelli. And I'd bet anything, part of his job as fixer for this crew is to keep me safe. "Okay," I whisper, remembering that when I first met Cerelli, he was leading a spec op, or maybe it was a black op. Did that include partying with boys? No. He might have gone to a party, but he'd never, ever abuse a boy.

"Annie? You never give up this easily."

"Maybe I don't want to know that part." And I sure as hell don't want to picture a kohl-eyed Ajmal dressed up as a girl, perhaps with fake breasts, dancing seductively in front of righteous Pashtun and Taliban men. Oh, God, those men, salivating as they watch their *bacha* boys twirl and shimmy, slipping money into their hands, and all too often waiting their turn for sex with the boys—for more desperately needed money, of course. I comb my fingers through my hair—still a little damp. Probably because I'm back to sweating.

"Okay. Good. That's good." He sounds dubious. "Now, would you please finish telling me about your meeting with Siraj?"

So much for hoping he'd given up—for once. "There's really not that much more to tell."

"Why do I not believe you?"

I shrug, even though he can't possibly see me. "I can't answer that question."

Cerelli lets out a sigh of clear exasperation. "Were you scared?" Leave it to him to try another strategy—he's trying to outflank me.

"Absolutely. Wouldn't you have been?"

"Unlike your Afghan general, I don't think my uniform gives me superpowers. Yeah, I would've been scared."

Okay, that tells me he's watching everything TNN airs about Afghanistan. "I told you. I was scared. But then nothing happened. In fact, the guard who was acting as his translator actually smiled at me. That was a first from a Taliban militant. At least I've never had one smile at me."

"Back up, will you? A Taliban guard was the translator?"

"Yeah, pretty strange. But get this. The guy had perfect English with a Cambridge accent. Nic found it pretty funny." I did, too, now that I think about it.

"What did you just say?" Cerelli's on high alert. I can actually hear the creak of his desk chair as he stands and starts to pace the room.

"The guy spoke perfect English? A Cambridge accent?"

"You're sure? Cambridge?"

"Definitely. Nic sure noticed."

"Annie, if this guy's who I think he is—"

"Who is he?" My voice sounds strangled.

"One of their top bomb makers. He's recently been trying out miniature devices."

"Fuck! He searched my Lowepro."

"Get it out of the apartment! Now!"

Pushing myself off the sofa, I yell for the guys, grab my flashlight and the Lowepro, and rocket out the door. Damn, these nonfunctioning elevators!

There's nothing for it. I'll have to run down all these flights of stairs.

Flashlight on, I gallop downstairs as fast as I can. I've got to get the pack out of this building. There's no way I can let anyone get hurt—or killed.

Down and down I go, pounding down the stairs, praying that my legs are strong and my feet land solidly on each step. God, please don't let me slip!

The stairs keep going and going. Endless. How many are there? It feels like I should be at the first floor by now. Always another landing, another flight.

I keep up my pace until my lungs are burning. I'm gasping for air, but I can't let up. Lives depend on me getting the Lowepro out of the building.

I'm not sure how, but finally I reach the lobby. Then, my heart in my throat, I'm out the front door. The guards are here tonight, for once, and jog over to see what I need.

"Get back!" I yell, straight-arming them away from me. "This could be a bomb!"

Wrenching open the gate, I hurl my Lowepro into the middle of the street and pray that a miniature explosive device won't be powerful enough to bring down the buildings on either side of the road.

But then, the unbelievable happens.

As in, nothing.

My pack just lies there. In the middle of the road.

Bent over, hands on my knees, I breathe deep, trying to get air into my lungs. But I can't move away from the sidewalk, can't bear to leave my pack. Which is beyond stupid. Still, I stare at it. Over twenty years old. No frays. No broken zippers. I've carried it on every single assignment. It shared a Pulitzer with me back in 2007. Then, in 2015, when I stuffed it under the seat of Cerelli's pickup before we hiked up into the Hindu Kush to escape a

Taliban roadblock, figuring I'd never see it again, Sawyer rescued it for me.

Still, all is quiet. What if this is a false alarm? Maybe the Cambridge Taliban bomber really just searched my pack. Maybe there's more than one Taliban militant with a Cambridge accent.

Besides, he smiled at me. And seemed concerned when I hit my head. Genuinely concerned.

Maybe he wanted to be the one to kill you? Sometimes my inner voice is a little too perceptive.

I don't want my Lowepro to be a bomb. Taking a step forward, I'm half thinking to retrieve it, to search it myself. The bomb would have to be obvious. The Cambridge bomber only had my pack for a few seconds. Just enough time to burrow something down to the bottom, where I'd be unlikely to find it—if I hadn't been talking to Cerelli. Something none of them had counted on.

"Madam?" One of the guards comes to stand next to me. "You should come back inside the wall." Smiling nervously, he beckons me to follow him. "Please?" The poor guy probably thinks I'm a lunatic, running around in the middle of the night, screaming about a bomb, and throwing my perfectly good backpack into the middle of the street.

I follow him back into the courtyard just as Ajmal charges out the door. Nic and Sadim and Aziz are right behind him. Their mouths are open—shouting something, but I don't hear what they say.

The blast is too loud.

20

August 15, 2021

MY BODY IS STILL REELING. My ears are ringing. Damn! These assholes really want me dead. Sawyer sits down next to me on the sofa in the TNN apartment. Sawyer's here? "How did you know what happened?"

He puts an arm around my shoulder. "I got a call. In fact, two calls." He nods at Ajmal.

"I can guess."

He hands me his cell. "Someone wants to talk to you. Be gentle."

I glance at him quizzically and see the worry in his eyes. Worry for me? Or for Cerelli? Something tells me it's for Cerelli.

"Annie?" Cerelli's voice breaks.

"Hey." I try my best to sound upbeat. "I did what you said. Got the Lowepro out of the building." Even though I'm feeling pretty heroic, I'm also totally done in. And I sound like it. My voice is ragged.

"Sweetheart. I meant for you to throw it out the window."

"Yeah, well, that wasn't an option." Glancing down at myself, I suddenly tune in to what I'm wearing. Not much. A T-shirt and short leggings. Sawyer and Nic couldn't care less, but the Afghan men can't be too happy.

"Why wasn't that an option?" His patience is wearing thin.

"They don't open."

He swallows the words he was planning to yell at me. Which is probably a very good idea.

I totally expect him to say something along the lines of "that's why we smash windows." But he doesn't.

Sawyer takes back the phone. "It was remote-controlled. He waited until late at night to detonate—when he figured everyone would be asleep." Looking grim, Sawyer sifts through the few pieces of debris he was able to find, now spread out on the coffee table. There isn't much. A few charred bits of my Lowepro. The remnants of my cell phone and yet another camera that's bitten the dust. And a tiny coil of wire. He seems very interested in the notch that's barely visible on the wire—the bomb maker's signature. According to Sawyer, they all have one.

I look around the room at my four guys. Ajmal is still pale, but his eyes are blazing. Knowing what I now know about him having been a *bacha bazi* boy, I try not to stare at him too long. I try to imagine him dancing for the entertainment of some Taliban men, but I'm just not seeing it. Then, I sneak another look. He's more slender than many Afghan men. Fine-boned. Take thirty years off his face . . . fuck. And that's what they did to him.

Ajmal catches me looking at him, so I shift my gaze to my other three guys. Aziz, his head bowed and resting against his splayed fingers, is most definitely shaken. Nic, though, is in full reporting mode. So is Sadim. They insisted Aziz film Nic standing in the middle of the street where the blast occurred. Nic ran with an impromptu story. Against my wishes. I absolutely do not want to be part of a story, especially one that will be seen around the world. It totally compromises my role as a journalist. But they've already wired it to D.C. I'm hoping Cerelli and Chris pull it before it airs.

"How powerful?" Cerelli's voice sounds very far away. From what I can hear, he's still struggling to regain control. I'm grateful that Sawyer doesn't have the conversation on speaker. No one else needs to know what this is doing to the man.

"It didn't do much damage to the street. None to any of the apartments. But if it had gone off in here? My best guess? It wasn't powerful enough to bring down the building, and the interior walls probably would've contained the blast." He pokes at the coil. "But Annie wouldn't be with us anymore." Sawyer does know his explosives. "Unfortunately, it's a great assassination tool. We got lucky this time."

My adrenaline surge is on the wane, and I'm crashing big-time, so I'm not paying full attention to the conversation between Cerelli and Sawyer. I'm kind of surprised when he hands the phone back to me. Even more surprised when he points down the hall. I take myself back to Nic and Aziz's room. Sitting on the edge of one of the cots, I try once again to sound upbeat.

"Hey!" One word and I can't manage to say it without sounding slightly drunk.

"Annie? You okay?" How could the man sound even more concerned than he did earlier?

"I'm good. Just tired. And, well, thank you for saving my life. Again."

"That all?"

I'm not quite sure what he's referring to. "Look, I'm sorry this happened. But they didn't get me."

"Not this time." It sounds like he's breathing heavily. I wait for him to say more. But he doesn't. The heavy breathing seven thousand miles away goes on for another few seconds before I realize Cerelli's crying.

Now I'm close to tears. "Oh, God, Cerelli. I love you."

"Sweetheart . . ."

I wait another ten seconds.

"I can't . . ." His voice is still cracking. "Whatever I say, it'll be the wrong thing. Look, I'll call you in a few hours."

THE GUYS CLEAR OUT of the lounge and let me sleep. And for the first time since I've been in Kabul, I sleep soundly. Like the dead.

It's nearly eleven when I finally wake up, and the apartment is silent. Because, I discover, no one's here. What the hell? They're following up on a story and left me behind?

Maybe they think they're doing you a favor. As in, you need sleep and time to recover from the trauma of almost being blown up.

Damn! I wish I could silence the voice that's wormed its way into my brain.

I'm exploring the meager contents of the refrigerator—a couple *mantu*, dumplings that are much better hot than cold, and a container of *palaw*, the rice now hard little pellets. My heart sinks until I notice the paper packet on the counter. Opening it, I discover a couple rounds of *nân*, still reasonably fresh. I'd bet anything Ajmal bought it this morning and made sure to save these for me. Good man.

I'm back in the lounge, munching my way through the first flatbread, when my sat phone rings. Please let it be Cerelli. Picking up on the second ring, I listen as Sawyer's voice fills the room.

"I'm your wake-up call." His cheer is more than welcome.

I smile. "I'm already up. And doing fine." My way of preempting the constant worried questions.

"Then you're okay if I come up?"

"Absolutely."

I figure I've got about five minutes to change out of my T-shirt and leggings and into a *shalwar kameez*. Pulling a lightweight one out of my duffel, I just finish dressing when Sawyer knocks. Beyond happy to see him, I swing open the door.

"I come bearing gifts." He grins, nudging the door closed with his foot. Turning, he stops to look at my forehead. Or rather the black-and-blue lump on my forehead. "Didn't notice that last night. Does the admiral know?"

"You don't have to tell him, do you?"

"Annie."

Which I guess means he's going to tell Cerelli just as soon as he leaves. Nothing I can do about it. So instead, I smile and move on. "Whatcha got for me?"

He walks ahead of me to the middle of the lounge, his eyes darting from the now clean top of the coffee table back toward me. "You scare me. Almost get yourself blown up a few hours ago, but you're right back at 'em this morning. As if nothing happened."

I feel my face redden. "That's not quite the case. But I'm sorry I'm not a frail weakling."

He laughs. "It's a compliment, Annie. And just so you know, the admiral is also doing much better this morning. He was adamant I get you a new cell." He pulls it out of his shirt pocket and hands it to me. "Although he and I both strongly caution you not to use it. Too easy to hack into. Stick with the sat phone when you can."

"Got it."

He slides the backpack off his shoulder. "I thought you could use this. It's not a Lowepro, which I know is what you had, but it was all I could get."

"It's perfect! You are an angel."

"You still have the *burqa*?"

I grimace.

"I take it that's a yes. The admiral and I both think it would be a good idea for you to start wearing that instead of the *abaya*. You'll be a little more concealed. That is, if you're staying in Kabul?"

I file away the *burqa* request and focus on the question. "Of course I'm staying. As long as Mel's here, I'm here."

"You've seen her?" He sounds more than curious. Eager?

"Only once. And let's just say it wasn't my finest moment." My voice is flat. "But I have high hopes I'll see her again, and we'll actually be able to talk to each other. Anyway, I've got a job to do. I've never left an assignment early"—okay, so that's not exactly true—"and I'm not about to start now."

"Yeah, we bet you'd say that."

"You two are *betting* on me?" Oh, God. What next?

"It helps ease the stress."

"You mind explaining?" Although I'm pretty sure I get his point.

He pauses for a few seconds, studying me, obviously debating how much to say. "Look, this is between you and me. Not a word of this to the admiral."

I think about that for a moment and counter with, "So long as you keep the bruise on my forehead to yourself."

"Deal." He tips his head.

"Okay."

"You've got that man tied up in knots—like I've never seen him, and we go way back. He hasn't told me much, but I know he's never going to tell you to stay out of Afghanistan. I'll tell you, though, and I'll be dead honest: this is all but killing him."

I sink down onto the sofa. "He knows what my job is."

Towering over me, Sawyer nods. "He does. And he's trying hard to respect that. But at the same time he wants to keep you alive and safe. We both do. But as you saw firsthand yesterday, we don't always succeed."

"What a clusterfuck!" I bury my head in my hands.

"Great military term." Sawyer joins me on the sofa. "Although not exactly apt for the present situation."

"Damn! I love him. I just can't . . ."

"Believe me, he knows."

"So?"

"Think about it. Decide what's important. What you can compromise on."

I try to smile. "How come you never married?"

He looks away, but not before I see him blush. "I've been waiting." And it's clear, that's all he's going to say on the subject. "So, Annie Oakley, you still got your gun?"

I groan. Cerelli once told me that Sawyer and some of the other SEALs gave me the nickname Oakley. It hardly seems appropriate at the moment.

"Ajmal told me he gave you the MK 3." His glance is full of questions. As in, how much do I know.

"He did." I leave it at that. The last thing I want to talk about right now is what Cerelli told me about Ajmal.

"Anything else you need?"

"No. Other than seeing Mel—the way she used to be back when we had a good relationship, when we were actually speaking to each other."

"Sorry, no can do. Although I like to think she'll come around."

I take a few moments to run through the rest of my mental list. "Do you happen to have a spare camera and lens? Mine keep getting destroyed."

"You're kidding, right?"

"Sorry, I'm not. I've still got a couple bodies and lenses, but at this rate, who knows. Anyway, it would probably be a good idea for me to get another cheap one—so I don't mind quite as much when the next Taliban militant smashes it. Other than that, I'm good."

"I kinda doubt I'll turn up anything. For now, let me pass on a few messages. As you probably already know, the Taliban are just outside the city. The minister of the interior has been on television several times already this morning, assuring the residents of Kabul that the militants will stay out. He says the deputy head, whom I believe you met yesterday, has assured him repeatedly that they won't enter the city."

"Yeah, the deputy head is so very trustworthy."

Sawyer laughs his agreement. "And your crew is out patrolling the streets, seeing what they can dig up. I talked to Sadim half an hour ago, and he said they'll be back here soon for lunch. They plan to eat while the Afghan president and his ministers break for a meal. Then, you'll all go back out."

"Sounds like a plan."

JUST AS I FINISH stuffing my gear into my brand-new pack, Nic rushes into the apartment. "You ready to go?" He's trying hard to catch his breath.

"What about lunch?"

"No time." He's still breathing hard. "We just heard rumors that the president and his cabinet are en route to the airport, and the Taliban will come into Kabul in the next hour."

I shoulder my pack. "Let's go!"

We all but run down the stairs and across the front courtyard. As soon as we climb into the Humvee, we're off, heading toward the airport. Ajmal isn't taking it slow. Once we're outside the city center, though, traffic gets heavier with armed Taliban parading in a convoy of white pickups and motorcycles and camo-painted Humvees, their white flag with the *shahada* flying proudly from every vehicle. Although he weaves in and around the other vehicles, often with just inches to spare, it takes hours to get to the airport. Where the Taliban are patrolling the entrance as well as blocking the parking lot and terminals. Ajmal manages to talk his way past the first couple checkpoints, but then we're stuck.

Nic, Azizullah, and I bolt out of the car and jog toward the airport. The roar overhead signals a plane taking off. From the looks of it, an Emirates jet. I point my camera and fire off a shot, managing to get the plane in a steep climb, its logo clearly visible. "You think Ashraf Ghani's on board?"

Aziz is also filming.

But Nic shakes his head and points in the opposite direction, back toward the city, at a helicopter hovering briefly then turning toward Pakistan. "I bet that's him. Probably also the general. And a few key advisors."

"The first to leave." I dig out my big lens and focus on the copter.

"And despite the general's promise, they're not staying to defend the city. Or to power share with the Taliban."

"It would never have worked." Aziz takes a break from filming to shake his head. Then laughs. "They were idiots to believe it. The Taliban are ruthless." He tilts his head toward the helicopter, now barely a dot on the horizon. "If they had stayed, they would be dead by now."

21

WE STAY AT THE AIRPORT well into the night, as do many of the other news crews. This is a story none of us can leave, so it's kind of odd that I don't run into anyone from Al Shabakat, specifically Mel. And it's not for want of trying and asking around. But it seems no one's seen them. Or if they have, they're not saying.

It's after midnight by the time we finally return to the apartment, and I've still got to send my images to D.C. I'm way too tired to do more than the most cursory review of my photos to see if there's anything worthwhile, but find nothing that excites me. A few minutes later, upload complete, I search my duffel for some clean clothes, only to discover that I'll have to do laundry. Soon. Except I can't imagine when I'll find the time to do more than shower and catch a few hours' sleep—if I'm lucky—before we head back out.

I change into one of my few remaining clean T-shirts, and since the guys are still in the lounge working on today's video, I decide to check in with Cerelli. Based on what Sawyer told me this morning, the man is pretty upset about what happened last night. I need to talk with him—to make sure he's okay. I also want to find out if he's heard anything from Mel. Leaving my new and unsecure cell phone in my pack, I grab my theoretically more secure sat phone and head into the kitchen. Sitting cross-legged on the floor, I bring up Cerelli's number.

Seven thousand miles away, his phone rings and rings, but he doesn't answer.

I glance at my watch and count back the hours to D.C. time. Sunday late night here, which makes it Saturday afternoon there. He's probably in a meeting. I can imagine the top brass are scrambling given what's happening in Kabul. Their plan of an orderly departure of coalition forces in September just went sideways. Big-time.

I'm giving myself ten minutes before calling again when the sat phone rings. "Hey!"

"Annie? This is Sam. Sam Harris. Admiral Cerelli's aide-de-camp."

"Sam." I try to keep my voice upbeat, but my heart is tightening. I've got this thing with other women answering Cerelli's phone, much less actually calling me on his cell—as he well knows from a few years back when his former lover, Fatima, picked up late one night to tell me that he was 'otherwise occupied.'

Sam puts an end to my wriggling worm of paranoia. "It's not what you think."

"Wait a minute. What do you think I'm thinking?"

"That something has happened to the admiral. He's fine."

"I'm glad to hear that." Even though that wasn't exactly what I was worried about. "He was pretty upset last night." As soon as the words are out of my mouth, I know I shouldn't have said anything.

"Oh." She sounds surprised and a bit perplexed. "He didn't mention anything."

Cerelli's discretion makes me smile. Even if he has been talking to Sawyer about us, he's mostly keeping his feelings about me to himself. And his therapist.

Sam waits a moment for me to respond but then continues herself. "Look, as you can imagine, things here are pretty chaotic. The admiral is tied up in meetings with—never mind about that. But it's pretty much twenty-four seven. When your call came through, he just couldn't answer. He handed me his phone and asked me to call you."

"Thanks for doing that."

"No problem." I imagine her batting her hand through the air, much like Darya used to. "It was easy enough. You're number one on his call list. Above the president and all the other top brass."

I sit up a little taller.

"He'll be in touch when he can, but it might be a while. As I said, the meetings here are nonstop."

"Thanks, Sam." I can't help the sadness in my voice.

"Hey, are you okay?"

"Fine. Nothing new to report." But my heart is aching. I clutch the fabric of my *Afghan Women Strong* T-shirt, wadding it up tightly in my fist. I seriously wanted to talk to him. Not that I call all that often from the field. Correction: I do call a lot when I'm in Afghanistan. The nightmares and hallucinations and sometimes just the sheer reality of the place can get the better of me. Not only do I love him, he's my lifeline. And now, hearing what Sawyer had to say this morning, knowing that Cerelli is tied up in knots—quite honestly, that's got *me* tied up in knots. And never-ending guilt. About Cerelli. Mel. Malalai.

"Is it okay for me to ask?" She lowers her voice to a whisper. "Any episodes? You know what I mean?"

I know exactly what she means, but I sure don't want news of my PTSD moment in the Taliban Humvee yesterday making its way into Cerelli's ear. Not until I tell him myself. That is, if I do tell him. "All's well. And you?"

"Glad to hear it. No worries here. I haven't had an episode in quite a while. That massage therapist I told you about? She's helping a lot. Really turning my life around." She pauses for a count of three. "Did you . . . uh . . . have a chance to call for an appointment before shipping out?"

I don't like being pushed but decide to keep my irritation to myself. "Nope, not yet."

She muffles the phone for a couple moments. "Sorry, I'm being waved back into the room. Any message for the admiral?"

"Tell him to take care of himself."

She laughs. "As if."

22

August 16, 2021

FIRST THING IN THE MORNING, we're back in the Humvee heading toward Hamid Karzai International Airport—soon to be renamed, I'm sure. We're not even out of the city and traffic is beyond awful. Bumper to bumper. Clearly, word is spreading that anyone who wants to get out of Kabul better do it now, if not a week ago. Especially Afghan citizens who've worked with the coalition forces. In fact, anyone who's worked with anyone from the West—news outlets, NGOs, whatever—is at risk. People like Sadim and Azizullah and Ajmal.

Western journalists—Mel and Josh, Nic and I—could also be targets, although I still believe the Taliban know it's in their best interest to make sure we all stay alive. The last thing they want right now is Westerners dying on their watch. Besides, there are a whole lot of government ministers and police officers they want to nab before they'll come after the likes of us. More likely, they'd be happy to see us get on a plane and leave the country. Which is exactly what I'd love to know my daughter is doing. Maybe today I'll actually get to see her—at the airport, standing in line, ticket in hand, waiting to get on a departing plane headed stateside.

On the off chance that Mel has decided to get in touch, I dig out my cell. Nothing. Then I remember my smartphone was blown up the other night. Which means my daughter has no way of reaching me. So, under the pretext of giving her my new number, I text her. Just to make sure she's got a way to contact me.

Hey, sweetie! My new cell number: 93 79 129 2032. XO, Mom.

No need to tell her why I've got a new number. Then, since I'm on a roll, I send another.

I'm on my way to the airport. Maybe I'll get to see you there!

Not a word about how dangerous things are getting. About how she should go home. About Josh. No interference whatsoever. Returning my cell to my pack, I cross my fingers that she doesn't get even more pissed off. Then, Sawyer's caution against using the phone floats back. I just as quickly dismiss his warning. Those two texts? If the Taliban do intercept them, they could care less.

Sadim's cell rings. The call lasts less than a minute, but long enough to explain why we're at a standstill. "The Taliban have checkpoints all along the road out to the airport. They are also at the entrance to the airport and turning most people away."

"I know another way." Ajmal grins and, slowly inching the Humvee onto the empty sidewalk, drives half a block then turns onto a nearly empty side street.

Cruising past bakeries and grocery stores and other shops, I notice that everything is locked up tight. No lights on. No doors propped open. No pedestrians out and about. And definitely no police or government troops. They've all gone to ground. Anyone not trying to get out of the country is hunkering down indoors and holding their collective breath.

Another call comes in on Sadim's phone, this one considerably longer with a great deal of back and forth. He finally disconnects and turns around so he's facing the three of us in the back seat. "Change of plans."

Nic immediately shakes his head. "The big story is at the airport. We need to be interviewing the people putting their lives on the line to get out of the country."

"Hear me out. There's a protest march against the Taliban that's about to take place on Wazir Akbar Kahn or maybe Sulh Road. I think we should cover it. Every other news organization will be at the airport or stuck in traffic. This could be a great exclusive."

"That's the Arg!" Aziz grins with excitement.

Otherwise known as the presidential palace. I give two thumbs up. "Sounds like the people are taking it to the Taliban. I'm in."

Nic raises his hands in surrender. "I know when I'm outvoted."

Ajmal shoots me a smug glance. It's pretty clear he's happy the vote went my way—especially if it means Nic comes out on the losing end.

With very few other vehicles in sight, Ajmal drives faster, taking corners with a screech of the tires. Which was nothing unusual in the past when we were rushing to cover a story, but I'm kind of surprised now. The way he's driving will definitely draw attention to our Humvee. Taliban attention.

Sure enough, as we get closer to the presidential palace, there are more camo Humvees and white pickups with armed men in the flatbeds. As well as some big guns that look like they could easily bring down a helicopter or even a plane. Those guns could probably do quite a job on buildings, too, not to mention crowds of people. And there are people clustering on sidewalks here. Mostly bearded men in camouflage fatigues, guns slung over their shoulders. Plus, there are men wearing white *shalwar kameezes* and long vests. Definitely Taliban. But there are also men who, until yesterday, I would have said were everyday civilians—not militants. Then again, who knows? There's no way the government could've collapsed this quickly without the Taliban, clean-shaven and in Western clothes, having infiltrated every level of life and society.

Ajmal slows the Humvee until we're well under the city speed limit. A truck full of Taliban militants drives right past us, continuing on their way to . . . well, probably the protest march. Another turn and Ajmal pulls up to the curb.

"From here, we will walk," says Sadim, opening his door. "If we get separated, let us meet back here"—he glances at his watch—"no later than noon."

Two hours from now.

Pulling one of my better cameras and lenses out of my pack, I murmur a little prayer. *God, please keep the Taliban from smashing this camera.* Next to me, Aziz carries the Sony at hip level, rather than on his shoulder. He's doing his best to draw as little attention as possible until he's ready to film. Tripod in hand, Nic follows behind us with Sadim, probably discussing how they want to cover this protest.

"Ajmal?" I look farther back and see him leaning, ankles crossed, against the Humvee.

Sadim glances over his shoulder. "He thinks he should stay

with the vehicle. I agree. There's no telling what could happen and how quickly we might need to get away."

Or who could hot-wire and steal the car. I imagine the Taliban would be only too happy to get their hands on the Humvee.

We hear the crowds before we see them. Quite an excited roar. Not wanting to miss anything, Aziz and I break into a jog.

Then, as we round the corner, the masses come into view. A lot of men, but a good number of women, too. They're lining both sides of the street, maybe four or five people deep.

Aziz and I work our way through the onlookers until we reach the front. Once they see our camera gear and MEDIA spelled out across Aziz's chest, they make way for us. A few even cheer us on with *"Zhornâlist!"* Or *"Tashakor!"* It's clear these people want their fellow Afghan citizens and the rest of the world to see this protest.

I bunch my floor-length *abaya* up, doing what I can to tuck the hem into the waist of my baggy pants. The black cloth promptly cascades down to my knees. Awkward, but still better than the way it was before. Kneeling next to the curb, fiddling with my camera to get my settings right, I wonder who the hell is brave enough to take on the Taliban by appearing in this parade. The next time I look up the street, I have my answer: women.

And here they come.

Women. So many women. Those in the front line are carrying a banner proclaiming the rights of women.

The right to education. To health care. To jobs. To determine their own lives.

The right not to wear the *burqa*.

I run into the middle of the street and snap a series of pictures. As the women march closer, cheered along by the crowd, I back up, still capturing images. Then, I focus on several of the women

marching in the center of the front line. Not wearing the *burqa*,
they're all still modestly dressed, their hair mostly covered. I stare
into the viewfinder. The young woman in the very center—I know
her. It's Bahar. I'm sure of it, even though I haven't seen her in nearly
six years, and when I did, she was wearing a rosy-pink *burqa*. Not
today. Her *shalwar kameez* is a deep tan, her headscarf a mint green.
Her shoes—I do a double take when I recognize lug-soled boots
that look a lot like what I'm wearing. I power a burst of shots,
then scurry back to the side of the street so that she and the other
women can march past me.

*I went to a demonstration with Dr. Faludi. It was for the rights of
women.* Bahar told me this as we chatted all those years ago in her
room at her parents' house in Wad Qol.

I remember saying, *That was brave.* It was certainly brave then.
But now, it's beyond brave. She's absolutely taking her life in her
hands.

Glancing around, I see Nic keeping pace with the women near
the front of the march—clearly hoping to interview some of them.
Aziz is right alongside, periodically stopping to film the protesters
as well as the people lining the street.

I take another look. Not everyone is here to cheer on these
women. I'm starting to see more men in the crowd. Definitely
not dressed like the typical Afghans living in Kabul, but wearing
shalwar kameezes or camo fatigues. Some of them are armed and
obviously Taliban. Others have notebooks and are writing. What?
Do they recognize the protesters? Are they jotting down names?
Descriptions of the women? Still others have cell phones pointing
directly at the marchers. But also at the women standing along the
sidelines. At me.

I hurry after Nic and Aziz. By the time I catch up to them,

the lead marchers have stopped. They're gathering in front of a temporary dais on the sidewalk. Making my way to the front of the crowd, I'm just in time to photograph the first of the speakers: a professor from Kabul University. She lets her scarf slide off the back of her head, revealing short, graying hair. Her fist pumps in the air as she demands that the Taliban respect women and the gains they've made in the last two decades. The crowd cheers, but I get the sense they're holding back, waiting for someone else to rouse them to action.

After several other speakers—a doctor, a lawyer, a news reader for a local Kabul TV station—they're still waiting.

Then Bahar climbs the short ladder to the platform. Barely five feet tall, she looks so small, too small, and way too young to have the voice she lets loose through the megaphone she carries. In just a few words, she demands that girls and women be allowed to continue to attend school, from elementary to high school to university.

"Without education, there will be no doctors to provide our health care. No lawyers to ensure women's legal rights are respected. No education for our daughters. No peace. Only poverty and ignorance! We will not be silenced! We will fight to retain what is ours." She doesn't raise her fist in the air. She doesn't have to. Her words have everyone in the street worked into a frenzy of support, ready to join her in the struggle.

As I work my camera, capturing images of her, my thoughts return to 2015 when she was a senior at Wad Qol Secondary School for Girls and I was there to teach a photography workshop. She was an amazing student with enormous potential but also quite a flirt with one particularly cute high school boy. Back then, she was determined to win a scholarship to university—to study literature: *One day I'll be able to teach girls. Like my mother and Mrs.*

Faludi. But less than one semester of college later, she was attending rallies for women's rights with her literature professor. And now, here she is. Taking her platform to a higher stage. A national stage.

I can almost see her untying her headscarf and swirling it above her head as Malalai of Maiwand did a hundred and forty years ago when she rallied Afghan warriors in their fight against the British. My heart clenches as I remember that Malalai died in that battle, killed by a British bullet.

Glancing around, I'm troubled to see so many cell phones raised in the air. I'm sure some people are recording what feels to us all like a historic moment. But I also see Taliban recording her. Maybe Bahar sees the enemy in the crowd. Maybe she doesn't. But I do. I also feel that horribly familiar cold chill inching up my spine and the hairs on the back of my neck prickling until my skin hurts.

Looking up to the dais again, I see that Bahar is climbing down from the platform—her job done for today. No, not quite. There's Nic intercepting her, leading her off to the side. Questions at the ready. And Azizullah, Sony securely on the tripod, is there to record it. An Afghan media crew stands nearby, waiting their turn to interview her. But there's no sign of anyone from Al Shabakat.

I make my way over. Bahar's eyes brighten when she sees me, but she keeps right on answering Nic's questions.

"What you said up there was very brave." Nic must have more than twelve inches on Bahar and is doing his best not to look down at her.

"There are many courageous women in Afghanistan. We will not be forced back into our houses."

"Could you tell us who some of these women are? Who inspires you?"

She pauses for just a moment, then smiles. "I have had powerful teachers in my life. One even died so that girls could be educated. There are strong and brave women today who are watching us and speaking the same words I am. They will have to step forward on their own. I will not give up their names."

Oh, God! She knows exactly what she's up against. What could happen to her. My heart tightens painfully even as I frame the image and click the shutter button.

"You just said 'give up their names.'"

Bahar nods. "I did."

"What do you think could happen to them? To you?"

She laughs, grimly it seems to me. "We all know who the Taliban are, what they believe, how they have perverted Islam into medieval torture aimed at dehumanizing women and girls. I have no illusions."

"Are you frightened?"

Again, she laughs. "Of course I am frightened. Who would not be? Only an ignorant fool. But that is what they are depending on. They will win if we are too afraid to fight back." She turns to look directly into the camera. "I am frightened, but I am not so frightened that I will stop fighting." Damn! She sounds so much like Gulshan. Her mother raised an amazing daughter.

Another picture. And instead of Bahar, I see the photograph she submitted to me years ago. Unlike the images of sulky teenage angst that most of the girls handed in, Bahar's showed the village butcher standing at the service window of his shop with lamb legs hanging on either side of him. He was looking off to the side where his toddler son was playing with a live lamb.

The image and her interpretation of the shot as a metaphor for the fragility of life in Afghanistan made me swallow hard then, just as I'm swallowing hard now. She's so smart and brave—

exactly the young woman this country needs to move it forward. But she's putting herself right at the front of the struggle, square in the crosshairs of Taliban guns, even though she knows what's likely to happen.

I want to stop the interview, the filming. The last thing that should happen is for this to air tonight. Definitely not in Afghanistan, but nowhere else in the world either. Running this on television will very likely be signing Bahar's death sentence. The Taliban aren't going to tolerate her speaking against their beliefs, their vision for this country, their newly reclaimed power. They won't arrest her now, not today, not in front of our cameras. But they will. Possibly tonight. Or tomorrow. Sometime soon, before she gains any more visibility, any more followers.

They'll come in the dark and slit her throat. Or execute her with a single bullet to the head.

And then deny it.

After a few more minutes speaking with Nic, Bahar nods her thanks and makes her way to me. "Annie!" She throws her arms around me, and I half imagine she'll grab my hands and dance us in a circle of celebration. "When I saw the television camera, I was hoping it would be your crew. I am so happy to see you."

I blink back threatening tears. "I have so many wonderful memories of you. And to see you now! To hear you!"

"Bah!" She waves her hand through the air, exactly like Gulshan would do. "I am just saying what is needed. Do you remember that night we spent at my parents' house in Wad Qol? I told you then that Dr. Faludi had taken me to a protest march."

"Of course I remember. I was just thinking of that."

"That was when it started for me. Then, after I graduated university and started teaching, the call was too great. I had to speak up."

"You have a very powerful voice!"

She smiles until her eyes shine. "Really? Do you think so?"

"I hear your mother in you."

Her eyes take on an earnest expression. "I hope you also hear yourself. You are one of my greatest inspirations. But you must realize that. You are one of the bravest women I know. You believed in Seema and never gave up. My mother told me how you rescued her from the Taliban, how you carried her for miles to the hospital and saved her life."

I wave my own hand through the air, but it feels like a poor imitation of Bahar's much more expert gesture.

"Annie? Please, you will tell me the truth?"

I nod warily.

"You are afraid for me? Afraid they will arrest me? Perhaps kill me?"

I bite my lip, then nod. "I am."

"You would rather I not speak out? That I stay safe? Even if I stay hidden in a house somewhere, never going out to work, letting a husband rule my life?"

I pause. More than anything, I want to tell her to hide. To get out of Kabul, out of the country. To fight this battle from outside Afghanistan where she'll be safer. But I don't. I can't. There are some battles that must be fought from the front lines, and I know this is one of them. So instead, I shake my head. "From what I heard today, you are the strong woman this country needs."

She takes a moment to think about that. Then, clasping my hands in hers, she pulls me to her. "Thank you," she whispers in my ear. "Oh, and before I forget, I want to ask, how is Seema? Is she doing well?"

"Much better, I think. Awalmir put her through a lot. But

when she and her father got back to Boston, she started seeing a therapist, and that seems to have helped."

"What is she doing now? Did she go to university?"

I smile. "She's in college—studying English, creative writing."

Bahar claps her palms together around my right hand. "That is exactly what I always thought she would do. We were such good friends . . . I am very happy for her." Then she moves on to talk to the Afghan TV crew.

I close my fingers around the folded square of paper she pressed into my hand and casually slip it into the pocket of my baggy pants. Then, I pull the bunched-up *abaya* out of my waistband, letting it drape down around my legs. I'll look at her message when Taliban eyes aren't watching.

23

BACK IN THE SAFETY of the apartment, far from watchful Taliban eyes, I boot up the laptop and look through my photos of the protest march and the various speakers. I'm studying an image of Bahar, very recognizable at the front of the parade, when I sense someone behind me.

"Powerful capture." Nic's voice. "Reminds me a great deal of the picture of that young girl. The shot that won you the Pulitzer."

My breath catches in my throat. He's right. Although Bahar doesn't look anything like Malalai, this image is equally staggering in its power, its energy. I can feel it. Even studying it now, I can feel the tingling in my fingers, just as I could with the picture of Malalai that I took so many years ago. She was about ten years old back then—she didn't know for sure; people in remote Afghan villages often don't record birth dates. Ten years old. That stops me. If the Taliban hadn't killed her that day, she'd be twenty-five now. Just a year older than Bahar. Both of them strong women committed to education. Strong women who have no place in a patriarchal culture.

"Sadim!" Nic calls to the other side of the room. "Make sure TNN runs with this pic, will you? And talk to Chris Cardona about showing it to *Time* or maybe the *Washington Post.*"

Sadim and Azizullah look up from the raw footage they're watching. A few moments later, they're standing on either side of Nic, looking over my shoulders. Aziz inhales sharply.

"Annie, I think you have just won your second Pulitzer." The smile in Sadim's voice echoes around the room. "Send it to D.C. Now."

Something in me doesn't want to hit the SEND button. Although I know if I don't, one of the three men behind me will. It's a great image. One of the best I've ever taken, but just like that day with Malalai in Khakwali, I sense the danger this image carries. Bahar has become a huge target. This photograph will give more power to her voice, but it will also heighten her visibility with the Taliban, giving them more reason to hunt her down.

"Hey, old thing. You okay?"

I take a deep breath and remind myself that I'm a war photo-journalist. I report from conflict zones. It's my job to tell the world what's going on here. To share today's story of women struggling to hold onto the rights they fought for and won over the last two decades. If I don't upload this image, I'm effectively silencing their voices. Bahar as good as told me to run with this image.

I send it.

A half hour later, while the guys are still debating moments in the video, I dig Bahar's scrap of paper out of my pocket and unfold it. 93 79 129 3930

A phone number. Probably Bahar's. I refold the paper, tap it against the heel of my hand, and finally stuff the square back into my pocket. Then, thinking better of it, I move it to the pouch with my passport hanging around my neck. Where it'll be safer.

24

August 26, 2021

ON EACH LONGER-TERM assignment, there comes a point when the days and nights take on a rhythm. They run together, making it impossible to discern one day from the next. It's pretty much a rush to get out of the apartment first thing in the morning, or even earlier. Then home again often late at night. Sometimes we're lucky to get five or six hours to eat and sleep. Time to ourselves is at a premium. So is the chance to wash my hair, which is once again dirty and matted.

This morning, Nic is gung ho to get back to the airport. Much to his displeasure, we haven't gone in a week. Most of the other media outlets have been there, so we decided to chase down other stories around the city and out in the countryside. But Nic is convinced that the airport is where something could happen. When he gets fixated like this, the rest of us know it's best to humor him.

Somehow, Ajmal manages to get us close to the checkpoint. Opting not to venture into the parking lot where he could well get blocked in, he pulls the Humvee as far off the road as he can.

The four of us get ourselves organized with press passes on lanyards around our necks, then pull on flak vests with MEDIA printed in large letters across the chest. I shoulder my pack—a camera slung around my neck. Tripod in one hand, Aziz hefts the Sony to his shoulder. Ready, we set off on a power walk toward the nearest Taliban checkpoint into the airport.

Like he did yesterday, Ajmal opts to stay with the car. I can tell he's worried it could go missing. Everyone is desperate to get out of Afghanistan, but only a chosen few are managing to get on the planes. So, if there's a vehicle left unattended, some could see it as a means to escape. Anything is fair during wartime.

Even though it's early morning and still fairly cool, I'm dripping sweat by the time we reach the checkpoint and take our places at the end of the line. A good hour later, at 8:00 a.m., we're finally the next to enter. Sadim takes the lead. Holding up his media credentials, he explains that we are all four together.

"Your passport and visa and plane ticket?" The guard in olive camo fatigues nearly snarls.

Much to the guard's surprise, Sadim immediately pulls out his passport.

"Where is your visa? Your ticket? You cannot get on plane without them."

"I do not have a visa or a ticket because I am not flying. I don't want to leave this country. I am a member of this TNN media crew. We are here to film other people leaving Afghanistan."

The guard looks momentarily confused and motions over another guard, this one with stripes on his shoulders—a higher rank. The insignia doesn't make a lot of sense, but that really doesn't matter. Whatever he is, he's in charge. It takes him less than a minute to decide we're who we say we are. Then, clearly realizing that we'll make less of a disturbance if he lets us through, he does exactly that. With a caution. "I tell all media: you stay one hour. That is all. I will watch to make sure you leave. One hour."

All the media crews. I sure hope we don't have to jockey with other outlets to find civilians to interview. On the other hand, Al Shabakat is sure to be here. Which means Mel will be here. With any luck, I'll actually get to talk to her and take a step toward repairing our relationship.

Sadim nods solemnly, as if he's agreeing to the one-hour time limit, and ushers us down the drive to the nearly full parking lot. So many vehicles. I look ahead to the terminal and the lines of people snaking out the doors onto the sidewalks and into the street. Many have suitcases. Others just a large tote bag. Some have nothing but the hand of a child holding tightly to a long tunic. They're all waiting their turn to beg a seat on a plane out of Afghanistan. But piddling mistakes on their visas will prevent many of them from boarding the few planes on the tarmac. Keeping them in order, U.S. Marines, automatic rifles slung over their shoulders, walk along the lines, doing what they can to keep people calm. And safe, of course.

Closer to the terminal, Nic and Sadim approach a middle-aged couple standing in line. Four children, looking to range in age from perhaps five to fifteen and each with a backpack, are gathered close around them. The mother is holding a fifth child—a toddler—on her hip, a large plastic bag in her other hand. The father nods that he's willing to be interviewed. Aziz stands back, setting up to film.

I move further on, ready to work the line. But most of the people I ask don't want me to take their picture. They turn away or put up a hand—the universal sign that every photog recognizes as no. Could be because I'm wearing the *abaya* and a headscarf. In other words, despite my media flak vest, I don't really look the part of a Western journalist. Before they turn away, I can see in their eyes and smell it in their sweat: these people are frightened. Scared they won't get on a plane. Scared they'll have to return home. Scared they'll be stuck in this country. Scared that a seemingly innocent woman is taking their picture—proof that they've been at the airport and tried to leave. All the evidence the Taliban will need to knock on their door and take them away.

It's 8:30, and I've managed to capture only a few images. None of them remarkable. I sure hope the guys are doing better. Looking toward the terminal, I see that Nic has buttonholed another family and Aziz is filming. I'm just about to admit defeat and head over to them when a commotion farther back in the line catches my attention. Apparently, the Marines are also aware because six of them jog past me. I see another six crossing the parking lot.

My cue.

As I make my way toward the gathering of military men, people in line are pushing their way forward, frantic, skirting around me, trying to get away. As if they know what's about to happen.

The blast is loud and big—much worse than the mini-bomb that was in my Lowepro. The percussive wave rocks into my chest, causing me to reel backward and then down. My first instinct is to check my camera. Intact. Even the lens seems fine. Not shattered like I would've expected.

Then, ears ringing, I'm on my feet and running toward the bomb site.

Bombs are never a one-off. The bomber waits for people to respond, then they detonate a second one. A third. My inner voice demands that I be reasonable. That I stay back for at least a few minutes. Until it's clear there won't be any more explosions.

It's good advice. I know this. I wait a moment. Or ten. But not the requisite three to five minutes.

I'm off again, cursing the entire way. *Fucking Taliban!* So, this is what they've resorted to. Killing people to keep them in Afghanistan.

There are bodies everywhere. Men and women and children still clutching their Mighty Mouse backpacks.

I keep on. Closer to the center of the blast, there are body parts. Arms, legs, torsos.

And shoes. Lots of fancy, patent-leather party shoes—the plastic flowers that once decorated them incinerated in an instant.

Glancing up ahead toward the parking lot, I wonder if I might see someone in a periwinkle *burqa* running away, holding up the fabric to make running easier, flashing his lug-soled boots. A too-vivid memory from the bombing at Dalan Sang years ago. But I see nothing, except uniformed Taliban guards running toward me.

Too soon, I'm rocked again, this time by a wave of blood and death. It's about to crash over me, take me down to my knees.

Lower your head until it passes! Cerelli's voice.

I bow my head and fight against the blood that's about to drown me.

The Taliban officer in charge reaches me, eyes open wide in astonishment to see me alive, standing unscathed in the middle of so much carnage. "Madam?"

The irony of this man being the link I need to stay in the here and now doesn't escape me. "I just got here," I say in Dari as I pull my camera off my neck and stuff it into my pack. "I want to help."

One curt nod, then he points me back toward where I was a few minutes ago, where survivors are most likely to be. I look down at the body parts and briefly close my eyes. There are no survivors here.

I follow the sound of the first moan I hear. A young Marine. Kneeling next to him, I find myself struggling again. This is not Murphy, not Lopez—my Marine escorts from when we were ambushed in Khakwali.

This young man's eyes find mine. I can see the fear. He could be in his early twenties, and he knows, oh God, he knows he's not going to get any older. I reach for his hand. His left arm is gone. So, I gently pick up his right hand. And hold it.

"Cold." His voice soft, just a whisper. "Hold me."

"You bet." I thread my arm under his shoulders and cradle him against my chest until he stops breathing. It doesn't take long.

I'm heading toward another body when I remember the sat phone in my pack. Digging it out, I call Cerelli, hoping for Sawyer, who's in Kabul and might actually be able to help.

"Annie?" It's Cerelli. "Please tell me you're not at the airport."

"Sorry, I can't do that. But I'm fine." I glance down at my hand, covered in blood. Just like my *abaya*.

"Look, we're aware. Help is on the way."

"Could you get in touch with Sawyer?"

"He's already at the airport. Has been since early this morning. I'm waiting for him to check in."

A shudder runs through me as I realize that he could be among the dead. The body parts encased in singed khaki. No dog tags because Sawyer doesn't wear them. Unidentifiable until they get him to Dover Air Force Base, where the casualties of war arrive back in the U.S., where they'll run DNA tests, check dental records. "I'll look for him."

"Promise me you're okay."

"I am. Trying to keep my head above the waves." No need to explain; Cerelli knows exactly what I mean.

"Do me a favor? Get your crew together and leave the airport."

"Cerelli."

"It was worth a try. I'll call you later."

Now I'm looking for Sawyer. Please let me not find him among the dead—or dying. Or even among the wounded. Looking toward the sky, such an eye-achingly azure blue, I murmur a prayer for help. *God? Darya? Whoever's listening! Some help here! Please?*

As if in answer to my plea, I see someone who looks amazingly like Senior Chief Warrant Officer Sawyer. He's kneeling next to someone who's lying on the sidewalk. Not too close to where the bomb went off, but close enough for the person to be injured.

I head over.

It *is* Sawyer, and he must hear me because he glances up. "Annie, I've got this. Go help someone else."

I take another step.

Sawyer's hand is instantly in the air, practically in my face. "I'm serious, Annie. Back off!" He shifts his position so he's effectively blocking my view.

Sawyer? Okay, this is a bad situation. Really bad. But what the hell? He's never talked to me like this. Maybe he's afraid I'll faint? No, he knows I'm pretty good in a crisis.

I'm about to turn away, but instead I watch as he starts mouth-to-mouth. Then chest compressions.

My eyes wander away from Sawyer and down the long, long legs of the person he's trying to save. Past the large, horrible gash in the slender, muscled leg to the lug-soled boots that look suspiciously like mine. For good reason. Mel copied my wardrobe when she went into the field.

I take a deep breath, struggling to pull as much air into my lungs as I can while the biggest wave ever threatens to crash over my head. No! I absolutely cannot collapse. I've got to help Sawyer save my daughter's life.

Moving sideways, I see Mel. Eyes closed. Chest not rising and falling.

In an instant, I'm on my knees next to her. "Tell me what to do. How to help."

"You have a knife?"

I pull the MK 3 out of the sheath in my boot.

"Cut me some tourniquets from your *abaya*. We need to stop the bleeding."

Stabbing the knife into the fabric, I start slicing the *abaya* into strips. "Her leg looks bad."

"That's not what I'm worried about. Her arm. Don't look. Let's get her breathing again."

'Breathing again.' Oh, God.

I rip my tourniquets and try hard to keep my thoughts in the here and now.

But I can't help seeing Mel's gorgeous arms, climbing grace-fully through the air as she dances the *Attan*. When she was even younger, a little girl, those arms would wrap tight around my neck as I carried her up to her room at bedtime or did what I could to calm her out of a tantrum.

"Annie? How are your resuscitation skills? Can you take a turn while I work on her arm?"

My mouth is on Mel's, breathing into her. Willing her to take a breath on her own. To live.

I refuse to think about a future without my daughter.

Then, shifting my hands to her chest, I start the compressions, trying hard to pretend I'm working on the Red Cross doll. Not on Mel.

I keep compressing until my hands are nearly numb, until my arms ache.

Please let this be the right pressure, the right depth, the right rate. Oh, God, don't let me crack one of her ribs, pierce her lung.

Still, I work on. Breathing into her mouth. Then more compressions.

I'm not about to give up.

I will not let my daughter die.

Then, Sawyer is grabbing my wrists.

I fight him, but he's far too strong for me.

"Annie!"

I glance up at him. He's smiling.

"She's breathing on her own."

Staring down at her bloodied tunic, I'm ready to laugh at the slow rise and fall of her chest. Too slow. Too shallow.

Breathe, I want to tell her. *Take deeper, stronger breaths.* But, of course, I don't. I just smile into her now open and very confused eyes.

"Mom?" She gasps out the word, her voice ragged, so very weak.

"Mel!" Clasping her hand, I very nearly burst into tears when she squeezes back.

"What . . ."

I look to Sawyer. What do I say?

He takes over, turning her head oh so gently toward him. "Mel. We're at the airport."

"Kabul?" Her voice is still hoarse, barely there.

"You got it in one." His smile is amazing. "There's been a bombing. You were hurt, but we got you back. Your mom did, actually. Now, I need to get you out of here. To a hospital."

She wrinkles her brow as if trying to figure out what Sawyer just said, then opens her mouth to say something, but the words aren't there.

Sawyer points to his ear.

I nod. Of course. Her ears must be ringing. Highly likely given how close she was to the blast. Or maybe she's just not strong enough to speak.

I'm ready to push myself to my feet. "Let's go."

Sawyer rubs Mel's hands as he speaks. "There are a couple possibilities where we can take her. By far the closest is Wazir Akbar Khan. It's the best hospital in Kabul, and right by the American Embassy."

"Okay." I can hear the 'but' coming.

"But doctors and nurses are bailing. Like everyone else, they're trying to get seats on planes out of here. All these wounded here?" He looks around at the carnage. "They'll be trying to get into that same hospital. I don't want Mel or any wounded Marines having to wait in a hall somewhere for surgery a day or two from now."

"Oh, God. So then, where?"

"I figure we've got two choices. From what I hear, no staff have fled Anabah yet."

"That's too far. What's the other choice?"

"Try to get her on a plane to Landstuhl. But that's a much longer flight, and I don't think Mel or the Marines are in good-enough shape. The docs at Anabah can stabilize them, and we'll go from there."

I don't have to think about it. "Anabah sounds like the best bet."

"I think so, too. But just so you know, the only copter I can get won't have room for you. Just Mel, the other Marines, the pilot, and me."

I should think this through carefully before putting my

daughter's life in Sawyer's hands. She's just returned from the dead, and she's in very serious condition. Probably critical. What if she dies on the flight up to Anabah? I should be with her. But I know firsthand the miracles Sawyer is able to work. Once they stabilize her at Anabah, he'll be able to medevac her. I won't.

So, even though giving her up now that I've just gotten her back is the last thing I want to do, I clutch my hands into tight fists and nod once. "Take her. And please . . ." My hands shake as I wipe away tears. ". . . take care of her."

"You're sure?" He closes his hands around mine.

"I'm sure."

"Annie, I swear to you, I'll do whatever it takes to save her."

I try to smile, but my lower lip is trembling furiously. "I know you will. Because we both know Cerelli will kill you if anything happens to her."

"Yeah." He draws out the word in appreciation of my attempt to lighten the mood. "But as I've told you before, you scare me a lot more than the admiral does."

Sitting on the ground next to Mel, I hold her hand, my thumb resting unobtrusively on her pulse point, which is still weak and thready. Meanwhile, Sawyer calls for a litter and pulls whatever strings he needs to hurry up the helicopter. To keep her conscious, I ask Mel questions about what happened leading up to the blast—not really expecting her to answer. And she doesn't. But at least her eyes are open, and she's watching me.

Then I realize that no one from Mel's crew has come to check on her. Are they injured, too? "Sawyer?" I ask between phone calls. "Have you seen anyone else from the Al Shabakat crew?"

He shakes his head.

But Mel's eyes shift first to the left, then to the right, as if she's trying to understand what I'm asking. Finally, I see what looks like a glimmer of recognition. She's got an answer for me. "Gone," she rasps. "Yesterday."

What the fuck?

I glance at Sawyer and see the murderous look in his eyes. He wants to kill Josh Forbes. I do, too. And I wouldn't put it past Sawyer to follow through. Instead, he helps another Marine lift Mel onto the litter that's just arrived. When Mel cries out in pain, he rests his hand on her shoulder, a gentle caress. I walk alongside as the guys carry Mel's litter to the waiting helicopter that has come to ground on the far side of the parking lot. The rotors are still whirling, sending dirt and pebbles flying and making way too much noise for me to say anything to Mel, who looks very small and very frightened.

Sawyer seems to know that I need some comfort, too. After Mel is loaded into the last available spot in the back of the helicopter, he squeezes my hand, then makes the sign of a telephone—middle fingers curled under, thumb and pinkie extended—and holds it to his ear. A moment later, he's in the copter. The rotors pick up speed, and they're off, kicking ass to get to Anabah Medical Center at the far end of the Panjshir Valley. So very far.

I wave them on their way, keeping my eyes glued to the helicopter long after it's become a mere dot on the horizon. And now, all I can do is wait. My knees give way, and I sink to the ground. The tears I've managed to hold back finally spill down my cheeks.

She'll make it! She'll make it!

But no matter how much I tell myself that, I can't seem to ease my pounding heart. A deep breath. Then another. Still, my heart is close to launching out of my chest. How the hell can I possibly wait until Sawyer calls?

25

TWO HOURS LATER AND Sawyer hasn't called to let me know they've gotten to Anabah. Still in my bloodied, ragged *abaya*, I pace around the inside of the terminal, snapping a few random photos, nothing thought out, nothing that tells a story. Just anything to keep myself from going crazy. But everywhere I look, I see Mel. Her leg and arm gashed open. Her eyes terrified. Her mouth open in a cry of pain.

My fingers tap nervously on the camera body. Why hasn't he called?

Maybe Mel's condition deteriorated on the flight up there. Maybe she didn't make it. Maybe he figured it would be better for someone on the ground here to tell me.

Stop it! This isn't helping. I keep pacing, trying desperately to silence my inner voice.

Finally, I head outside to where Nic and Aziz are filming another interview—likely with someone who was near the bombing. In the background, I see medics working on the injured, loading bodies into ambulances or the backs of pickups to go to hospitals. Please let there be enough doctors and nurses.

The guys finish the interview, and Nic wanders over to stand next to me. "Have you heard anything yet?"

"No." My voice cracks.

Nic gathers me to his chest, and I hold on tight. For some crazy reason, I'm afraid that if I let go, my world will splinter apart, that something will go deadly wrong with Mel. God almighty, why doesn't Sawyer call?"

"Hey, old thing. Sawyer's a good man. He'll call as soon as he can."

I push myself off Nic's chest. "I know. This waiting . . . I'm worried . . . and I'm quickly going insane. Damn it all, I'm her mother. I should be with her. All those times when she was growing up, the big events and every other day in between, I wasn't there. This is one more time when I'm not there for her. And now, it's all crashing down around me."

"I can see that." Nic plants his hands on my shoulder. "Call Finn. If anyone can sort through this, he can."

Of course he can. Why the hell didn't I think of calling Cerelli? Because I'm not thinking straight, that's why.

I WALK AWAY FROM the maddening noise of the crowds and just keep going. Past the vehicles in the parking lot. Almost to the checkpoint, where Taliban guards are now sending everyone away. One guard glances up at me, his eyes dropping down the length of my *abaya*. The blood. I know he sees the blood. And the jagged hemline where I knifed scraps of cloth for tourniquets to save my daughter's arm.

Finding a quiet place away from the still-chaotic checkpoint, I sink cross-legged onto the ground and lean against the wire fencing. "Two minutes," I murmur to the sat phone. "I'll give you two more minutes, and then I'm calling Cerelli."

I count down the time, my heart nearly splitting in two by the final ten seconds. Nothing. So, I press the number one. Please, please let Cerelli pick up. I'm not sure I've got the energy to talk to Sam, to convince her to pull him out of whatever meeting he's in.

"Annie?"

"Cerelli." And that's all I can say. My tears are coming fast and furious.

"Sweetheart."

I choke out the only thing I want to know. "Have you heard from Sawyer? Do you know how Mel's doing?"

"I just heard from him. They're at Anabah. The doctors have taken her in and are assessing what to do first. From what they told Sawyer, she's in bad shape, but they're cautiously optimistic."

"How bad is she?" I gulp, wishing I'd insisted on squeezing into the helicopter with them.

"It was a tough ride, but she's holding her own."

I let myself relax. A little.

"He said she wasn't breathing when he found her." His voice is gentle, oh so gentle. But also matter-of-fact.

"Yeah. That was right when I found them."

"Sawyer said he tried to get you to leave?"

"He did. Ordered me to leave. I'm guessing he . . . uh . . . didn't want me to see her like that."

"He said you saved her life."

"I don't remember it quite that way. No, he was tying a tourniquet, trying to stop the bleeding from her arm. I just did what I had to do. My Red Cross training kicked in."

"Thank God. You're good to have around in a crisis, you know. I'm living proof. So is Mel."

"Thanks. But hey! Sawyer—he promised to call me. Why'd he call you?"

"He tried calling you. No answer."

"What? That doesn't make sense. I've been sitting here with my phones out, staring at them, willing them to ring."

"It could be the wonky reception in the valley. Or maybe the Taliban are blocking calls at the airport. Make sure you keep the sat phone on. Your cell, too."

"If he can't reach me, what am I going to do? Damn it! He should've taken her to Wazir Akbar Khan. We talked about it. But he said—"

"She's in the right place. Not only is the medical care good—as we both know very well—but there aren't any Taliban around. She's safer at Anabah than in Kabul."

There's something he's not telling me. It's not just that the Taliban are in control here. "What do you mean 'safer'?"

He takes a deep breath. "Mel will be on heavy-duty pain meds. Who knows what she might say. If she happens to mention your name or mine, she could be in danger."

"Because?" But as soon as the word is out of my mouth, I know.

"Because of her relationship to me, I wouldn't put it past the Taliban to kidnap her and hold her for ransom."

"Fucking Taliban." My hand tightens on the phone. "First, they blow up the airport, then they want to kidnap Mel?"

"I don't think it was the Taliban."

"What? You just said—"

"Sorry. I don't think the Taliban bombed the airport."

"I don't follow."

"We think it's ISIS." The 'we' is telling. Not just Cerelli, but probably the joint chiefs. And they advise the president. "It'll be out on cable soon enough, but until it is, keep that to yourself, please."

"I'm beginning to think a great deal of my life is off the record."

He chuckles. "Welcome to my world. Anyway, being out of reach of the Taliban, or for that matter ISIS, is another reason why Mel's better off at Anabah."

"I wish Sawyer had told me."

"Probably should have, but he had a lot on his mind—what with all those Marines. And just so you know, he's aiming to medevac Mel as soon as she's able to handle the flight."

"They'll come back to Kabul?" I can hear the hopeful note in my voice.

"I doubt it. Kabul's total chaos. The last thing Mel needs is to get caught up in the mess at the airport there. He's already talking about flying her to Pakistan or Tajikistan and then to Landstuhl. After that, here."

"Good. Any idea when?"

"None. A day? A week? It all depends on Mel. But he'll stay with her and the Marines. Annie, I'll feel a whole lot better when she's in a hospital stateside."

"Oh, tell me about it. Stateside sounds really good."

"She will be. Soon. Sawyer's well aware he needs to get her out of Afghanistan. And he'll tell you all this himself as soon as he can get through."

"Yeah. When he gets *through.*" Whoa! That sounded way too critical. So, I'm frustrated that Sawyer hasn't been able to reach me.

The important thing is that he's with Mel and moving heaven and earth to save her life.

It's probably a good thing that Cerelli ignores my last comment. "Oh, one more thing. Should I call Todd and Catherine Elizabeth? It's early there, but they'll want to know."

I take a few seconds to think that through. Of course they should know. Mel's their daughter, too. "Maybe we should wait until Sawyer calls with more news? Something definitive about how she's doing? What do you think?"

"You tell me. It won't hurt to wait until tonight. Or even tomorrow. I doubt her name will be on the news—"

"Let's wait until we know more. And could you call Bonita, too?"

"Of course. Anything else?"

"Oh, jeez, I almost forgot to tell you." Mel's horrifying few words about being left behind echo through my brain. Zero to sixty, I'm once again so angry that I can barely hold onto the phone.

"Okay. Clue me in." He doesn't sound happy. I can imagine him yet again jamming his fingers through his hair in anticipation of the next round of joy I'm about to lay on him.

"While Sawyer was off getting the helicopter, Mel told me—tried to tell me—that the Al Shabakat crew basically abandoned her in Kabul."

"They fucking *what?*" Cerelli's voice rockets into the stratosphere. "Did I hear you right? They left her behind?"

"You heard me right. At least, I think that's what happened. She was hurt, seriously, hardly able to say much. Just 'gone' and 'yesterday.' I'm kind of filling in the blanks. To be honest, people on a team can cycle home at different times. That's a given. But to leave an inexperienced, vulnerable member behind on her own . . . in a war zone? Goddamn, why not just hand her over to the Taliban? Or ISIS?"

"I'll find out what happened. Believe me."

I have no doubt whatsoever. "What are you going to do?"

"Probably best you don't know."

I let that spin in my brain for all of ten seconds. Looking down at my *abaya*, I watch my index finger trace the smears of blood. Mel's. And the Marine's—a young guy who was just trying to help Afghan civilians get on a plane and emigrate to a place of safety. Both of them young—their lives ahead of them. Both of them just trying to do their jobs.

Mel's job. Which somehow included being seduced into her boss's bed. Then left behind. God, what were they thinking? And where was the producer in all this? Wasn't he supposed to be keeping an eye on her? Even if by some chance he didn't know Josh was sleeping with her, didn't he notice she wasn't on the plane out? As for Josh, I told him what I'd do if I ever caught him hazing another woman. *Next time I won't stay silent.* Maybe fucking my daughter doesn't count as hazing in his book. Maybe Mel was a willing participant. But in my book, this qualifies.

The telling starts now. "Josh Forbes was one of the guys who hazed me back in '06."

Cerelli doesn't say a word for a good ten seconds. "I wondered when you'd tell me. Not for yourself. For Mel. I should have known."

I decide the best defense of Nic is to name him now, too. "Nic Parker Lowe was also in on it."

Another long silence. "I know."

"Excuse me? Your mind-reading skills extend beyond me?"

He laughs. "Hardly. Nic took me out about five years ago,

bought me the best scotch available, and told me. Brave of him considering he was expecting me to deck him."

I'm practically speechless, but after a few false starts, I muster my voice. "You've frigging known all this time and never said anything? I mean, seriously, the man played poker with us every time he was in town, and you never let on?"

"I was waiting for you to tell me. I'm a very patient man."

He is. Very patient. "Like I've said before, you're a saint." And we both know it's not Nic we're really talking about.

A helicopter passes overhead, probably ferrying more wounded to a hospital. The noise of its rotors makes conversation impossible for a very long minute. When it finally passes, I hear Cerelli say quietly, "She's going to make it. The medical staff at Anabah and Sawyer will get her through this. Besides, I can't imagine a world without her."

"Neither can I," I whisper, my heart clenched into a painful lump.

26

AJMAL INSISTS I GO with him to get our take-out dinner. "Doing this, it will help you relax." He smiles kindly. So sweet. Nic, Sadim, and Aziz look up from the video they're working on and nod. They've all been attentive and concerned and clearly think getting out of the apartment will take my mind off what happened today.

They're wrong. Nothing will stop me from worrying until I hear from Sawyer that Mel is out of surgery and on her way to a full recovery, back to how she was before coming to Afghanistan. Or maybe I'm jinxing things. Maybe I'm asking too much. Maybe . . .

Stop it! All this obsessing won't help Mel. You're just wallowing in your own fears.

I'm her mother. I'm supposed to worry.

Yeah, well, you never worried enough in the past to stay home and take care of her.

If I could do it over . . .

You'd what? Stay home?

Honestly, no. But I would've spent more time with her. A lot more time. I wouldn't have taken all those assignments. I wouldn't have told myself she was better off with Todd and Catherine Elizabeth. Damn, I've got enough guilt to last the rest of my life. Burying my face in my hands, I breathe deep, trying hard to keep the tears at bay. If I give in to crying now, there's no stopping.

"Annie? You are ready to go for the food?"

I look up. He's standing at an acceptable, a respectful, distance. Such a kind man. The torture he endured as a teenager is yet something else that I'm carrying in my heart. Fucking Taliban!

Eating is beyond what I'll be able to do tonight, but I can definitely let him help me. "Yes. Let's go!"

Even though I could swear I heard the mechanical rumble of the elevator a few minutes ago, it's not working now. So, I follow Ajmal down the stairs, not looking forward to the climb back up with stacks of food. When we reach the street, no longer under the watchful eyes of the guards who've abandoned their posts and their jobs to flee from the Taliban, Ajmal asks me to wait while he goes to the secure parking lot to retrieve the Humvee.

Alone outside the gate, I become acutely and uncomfortably aware that I'm the only person out here. Well, the only civilian. There are a couple armed men further up the block. Taliban, of course, and they're quite fixated on me. Probably because I'm not wearing my *abaya*. Sadim and I figured that far from protecting me, a bloody and torn garment would likely raise too many questions and bring unwanted attention. It went into the garbage. Ajmal promised to do what he could to find me another. Of course, I still have the *burqa*, buried in the bottom of my pack, but since the Taliban haven't yet officially decreed that women must wear it, I opted for not. My headscarf is tied on securely, and I checked before we left the apartment: not a single hair is visible.

When Ajmal pulls up to the curb, I open the front passenger door and start to climb in.

"No." He lifts an index finger off the steering wheel to point up the street. The Taliban guards are now very interested in my actions. "It is better you sit in the back."

"But—"

He shakes his head with decision. "I am your driver. It is better this way."

I gently shut the door and make my way into the back seat, taking care to sit on the opposite side of the car from Ajmal. That should satisfy the Taliban. Even if it's making me feel like an entitled Westerner.

Ajmal drives under the speed limit, careful to avoid giving the Taliban any excuse to stop him. Not that they need a reason. We're heading to *Shandiz*, a Persian restaurant for a change. And actually, their *chelo morgh* might just tempt me to eat. I suddenly realize he's taking a very circuitous route.

I lean forward and rest my forearms on the back of the front seat. "Are we still going to *Shandiz*?"

"Yes." He nods.

"Are they still on Wazir Akbar Khan Road?"

"Yes."

"So why are we heading in the opposite direction?"

"Because the ambulances from the airport block the road between us and the restaurant."

So, Sawyer was right. The hospital and the streets around it are a madhouse. If he'd taken Mel there, I would've been able to go with them, but we'd likely still be sitting in a hallway—or maybe even out in the street—waiting for a doctor to see her. I pat the cell phone in my pants pocket. Still there. Then grip the sat phone more tightly. *Ring, damn it!* It's been hours since I last heard anything. They can't possibly still be operating—not after all this time. Can they?

We finally pull up in front of the restaurant. Neither of us says a word as we stare at the unlit front window, the *BASTEH* sign hanging on the door. Closed. So much for their famous chicken with berries.

"What now?" I sound ridiculously discouraged.

"You are not to worry. I know of a place that is open." The confidence in Ajmal's voice is welcome.

I lean back against the seat and try hard to relax. Which is pretty paradoxical. But there you go.

More slow driving. Many more white pickups and camo Humvees with big guns mounted in the flatbeds cruising the streets. Both of us looking determinedly away from the Taliban militants who are staring at us, probably deciding whether we're worth stopping. It feels like forever until we reach the next restaurant. Secure behind its high cinder block walls, but no guards in sight.

I'm suddenly feeling vaguely unsettled. Nothing to do with the Taliban, but something has me on edge. I take another look and finally recognize where I am. *Khosha* restaurant. Years ago, I ate lunch here. After spending a very long, very hot hour having the owner Fatima drill me in the proper way to wear and walk in a *burqa*. It was my first time meeting her. She was perfection, the way she moved with that confounded tent over her, whereas I was . . . not. Pretty much a limping donkey, I ended up doing a face-plant. In my defense, I was having one of the first of my increasingly frightening PTSD moments. But at the time, I was also acutely aware of the sexual attraction between her and the man who brought me here—Captain Finn Cerelli. Her former lover. Shortly after that, Cerelli and I got together, and since then he's told me again and again, he's all mine. I'd like to think I'm looking forward to seeing Fatima again, but I'm not.

The intoxicating aromas of chicken and lamb kebabs and *palaw* assure both Ajmal and me that *Khosha* is open. And by the time we reach the front door, I'm practically salivating for Sami's *borani banjân*. Eggplant with tomato and garlic-yogurt sauce is one of my favorite foods in the world, and no one makes it like Fatima's husband Sami.

The dining room is far from empty. A contingent of camo-uniformed Taliban lounge on large floor cushions at nearly every table. Is that the Cambridge Bomber sitting in the corner staring at me, eyes cold, lips pursed? I'd bet anything that's him.

Fatima herself steps out of the kitchen and welcomes us. She smiles broadly when she sees Ajmal; it's clear that she knows him. Probably from his several previous visits to get food for our crew. But then her eyes widen ever so slightly when she looks in my direction—a sure sign she recognizes me. I offer a small smile in return, then a silent nod when she inclines her head toward the men in the room. Message received. I won't say a word about having met her in the past, about Cerelli, about anything. The Taliban certainly won't look favorably on any association she might have with Westerners. And I'm positive that the last thing she wants them or anyone to know is that she used to be one of Cerelli's operatives. Or maybe she still is.

Ajmal places our order. All my favorites. Meanwhile, I sit on the chair next to the front door and savor the cup of *chai* Fatima serves while we wait. All the better to keep me occupied and my mouth shut.

Fatima is in and out of the kitchen, back and forth across the dining room as she attends to the men's demands. I'm not sure what causes me to glance up when I sense the soft flutter of the curtain at the back of the narrow hall. A little girl, maybe four years old, is clinging to the fabric. She's watching me closely, but as soon as she realizes I'm looking back at her, she dips her head behind the curtain.

A few moments later, dark eyes are peering at me again. This time, she doesn't hide. If ever there was a mini-me, it's this little girl. There's no question that she's Fatima's daughter. The same lustrous dark hair, heart-shaped face, wide mouth.

I smile at her and flutter my fingers.

She waves back. And grins.

What a beautiful child!

Then, that dreadful, jealousy-ridden worm starts boring into my brain, reminding me that in 2015, Cerelli was working with this child's mother. And he's been back to Afghanistan since then. He's always assured me there was nothing for me to worry about. But I've heard more than one man say that. It doesn't mean they're not sleeping with someone else. It really just means the woman—in this case, me—shouldn't worry about it.

Oh, get real! Cerelli told me they'd slept together once, long ago.

Yeah, well, what man returns to a former lover, spends the night, and doesn't . . .

I trust Cerelli. I do. He told me there's nothing romantic between them.

Does the girl look like Cerelli?

I'm still playing peekaboo with Fatima's daughter when the woman herself carries a stack of aluminum containers from the kitchen and presents them to me. Ajmal pays. This time when I wave to the little girl, she steps out from behind the curtain and comes to join her mother, reaching up to hold on to the long green tunic.

I'm about to say goodbye, but I remember the Taliban in the room and stop myself. Would 'goodbye' suggest that we know each other? I decide it'd be safer for all concerned to say *"Tashakor."* The look of relief that flits across Fatima's face confirms I made the right decision.

27

EVEN THOUGH I WAS CONVINCED I wouldn't be able to eat a bite, I do—voraciously. The way the guys are looking at me, indicates they think I'm doing better. The occasional sideways glances, the knowing smiles, the nods to one another. I see it, and feel doubly guilty. How could I possibly eat when I still don't know what's happening with Mel? She must be alive. I'd feel it if she weren't. Wouldn't I? But my heart isn't clenching quite so much—a sure sign that she must be handling the surgery well. Besides, Sawyer would've called if she'd died, wouldn't he? Or, if not me, then Cerelli. And Cerelli would absolutely have called to break the news.

She's alive. Definitely.

Then why hasn't Sawyer called?

By eleven, one by one the guys give up waiting, and I wave them off to bed. Someone should get some sleep. Nic is the last to go.

At midnight, I'm curled up in the corner of the sofa, unable to think of anything except Mel. I've tried Sawyer—repeatedly—but he doesn't answer. My eyes are burning from being awake so long. I can barely keep them open. I need sleep. Desperately.

But more than sleep, I need Sawyer to call. Or maybe I should call Cerelli?

I close my eyes—for just a moment. But the day catches up with me, and I feel myself sinking into sleep. Restless. Interrupted by the oddest sounds. And finally, I hear ringing—from far away. In my dream, I think it's a phone and race to answer it, my legs slogging through water or quicksand, I'm not sure which. Each time I think I'm close enough to answer, the phone goes silent. Whoever was calling is gone.

Someone is gripping my shoulders, shaking me. "Annie? Annie! Wake up!"

I open my eyes, confused. "Nic?"

"Your sat phone's been ringing, and you never answered. It's Sawyer."

Grabbing the phone from Nic's outstretched hand, I nearly yell, "Sawyer!"

Shaking his head, Nic retreats down the hall but doesn't close the bedroom door. I'm pretty sure all four guys are listening.

Sawyer's laughing. "Sure took you long enough."

"Sorry. Really. Adrenaline crash. It's been a long day."

"Tell me about it. But look, I've got good news for you."

I've been curled into myself, digging my fingers into the sofa cushion, bracing for him to say something bad, something so horrible I couldn't bear to hear it. But the uptick in his voice has me smiling. "Mel's okay?"

"Not so fast."

My heart skids to a stop. "What?" I whisper, barely able to get the word out.

"She's out of surgery. But okay isn't exactly the word I'd use."

Oh my God. "What's the prognosis?"

"She's definitely going to make it. No worries about that." He takes a deep breath, almost as if he's leading up to breaking the bad news.

She's going to make it. That's all that matters. Closing my eyes, I whisper a short prayer of thanks to the universe. Then, I stop. "I hear a lot of reservation there. Tell me."

"Annie, I'll be honest. She's in for a long haul. Months of rehab. You remember how Finn—"

"No! Please, no! Don't tell me she's lost her leg."

"Annie—"

"Her arm?"

"Stop! Would you just stop so I can tell you?"

"Sorry, sorry. Tell me." I look down the hall and swear I see shadows hovering in the doorways. Thank you, guys, for keeping me company. For making sure if this goes sideways, I'll have shoulders to cry on.

"I don't know how the admiral does it."

Whiplash. Damn. Sawyer's as bad as Cerelli at changing subjects. "What are you talking about?"

"You. You must drive him crazy." But the way he says it sounds almost wistful. Like he wouldn't mind being driven crazy—occasionally. "Look, I'm not gonna lie. I was worried, too. But not anymore. You raised a strong girl. In fact, she's amazing. I'm not sure I would've pulled through what she's managed so far."

"You going to tell me?"

"She was in surgery for a long time. Hours. Her heart's strong, but it wasn't all smooth sailing. She"—he adds before I can interrupt—"rallied and came through."

"Details, please?"

"Of course you want details." He makes a noise that's half chuckle, half groan.

I stare cross-eyed at the sat phone. Does he honestly think I wouldn't want to know every last thing that happened?

"Here goes. There's significant muscle damage in her left leg. She took some shrapnel from the bomb, and they . . . uh . . . did their best to repair it. But she'll be facing another operation as soon as I can get her back CONUS. Or more probably to Landstuhl."

My heart starts beating faster. Something tells me what he says next could be even worse.

"Her arm. Before you think the worst, they were able to save it. But there's a lot that still needs to be repaired."

"Okay." I'm struggling to keep my voice calm, measured.

"Like I said before, she's got a long road ahead of her."

"Yeah, I get that." There's something more. I can hear it in his voice. "What aren't you telling me?"

He clears his throat. Oh God, this is going to be bad.

"Sawyer?"

"Okay. It's pretty iffy whether she'll be able to dance again. She'll probably have a pronounced limp and . . . may need . . . help walking."

His words knock me sideways. I clutch the sat phone, my fingers tightening until I'm sure the knuckles are colorless. Calm and measured disappear. In my mind's eye, I see her dancing. So beautifully. So effortlessly. The flow of her body as she moves through space, pirouettes across my kitchen in Bay View. She always became the dance. That's who she is—a dancer. And now? Not able to dance? A thousand questions swirl through my mind until I settle on what's probably most important. "Does she know?"

"Not yet."

Tears are burning my eyes, but I blink frantically, determined not to give in. "Dancing is her life."

"Yeah, I know."

"You do?"

"The last thing she said to me as they were wheeling her into the OR was something along the lines of 'Don't let them take my leg. I'm a dancer. I have to be able to dance.'" He lets Mel's words sit between us. "Annie, I did everything I could. I told the surgeon. Hell, I begged the surgeon. She was aware. But, as I said, the damage was significant."

I roll that thought around in my brain before I give voice to it. "Will you tell her?"

He pauses. "Shouldn't you?"

I nod. "Probably. And if I could get to Anabah—"

"That's a hard negative—at least, for now. I've already talked to Finn, and he agrees, so don't you dare even think about it."

"So, you and Cerelli decided—"

"Sorry. I know how you feel about men telling you what you can and can't do." He really does sound abashed. And I'm sure the last thing he needs tonight is for me to argue with him. "The Taliban are trying to take the Panjshir Valley. You won't do anyone any good, least of all Mel, if you try to get here and get caught up in that."

I breathe out slowly. "Understood." I let that sit for a minute, wondering yet again if I should have insisted on getting on that helicopter. Which is a crazy thought. If there'd been room, Sawyer or the pilot would've told me. "Back to Mel, okay? She's sort of single-minded. I wouldn't be surprised if she asks you about dancing. Soon."

"She already has. As soon as she came to."

"She's awake?"

"That's why I waited. She made me promise—so she can talk to you, too. Be forewarned: she's pretty doped up on painkillers and a little loopy. But the drugs are doing their job. So, she can talk. But keep it short? Please? Let me get back in her room."

I listen as he opens then closes a door. "Sawyer? Is that my mom?" Mel's voice—not so much groggy or weak, more tired than anything.

"It is." Two words. But I've never heard Sawyer's voice sound like that before. The gentleness, the sweetness.

I think back a few days to when he brought me the new phone and backpack. Half-jokingly, I asked him why he never married. "Waiting," he said. God help me, has he been waiting for Mel? Another memory surfaces. Farther back. When Cerelli was recovering at Bethesda Naval Hospital from the transtibial amputation—and refusing to see me. In an attempt to mediate between us, Sawyer and Mel had teamed up. It was enough of a team that I came away thinking she was crushing on him. In a big way. At the age of fifteen.

Now, Sawyer sounds for all the world like he's got a crush on her. At the same time that Mel's been jumping into bed with Josh Forbes.

"Mom?" Mel sounds a lot stronger than I expected. Thank God for pain meds.

"Sweetie. I wish I could be with you." My heart is a painful lump in the middle of my chest.

"No worries. Sawyer's here. Get this: he got us a private room."

"Us?"

"He's worried some Taliban maybe slipped in with the wounded."

I think about that. It's good that Sawyer will be there, guarding her, but . . .

But what? There's no way Sawyer will put the moves on her. Good God, she just came out of surgery!

"Good. I'm glad he'll be there with you." And I am.

"Mom, I'm really sorry about . . . everything."

"Shhh. It's okay. And I'm sorry, too."

I wait. My heart in my throat.

"I . . . I trusted him, Mom. But he lied. It was all . . . oh, fuck, I don't know what it was."

"We'll talk about it. Later."

"Yeah. Okay." The rustling of cloth muffles her voice. "Oh, Mom? Sawyer wants to talk to you again."

"Sure, sweetie. Hey, I love you."

"Me . . . too." She sounds like she's fading fast.

A few moments later, Sawyer's back on the line. "Listen, Annie. It's pretty fluid here. The doctors have told me I'll need to medevac Mel as soon as possible."

"Seriously?"

"Yeah." He doesn't sound pleased. "A lot of wounded are being brought here. They need the room. I won't let them kick her out before she's able to fly, but just be prepared that we may have to leave soon. As soon as she's strong enough."

"Okay." I take a deep breath. "Oh, one more thing?"

"Yeah?"

"Are you about to call Cerelli?"

"I am."

"Could you please ask him to call Mel's father and stepmother? And Bonita? He's got the numbers."

"Will do."

"And Sawyer, thanks for everything you've done today." I can feel tears welling. "I'll . . . never be able to—"

"Annie, there's no need . . ." He doesn't say anything for a few moments, leaving me to wonder if I should say more. Then, he's talking again, his voice so low that I'm sure Mel can't hear him. "I swear to you, I'll protect her with my life."

28

August 27, 2021

NOTHING COULD HAVE PREPARED me for the sight of so many wounded civilians on gurneys and litters in the halls and lobby of Wazir Akbar Khan Hospital. Family members sit with patients, doing what they can to comfort them, giving them sips of water, reciting verses from the *Qur'an*. Several nurses and a male doctor in a blood-soaked jacket and latex gloves move from patient to patient, doing their best to triage the most seriously wounded. But the whole thing is nothing short of a nightmare. The fusty smells of blood and urine and feces. The moans and groans of pain. The contortions of broken bodies. The missing limbs.

Yesterday, people at the airport shook their heads when I asked to take their pictures. This morning, they shrug and nod sadly. *Why not? We have nothing left to lose. Yes, show the world what happened.* I take their pictures, trying to frame them to crop out protruding bones, deep gashes, and bloody stumps. But it's always a delicate balance. My pictures need to tell the story of what happened, and the people seem to know that.

The doctor thrusts a jacketed arm in front of my camera to block a shot. "Please, you must stop. This is upsetting my patients."

I raise my camera above his arm and take the shot. "I disagree, Doctor. They gave me permission when I asked."

"Madam, I asked you to stop. Your story will say that we are a full day behind treating these people who are badly wounded. That is what people around the world will see: the incompetence of Afghan doctors." The doctor sounds exhausted, as if he could crack at any moment.

"As you just said, you're twenty-four hours delinquent in helping these people. Would you have me say they're getting good care?" Thank God Sawyer knew this hospital would be the wrong place to bring Mel. I'd be frigging insane if she were lying on a gurney out here waiting for surgery.

"They are getting the care I can give them. I am only one doctor."

I turn to face him. A young man, he looks to be not long out of med school. Oh my God, I know him. "Farrakh? Dr. Farrakh Abdulin?"

He looks at me through bleary eyes. Then, recognition dawns. "Annie Hawkins? I cannot believe it is you." A tired smile creases his face. "But of course you would be here. This is exactly the kind of work you do."

I lean in closer and lower my voice. "Tell me, honestly. What's going on here? Why is this triage taking so long?"

He closes his eyes. A ten-second nap. Then, he swings his arm around half the room. "As you can see, there are so many wounded people. I am one of the few doctors still here. Only three doctors are operating, but most of these surgeries, they are complicated and take many hours. There is only so much we can do."

"But where—"

"Many doctors—and nurses—they have fled. Some left weeks ago. Others are at the airport now, trying to get to the U.S. or Qatar. Or they are driving to Iran or even Turkmenistan."

"You stayed."

He nods. Sadly, it seems to me. "Someone has to. This is my country. I am not ready to leave."

We watch each other warily for another few moments, then each of us goes back to our jobs. Truthfully, though, I find myself second-guessing what Farrakh said. Am I upsetting the patients? They actually seem to welcome the opportunity to be photographed, but how could they when they're wounded, perhaps even dying?

Soon after, Sadim signals me that they're wrapping up the interviews and filming. I nod that I've gotten all the photos I need. I'm turning to follow the guys back outside when Farrakh steps in front of me. He's careful not to touch me, but he's close.

"One moment?" he asks quietly. "In private?"

"Of course."

We look for a corner away from patients and families, but there isn't one. Not inside the lobby. He nods toward the main doors, and I follow.

He looks around carefully. I'm guessing he wants to make sure no one can overhear us. Finally, his voice barely audible, he says, "It is about my sister. Bahar."

My heart thuds, and my mind races, imagining all kinds of horrible possibilities. *Don't make assumptions!* I block out my thoughts. "Has something happened?"

"You know she is a feminist?"

"Yes, I saw her the other day."

"So, it was your crew that filmed her leading the protest?"

I nod. "And I photographed her. Reluctantly, believe me. But she was adamant. She insisted that we publish the images."

"That does not surprise me. She has been taking risks for several years. But now, it is even more dangerous."

"I know. I told her exactly that."

"It is even worse than she knows. The Taliban came to the hospital last night looking for her. You see, they know who I am—that she is my sister. They think maybe I am hiding her here. They searched the hospital and my apartment but didn't find her. Of course. Now they want me to tell them where she is." He bows his head.

"Oh, Farrakh!"

He looks up sharply. "I would never tell them. Even if I knew. It would not matter what they do to me." A moment later, he adds, "This is so difficult for my parents. She is the youngest, and they want . . . they expect me to protect her."

I think back almost six years to my last visit to Wad Qol. Farrakh and Bahar drove me from Kabul to their small, sleepy village. I worried when they left to drive back early the next morning, before the early gray light of dawn had found its way past the high Hindu Kush Mountains into the valley. Their mother, Gulshan, dismissed my concern with a laugh, telling me how devoted Farrakh was to his sister.

I search for words to ease Farrakh's struggle. "You know, sometimes we have to let the people we love make their own decisions, live their own lives." Oh, God! I sound ridiculously preachy, as if I've got all the answers. Which is far from the truth.

He wipes his palm across his eyes. "They will arrest her. And,

I am certain, they will kill her. They are rounding up people who worked for the government, but also many others, especially women. We have heard stories of bodies being found in the street with their throats slit open."

This young man has so much riding on his shoulders. The least I can do is let the rest of the guys go on to their next assignment and ask Ajmal to drive me to some of Bahar's usual haunts. If Farrakh has any idea where I might search. "What can I do?"

His bloodshot eyes brighten. "I have tried to call her, but she is not answering. A few days ago, I took time from work and went by her apartment, but she wasn't there. I am very worried, but I can no longer even try. The Taliban know to follow me. Could you . . ."

"I'll do what I can, but they might follow me as well."

His shoulders sag. "I know I am asking a lot. Too much. But if you see her, please tell her to leave Kabul." With that, he sits for a moment on a concrete bench, his face buried in his hands. Then, standing, he strides back through the glass doors into the hospital lobby. "Thank you anyway. *Bâmân-e khodâ.*"

"*Khodâ hâfiz,*" I murmur automatically, more to myself than to him. I'm about to call after him. I need some directions, some idea of where to look. That's when I glance down. The sidewalk in front of the bench. A piece of white paper, folded small. A quick look around, and I see no one watching. So, I sink onto the bench, my lug-soled boot clamping hard on top of the paper. Raising my camera, I focus on the front of the hospital and make as if I'm pressing the shutter. Again and again. Jammed. I examine the camera, eventually opening the SD card slot. Pulling it out as if the problem could be related to the card, I fumble it to the ground next to my boot.

Exhaling sharply, I lean down, shift my foot, and scoop up both the paper and the card. I slip the card back into place and palm the paper behind my watchband, praying to God it stays there until I can get to the Humvee.

Back on my feet, I see Sadim waving at me from a block away. But I sense someone else watching me, too. There, in the near distance, I focus on a bearded man. He's not wearing a camo uniform, but that doesn't matter. He's Taliban.

Making sure the lid to the card compartment is secure, I head toward the vehicle, praying the man didn't see the square of paper.

SECURE IN THE BACK SEAT of the Humvee and safe from prying Taliban eyes, I unfold Farrakh's note. An address. Exactly what I expected.

"You going to tell us what that was all about?" Nic tries to play it cool, but his curiosity is insatiable. There's no point fobbing him off.

I hold up the white paper and tell them about Farrakh's concerns. "He asked me to check on her, to make sure she's okay. He also wants me to convince her to stop drawing attention to herself and go into hiding."

Nic purses his lips. "Not exactly your line of work."

"Not at all. But I'd like to help if I can. Plus, this could give us the chance to see what the Taliban are really doing to ordinary civilians." I'd love to convince the guys, especially Sadim, that this could be a worthwhile investigation.

Nic nods thoughtfully. "We've been hearing rumors that they're rounding up anyone who worked for the coalition forces or the national police as well as women in any position of government. In fact, any women who speak out against the Taliban."

"I've heard from a few women who are news anchors and journalists," says Aziz. "They are telling me that the Taliban are showing up at their homes and warning them not to go back to work."

Nic's sharp intake of air is audible. "I say we follow this lead."

It'd be great to have the guys along with me. A lot less to worry about. Plus, I'll have more pairs of eyes keeping a lookout. I reread the address, committing it to memory, then pass the note forward to Ajmal. "Do you know where this is?"

Ajmal reads the address. "Yes, it is very near to here." Then he looks in the rearview mirror. His eyes narrow. "Perhaps it will take a long time to get there." He pulls away from the curb and sets off at a slow pace.

Glancing back, I see a Humvee with darkly tinted windows following a few lengths behind us. The Taliban. Who else? "You know, after Farrakh dropped the note on the sidewalk and I picked it up, I . . . uh . . . noticed someone watching me."

"You do tend to draw attention to yourself, old thing."

Driving well under the speed limit, Ajmal makes a sharp right turn, then another right. The other vehicle is still with us. And now I see two other vehicles. Backup, just in case we manage to get away from the lead car.

Sadim reaches for the note, then lights a cigarette. Rolling down the window a few inches, he breathes out some smoke and very carefully holds the burning ash to the white paper. It takes a moment, but finally catches. Holding it a few seconds longer, he opens the ashtray, and with a pen tamps down the flame until it's nothing more than smoldering ash—indistinguishable from the remains of the cigarette.

"Thanks, Sadim. That was smart. You think they're going to stop us?"

"I think it would not go well for us or your friends if the Taliban were to find this."

Aziz shoulders his camera and starts filming through the back window. Nic provides some impromptu commentary. "We have just left the Wazir Akbar Khan Hospital and are being tailed by the Taliban." He goes on to talk about how the Taliban are thwarting our visit to the home of an unnamed Afghan.

We continue driving in circles for a good forty-five minutes until Sadim calls a halt to our attempted mission. "We'll try this again later. For now, let's go out to the airport."

A savvy driver, Ajmal continues his meandering pace, only now in the direction of the airport. Nothing to give away our original destination. He's worried though. I can hear it in his voice. "They are still following us."

At the airport, we're able to get all the way into the parking lot only to have one of the trailing Humvees pull into the space in front of us. The other—with the very dark, tinted windows—comes to a stop directly behind us. A car door opens, then clicks shut.

Ajmal keeps his hands on the steering wheel.

Aziz shoulders the Sony again.

My heart is in my throat. The camera still hanging from my neck is on, ready to shoot. Trembling more than I'd like, my right hand snakes down into my pack in search of the Sig. Finding it, I make sure the safety's off and that I can easily pull it out.

Nothing happens for a very long minute.

Then, the expected tap of a gun barrel clicks against glass. My window.

My heart thuds.

I don't move.

Nic leans close. "You sure you want them to find that Sig you're holding?"

"No."

"When you get out, pass me your pack."

Another tap of the gun. Then, the door swings open.

"You will get out, please."

I know that voice. The Cambridge accent. It's the fucking bomber.

Nic deftly shifts my pack onto his lap. I can only hope he realizes that I've switched off the safety. And if he shoots, please let his aim be good enough to spare me.

I slide out of the Humvee and find myself face-to-face with the Cambridge Bomber. Half expecting him to hold the gun to the side of my head, that spot just above my ear that the Taliban seem to favor, I'm kind of surprised that he keeps his automatic down by his side.

Don't kid yourself! That gun could end up against your head in a split second.

"You will come with me."

"Wait!" Sadim's voice. "Where are you taking Ms. Hawkins? She's an American citizen and works for TNN. The media."

I can feel the bomber's body tense.

But his voice doesn't. "It will be just a minute or two." Then, to me, "Please? You will come?" His extended hand invites me to the vehicle in back. Such courtesy. Such pretense. As if I have a choice.

Another Taliban guard opens the rear door. Again, the bomber's perfect English. "Please, you will get in."

I do. There's no point even debating the 'invitation.' They've got all the guns.

Even though I spent hours with the deputy head of the Taliban a few days ago, it takes me a moment to recognize Sirajuddin Haqqani curled against the opposite door. This time, he's draped the tail of his turban across the lower part of his face. And underneath, he's wearing an N95 mask. To avoid being recognized? Or as protection against COVID? But there's no disguising his eyes. Murderous.

He speaks in Pashtun, so quietly that I can't begin to understand him. But the bomber, one knee on the pavement next to the open door, translates. No niceties, no formal greetings. Just, "No pictures."

I nod. He doesn't have to worry. I couldn't care less about taking his picture.

Again, Siraj speaks, his voice a little louder this time, but still moderated.

"It was not the Taliban who bombed the airport. It was ISIS. We believe there was only one suicide bomber."

I can't begin to imagine why they're telling me this. Or what they want me to say.

"We would like you to tell this to your government."

The all-too-familiar cold charges full bore up my spine. 'Tell your government.' Not, 'Put this on the news.' Which means they know—about Cerelli and me. That I've got a direct line to a U.S. Navy admiral and hence the U.S. government. Otherwise, why tell me? It would've made a lot more sense for them to give this message to Nic. To put on the air. It takes me a couple seconds, then the puzzle pieces fall into place. This is a lot more than a 'message' to the government. This is a warning to me that they know who I am. And that they're coming for me. Again.

And now, I really do have to say something. Only what?

Don't overthink it!

"All right," I say. I intend for my voice to be noncommittal, vague, and fearless. No wobbles. Even though there's a loaded gun inches from my back. "If that's all . . ."

"Na," Siraj answers. Which tells me that he must understand at least a little English. "Stä yur."

My heart stops. 'Your daughter.' I don't need this translation. But Siraj says a few more words. Then more. And more. All of which go right past me. I'm still back on 'your daughter.' When he finally finishes, he bows his head forward just a bit. So slight and so quick that I'm not really sure whether he actually did.

"The Taliban did not injure your daughter," the bomber says at my shoulder. "It was ISIS. It is a terrible thing to lose a daughter."

I'm rigid with terror. Mel. I haven't lost her. Have I? Did something happen today? She took a turn for the worse. She stopped breathing again, and the doctors at Anabah couldn't save her. Somehow, the Taliban found out. Because the Taliban are everywhere. Even at the medical center at the north end of the Panjshir Valley.

Or maybe they're just trying to get to you.

THE TWO TALIBAN VEHICLES power their way out of the parking lot while I barely manage to walk the twenty feet back to the TNN Humvee. As soon as I climb into the car, collapsing against the back of the seat, I tell the guys Siraj's message. Nic shoves my pack into my lap. "Call Sawyer!" he says.

I know she's fine. Sawyer would've called me if something had happened. Or Cerelli. Someone would have. But that doesn't stop my hands from trembling as I fumble my way through the contents of my pack in search of the sat phone. Only to suddenly freeze in place as I remember that unless Nic put the safety back on, it's most definitely off. And the gun is sitting somewhere in my pack, just waiting for an errant finger to pull the trigger. Slowly I pull out the sat phone, then the *burqa*, which feels a whole lot heavier than it should. Damn. The Sig's gotten wrapped up in all this fabric. Taking a deep breath, I lift fold after fold of cloth until the gun shows itself.

I switch the safety on.

Now I can breathe.

"Are you seriously telling me I've been holding a loaded gun with the safety off?" Nic sounds ridiculously amused.

"Sorry. But yes. Apparently, I'm not so great with weapons."

Nic takes the gun and hands me the phone. "Call."

I push #2 for Sawyer's preprogrammed number and listen through ring after ring until it's clear that no one's going to answer. Cerelli's my next call. What are the chances he won't be in a meeting? I've talked myself into expecting Sam to pick up when the man himself comes on the line.

"Annie?"

"Hey." My voice sounds deflated and pretty weepy. I'm really not aware of the guys getting out of the Humvee until Nic squeezes my shoulder, eases across the seat, and shuts the door.

"You're not okay. Tell me."

For once, I start at the very end of what happened. With the Cambridge Bomber's chilling warning about Mel.

"No worries. I heard from Sawyer maybe an hour ago. He's in the air headed to Landstuhl with Mel and three Marines. Everyone's stable, but they've got medics on board with them. They should be landing in another five or so hours."

"But the Cambridge Bomber said . . ."

"Maybe he wasn't referring to Mel as the daughter it would be terrible to lose? Any other daughters? Or maybe Siraj lost a daughter?"

Another chill inches up my spine. "Bahar." I fill him in about our stopping by the hospital, running into Farrakh, and his passing me her address. "I have a feeling the Taliban may have been watching."

"Highly likely. Promise me you won't get involved."

"Cerelli." I move ahead to the other part of that charming conversation with Siraj that has me worried. The 'tell your government' part.

"Hell."

"Yeah, that's my interpretation, too. But honestly, I don't have a clue how the Taliban could've put us together."

"Let me count the ways."

"What?"

"Are you forgetting Uncle Omar? The bugged sat phone?"

"Well, yeah, but all that was years ago. We could've gone our separate ways."

"We haven't." For those two words, his voice is warm and loving, and he's making sure I feel every bit of it. Then, he's back to business. "But it's clear they know about us. Could be you've got another bug in the sat phone. Or maybe in the cell? Some kind of malware?"

"Great! Just great! So, what should I do?"

"Short of coming home?"

"Another six days and I should be on a plane—if Nic and I can get seats."

"Try not to use either one of those phones. Unless there's an emergency."

"Done."

"One last thing. I've spoken to both Todd and Bonita. Todd's flying to Germany to meet up with Mel in Landstuhl."

I almost smile. "Good. I'm glad to hear he's rising to the challenge."

"And as for your phones, we probably shouldn't be talking now." He sounds wistful.

He's right. But I seriously don't want to end this call either. Still, prolonging it will only make it harder to hang up. Not to mention that the eavesdropping Taliban will get an even clearer picture as to how close our relationship really is.

"Okay then," I say as cheerfully as I can manage. "See ya around campus." I dare the Taliban to figure out what that means.

"Only you." Cerelli laughs, then disconnects the call.

29

"ANNIE? YOU ARE AWAKE?"

I've been awake for hours, turning and tossing on the sofa, trying to stop thinking about Mel—and now also Bahar—just so I can get some sleep. And failing. Now, I open my eyes to the dark gray of early morning. The sky is just beginning to lighten, but it won't be dawn for a while yet.

"Annie? It is Ajmal."

"Yes, I'm awake." Although lack of sleep has me a bit dazed. "Has something happened?" Oh, God, have I missed another phone call? I push myself up so I'm sitting. Beneath me, the sheet is damp. So is my T-shirt. I'm still not used to sleeping in this confounded heat.

"There is nothing to worry about. Everything is all right. Do you still wish to go look for your friend Bahar?"

"I do."

"Then I am thinking this would be a good time for us to go. It is likely there will be fewer Taliban out this early. And we will have a better chance of catching her at home."

"Ajmal, you're brilliant. Thank you for this."

"We should leave soon. I will tell the others to come?"

I consider that for a few moments, then shake my head. "I think not." It was another late night, and we're all exhausted. The guys would probably appreciate some sleep. Then again, if we discover anything, they'll want to be in on it. In fact, they'll be downright pissed at me for leaving them behind. But what could we possibly discover? I'm pretty sure Bahar has gone to ground—probably far from Kabul. I hope so, because if the Taliban find her, it's not going to end well.

Pulling on my clothes and shouldering my pack, I hurry down the stairs to find Ajmal waiting for me out front. Or, I think he is. It's not our regular Humvee. Instead, he's behind the wheel of a rusting white pickup—the Taliban's vehicle of choice. Rolling down his window, he waves me over. "Get in. I will explain."

Hoping I'm doing the right thing, I open the passenger door.

"You have your *burqa?*" The reluctance in his voice is obvious.

He's right. If the Taliban were to see me sitting next to Ajmal in the front seat—just the two of us—it wouldn't matter to them that we work together. They'd likely arrest both of us. I dig the periwinkle *burqa* out from the bottom of my pack and drape it over my head.

"If they stop us, please you will let me do the talking? You agree?"

I appreciate that he's asking my opinion. Then again, what opinion could I possibly have? Turning toward him so I can see him through my micro-crosshatched eyepiece, I speak a little louder than I normally would. "Yes, I think you're right. But what if they ask me a question—directly?"

"Then, you answer. But you will speak in Dari, I think?"

"Point taken." Fingers crossed that my accent will be passable. If not, I could get us both in a lot of trouble—sneaking around in a *burqa*, pretending to be an Afghan woman. Best hope that if someone stops us and demands I say something, he speaks strictly Pashto.

No matter that he's not driving the TNN Humvee, Ajmal meanders through the maze of city streets. A straight line would get us to Bahar's apartment in under fifteen minutes. We cruise through neighborhoods all over the city and see very few other cars. And just a few Taliban guards patrolling the streets. Finally reaching the university and then the side street nearby, Ajmal drives several blocks, then turns right, another right, a third and then a fourth right until we're back on her street. Stopping at the curb, he turns off the engine and headlights, then points to a four-story apartment building halfway up the block. "There. You see? That is where Bahar lives."

I count off the buildings. "The third one?"

He nods. "Yes." We wait a few minutes until we're sure there are no Taliban in sight. No guards either. He quietly explains his plan. "Take this with you." He hands me several rounds of *nân* wrapped in white paper. "In a few minutes, the *mu'adhdhin* will call the *adhan*. That is when men will leave the building. You wait by the door. They will let you in no problem, because of your *burqa* and this bread. They will think you went out early to get it. Bahar's apartment, it is on the second floor. You climb two flights of stairs. She is number three. You understand?"

"Number three. Where will you be?"

"I will stay with the truck. If I see any Taliban, I will leave and turn right at the next block, then right again. You will find me there—one street over. You understand?"

"Got it. And if you're not there?" I'm putting a helluva lot of trust in this man.

"I will find you." He smiles reassuringly. "Unless they arrest me first."

I reach for the door handle and climb out. Then, shouldering my pack under my *burqa*, I focus on walking like an Afghan woman. It's unlikely that anyone in this building will care about me obeying the as-yet unannounced new dress code, but who knows? There are spies everywhere in Kabul. The Taliban are counting on people turning in their errant neighbors and colleagues, even family members.

I make it to the door just in time to see the light in the foyer come on and a scruffy-bearded man in his *shalwar kameez* approach the door. *Do not nod! Do not say a word! An Afghan woman wouldn't.* Exiting first, he holds the door open for me. Careful not to let my fingers touch his, I pull it shut behind me, my thoughts focused on his beard. Hardly a beard. More like several days of not shaving in the hopes of going unnoticed by the Taliban. Another thought stops me cold: all those undercover Taliban—clean-shaven and dressed in Western clothes, who for years successfully infiltrated every aspect of Afghan life—they would now be growing back their beards and wearing their regular clothes.

Stay in the moment. Cerelli's voice, reminding me to rein in my imagination.

Easy for you to say.

There's no elevator, so I open the door to the stairs and climb two flights to the second floor. Stepping into the dimly lit hallway, I count off the Arabic numbers on the doors. At number three, I take note of the two names on the card taped to the wooden door. Turning on the flashlight on my cell, I study the names. Yes, one of

them is most definitely Bahar Abdulin. I'm about to knock—softly
first so as not to wake the neighbors—when I see the gauge marks
around both the doorknob and the deadbolt lock. Someone tried
to break in. It's impossible to tell whether or not they succeeded.

I knock.

There's no answer.

I knock again—a little harder.

Still no answer, but I'm sensing someone standing on the other
side of the door. "Bahar?" I keep my voice low and gentle. I'm fairly
certain Bahar isn't in the apartment, but it could be her roommate,
and I don't want to scare her. "Bahar," I say again. "It's Annie. Annie
Hawkins." A definite risk, but maybe she's mentioned my name to
whoever she lives with.

"Bahar is not here." The words are in heavily accented English.
The whisper barely audible.

Then I hear the deadbolt sliding. A moment later, the door
slowly opens—just a crack, enough for me to see two dark eyes,
wide and frightened. I stand back so she can study me in my
periwinkle *burqa*. Finally, the door opens wider. Her arm snakes
out and reaches for me. "Come in. Quickly."

Once I'm inside the apartment, she shuts the door and clicks on
the overhead light, which doesn't do much to illuminate the front
room. But after I throw the front of my *burqa* back over my head,
I see enough. The place has been ransacked. The upholstered sofa
has been slashed open, polyester stuffing hanging out. Cushions are
strewn about the room, also slashed. Bookcases have been toppled.
Pages ripped out of books and spines broken. Looking toward the
tiny kitchenette against the far wall—nothing more than a burner
on a counter, a sink and mini fridge, and some shelves—I see shards
of dishes littering the floor. And the smell. Food has been dumped

on the floor as well, and bottles are smashed—their contents stain-
ing the woolen rug. I'm just now becoming aware of how hot it is in
here, and that's definitely making the stench even worse. I've got a
pretty good idea of what the bedrooms look like—clothes slashed
and furniture smashed. My imagination is starting to take hold.

Stop! Stay focused!

Turning in a full circle, I'm back to facing the roommate. To
say she's scared isn't nearly sufficient. Dark circles under her eyes
tell me she hasn't slept in at least a day. Her long dark-brown hair
droops unbrushed. And her clothes. Black pants and a short-
sleeved shirt. Rumpled and dirty and much too big for her. Almost
as if they're not hers. She probably borrowed whatever she could
from a friend. Looking closer, I see on her upper arm, peeking out
from under the sleeve, a flowering of bruises. I'd bet anything one
of the men who was here held her while the others destroyed the
apartment.

"The Taliban. They came yesterday, looking for Bahar." Her
voice is barely audible.

Oh, God. Farrakh's nightmare came true. I don't want to ask,
but I do anyway. "Was she here when this happened?"

She shakes her head. "No. She has not been here for more than
a week. Not since the parade."

I look pointedly at her arm. "But you were here." It's not a
question.

She quickly reaches her hand up to cover the bruises—proof
that they abused her.

"I'm so sorry. That must have been terrifying."

"Yes. I know you understand. Bahar told me about what
happened the last time you were in Wad Qol."

That stops me. Bahar told her about the man at the Bazarak

market grabbing me? Or did she tell her about the Taliban kidnapping me? Why would she do that? But there's no time to pursue that thought. I need to move this along. Ajmal is waiting downstairs, and who knows if or when the Taliban will return. "Do you know where she is?" As soon as I ask the question, I know it was the wrong thing to say.

She claps her hand over her mouth. Terror returns to her eyes.

Stupid! I chastise myself. God only knows what kinds of listening devices the Taliban put in here. Maybe even a video camera. Afghans seem to like videotaping women in compromising situations—something else I well remember.

Okay, so how do I get information from this woman? Still holding the wrapped rounds of bread, I scan the room, searching for the likeliest places for a camera. They probably weren't in here very long, so any bugs or recorders would have to have been easily planted. Finally, my glance lands on the one lamp still standing. I turn my back to it and point.

She responds with one clipped nod.

Everything in me wants to throw the lamp on the floor and stomp it to teeny, tiny pieces. But that would only give us away. Instead, I steer her to the opposite end of the room—the kitchen. I stuff the rounds of *nân* into my pack, then start to pick up pieces of plates.

She reaches to stop me.

I turn on the water in the sink—full blast. Then whisper, "I want them to think I've come to help you clean up." Righting one of the plastic crates to use for trash, I toss in what I've collected so far.

Her lips form a perfect 'o.' Good, she understands. And now she's following my lead, picking up shards. And every so often, one of us says something—brief and as quietly as possible.

"Do you have any idea where she might go?" I ask. "Somewhere at the university maybe?"

"The university?" She looks puzzled. "I do not know. We never talked about things like that. I was hoping you might have an idea where she could be. You are her good friend."

"Me? Sorry, I don't have any idea where she might have gone." I pick up another broken dish and add it into the crate, then glance up at the roommate. "What about her Afghan friends? Would she stay with one of them?"

"Maybe. Do you know their names?" She sounds almost eager.

Which strikes me as a peculiar question. Wouldn't her roommate know the names of her friends? Especially since she knows about me?

A moment later, she touches my arm. "One woman, she did come by, looking for Bahar. But she also did not know where she could be."

"Do you think she could've gone to Wad Qol?"

"Maybe. Yes, her brother could have come and driven her there. I remember he came one time in June, and they went there."

Another odd answer. "He told me he came here looking for her the other day, but no one answered."

She looks confused for a moment. "Oh! Yes, now I remember. I was afraid it was the Taliban coming back. I did not answer the door."

I keep picking up shards, taking care not to cut myself. The last thing I need is a deep gash on one of my fingers.

"Wait! I thought of something!" She turns toward the bedroom, which is when I realize there is only the one door. So, only one bedroom. They must share.

I start to follow.

"No! Stay there." She runs into the bedroom, and a moment later, I hear the rustle of sheets. When she comes back into the front room, her lips pressed tightly together, there's a small black notebook in her hand. "They found it," she whispers, lifting the front cover to show me the tattered bits of paper glued to the binding.

"What is this?"

"Her address book."

I step back in stunned surprise. Bahar left her contacts' info behind? It's hard to believe she'd be so naïve, even if she had to leave quickly. The girl I taught in high school, the young woman I talked to at the protest march ten days ago was smart and savvy. She knew the risks and that her own arrest and death were possible, even inevitable. But she would never have subjected anyone else to that fate. In fact, during her interview with Nic, she refused to name names.

But this woman in front of me seems equally certain that this is Bahar's address book. Which leads me to wonder if Bahar left this book as a decoy of sorts, to make the Taliban think they now know where to look. That sounds exactly like something Bahar would do. However much I want to tell her distraught roommate that all is not lost, to reassure her that Bahar might yet survive, I can't say the words. Not with who knows how many bugs or miniature videocams recording everything we say.

Instead, I hug her and whisper, "I've got to go. If you remember anything, please contact me through TNN. Or through Afghan TV. Also, if you have any place you could stay for a few days, a place that is safe, I think you should go."

Teary-eyed, she manages a weak smile.

There's nothing more I can discover here, so, draping the *burqa* in front of my face, I open the door. I take a moment to glance both ways down the hall and listen for footsteps, any noise out of the ordinary. Hearing nothing, I pull the door closed behind me and head toward the stairs.

I've already reached the lobby when I realize that the roommate never told me her name. Which strikes me as beyond strange. That just doesn't happen in Afghan culture. Then again, she was so upset, it probably didn't occur to her to say. And I was so blown away by the ferocity of the destruction that I focused only on trying to find some clue to tell me where to look next. Then I remember that the best clue to where Bahar could be has been in my passport all along. And as soon as I get to someplace safe, I'll dig out that folded piece of paper she slipped to me at the demonstration. For now, though, I've already been here way too long. Ajmal must be wondering where I am.

Opening the front door of the building, I again look in every direction for any Taliban militants who might be lurking. I take a few steps and listen. All is quiet. No sandals slapping on the sidewalk. No one out and about. Not even an idling pickup. And there are hours to go until the *mu'adhdhin* sings the next *adhan*. Except then, I do hear something: someone turns on a vehicle and guns the engine. Tires burn as the car races up the street, then shrieks into a turn.

Ajmal? It must have been him. Somehow, I know he spotted the Taliban Humvee that is just now pulling up in front of the apartment building, and he made as much noise as possible to warn me. What the fuck are they doing back here? Didn't they terrorize Bahar's roommate enough yesterday? But I know why they're here. Despite the precautions I took, they must have heard some of what I said. What we said. Or, oh God, maybe they recognized me on the video. I do what I can to fade back around the corner of the apartment building into the narrow alley, retreating as far back as I can. And just in time. Booted feet run up the walkway to the front door. Throwing it open, they disappear inside.

Should I run?

No, chances are that other Taliban are waiting in the vehicle out front.

And chances are really good that the Taliban who ran into the building will search for me when they come back out.

30

BARELY TEN MINUTES AFTER the Taliban slam their way into the apartment building, they're back, their heavy lug-soled boots pounding the concrete walkway again. I ease my way forward until I can peek around the corner of the building. Several bearded men in camo uniforms are hurrying toward the Humvee that's waiting at the curb. To my relief, they don't prowl around the outside of the building looking for me. In just a few moments, they're all in the vehicle and on their way.

Could one of them be the man who was staring at me yesterday at the hospital? Or maybe the Cambridge Bomber? Whoever they are, I'm positive they've been in Bahar's apartment. Again. My heart sinks. I can't bear to imagine what they did to that poor woman this time. More bruises? A blackened eye? Something worse? Or maybe they just grilled her on what we talked about. They must have been somewhere close by, listening in, probably also watching us.

I lean against the wall of the apartment building. My sense of relief is gone, replaced by prickling on the back of my neck.

Something is definitely wrong. My heart tells me to go back up to the apartment to make sure the roommate is okay. But then I rerun my mental videotape of the visit to the apartment. In retrospect, there are way too many red flags that I somehow missed—all of them having to do with the roommate. Bahar may have trusted her enough to share the apartment, but this woman seemed to know precious little about her.

And that black address book. Why would the Taliban rip out the pages and leave the covers and binding? That makes no sense. Loose pages would be much harder to keep together. The answer: I don't think they would. They would've taken the book intact. Unless they wanted something for this woman to show me. Maybe they were thinking that I'd know something, give them some names.

Something else that's troubling me: going into the bedroom to get the address book, the roommate was gone for all of one minute max, which means she knew exactly where it was. That doesn't seem at all like Bahar. No way she'd leave a book of her contacts lying around for the Taliban—or her roommate—to find.

And when did the apartment invasion actually happen? She seemed a bit confused on that score, too, saying the Taliban came yesterday, but later that they were there two days ago. Whenever they ransacked the place, from the look of things, she hasn't done anything to set the place to rights—even leaving food to rot on the floor. All of it very odd.

Nothing is adding up.

Cut her a break! She was obviously scared to death. And bruised!

I'm not sure what's really going on here, but something tells me it's not good.

I wait a few more minutes, then make my way out of the alley and onto the sidewalk. There, halfway up the street, I see a white pickup. Ajmal? It could be his truck, but from this distance, it's impossible to tell. I walk in that direction—slowly, trying to scope out where to run if I have to.

I'm still two buildings away from the truck when the driver opens his door, climbs out, and waves. Ajmal! Thank God. Waving back, I pick up my pace. Best get out of this neighborhood as fast as possible.

As soon as we're back in the truck, he keys the ignition and pulls away from the curb. I take the package of bread out of my pack and unwrap it. No longer warm, it's still something to eat, and I bet Ajmal is every bit as hungry as I am. He takes the top round and rips off a piece to chew. I do the same.

Turning left at the corner, we pass another white pickup idling by the side of the road with two men in the cab and two more hunkered down in the flatbed. Like us, they're all gnawing their way through rounds of bread. As soon as we pass, they pull in behind us. Ajmal's hands tighten on the steering wheel, and he keeps an eye on the rearview mirror. His frown deepens—a sure sign that he wishes he'd made a U-turn when we left the apartment building.

After several glances in the rearview mirror, Ajmal makes another turn, and I look in the side mirror. Yes, indeed, the Taliban in their white pickup are still behind us—and getting closer.

Ajmal doesn't increase his speed. "I am thinking we should return to the TNN apartment."

I let that roll around my brain for a few moments. "Good plan. We need to get back there anyway. The guys must be up by now and have to be wondering where we are."

"Do not worry about the crew. They know I drove you to Bahar's."

I turn a full ninety degrees so I can see him through the *burqa's* netted eyepiece. "You told them?"

He shrugs. "Sadim, he is the boss. I did not want to risk losing my job."

Of course he told Sadim, who undoubtedly shared with Nic and Aziz. This is a patriarchal culture. Best not forget that, even though the guys I'm working with are among the more enlightened.

Ajmal's now staring intently in the rearview mirror—his brow furrowed.

I start to turn around.

"No. Do not. They can see you and will know we are worried."

"You mean that will give them all the more reason to stop us— to find out why we're worried."

He grins, but just for a second. "You know them well."

"Too well."

"There is something that I should know?"

Should I tell him about them kidnapping me six years ago?

Absolutely not! Cerelli's voice. *That's on a need-to-know basis, and everyone who needs to know already does.*

He's right. I know he is. But it gets tedious having him tell me what to do, especially when he's not even here and couldn't possibly know what I'm thinking.

"Annie?"

"Sorry. No, there's nothing to tell other than the Taliban scare me. Which is why they're called terrorists. ISIS is even worse, though. You think we can believe what Siraj said at the airport yesterday? That it was ISIS behind the bombing?"

"I think it does not matter who was responsible. The dead do not care. Their families do not care. It is a great evil."

After another minute of following us, Ajmal's slow and steady driving must convince the militants that we have nothing to hide, nothing to share—even if they torture us. They peel off down a side street. Both of us release our collectively held breath.

"Truly evil," I agree. Now, I turn around and look out the back window. The street behind us is clear of white pickups and camo Humvees. I scan the sidewalks and don't notice more than the occasional bearded man in a *shalwar kameez* patrolling. A few pedestrians hurry along, definite destinations in mind, perhaps looking to buy bread or whatever other food they can scrounge up. Normal. Or as normal as life in Kabul can get these days. Something that used to be as easy as going to buy morning bread is getting harder and harder. Pretty soon, there could be serious food shortages, hunger, even starvation.

"You will tell me now about Bahar's apartment?"

I should probably wait until we get back to our apartment, when I can tell all four of the guys at the same time. But no, that wouldn't be fair to Ajmal. He's the one who cut short his sleep to drive me, besides taking any number of risks to get me there and back. I owe him. So I tell him what I can. About Bahar's apartment having been ransacked. Her roommate having been terrorized and totally clueless as to where Bahar could be. But I keep the things that are really bothering me to myself.

FIRST THING WHEN WE get back to the TNN apartment, I whip the *burqa* up over my head and off. I almost sigh in relief as my body temperature slowly drops. Then, I have to repeat everything. I keep it simple, still avoiding the things that are troubling me. When

I finish, Nic raises his eyebrow—a sure sign that he, at least, knows there's a lot more to the story. And he looks determined to find out.

"Look here, old thing—"

I bat away his question, exactly like Darya used to do, and, amazingly, it works. "What's on the agenda for today?" I direct my question to each of the men in turn.

But Sadim's ringing phone silences their potential responses. A contact calling in the latest events happening around Kabul, I'm sure. And from the excitement in his voice, it sounds like something big is in the works.

Slipping his cell into his pocket, Sadim pushes himself to his feet. "Our visit to the university will have to wait."

Nic clarifies. "We were planning to interview a few professors—women—who look to be losing their jobs."

Sadim nods. "First, we're heading back to the Wazir Akbar Khan Hospital."

"What's going on?" Aziz is already on his feet, reaching for his camera.

"Word is that the Taliban are rounding up doctors and nurses."

"Any idea who?" *Please*, I pray to the universe, *not Farrakh*. I can't help but worry that the Taliban militant who saw us talking the other day connected the dots from Farrakh to Bahar and even to me. Could he have been one of the militants who showed up at the apartment this morning? This is all way too much of a coincidence. And as Cerelli always says, *I don't believe in coincidence*.

I make a quick detour into the kitchen to grab a bottle of water from the fridge only to find Nic following me.

"You will tell me what happened this morning." It's not a question. "And careful with the water. Sadim read us the riot act this morning while you were out gallivanting."

I ignore the first part of his statement. "What's wrong with the water?"

"There's not much left. Unless you want to drink from the tap."

Perish the thought. The last thing I need is creepy-crawlies swimming in my gut. I leave the water in the fridge and follow Nic out of the apartment, clomping down flight after flight of stairs.

By the time we reach the lobby and then the sidewalk out front, Ajmal is pulling the Humvee up to the curb. This time, he doesn't drive slowly, meandering through every neighborhood of the city. He's on a mission, flying through the streets in as straight a line as he can manage. Fifteen minutes and we're almost at the hospital. Except as we're passing the grounds of Omid High School, about to turn into the drive to the hospital, we nearly collide with a line of white pickups and Humvees blocking the road. The Taliban are most definitely here. And we're at a standstill.

We've barely stopped moving, and Aziz has the back door open. Sony in hand, he hits the ground running. Nic is right behind him. My camera already around my neck, I shoulder my pack and set off. I'm keeping pace with them, because, I suddenly realize, I'm not wearing the *burqa*. Sadim brings up the rear. He shoots me a look but doesn't say a word.

"*Dresh!*" An angry militant shouts at us to halt.

But we don't stop. Now, we're running flat out along the pathway leading up to the hospital. Another armed and bearded Taliban militant steps in front of us, his arm raised, but we skirt around him and keep on until we're almost to the front doors of the building. Along with more Taliban than I ever want to see.

The Cambridge Bomber, in his camo fatigues, steps in front of me. Then points his gun at the middle of my forehead. And smiles.

I skid to a stop.

"Ms. Hawkins, I believe." His accent really is cultured and every bit as formal as Nic's. Which makes him even scarier. And his frigging gun is still pointed at me.

Stay calm! Cerelli's voice. *And don't irritate him.*

I see the backs of Nic's and Aziz's heads as they somehow manage to zig and zag their way past militants and into the hospital. And then Sadim's head. But I'm stuck here with a world-class murderer aiming a gun at me—at point-blank range. Somehow, I manage to muster my nerve. "Would you please lower that gun?" My voice doesn't wobble one iota. I'm inordinately impressed with myself.

He stops smiling. Actually, he looks surprised. At what? That I asked? That he's still training his gun on me? Whatever, I've caught him off guard, and he actually lowers his gun, returning it to his holster. "My apologies, madam."

Which throws me off-balance. This murdering asshole sounds for all the world like he's an officer in the British military. I decide to rely on his apparent training as a gentleman. "I understand that you are arresting medical personnel." Okay, so Nic would probably have a better opening line, but interviewing isn't in my skill set.

The smile is back, broader this time. "I am not certain where you heard this."

Now, I'm smiling. "An anonymous source."

"Ah, perhaps you should take greater care than to believe such sources."

I study his teeth—really amazingly good for a militant. I'm guessing his family had some money. A British education and uncommonly good dentistry. Actually, with his well-styled dark hair and full lips, some people would say he's attractive. I wouldn't. It's hard to get past the fact that he likes to kill people. And tried to kill me. "I have every confidence in this source." Sadim's contacts almost never steer us wrong. I lift my camera. "A photograph, perhaps?"

His eyes widen—for just a moment. I've surprised him again. Good. "I think not, madam. This is not what you would call a photo op."

I lean in, closing the slight distance between us. "I don't go in for 'ops.' I specialize in capturing images of major events. Photographs that tell a story."

He inclines his head. A point for me? "Yes, I've heard that about you. Stunning. I think that is the right word to describe some of your images. I particularly admire your picture of that young Pashtun girl who died—Malalai, that was her name, was it not?"

Although he raises his voice just a bit, I know damn well he's not asking a question. I also know that, just like Cerelli, this man has dug into every nook and cranny of my life. And that really pisses me off. I'm not one of the fighters in this insane war. I stay behind the lens and record what happens. But this man means to terrorize me, to put me front and center in his ongoing battle.

My best course of action would be to ignore the bait he's dangling in front of me. And for once, that's exactly what I do. "Well, then, if you could let me pass? As a member of the international media, I would like to get some pictures of what your men are doing here."

Again, the smile. And although it's smaller this time, I'm positive his eyes are softening, shining. Then, the kicker. "Yes, I can see why he is so taken with you." Finally, he frigging steps aside—to let me by.

And none too soon. His parting shot has left me seriously rattled. I absolutely cannot be here, in Afghanistan, in the middle of this chaos, with one of the world's most wanted killers who knows about Cerelli and me. That's just too big a target, too much danger.

Somehow, I manage to keep my nerves at bay, and, shoulders back, I walk away, wending my way between Taliban and doctors and nurses tending to patients. Behind me, I can feel the Cambridge Bomber's eyes boring into the target on my back. He'll come after me. Not today, but soon. Does he plan to take me by surprise? Or will he want me to suffer? Or maybe he'll demand Cerelli in exchange for me.

Will anyone be able to stop him? Do any of the good guys even know what he looks like? Probably not because no one's ever managed to get a picture of him.

I stop, then turn around.

He's no longer watching me.

I take my shot. And a second. Then quickly slip out the SD card, load in another, and format it. The work of ten seconds. A few moments after that, from the corner of my eye, I catch him looking up, almost as if he heard the shutter click on my camera.

I turn to the side, pausing to capture some images of Taliban brutality. Are they even aware that by arresting and torturing these doctors and nurses, they're seriously curtailing the medical care available for the Afghan people? For themselves? Yeah, they probably are and simply don't care.

A few more shots. Then, I stop. 'I can see why he is so taken with you.' I may look calm and steady, but that . . . that . . . monster has well and truly gotten to me. And knocked me sideways.

I take a few more shots, but for the first time in my career, I don't even care what I'm getting. Pretty much on autopilot, I move toward the front doors of the hospital, hoping against hope that I come across Farrakh—well and unscathed.

31

I DON'T FIND FARRAKH. Even though I ask everyone who's rushing by. No one's seen him. It's possible, one photog for another media outlet says, that the Taliban arrested him and took him away early on. One thing he's sure of: the militants were definitely looking for Dr. Farrakh Abdulin.

My heart sinks.

My fingers can't even find the shutter button. I couldn't frame or meter a shot if my life depended on it. My camera feels like a useless stone hanging around my neck. An unnecessary weight that's sinking my life. What the hell kind of photographer am I, anyway? I should be keeping my cool. Working. Capturing images so TNN can show the world that the Taliban are every bit as brutal as they've always been.

But I can't.

I'm done. Wasted.

Looking around, I don't see any of my guys. Nic and Aziz and

Sadim must be somewhere close by, getting the story, but I can't find them.

"Annie." Ajmal is next to me, probably standing closer than he should. Way too close by Taliban standards. "You come with me back to the vehicle."

I don't say a word, just mutely follow him out of the hospital lobby, through the increasing crowd in front of the doors, and back to the Humvee. Climbing into the back seat, I slide over to the far side where I hunker down, not sure what to feel, what to think. Mostly, I'm numb. Which isn't a good thing for a war photographer.

Cerelli. I need to talk to Cerelli. To let him know what the Cambridge Bomber said. To tell him about Bahar. And Farrakh. More than that, I need to hear his voice—to keep me tethered to the world—before I totally lose it.

I'm not yet so completely out of it that I've forgotten my phones are potentially compromised. Cerelli warned me not to call unless there's an emergency. It takes me all of five seconds to decide this comes close enough to being an emergency.

As soon as he sees me with the sat phone in hand, Ajmal gets out of the Humvee. He doesn't go far, and he keeps his eyes on me.

It's way too early to call, but as I well know, Cerelli never sleeps. Then again, chances are good that he's in an all-night meeting, and that would mean he won't be able to take my call. I could very well end up talking to Sam. Nice enough, but I *need* Cerelli.

"Annie?" He sounds rushed. Damn, things must be crazy in D.C. He hardly ever sounds rushed. Only when he's 'in deep.'

"Hi." The sound of my voice surprises me. Flat. Monotone. Yeah, dead.

"Tell me." He doesn't sound rushed anymore. In fact, I hear his voice saying that the rest of the world can go on without him. He's totally there for me.

I take a few deep breaths, more to get oxygen back to my brain than anything else.

He waits patiently, until he's not waiting any longer. "Is someone with you?"

"Ajmal."

"Let me talk to him, please." The gentleness, the worry in his voice come close to breaking my heart.

"I will. In just a minute. First, the Cambridge Bomber."

"What about him?"

"He definitely knows about us." I repeat as much of the conversation as I can remember. Which is impressive considering how hard I've been working to bury it so I don't lose what's left of my sanity. "I'm spooked. Well and truly. And the worst part is . . . I . . . uh . . . can't take any photographs."

"Annie." When he says my name like that, I know he's concerned.

"That's what has me the most upset. He got to me. For the first time in my life, I can't. I just can't. I mean good God, I've taken pictures of people being shot, people dying, and now . . . I look at the camera and can't figure out what I'm supposed to do with it."

"You staying in the moment?"

"I'm trying to. But it's not working."

"Sweetheart, listen to me. He's not going to come after me. Hell, he'd have to have very long arms to get me in D.C. He's not after you either. He's playing with your mind, and he's good at it. One of the best. Don't let him. Beat him at his own game. You've got two more days—"

"Three." I don't say anything about still not having a confirmed seat on the plane.

"Wishful thinking on my part. Okay, three. Just lay low and keep your head down."

I actually manage to snort out a laugh. "You told me that once before."

"You were in Wad Qol—the first time, right? Did you listen to me then?"

"Kind of. Not really."

"I didn't think you would. What else did I tell you then—to calm you down?"

"Not to wear makeup."

"Seriously? I said that?" He chuckles. "Not very helpful, was I?"

This time, I laugh for real. "You're actually helping me a lot—now."

"Good. You sound better. You up for some good news?"

"Please."

"Mel's in Landstuhl. She had more surgery and is doing better than expected. Todd is with her and actually behaving well—like a concerned father. I think she's happy to have him there."

Oh my God. How could I not have given Mel a single thought this morning? What kind of mother am I? My questions spill out. "How well is she doing? Do you know if she'll need any more operations?"

He takes a deep breath, which has my heart tightening. "They've been able to save her leg and her arm."

"You told me they did that at Anabah."

"Weeelll, I may have overstated the prognosis just a little. I didn't want you worrying. But this is a sure thing. And yes, there will be more operations, but I think they want to ship her CONUS for those. After that, she's got a long road of rehab ahead of her."

"I can do long roads," I whisper.

"I know you can. Believe me. But for this, you might have to stand in line." He sounds—I'm not at all sure how he sounds.

"What do you mean?"

"From what I hear, there may be a romance brewing."

"Oh, please tell me it's not with Josh."

"It's not Josh."

"You going to clue me in?"

"It seems that Sawyer and Mel . . ."

Even though I've been wondering about exactly that, actually hearing Cerelli say it takes me aback. "You're kidding, right?" I did hear something in Sawyer's voice the other night, but sometimes I let my thoughts run away with me. A real romance?

"I'm not kidding. And it sounds mutual."

"You've talked to them about this?"

"Both of them. And before you get upset that they told me first, let me explain that Sawyer was checking in. He put Mel on the phone. It seems they'd been trying to call you, but not getting through."

"Damn these phones!" I wave my hand through the air, as if that could possibly do away with the absurdity of telephone communication in Afghanistan. "Are they . . . I don't know . . . do they sound happy?"

He laughs. "Oh, yeah."

"So, this is a good thing?" Then I remember that Sawyer's been 'waiting.' And years ago, Mel was crushing.

"Annie, I know what you're thinking. Stay in the moment. Please?"

"Yeah. Okay."

"Now, let me talk to Ajmal?"

My mind is spinning as I try to comprehend Mel and Sawyer together, but I dutifully roll down the window and wave Ajmal over.

"Here you go," I say to Cerelli, about to pass the sat phone to my newly appointed bodyguard.

"Wait! Sweetheart. I . . . come home to me."

My heart eases in my chest. "Always."

Ajmal takes the phone.

I go back to thinking about Mel and Sawyer. How exactly is this going to work? I mean, he's got to be nearly two decades older than her. For a moment, I remember Todd warning me away from Cerelli. *You know what those military types are like. A girlfriend in every port.* Sawyer is a hunk of a man. And he's been around. I have no doubt he's shared his bed—many times. Then again, Mel fell into bed with Josh Forbes. And I'm sure Sawyer knows about it. *I've been waiting.* Could it work?

I look out the window to see Ajmal, the sat phone to his ear, walking a few meters away, then a little farther. And turning his back to me—a sure sign that neither he nor Cerelli wants me eavesdropping. Even so, I listen intently. But I can't hear a thing Ajmal is saying. Leaning back in the seat, all I can do is imagine their conversation.

Keep a close eye on her, please?

Yes! Of course, I will go everywhere with her. Never will she be out of my sight.

Loop Nic and Sadim in on this.

That I will do. Yes.

Or something along those lines. Exactly what I don't want him saying, and he knows it'll piss me off. And maybe that's the point. He wants me angry—at him. Not feeling done in by the Cambridge Bomber. Talk about mind games. Cerelli's a master—as he reminds me every Friday night when we're able to get the crew together to play poker.

I study Ajmal's back—a bit hunched over—and realize he's been talking to Cerelli for a lot longer than 'watch her' would require. So, what the hell are they talking about? Me? Or something else? And exactly what kind of relationship do these two have, anyway?

My thoughts return to Farrakh. And Bahar. Suddenly, I remember yet again the folded square of paper Bahar gave me so many days ago. I pull the neck pouch out from under my tunic. There, nestled behind my passport, is the bit of white paper.

Unfolding it, I stare at the phone number. I know better than to use the cell, so when Ajmal returns to the car and gives me back the sat phone, I punch in the number, hoping that Bahar herself answers. If someone else, anyone else, comes on the line, I'll just hang up. Besides, both Sawyer and Cerelli told me to be careful using this phone.

The call goes through, and I listen to one, two, three rings. Finally, someone answers.

"*Salâm. Khosha rastôrân.*" A woman's voice, but definitely not Bahar's. This voice is feminine and sexy as hell. And belongs to the last person I expected to pick up my call. Fatima.

32

I DON'T SAY A WORD. Just disconnect the call. Bahar and Fatima. What kind of sense does that make? But the more I think about it, there's a certain inevitability that these two women would know each other. Two strong women in Afghanistan. And given that Fatima is an operative working for the U.S., she'd be sure to keep an eye out for a young woman leading the fight for women's rights against the Taliban, maybe even help her escape Kabul. Bottom line, there has to be a reason Bahar gave me the phone number for *Khosha*. She obviously wants me to have a way of getting in touch with her should things go wrong. And things have most definitely gone sideways. So, how do I call Fatima without using one of my wonky phones that could very possibly be bugged?

Hours later, when Ajmal says he's going to get takeout from *Khosha*, I offer to go along. From the way he smiles in response, I figure Cerelli really did tell him not to let me out of his sight. Good. I'm making both men happy. Although the frowns that the rest of the guys are shooting my way tell me they think I should stay put—in the safety of the apartment, where all of them can guard me.

Ajmal takes the direct route to *Khosha*—all of fifteen minutes. We're still a couple blocks away—I can see the wall in front of the restaurant up ahead—when he slows down. The street is eerily empty. No cars or pickups or motorcycles parked along the curbs. Unusual for this time of day, when people should be showing up for dinner. Except absolutely no one is out and about.

Another two blocks to go, but Ajmal parks and shoots me a troubled glance. "This I do not like. We should go."

I actually agree with him but am already salivating in anticipation of Sami's delicious food. Plus, there's my real reason for tagging along. I need a few minutes alone with Fatima to find out what she knows about Bahar. "It'll be okay. Look, there's no one around."

He rubs his jaw, clearly debating what to do. Upset me or upset Cerelli? He's got to decide. And if we don't pick up our order here, that means driving around to find some other restaurant that's open. Finally, he turns off the car and opens the door.

Shouldering my pack, I climb out—into silence so complete that my ears are ringing. The street is empty enough that our footsteps thunder against the cracked macadam, echoing between storefront walls.

When I push open *Khosha's* front door, the jingling of the rope of small, tarnished brass bells nearly deafens me.

I expect to see Fatima, her pale-blue *hijab* in place, covering all her lustrous dark-brown hair, her darker blue or maybe green *shalwar kameez* draping elegantly over her voluptuous curves, coming out to greet us.

I expect to see Taliban in camo fatigues lounging on floor

pillows and beckoning Fatima to bring more food or to refill their
pialas with *chai*. And all the time, undressing her with their eyes.

Fatima doesn't appear.

Neither does Sami, who's always in the kitchen creating dishes
that entice with their delectable aromas.

There are no aromas. Instead, there's cold dread charging up
my spine.

Ajmal ventures into the dining room and is back in a moment,
looking down the back hallway, then toward the kitchen—visibly
worried. "There is no one here. I called with our order an hour ago,
and Fatima told me to come ahead. This is not good." He heads
toward the front door. "Come! We must leave."

I do my best to ignore him as well as the terror that's twisting
around my heart. "Fatima?" My voice isn't above a whisper. I clear
my throat and try again. A little louder. "Fatima?"

No answer.

"Sami?"

I make my way to the kitchen door and, taking a deep breath,
push my way through.

There he is.

Sprawled on the floor. His head thrown back. His throat slit
open.

Did he hear them coming? Did he call up the stairs? "Fatima!"
I can hear his voice bellowing across the years from when Cerelli
first brought me here. Sami was prepping for the lunch crowd that
would be flooding into the restaurant in another thirty minutes.

Although he's quite obviously dead, I take a deep breath and
touch his hand. Still fairly warm, and rigor mortis hasn't yet set in.
The Taliban must have killed him soon after Ajmal called to place
our order.

"Fatima?" I call again. Then I glance over my shoulder at Ajmal. "I'm going upstairs to the patio. Maybe Fatima and her daughter are hiding up there. Be right back."

"Annie . . ." He shoots me a troubled look but lets me go. Sig in hand, I thread both arms through the shoulder straps to secure the pack on my back. Then I ease my way as quietly as possible to the back staircase. Slowly, I make my way up the stairs—as if I'm climbing a steep mountain. One foot up and solidly planted before I lift the other. And all the while, I'm listening for anything that sounds the least bit out of place. But there's nothing to hear.

When I get to the top of the stairs and onto the patio, I half expect to see Fatima front and center, dressed as she was years ago in a *burqa*, ready to show me how to walk like an Afghan woman. But the rooftop is empty—except for the many terra cotta pots filled with *sabzi* and all sorts of herbs.

"Fatima?"

I seriously hope no one's up here. Please let Fatima have had enough time to grab her daughter and get away.

Then, I see the blood on the tiled floor. Not a lot, but what must have been a steady drip, drip, drip. They lead to a door that I don't remember from the one and only time I was here all those years ago.

I knock softly. "Fatima? It's Annie."

Do I hear a groan? Or am I just imagining it?

It could be Fatima. But it's just as likely a Taliban militant. Maybe holding a knife to Fatima's throat, trying to lure me inside. Half wishing I'd listened to Ajmal's plea for us to leave while we were still in the car, I make sure the Sig's safety is off. I reach for the doorknob. And stop.

Open the frigging door! Once again, my inner voice is riding roughshod.

But I don't know who's in there. Hell, it could be the Cambridge Bomber. And no matter what Cerelli said, I know he wants me dead.

But it could be just Fatima. Seriously injured. Needing medical help. And God only knows what they've done to her daughter. Have you given any thought to that little girl and what she's going through?

Oh, damn.

I turn the knob and shoulder open the door, my pack laden with my camera, phones, and extra ammo clunking hard against the painted blue wood. The small front room is empty, but for the trail of blood leading diagonally across to a fading curtain hanging in a doorframe. I definitely hear something now.

"*Ne! Ne!*" Fatima's voice? I'm not sure.

Then, a shuffling sound, as if a body is dragging across the floor. It's coming from the back room. I move forward as quietly as I can, then push aside the curtain hanging in the doorway. The back room opens in front of me. In the near corner, a child's cot low to the floor and against the front wall, a double bed, neatly made. And there, on the far side, I see a little girl in a light-colored *shalwar kameez*, standing as tall as she's able in front of the body curled on the floor.

In the dim light, I think I see her face soften, losing some of the fierceness she's trying hard to convey. She's seen me once before, when Ajmal and I stopped by for takeout, but she must see scores of customers. I can hardly expect her to remember me out of so many.

The safety back on, I slip the Sig back into my waistband. Then, kneeling down to her height, I do my best to sound motherly and reassuring. "*Salâm. Nâm-e shomâ chist?*"

Fear now filling her eyes, she scowls back at me, her lips clamped firmly together. No one is getting past her.

I try again. "*Nâm-e man Annie ast.*" Please let her mother have mentioned my name.

Still nothing.

But from behind her comes a groan. Fatima. I push myself to my feet and try to skirt around the girl to the right. But she shifts her position to block where I want to go. She's absolutely going to protect her mother.

Another groan, but this time Fatima says something. "Zanna, this is Annie. It is okay. She will help."

The little girl still looks wary, and now I see a flash of something bright. Oh, dear God, she's got a knife! I don't want to begin to imagine what she could do with that.

"Zanna. That's a beautiful name." I try to use my most cajoling mother voice. It didn't always work with Mel, but please let it work now.

Finally, she takes one small step to the side, letting me see her mother. And the smear of blood on the floor. What the hell can I do to help? It's clear the best thing I can do is get her to a hospital. First, though, I need to see where she's wounded and then try to stop the bleeding. But I can't do anything with Zanna holding that knife.

I hold out my hand. "Sweetie, could you please let me have the knife?"

Fatima seems to understand. "My darling, give Annie the knife." Her voice is low but firm. Thank God I don't hear any blood gurgling. But the shallow, raspy breathing tells me she's seriously wounded.

Finally, the girl puts the knife on the floor and scampers around me to sit by her mother's shoulder.

I kneel down next to Fatima, but take a moment to speak to

Zanna. "Thank you. You are very brave. Now, we need to help your mother."

She nods.

"Fatima, can you tell me where you're hurt?"

She holds up her hand. Blood is oozing from the deep gash across her palm. Taking hold as gently as I can, I nearly gasp. Bone. Pulling the sheet off the bed, I slowly reach for the knife, only to hear Zanna growl. "It's all right. I'm not going to hurt your mother. I'm going to make bandages. To stop the bleeding."

But Zanna isn't looking at me. She points to the doorway.

My heart clenches in fear. A man backlit in the doorway, holding the curtain aside.

"Annie?" Ajmal's voice.

A respectful Afghan man, he seems hesitant to come into the room.

"It's Fatima," I say quickly as I slice the knife through the sheets—all the while hoping they're clean enough, that my bandages aren't full of germs that will worsen her condition even more. A quick glance at Zanna and I know I have to weigh my words carefully. "They've hurt her, too." Best not to say anything about Sami. Who knows what either Fatima or Zanna saw in the kitchen. I wrap the cloth around and around her hand, then knot the ends.

Fatima rests her bandaged hand on her belly. With her good hand, she points to her shoulder. "Here." The pain in her voice slays me.

I look but can't see anything. The room is darkening by the minute, and her navy-blue tunic isn't helping. Slowly I unbutton the neck and inch it to the side to reveal her upper chest. More blood oozing from what looks like a bullet hole. And right above that, the jagged ends of her broken clavicle have pierced the skin. I take a deep breath, hoping to calm my nerves.

"You need to be in a hospital." I keep my voice low and steady.

"No! In hospital, they will find me."

She's right, of course. Take her to the hospital, if we can even find one that has a spare bed, not to mention doctors still working, and the Taliban will most definitely find out. They've got spies patrolling the wards, looking for people who collaborated with the coalition forces.

From the looks of her wounds, she was probably in the kitchen with Sami when the militants charged in. I'm guessing Sami did what he could to protect her. And paid with his life. Then, they went after her. Maybe she played dead? They must have thought they'd killed her; they never would've left her alive. She and Sami were obviously both targeted. Because they regularly served Westerners in the restaurant? Or had the Taliban somehow pieced together that Fatima was a U.S. operative? Maybe they learned of her connection to Cerelli? Or maybe to Bahar? Or to me? When Ajmal and I came for takeout the other night . . . shit, the Cambridge Bomber was in the dining room.

"I can't leave you here. Ajmal, any ideas?"

"Ajmal?" The relief in her voice is palpable. I'm guessing they know each other and not just as restaurant owner and patron.

A few long strides and Ajmal is across the room. I scoot back so he can kneel next to her. They speak quietly, almost breathing the words—just like Cerelli and Sawyer do in a crisis. I can only make out "safe house." Between the two of them, they decide that we'll take her and Zanna to a more secure location—wherever that is.

I do my best to explain to Zanna what's going to happen. She seems to understand. At least, she nods her agreement and doesn't try to grab back the knife.

Ajmal turns to me. "We must go quickly. I am worried they will come back."

"Fatima? Can you walk?"

She nods, but I have my doubts.

After I swaddle Fatima's upper chest and shoulder with bandages, Ajmal and I help her to her feet. She takes a few steps, but it's slow going, and she's groaning in pain. There's no way she'll be able to walk very far or very fast.

Our first hurdle soon presents itself: how the hell are we going to get her down the stairs? But miracle of miracles, we get her to the first floor, where she leans against the wall, looking like she could collapse at any moment.

A minute later, we maneuver her out the back door and into the alley that runs the length of the block. Zanna has no sooner gently shut the door than we hear the jingling of bells at the front door. Someone else has come for dinner. But the bells don't stop. The footsteps tromp heavily around the first floor. The voices are male and angry and very loud. Shouting in Pashto.

But one voice speaks in English. With a cultivated Cambridge accent. "You will come now to the dining room. One minute. I will be patient for one minute. After that, my patience is done."

Why isn't he speaking Dari—Fatima's first language? I doubt he even knows that she speaks English. She'd have been careful not to let him or any Taliban know that. Bottom line: he must know there are Westerners hiding somewhere in the building.

More heavy lug-soled booted steps. Someone is climbing the stairs to the rooftop patio and shouting again for everyone to give themselves up. Then come the shots from an automatic.

Fatima tightens her hold on my arm. "We must go!"

Yeah, but running is out of the question. How can we get Fatima to walk faster?

Remembering the rescue skills learned during my Girl Scout days, I show Ajmal how to cross our forearms to make a chair. Her good arm around my neck, Fatima balances herself as best she can. She's a big woman and not a lightweight, but with Zanna running silently by my side, we're able to move much faster now and manage to put an entire block between us and the restaurant. Then a second block. And a third, before turning into another alley. In minutes, we're deep into the maze, and I'm completely lost.

I'm beginning to tire. But we keep on walking, I'm guessing another half hour. My arms are giving out. Unless the safe house is very close by, there's no way we can carry Fatima all the way there. We need a car.

"I will go back for the vehicle." Ajmal sounds determined.

"Ajmal, no!" They could still be there. And they've got to be watching the street.

"I will be careful. I know these alleys. There is no worry."

But he's wrong. There is a worry—a huge worry.

Finding an alcove set back from the alley, we ease Fatima onto the ground. Then, Ajmal takes off running before I can talk sense into him. *Please*, I pray to the bit of starlit sky directly above us, *don't let anything bad happen to this man.*

33

AJMAL HASN'T BEEN GONE more than a few minutes when my cell phone rings, echoing loudly up and down the alley. It's got to be him, calling to tell me to sit tight, that there are still Taliban watching *Khosha*, and that he can't get to the Humvee for a while. I slip off my pack and dig out my phone as fast as I can. The last thing we need is for militants to hear the rings and track us down.

"Ajmal?"

"That's right, old girl." Not Ajmal. Nic. But what's with the 'old girl'? He always, without fail, calls me 'old thing.' In the beginning, I bristled at 'thing,' but he assured me that it's a term of endearment.

I play along. "So, Ajmal." I hear a soft click on his end of the connection, then a bit of an echo—as if he's turned on the cell's speaker. "Sorry about dinner. They were out of food. The shortages, you know. I thought I'd try *Herat*. They're sure to be open."

"Brilliant! That's at quite a distance, though, so we won't expect you anytime soon." There's a muffled pause. Nic must be holding the phone to his chest, but a moment later, he's back on the line.

"Oh, here's a thought. Why not try Silk Road? That's much closer, and some of us have a hankering for Thai food. You know what we like. Don't be stingy with the hot sauce. All of us are hungry."

And there it is. Silk Road. The code we settled on long ago—a warning to each other to stay away.

"Silk Road it is." Warning given and received. I end the call. A nice little flourish Nic thought to add at the end: hot sauce, as in this is a hot situation. Which I take to mean there are militants watching the building, ready to arrest me should I return. Or maybe they're actually in the building. In the apartment? Of course they are. That's why the phone's speaker was turned on. So the Taliban could hear what I was saying. Could this get any more complicated?

Sinking down to the ground next to Fatima, I invite Zanna onto my lap. She's still not saying anything, but when I wrap my arms around her, she nestles her head against my shoulder and relaxes her body against mine.

"Silk Road?" Fatima whispers. I'm guessing she doesn't want to draw attention to us either. "This is a code?"

"It is. My partner, Nic, and I settled on it years ago."

"So, now we will all three be at the safe house."

"If Ajmal's able to get the Humvee."

"He will get a car. It is arranged."

A car. As in any car he can get his hands on. Clearly, Fatima and Ajmal have set their own plan in motion. I bet he's not going back for the Humvee after all. Which is actually a huge relief because there's no way the Taliban wouldn't have already recognized our vehicle and its plates. There was probably someone watching from the moment we turned onto the street. They checked the plates against their master list, identified it as a TNN vehicle, and they knew. Plus, they saw a man and a woman. Since I'm the only woman on the team, the process of elimination was simple. Now I understand who the Cambridge Bomber thought he was talking to back at the restaurant. Not just any Westerner. Me.

Fatima breaks the silence. "You called the restaurant earlier today?"

Her question takes me aback. "I did. But how did you know?"

She watches me intently. "Your caller ID."

"But how—?"

"Phinneas gave it to me. He thought I should have it in case you called." She's gasping for breath after every word or two. But she's still able to pack a lot of sexiness and emotion into 'Phinneas.' I can't help thinking Cerelli might well have been wrong when he promised I had nothing to worry about. A horrible thought, given that Sami is sprawled dead on the *Khosha* kitchen floor. "You called about Bahar." It's not a question.

I ignore the 'Phinneas' part of her comment and focus on Bahar. "I ran into her at the protest march a couple weeks ago. She gave me the number."

"Yes."

"Then, she disappeared. Her brother, Farrakh, is worried."

"She did not disappear. As Phinneas would say, she is laying low."

One worry gone. "Well, it seems her brother has now gone missing. We weren't sure if the Taliban arrested him early on during the raid at the hospital or if he managed to get away."

She looks puzzled. "That I do not—"

We both hear the footsteps running. Toward us, it seems to me. As quietly as I can, I move Zanna behind me, whispering to her to scrunch down and stay hidden. Then, slipping the Sig from my waistband and flicking off the safety, I huddle next to Fatima as far back into the dark shadows as possible. We wait. A moment later, the running slows.

"Annie?" Ajmal's voice. "I am alone."

"Ajmal!"

A few seconds later, he peers around the corner of the building at us. "Come! I have a vehicle. It is not far."

Safety on, the Sig goes into my waistband again, my pack once more on my back. Together, Ajmal and I help Fatima to her feet. She does her best to stifle her groans, but they're loud. Too loud. The woman needs to be in the hospital getting serious medical attention. Not an option, so I save my words. Instead, Ajmal and I link our arms once more into a chair and carry her the several blocks to the car. She's sagging against me now—I'm sure that's not just my imagination.

An aging white Toyota Corolla with rust above the wheel wells, it couldn't be less noteworthy. Exactly the vehicle we need to make us anonymous. Gently, we position Fatima on the back seat. Zanna kneels on the floor next to her mother. With us about to cruise the main roads of Kabul, I decide it's a good time to pull the periwinkle *burqa* out of my pack. As soon as I drape it over my head, Ajmal nods his approval.

I have no idea where we're going, but it's a long trek. Ajmal is back to driving through every neighborhood in the city. Some of them multiple times. All the better to lose whoever may be following. I'm sure we both assume there are Taliban on our tail—even though neither of us manages to spot them.

Eventually, after an hour of meandering around Kabul, we near Chindawul. A neighborhood I never expected to see again. Built on the slopes of the Hindu Kush Mountains, the shanties are in even worse condition than I remember. Cobbled together of deteriorating mud bricks and whatever building materials the residents can scrounge together, they're now home to evacuees from other cities and the surrounding villages. This place was crowded before the Taliban assault; now it's absolutely teeming with people. With its lack of sanitation and food, I can't imagine a worse place for Fatima to go into hiding. Still, this should give us some anonymity.

Ajmal stops the car and waves over several of the young men standing around. Despite the dark, I see their gaunt faces. He offers them a handful of afghani dollars to guard the car.

And then we're climbing the narrow alleys of Chindawul, Fatima once again seated on our arm chair. Zanna sticks close to me, her hand clutching my *burqa*. The going uphill is slow, and sloppy. Puddles are everywhere, and the acrid smell of urine all but overpowers the more enticing smells of stews and soups cooked for dinner. I don't want to think about what we could possibly be walking through. Thank God I'm wearing my boots instead of sandals.

At each turn, I keep hoping we've reached the point where we'll slip out of the alley and into the safe house. But we never do. Half the time, we double back and go downhill, then into an alley that runs across to another uphill climb. Ajmal is taking every care he possibly can to get us safely where we need to go.

That's when I remember the car. Surely, those young men will give us away to the first Taliban militant who happens by. They already have their money. Did Ajmal promise them more when he returns? Probably. On second thought, I'd bet anything he has no intention of going back to that vehicle. Another ingenious decoy—something Cerelli would do. Eventually, the young men—and the Taliban—will realize they've been duped, but until then, they'll wait for him there.

God, please don't let them come after us. We wouldn't be hard to spot: a man and a woman carrying another woman. Besides which, we're moving slowly enough that they could easily catch up. My arms are aching to the point of trembling. If we don't get to the safe house soon, we'll have to take a break. But Ajmal keeps us moving. We set off on another climb, this one steeper than before. Now there are steps—of a fashion—carved into the rock of the mountain. I'm about to ask for a rest—just five minutes— when Ajmal tells me we can't stop. Too many people have noticed us. There will be questions. I stop thinking about how much my arms hurt and focus on putting one foot in front of the other, periodically glancing down to my side to make sure Zanna is still there, hanging on. An amazing little girl. What four-year-old would put up with this? No complaints? No whining? Not a whimper. I shudder to think she's experienced something like this before—a narrow escape in the middle of the night.

Finally, we reach yet another horizontal branch of the alley network. Ajmal steers us down a block, then guides us into the narrowest alleyway yet. Not even an alley. Barely wide enough for one person to pass, much less three. There is nothing for it but to set Fatima on her feet. Leaning against the wall, she shuffles forward, doing her best to swallow her groans. Ajmal follows close behind, ready to support her if she asks. She won't. This woman is fierce. I bring up the rear with Zanna still glued to my side. On an impulse, I reach down and, gathering her into my arms, lift her to my hip. She links her arms around my neck and hooks her feet at the small of my back. We just fit.

At long last, we're at the safe house. I'm ready to collapse, and I don't have a bullet in my shoulder or a broken clavicle. How the hell is Fatima still standing? I follow Ajmal through the doorway into a room divided in half by sheets of fabric hanging over a low-slung rope. Door locked and a two-by-four in place for added protection, he pushes the sheet aside, and we cross to the back of the room. In the near corner, he moves a cabinet of sorts aside to reveal a doorway. Shorter than normal. Probably for a child. Anyone taller than Zanna will have to crawl. Fatima will have to manage on her own. There's no way to help her. I hurt for her as she sinks to her hands and knees and maneuvers her way through. Ajmal stands back to let me go next. But Zanna doesn't want me to put her down. She tightens her hold around my neck.

"Sweetie, it's just for a few moments. I'll hold you again as soon as I get through."

She thinks about that, her eyes flicking back and forth from the miniature doorway to me and back to the opening. Finally, she loosens her hold and lets me lower her to the floor. Standing back, she mutely demands that I go first. Throwing the *burqa* back over my head and then pulling it off, I crawl through and turn, just in time to catch the little girl who rockets into my arms. Ajmal scrambles through with the speed of a man who's done this many times before. I'd love to know about his exploits and who he really is, but I know better than to ask.

With Zanna once again perched on my hip, clinging tightly to my neck and waist, I scout out the room. Small, but again there are sheets hanging across the room as a divider. No windows. And, I'm betting, no indoor plumbing, which means there will be a lot of crawling in and out of that hole whenever Ajmal or Zanna or I need to relieve ourselves. For Fatima, we'll have to find a pot.

At the far end of this side of the room, I see a kitchen of sorts. For a brief moment, my own kitchen in Bay View flashes before my eyes—modest by American standards. But this arrangement doesn't come close. A couple plastic crates with a pot and pan and bowl, some utensils. A single burner. Luxury! And a basin for washing up. I notice the large yellow jerry cans in the corner. Water. I hear rustling on the other side of the curtain. A kerosene lantern illuminates shadows on the sheet. Making my way through, I see Ajmal settling Fatima onto a mattress. There are other people helping. She's sitting, slumped against the wall while the man who's kneeling next to her carefully unwraps the cloth I wound around her shoulder. Practiced hands, he appears to know what he's doing. A doctor, or maybe a nurse. I can only hope. I take a step closer. He pauses briefly and glances over his shoulder at me. Farrakh.

The woman kneeling on the other side of Fatima also looks up. And smiles her welcome. "Annie!"

I heave a sigh of relief. "Bahar, I'm so glad to see you! And Farrakh, you're the answer to my prayers." Thank God the Taliban didn't catch up with him. I take another look at his face. Grim. It's the only word that comes to mind. It's a look I know all too well. It's what was on my face when I sat with Corporal Sean Murphy years ago, then again with the Marine at the airport bombing last week, waiting for them to die. But this. This is just a bullet in the shoulder and a broken bone. Painful and serious enough, but surely Fatima can survive?

Moving closer to the mattress, I slowly lower myself to the hard-packed dirt floor without disturbing Zanna, whose head is lolling heavily against my shoulder, her gentle snores ruffling my hair. Next to us, Fatima's breathing is rapid and shallow.

34

I'M NOT SURE HOW long I sleep. A few minutes. A few hours. But when I wake up, stretched out on the floor next to Fatima's mattress with Zanna curled on top of me, I find a thin blanket draped over both of us. And I hear soft voices from the other side of the room divider, their shadows projected on the sheet by the light of the kerosene lantern. Our side is darker, but I'm still able to see Fatima. Her chest barely rises and falls as she struggles mightily to breathe. Thank God she's still alive. But Farrakh is going to have to remove that bullet soon and clean the wound, otherwise she'll have to deal with a roaring infection. Not to mention he's got to figure out why she can barely breathe.

I ease a still-sleeping Zanna to the dirt floor, then push myself to my feet. Lifting her loose-limbed body back into my arms, I make my way around the partition to the other half of the room where Bahar and Farrakh are sitting on thin mattresses, more threadbare blankets draped over their shoulders. It takes me a minute, but then I realize that Ajmal isn't with them. I turn to look at the small doorway in the wall, then fix my eyes back on them. My confusion must show on my face.

"Ajmal left right after you fell asleep," says Bahar.

"But he'll be back." It's not a question.

"Perhaps." The tone of her voice tells me she could just as well have said no.

"Why not?" I can't help the slight whine.

"You must see how very dangerous it would be for him to return. People will notice. They will talk. From what I understand, they are already talking."

"Of course." Selfish of me. The man has put his life at risk time after time since I've been here. He has a family, a life. I want him to be able to live it. I rub Zanna's back through the tunic of her *shalwar kameez*. Pale blue, I can see now. Then my eyes lock on her pink patent-leather Mary Janes. A plastic pink flower on each toe box. Perfect for a little girl. One strap unbuckled. I try to remedy that only to discover that the buckle itself is broken.

I claim a corner of Bahar's mattress. "Before I forget, I went by your apartment a few days ago."

She rolls her eyes. "I think the Taliban must have been there by now. And destroyed everything."

"Oh, yeah. And your roommate was pretty much terrified. Someone had obviously roughed her up."

Now it's Bahar's turn to look confused. "Annie, I don't have a roommate."

All I can do is stare at her as all those red flags that were troubling me that morning start waving again. "But there were two names on the card on the door."

"Wait, I don't understand. Why did you think to go to my apartment?"

Farrakh answers for me. "I asked Annie if she knew where you were. I gave her your address. You see, I stopped by your apartment, too, and couldn't find you."

Bahar's shoulders sag. "I told you I might have to go into hiding."

"It is one thing for you to say that might happen. It is very different when you disappeared without letting me know. Our parents have told me to look after you. What was I going to tell them?"

She rests her hand on his arm. "You don't need to worry."

Sputtering to the point he could explode, he clearly wants to yell, but ratchets down the volume. "Of course I worry. We have all been worried about you."

I shift my position, trying to find a bit of mattress that has more cushion to it. Zanna stirs in my arms, opens her eyes just for a second, and then closes them again. No one says a word until she starts snoring again.

Bahar catches my attention. "Tell me about this imposter roommate."

I shrug. "About your age, I think, and a little taller than you. Dark hair. She was dressed in black trousers and a short-sleeve shirt. The clothes looked too big for her."

"It sounds like the woman who lives down the hall. She has always been nice enough, but I've had my suspicions about her husband."

"Does he have a scruffy beard that's just starting to grow in? You think he could be Taliban?"

She nods. "He told me he was a police officer, but I am sure he was one of the undercover militants."

I comb my fingers through my hair in frustration. "Honestly, I caught on that something wasn't adding up. Based on what she said, she sure didn't know you very well."

Bahar hugs the blanket tighter around her. "It is strange that they would have her in my apartment. But nothing they do surprises me. They probably were hoping I'd return. Or that someone else might show up." She looks knowingly at me. "Someone they could torture into revealing where I was hiding. You were lucky the Taliban weren't there when you visited."

I shake my head. "Oh, they showed up—just after I left. I had to hide in the alley for a while."

Bahar's eyes widen. "But how did the Taliban know you would be there?"

"As far as I know, only Ajmal and the guys on my crew knew. But I trust them."

Bahar furrows her brow. "Perhaps you are trusting too many people."

My heart sinks. This young woman has a hardened veneer. What happened to the sweet girl I knew six years ago? I shift Zanna's weight a bit. Then I remember how quickly the Taliban showed up after I left Bahar's. "I think they probably bugged your apartment. Either they were monitoring your place from somewhere close by or maybe the husband alerted them."

"Oh, well. It is not to worry about," she says emphatically. "I will not see them again."

She's right. Bahar won't be going back to her apartment. At least not anytime soon. And even though she swore a few weeks ago that she'd stay in Afghanistan and fight, I'm hoping to convince her to leave for the time being. Something to talk about later. For now, we have a bigger problem.

"There's something else we need to talk about." I lower my voice to a whisper, causing both Bahar and Farrakh to lean closer. "What are we going to do about Fatima?"

Bahar raises her index finger, then creeps to the curtain and pulls back the sheet. She's back in a few moments. "She is still sleeping."

Farrakh inches closer. "There really is not much I can do. I cleaned the wound as well as I could, but the bullet is lodged deep. From what I saw, there is a lot of damage to the muscle, and the clavicle is broken. Not just cracked, completely fractured. Bullets can move around inside the body. Her breathing is labored, which makes me think the bullet penetrated her lung. Or broke a rib, and that pierced her lung." His voice is heavy and sad. "Someone was a bad shot. Or he wanted her to suffer by not dying right away. The gash on her hand is also very deep. Unless I take her to the hospital and put her on antibiotics, she will develop a very serious infection."

"We cannot take her to the hospital!" Bahar sounds almost indignant that Farrakh would suggest such a thing. "Even if we register her under a different name, everyone knows Fatima. The Taliban will figure it out. They'll either kill her outright or arrest her and throw her into a prison cell to die."

Both Farrakh and I nod our agreement. She's right. That's exactly what will happen, and Fatima herself knows that. And yet she can't possibly want to die. Even with Sami gone, especially with Sami gone, she must want to live for her daughter. I can't believe she would've made that long and painful trek through the alleys of Kabul and then up this mountainside just to give up.

"Could you operate here? Take out the bullet? And sew up her hand?" I keep hoping to find a way to save the woman, but the doubt in my voice is apparent to all of us.

"Surgery without anesthesia? That is impossible. I would need to root around for the bullet. There is also her lung. No, I could not possibly do that here." He looks around the room—at the dirt floor and the stained mattress.

Not to mention that Fatima's screams of pain would alert the neighbors. "Maybe we should talk to her? Try to convince her to go to a hospital?" I suggest.

"A waste of words." Bahar slices her hand through the air.

"I could perhaps search for some medical supplies." Farrakh sounds torn, as though he doesn't want to venture out on a suicide mission but knows that as a man dedicated to healing, he should.

Bahar puts an end to that line of thought. "I am certain that when Fatima took on her work, like me, she knew it might come to this. She would not want either one of you to endanger your lives."

And yet we already have. Ajmal sure has. So have I.

Still holding Zanna, I push myself back to my feet. "I think it's time I had a talk with her. We know she's seriously injured, probably already fomenting some nasty bacterial infection, but she needs to understand the decision she's making."

Farrakh nods his agreement while Bahar takes a deep breath, then shrugs, as if to say again that I'm wasting my words. But she doesn't try to stop me.

Stepping quietly into the other half of the room, I stand next to the curtain, watching Fatima. She's gasping for air, but she doesn't seem any worse than last night. Still, I've seen many Marines as they near the end, and I think it'll come to that if we don't do something soon. I'm still staring at her when I notice that her eyes are open, and she's watching me in turn. Or maybe she's looking at Zanna sleeping soundly in my arms. Probably the latter because her lips soften into a smile.

"Come, please." She pats the side of the mattress with her good hand, then pushes herself up so she's sitting—actually more like slumping—against the wall.

I do as she asks, although for the life of me I can't imagine two women who have less to say to each other. "Do you want to hold her?" I whisper, leaning forward, ready to lay Zanna onto the mattress next to her.

But she shakes her head. Does she think it will hurt to have Zanna pressing against her? Yeah, it probably will.

"This will be hard for her." Fatima doesn't look away from her daughter, but she doesn't reach to touch her either. "She never goes to another person like she has . . . with you. Well, she goes to Phinneas."

I'm not quite sure what to make of that, so I just sit quietly and wait for her to continue.

"My time will come soon."

"Fatima—"

"No. Please, I speak."

"Of course."

"I have not slept. I think about . . . my darling girl. For her, I want . . ." Her voice breaks, and she takes a breath that causes her to shutter visibly in pain. "Please, you take her? You and Phinneas?"

My eyes widen. "You mean adopt her? But you're her mother and—"

She raises her hand to stop my words. "Do not tell me to have hope. I know . . . Farrakh is a good doctor. If we were in his hospital, he could operate, but . . ."

"We could get you to a hospital—"

"No! Taliban would come for me . . . they are already there."

"We could take you tonight. When it's dark. No one will see." Even as I say the words, I know it's pointless. Yeah, we might be safe ourselves, but Fatima wouldn't be.

She shakes her head. "They know me. They come after Bahar . . . Farrakh . . . you . . . Zanna. No."

I want to argue. To point out that her daughter needs her, that we need to try to get her medical help. But I don't. She's beyond wanting to endure an argument. It would take too much effort, and she doesn't have enough left.

"I need to make sure Zanna is safe. I want her to have . . . a good life. Phinneas can give her that. And you."

"Your family? Sami's?"

"Sami's family . . . all dead. Mine are in Iran—no, Zanna cannot go."

I don't have the words to respond. Just the thought of Cerelli and me adopting Zanna has me reeling. Me give another mother's daughter a good life? I've been a terrible mother to my own daughter, but at least Mel had Todd and Catherine Elizabeth. How could Zanna deal with me being away from her for weeks, possibly months, at a time? And it's not like Cerelli could stay home with her while I'm off on assignment.

She doesn't wait for me to think things through, to formulate an answer. "You must know . . ."

Why do I dread hearing what she's about to say?

"When Zanna was born, we made Phinneas . . . how do you say? Her guard?"

"Her guardian?"

"Yes. If something happens to Sami and me. Did he tell you?"

"No." He failed to mention that little detail of his life. Hell, I didn't even know Zanna existed until a few days ago.

"Ah."

I seriously don't like the tone of that 'ah'—as in 'so Phinneas keeps secrets from you.' But I decide not to follow that thought. This woman is trying to find a home for her daughter, a child she dearly loves, before she dies. This must be even more painful than her wounds. To know that her former lover and another woman will be raising her child.

"Now Sami is dead. And soon . . ." With her good hand, Fatima lifts the blood-stained, oversized silk pouch that's hanging around her neck. "Can you?"

I gently ease Zanna onto the mattress between Fatima and me, then slip the cord of the pouch up and over her head. When I try to hand it to her, though, she pushes it back to me. "You. Please."

The pouch is stuffed. I pull out four passports first and nearly gape. They're navy blue—close in color to the Afghan passport I was expecting to see. But these have an eagle stamped in gold and the words 'United States of America.' Then, a stack of papers—mostly in Dari, only a few in English. I shuffle past the birth certificate, and then the next document stops me. There in the middle of the page is Cerelli's name. And mine. "An adoption certificate?" I look up to see her watching me.

"We both signed. The lawyer . . . the judge agreed."

Turning to the second page, I see the signatures and the seals. I can't begin to fathom signing a daughter away to someone else. Then it occurs to me that Darya and Tariq probably did exactly the same thing for Seema. No one gets into this line of work without having an escape plan. Darya and Tariq both told me that. So, these are the good mothers, who prepared for every eventuality. I didn't. I blindly assumed Todd and Catherine Elizabeth would take care of Mel—that I'd just disappear from her life for good.

I keep paging through the documents until I come to another that stops me short. A second birth certificate. This one listing Phinneas Cerelli as the father of Zanna. And here her name is Zanna Cerelli. Just that suddenly, my heart starts to split open. He couldn't have. He wouldn't have.

There has to be an explanation!

I thumb back until I find Zanna's other birth certificate. Sami is the father. I hold the two certificates next to each other. Both look authentic. The signatures in ink. Stamps that look official. What the hell? Then I open the passports. One for Sami. One for Fatima. Two for Zanna, one with 'Cerelli' as her last name. Confused, my heart careening between disbelief and anger, I look up to see Fatima's eyes, full of desperation.

"I don't . . . understand." I try to keep my voice calm, but I most definitely hear the first notes of anxiety coloring my words.

Fatima tries to take a breath, but she's struggling. She reaches for my hand—as it happens, the one holding the birth certificate naming Cerelli as father. "It is . . . only way. Afghan"—she gasps for air—"law . . . no adoption . . . U.S. . . . . search for family . . . orphanage . . . on streets . . . sell her . . . my daughter . . . I can't."

The one thing she hasn't said is which certificate is fake. My heart tells me it has to be the one naming Cerelli. No matter how beautiful Fatima is or what he used to feel for her, there's no way he'd betray me. Clinging to that thought, I put my hand on hers to stop her from trying to force out words. The woman can barely breathe, much less speak.

But she's not done. "Please . . . you will love her?"

I brush Zanna's hair away from her face. And although she's still asleep, she inches closer to me, her hand now on my thigh. A quick glance at Fatima confirms that she sees it, too. And although I haven't yet agreed to adopt this little girl, and I sure as hell should discuss all this with Cerelli, I take the next step. Until he and I can talk. "Yes. I will. I promise." Silently, I slide the papers back into the pouch and hang it around my neck. "We won't let her forget you. Or Sami."

"Thank you," she whispers. Then, staring at a spot over my shoulder, she begins to slide down toward the mattress. "Could you . . . ?"

Cradling Fatima's head, I ease her gently back down onto the mattress. Then, thinking she might want to watch her daughter sleep before sleeping herself, I sit, and wait. But she closes her eyes, then turns her head toward the wall, although I know she's still awake. Finally, I stand and, scooping Zanna into my arms, walk toward the partition. I'm almost there when I hear Fatima moan softly.

Turning, I see her shifting on the mattress, clearly searching for a less painful position.

"I love him," she says softly, although I'm pretty sure she's speaking loud enough to make sure I hear her.

And oh, God. That's the last thing I want to hear.

35

"SHE SAYS SHE'S READY to die." I'm not whispering. Fatima deserves to hear what I have to say, to know that I'm accurately conveying the decision she's made.

Bahar nods, as if she's known this from the start. But I'm still trying to understand.

Farrakh raises his eyebrow. "Did she tell you that?"

I sink slowly to the floor, careful not to disturb Zanna. "Not exactly. She absolutely refuses to go to a hospital. And although I hate to say it, I understand. She doesn't want to give the Taliban a second chance at her. She's very aware of what could happen without having surgery."

"I must do something." Farrakh looks miserable—as though he has failed Fatima by being unable to create sterile conditions in this dirty hovel, by not having the equipment to operate.

"She's worried about putting us in danger. Especially Zanna. I think she accepts that she's going to die and just wants to make sure

there's someone to take care of this one." I rest my cheek on the top
of Zanna's head.

"Someone?" Bahar looks intently at me and then at the little
girl—the very image of her mother—clinging to me, her eyes open
now and locked on mine. "From what we could hear, she wants you
to adopt her."

I absolutely do not want to continue talking about this in front
of Zanna. One day—perhaps a lot sooner than I wish—I'll tell her.
With Cerelli. But for now, I comb my fingers through her hair. "Oh,
my sweet girl. You must be hungry."

"Of course she is hungry." Bahar scrambles to her feet and extends
her hand to Zanna, who promptly buries her face against my chest.

My stomach growls. "There's food here?"

"Yes, we have food." Bahar laughs. "Not a lot, but enough to last
a few days."

A few days? "How long do you think we'll be here?"

Bahar and Farrakh exchange a cryptic glance, then she shakes
her head. "I am sorry, but—"

"Didn't Ajmal say anything before he left? There must be a
plan. I mean, we can't stay here forever."

"We are fine here for now." Bahar smiles reassuringly—although
I'm not feeling all that sanguine. "Why don't we see about getting
something to eat."

"Anything would be wonderful." Zanna and I follow Bahar
to the plastic crates and watch as she sorts through cans and jars
of food. Everything seems to require cooking. And at this point, I
think we're all reluctant to fire up the burner. I know I am.

"Nân? Crackers?" I ask.

"I brought some bread with me." Farrakh opens his black medical case and pulls out several rounds. "Would you like some?" He

dangles one in front of Zanna, who seems singularly unimpressed with his effort to get her to talk.

Please let him not hold the bread for ransom, forcing her to say something in order to eat.

"Zanna! Can you say '*lotfan*'?"

In the face of Zanna's silence, I say, "*Balê, tashakor,* I would like some bread." Plucking the round from his hand, I rip off bite-size pieces and try to give them to the little girl, but she turns away. So, I stuff the pieces into my pants' pocket. She'll find them—when she's hungry enough. Eventually, I feel a hand crawling into my pocket, then stealing away.

Bahar shakes her head. "You are spoiling her. She really has to speak sometime."

"She will. When she's ready." And I well know that 'ready' may take a very long time. What this little girl has endured in the last twenty-four hours, no child should ever go through. I tremble with fury to think that the Taliban may have killed Sami with Zanna looking on. They may have attacked Fatima in front of her. Even if she didn't see the actual butchering, she certainly saw the aftermath of what they did to her mother. I can't even begin to contemplate the horror she witnessed.

"It is lucky she is so young." Bahar chews her way through her share of the bread. "*Inshallah,* she will not remember this."

Lucky? I close my eyes for a long moment, trying to tease out the words to answer, but I can't. Of course Zanna isn't the only child this has happened to. Many children in Afghanistan and in conflicts around the world have witnessed the same thing—their parents, brothers, sisters brutally murdered. But looking forward to Zanna growing up to be ten, fifteen, twenty, I'm not seeing anything lucky about her being only four years old when this horror happened to her. I'm also not convinced that a part of her will ever be able to forget everything. Won't she always have questions?

I feel Zanna's hand squirrel its way again and again into my pocket. Good! She's eating. Then, sneaking a glance, I see she's not eating after all. Instead, she's moving the pieces of bread from my pocket to hers.

Apparently Farrakh sees it, too. Sensing that he's about to say something, I raise my hand to stop him. She'll eat. When she's able to. For now, let her store up her food. At some point, she'll take out those crumbs. I hope.

I SPEND THE NEXT few hours worrying about what I can do to get us out of here. I don't have Ajmal's phone number but could try calling Nic or Sadim. Nix that. The Taliban probably have them all, including Ajmal, under surveillance. Cerelli is my best bet. Even though he's in D.C. and Sawyer's in Germany, there's got to be someone here who could help us escape. Sooner rather than later. Not only will food become an issue, but the longer we're here, the greater the odds that the Taliban will find us.

But there's absolutely no reception here. I'll need to go outside— even though anyone living nearby or just passing by will see me or hear me. Cerelli himself told me not to use the phones except in dire emergencies. Well, I think this counts—this is definitely an emergency, and it's dire. If I could get a few blocks away from the safe house, even just going straight up the mountain or down, I should be okay.

I wait for Zanna to take yet another nap and then tell Bahar and Farrakh what I've got in mind. They're both opposed.

Bahar plants her fists on her waist. "Annie, you will draw attention to yourself. And to us."

"Not so much if I wear the *burqa*."

"They will hear you." Farrakh joins the effort to talk sense into me. "If you speak Dari, they will understand exactly what you are saying. If you speak English, they will know you are a Westerner. I myself saw the Taliban outside in the alleys when I came here. They are beating people to get information. If they see you, they will not stop with a beating."

"We can't stay here forever. And I know someone who can help."

"Oh, Annie, Farrakh is right. It is far too dangerous." Bahar sounds for all the world opposed to my going out, but I sense a slight weakening.

So, I sketch out my plan.

They listen intently. I'll give them that.

Despite her obvious reluctance, Bahar finally acquiesces. "You must wait until tonight. I think around nine o'clock would be a good time. It will be dark enough that no one will be able to see you well, especially with the *burqa*. And it is not so late that people will think it is strange for you to be outside." Bahar seems satisfied.

But Farrakh isn't. "I will go with you. It is important for you to have a man with you, especially while you are talking. I will stand guard."

HOURS LATER, BAHAR SIGNALS that it's time. I bundle up the *burqa* to put on after I crawl through the doorway into the front room. From his medical bag, Farrakh pulls out a surgical mask. Given that COVID is running rampant here in Chindawul, it's a brilliant disguise. But none of us counted on Zanna's reaction. She refuses to be left behind. Her fear that I won't come back is quickly gaining strength, soon to become a major meltdown. As far as Zanna's concerned, where I go, she goes. In the end, I carry her, arms around my neck, legs around my waist. With luck, people will see a young Afghan family. I just hope to hell that there's no Taliban militant out there who ate at *Khosha*, who may recognize this beautiful little girl.

Farrakh seems to know his way around the alleys fairly well, so I let him lead us through the maze. Anything that makes the safe house harder to find is a good thing. There will still be people who hear me, though. Over a million people live here, and they're all on top of each other. Finally, after what feels like an eternity, he stops walking and nods. This is the place. I'm not sure what caused him to pick this exact spot, but I'm not going to question him.

Sat phone out, I punch in Cerelli's number and pray that he answers.

"Annie?" Sam Harris is on the line.

"Sam. Could you please get Cerelli?" The pleading in my voice certainly speaks to a dire emergency. At least to my ears.

She doesn't mince words. "Sorry, he can't talk to you right now."

"What?"

"Annie, I'm sorry, I—"

I rein in my panic. "I need him. Now. Believe me, this is important."

"Listen to me. And please, listen carefully. I can't tell you much, but he did leave a message:

I walk to the hill outside Kandahar
And see that tonight my Beloved's caravan has not gone far."

The *landay* Seema purportedly texted to me six years ago? This makes no sense. "What the hell kind of message is that?"

"Oh, dear. I honestly don't know, but he thought you'd understand. He was certain." Sam takes a deep breath. "I'm under orders not to say anything else. And I shouldn't have said even that. But look, if things are really that bad, you can always go to the embassy."

My eyes nearly cross. She can't be serious. The U.S. Embassy? That's exactly what the Taliban are expecting us to do. They must have lookouts posted all along those streets. We'd never make it. But then I wonder if she's saying that for whoever she assumes is listening to our conversation. So, I play along. "Oh, gosh! Yes! That's exactly what I should do. Thanks."

"Good. I'll let him know. Take care."

A moment later, I hear the complete emptiness of the line. Not even static. She's gone. Off to tell Cerelli to contact me at the embassy. Great, just great.

Farrakh leans in close. "You see those men a few doors away? They have been listening to your conversation. Now they are watching us closely."

"You think we should go."

"Yes."

He leads us on an even more complicated path back to the safe house. Turning corners, going uphill and down. All the while, we can hear the footsteps of the men trailing behind us. Perched on my hip, arms and legs wrapped tightly around me, Zanna is hanging on for dear life, but the uphill climbs are getting harder with all the extra weight attached to me.

Honestly, though, I'm not thinking about our seemingly endless trek. Instead, I'm trying to sort through the meaning of Cerelli's *landay.* Unable to successfully read between the lines, I'm close to giving up when I think to take it literally.

I could be Cerelli.

The *hill?* Well, I'm on a hill. Make that a mountain. But there's no point mincing words.

Kandahar—let's say that's a bit of misdirection and go with Kabul.

I suppose *tonight* could be exactly that. Right now.

My Beloved's caravan. Well, I'd sure like to think that's me—the beloved. And my posse. Meaning Bahar and Farrakh and, I guess, Fatima. Or could he mean Nic and Sadim and Azizullah and Ajmal?

I'm no poet, but I'm thinking this *landay* could be Cerelli's message to me that he's in Afghanistan. Kabul to be exact. But why the hell would the U.S. Navy send an admiral here? Now? Unless the Navy didn't send him. Unless Cerelli is on some kind of spec op. Or maybe he came on his own. Because Nic or Ajmal or maybe Sadim got through to him and told him what happened.

We walk through the alleys of Chindawul for another eternity until Farrakh finally sees a landmark that lets him know where we are, and after one more series of detours, we duck through the doorway into the safe house. And none too soon. Standing just inside the locked and bolted door, the lights out, and not even daring to breathe, we hear footsteps hurrying past. We still don't take deep breaths, although my lungs are in serious need of air. And Zanna is pretending she's dead. Not a peep.

"Stay where you are." Bahar's voice, a whisper from the corner. Quiet. Barely audible.

Next to us, there's a sound of rustling. Some minutes later, she gives the all clear and turns on the flashlight in her cell phone.

It's enough light to let us see that she's put a sheet over the one shuttered window and another over the front door. Pulling off my *burqa*, I look toward the back corner where the hole in the back wall should be, but the cabinet has been pushed in front of it.

Bahar signals Farrakh, and, as quietly as they can, they move the cabinet to the side. "Annie, you stay here." Then, she reaches for Zanna. "Just for a few minutes." And before the little one knows what's happening, Bahar whisks her into the back room. Farrakh is right behind them. Leaving me standing alone in the front room.

36

I HEAR THE SLIGHTEST noise from the other side of the sheet partitioning the front room in half. The click of a flashlight turning on. Now I can see the shadow of someone standing up from the mattress I imagine is on the floor over there. For one brief moment, my heart forgets to beat. Then I remember Bahar must know and trust whoever's over there to have let them into the safe house. No, she wouldn't set me up.

Just in case, I pull the Sig from my waistband and make sure the safety's off. Feeling a little more confident, I push the sheet aside and aim at the silvering bearded man in a dark-brown *shalwar kameez* standing just a few feet away.

"You've got the safety on or off?"

"Off. Definitely," I say, beyond relieved to see Cerelli.

"Good. Never pull a gun without making sure you're ready to shoot."

"Goddamn it, Cerelli, I know that. I learned my lesson six years ago."

"A little review never hurts. When was the last time you practiced at a shooting range anyway?"

I swallow hard. "It's been a while." The Sig is still in my hands, still pointed at Cerelli.

"Maybe we should do something about that when we get home."

"Maybe we should. Except, I don't do—"

"Guns. I know. You've told me before, many times."

"A reminder never hurts."

He quirks the corner of his mouth into the grin that makes my knees go weak. Still, after all these years. "You mind getting me out of your sights and putting the safety back on?"

"Making you nervous, am I?"

"Always."

"Sorry about that." I hand him the gun.

He gathers me in his arms. "Never, and I mean never, give your gun to a bearded man in a *shalwar kameez*."

A FEW MINUTES LATER, as Cerelli and I are sitting on the mattress, about to launch into a conversation about Fatima, I hear the scamper of feet across the dirt floor. Then, a dark-haired bundle of pissed-off energy hurtles herself across the room and onto the mattress between us. She blindly wraps her arms around my neck and buries her face against my chest.

In the flickering light of the kerosene lantern, I see Cerelli smile. "Who is this little princess?"

Zanna stops wiggling in my arms. Then, turning her head toward Cerelli, I can feel her body relax and her smile begin. "*Kaka Feen!*" She scrambles into his arms, nestling into his neck.

Kaka. Uncle. Family relationships in Dari are complicated, with a different word for 'uncle' depending on whether he's on the father's side or the mother's. Not that it matters since Cerelli isn't related to either Fatima or Sami. But I remember that 'kaka' would be for her paternal uncle. An insidious thought occurs to me. And there's that birth certificate. Try as I might, I can't unthink it. Cerelli wouldn't have. He couldn't have.

He takes one look at me, and, leaning past Zanna, he kisses me sweetly, then deepens his kiss. Finally pulling back, he says firmly, "I am not her father. I swear to you."

"But your name is on one of the birth certificates."

A thunderous cloud appears momentarily on his face. "What did you say?"

I pull the pouch over my head and dig out the two papers. "See?" I point first to Sami's name as father, then to his.

He scans each paper, then the rest of the documents. Finally, he turns his eyes on me. "She's a clever woman."

"You want to elaborate on that, please?"

"She faked a birth certificate and convinced a judge to sign off on it. Brilliant, actually."

"Excuse me?" I'm not so sure it's 'brilliant.'

"Fatima and Sami were covering their bases for Zanna—in case something happened to them, just like I told them to. They want her to be able to get out of Afghanistan." He picks up the adoption certificate. "Not that she ever discussed this with me, but adoption is a long shot. Even with the previous government, it might or might not have succeeded."

"What do you mean?"

"It's next to impossible for U.S. citizens to adopt an Afghan child, whether or not she's orphaned. The Afghan government says orphans belong to the country. The court orders a search for family that could go on for years. Even if they don't find any relatives, they insist that anyone adopting must be Muslim. With the Taliban now in power, I can only imagine they'll double down on that."

"So, they came up with plan B."

"They did. Named me as Zanna's father. Hence, no adoption necessary." He rests his index fingers on my lips. "And before you say anything, she didn't discuss this with me either."

I think about that for a few seconds. "You're saying she's a desperate mother doing whatever's necessary to protect her daughter. Yeah, I guess that qualifies as brilliant. Exactly what I would've done in her position." I can't help the snark that creeps into my voice.

He chuckles softly. "Sweetheart, I've told you before: one time. Many years ago. Before you and I . . . came together. Fatima and I weren't good together. She married Sami. And I sure as hell haven't slept with her again. Or fathered Zanna. I've been too focused on trying to marry you to be involved in any of this."

I decide not to tell him that Fatima still loves him. Maybe she'll tell him before she dies. Maybe she won't. But that's between them. Instead, I kiss him back. "About that marriage thing? Maybe you should try harder." I kiss him again. "Oh, and by the way, I like the beard."

"Do you now."

37

A WHILE LATER, WE all gather around Fatima's mattress. Zanna snuggles next to her mother, taking great care to stay away from her wounded shoulder. Cerelli has just finished a detailed explanation of why we've got to leave the safe house. Tonight.

"Getting up here, I saw too many militants. They're not just out on patrol. Word is they're here to round up some people. I don't want those people to be us."

"We'll need a vehicle." Trust Bahar to go straight to the logistics.

"My car should still be at my apartment. It's not big, but I think we will all fit." Interesting that Farrakh doesn't even ask where we're going. He's just ready to get the hell out of here. As for his car, I'm willing to bet the Taliban are keeping a close watch on it, if they haven't already seized it.

"I've arranged for a vehicle. We just need to get to the pickup point."

I make eye contact with Fatima and Bahar. "We should probably all wear *burqas*."

Cerelli laughs. "That's the last thing I ever thought I'd hear you say."

"Don't get used to it."

Beside me, Fatima stiffens, her breathing increasingly ragged and shallow. Not much longer. "I cannot. . ." She struggles to pull air into her lungs.

Cerelli's no longer laughing. "I'm not leaving you here."

I remember back fifteen years, when Cerelli and his team rescued me from the Taliban ambush in a small village near Kandahar. Unbelievably, they carried the bodies of Murphy and Lopez—my Marine escorts—for miles. U.S. Navy SEALs are beyond strong. If Sawyer were here, I know he'd be able to carry Fatima all the way to wherever we're going. But Cerelli with his prosthetic leg? Down these precariously steep and slippery slopes? I just can't see it.

He's watching Fatima closely, and the muscle at the corner of his eye is spasming like crazy. When he gathers Zanna in his arms and turns to me, all becomes clear. He's heard the shuddering of Fatima's lungs, too. And like me, he knows exactly what that sound means.

So does Farrakh, who reaches for Fatima's wrist. I watch as he puts his fingertips on her pulse point.

"Hey, my little princess." Cerelli turns so Zanna is looking at me. "Would you go to Annie? She wants to tell you a story."

Oh, God, Cerelli. You had to promise her a story? But Zanna twines her arms around my neck and pillows her head on my shoulder. Pushing myself to my feet, I make my way around the hanging sheets to the other side of the room, Bahar following close behind.

For the life of me, I can't think of a story to entertain Zanna.

But from the way she's pressing her body against mine, her wet cheek to mine, I'm guessing she may not be interested in anything except being held. She knows something bad is about to happen, and she's clinging to me to make sure I stay put.

All I can do is hold her. Just as my Grammy held me after my mother died so many years ago. My mother. Shot. Killed. When I was three years old—just a little younger than Zanna. At least I wasn't with her when it happened. And honestly, I don't remember anything about her. What she looked like, smelled like. The sound of her voice. Did she hold me like this?

Probably not. She wasn't exactly the most hands-on mother. From what I understand, she was far too busy with the rebel movement in southern Mexico, and I was raised with other kids in a crèche of sorts.

Nor do I remember anything about Grammy coming to get me and taking me home with her. I'm sure I was traumatized, at least in the beginning. Grammy said I didn't speak for months. Not a word. But she gave me space and was infinitely patient, figuring I'd start talking when I was ready. And she made sure I had lots of wonderful memories in the years that came after that.

I must've remembered my mother—and my father. At least in the beginning, after I moved to Wisconsin with Grammy. Missed them. Cried myself to sleep. But at some point, the missing as well as the remembering stopped.

By the time I entered kindergarten, I was happy and didn't give my dead mother or my absent father another thought.

But now I am.

What would it have been like growing up with my mother in that far-off place she'd embraced as her home? With a father who had too many other women in his life—women he didn't want to give up and so never married my mother? A father who apparently acknowledged my existence only under duress. When Grammy insisted he hand me over.

Sometime later, Farrakh pushes his way past the sheet and comes to join Bahar and Zanna and me. When I look my question at him, he gives one slight shake of the head, his lips pressed tightly together. Then, he leans close to me and whispers, "The end, it will be soon. She asked to be alone with him. Just the two of them."

"*Dôst daram.*" I think that's what Fatima says, but her voice is so breathy, so raspy, so quiet, it's hard to be sure.

I definitely hear the rustling of clothes and imagine that Cerelli has gathered her to his chest, maybe wrapping the thin blanket around the two of them, holding her close while she passes.

I don't really wonder what he says to her. As I well know from years ago when I told Private Murphy, "Yeah, we could've," as he lay dying, there are times when you say what needs to be said. What a dying person needs to hear.

Especially in a war zone.

Cerelli knows that, too.

38

CERELLI LOOKS DRAWN, ALMOST tortured, when he joins us. Even though he's told me that there's nothing between Fatima and him anymore, there obviously once was. And based on what she told me, there still is—was—on her part, at least. Damn, he must be hurting. He catches my eye, then looks away. I'm not sure what I'm supposed to take from that but figure we'll talk later. When he's ready. If we can get away from Chindawul and Kabul—a seriously challenging proposition.

Bahar pushes herself to her feet, turns to me, then reaches for one of the large yellow jerry cans of water. "We should wash her, I think?"

"No." Cerelli's voice is firm. "We don't have time."

"But we cannot leave her here. Not like this." Bahar sounds equally determined.

"We won't. I've made arrangements."

Bahar offers one curt nod. She and I both know time is running short. We also know Fatima wouldn't want us to sacrifice our lives—or Zanna's—to prepare her body for burial.

"Farrakh and I will take care of Fatima. We'll carry her body down. You two will take Zanna a different way." Cerelli goes on to explain in excruciating detail to Bahar and me the route we'll follow to get to the pickup point. "Go to the second water pump—the one that's broken. There will be a vehicle waiting. Likely a Humvee. Dark gray. Either Ajmal or Sawyer will be there."

"Sawyer?" I'm confused. "But I thought he was in Germany with—"

"Don't worry about Mel. She's doing well, and Todd's with her. I need Sawyer here. If you see someone else, anyone else, even talking to him or Ajmal, it's a trap. Keep right on walking and get to the safe house that's nearby."

I'm trying to stay calm and in control, but I can't help that my eyes widen alarmingly. "Another safe house?" My voice bears an uncanny resemblance to a mouse squeaking.

Cerelli puts his hands on my shoulders. Warm, heavy, comforting. "You can do this. I know you can, or I'd never let you go. This is the safest way for you three."

Somewhere between those words, I'm picking up on what he's not saying: *I'm the diversion. The Taliban are going to follow me. I want you to get away.*

It's not going to help anyone if I protest. If I tell him that I'm scared shitless. That I need him with me. Not just tonight, but forever. So, I swallow my fear and my need. "Okay. The safe house. Where is it? How will I know?"

He smooths my hair away from my face, his right index finger lingering on the tattoo just inside my hairline. "When you're at that second water pump, turn north—toward the mountain, then climb up the first path to the blue door with a crescent moon painted on it."

I smile. "Pretty obvious, don't you think?"

"Just to the people who need to know."

"That would be you and me?"

"That would be correct."

"So, what about you and Farrakh? Will you be meeting us at the pickup point?"

He takes a deep breath. "Better you don't know."

In case Bahar and I get stopped by the Taliban. I nod. "Two fewer people to get rounded up."

"Affirmative."

"Can you tell me your route?"

"No."

"But what if we need to backtrack to find you?"

"That's a negative. No backtracking."

Interesting that Cerelli has reverted to Navy speak. I'm guessing it helps him to think that what we're about to do is a military op. He's got to compartmentalize everything and everyone. Emotions and feelings cannot come into play. Still, if I know Cerelli, he's not at all happy about sending Bahar and Zanna and me off to very possibly land in the clutches of the Taliban. I'm not exactly happy about it either. But there's no alternative. If we head out as a group, we'll draw a lot more attention than if two women and a child go out. And then later, two men—carrying the body of a dead woman.

Damn it, Cerelli, you better make it.

A FEW MINUTES LATER, Bahar and Zanna and I are ready to go. We make our way through the opening into the front room. Cerelli brings up the rear. Before I can drape the *burqa* over my head, he takes me aside.

"Keep the Sig in your waistband."

"Got it."

"Extra ammo in your pocket."

"Yup."

"If you have to draw, get the safety the fuck off, point, and shoot. And I mean shoot to kill. No matter who it is."

"But what if it's—"

He pulls me close and presses his forehead to mine. "No matter who."

"Okay. No matter who." But I sure as hell know that if it's Cerelli in front of me, there's no way I'll pull that trigger. No matter what.

"You've got the MK 3?"

"In my boot."

"You still remember what I told you back in '15 about gutting pigs?"

"Yeah, I remember." I also remember the horror of waiting in that cave in the Hindu Kush Mountains when Cerelli and Sawyer and Massoud's men fought a battle akin to Armageddon with the Taliban. And now that my mind has gone there, I'm there, too. The darkness of the cave, the angry voices searching for me as I hide in the cubby at the very back of the cave. It's all starting to crash down on me. I'm fighting it as best I can, but there's no time to lower my head and let the wave pass over me. Cerelli needs me here, and he needs me now—in this moment.

"Annie! Look at me!"

I look at him. In his eyes. That are filled with worry. He wraps his arms around me, holding me in place, tethering me to reality.

"Sweetheart? Can you do this?"

I look away from him to Bahar already wearing a *burqa* and

Zanna waiting just inside the front door. They're depending on me. This little girl needs a mother. She needs me. I've also got a daughter in a hospital in Germany who will need me big-time in the weeks and months to come.

Turning back to Cerelli, I offer one clipped nod. "Yes." Then, leaning forward, I press my lips to his. Not in the least a military leave-taking, but it's the best I can do.

He hands me my pack, nearly empty with just one camera and the sat phone. "You should carry this. If you get stopped, you'll be able to make a better case that you're in Chindawul to take pictures of the refugees."

"Good point. But as it happens, I don't have any pics."

He presses an SD card into my hand. "Now, you do." Then, lifting Fatima's neck pouch over my head and leaving my own in place, he adds, "I'll take care of this. It's the last thing I want them finding on you."

"Another good point. I'll be fine." I kiss him again.

Burqa in place, my pack shouldered, I pick up Zanna, who immediately wraps her arms around my neck, legs around my waist. The best way for us to move quickly and the most likely scenario for people to see me as just one of the many mothers living in Chindawul.

And we leave. Bahar and Zanna and me. Out the front door that closes softly behind us and into the very narrow alley. A darkness so heavy, it weighs me down. The smell of stale cooking. And urine—so acidic, my eyes water. I take a step and hear the squish of my boot in the mud. Of course, there aren't any toilets inside the shacks this high up the slope. So, late at night, men just relieve themselves outside.

Thank God I've got my lug-soled boots on.

A short time later, I'm cursing myself for wearing my boots. A dead giveaway if we're stopped. No Afghan woman would be wearing U.S. military-issue boots. Shit! If I'd thought of sandals earlier, maybe someone could've found me a pair. Or maybe Fatima's would've fit me. Cerelli's going to kill me when he finds out. That is, if we both make it to the pickup point.

There's nothing for it but to continue. I hurry forward and manage to catch up to Bahar, but with my peripheral vision completely cut off, it's impossible to know how much space I've got on either side of me. A sudden, quiet whimper tells me that I've scraped Zanna's leg against the wall. Kissing her cheek through the cloth, I whisper for her to get down—just for a few minutes—until we get to the end of this alley.

Then, she's back in my arms. Clearly she figures that a promise is a promise. For a moment, I wonder about the promises Fatima made to her daughter—promises that will never be kept. Is that where this little girl's thoughts are? Back with her mother's body in the safe house? Or is she able to stay in the moment? Something Cerelli is counting on me to do, but a talent that keeps eluding me.

Bahar has a much better sense of the alleyways than I do, so I follow her lead along the maze-like path Cerelli has laid out for us. Somehow, she knows to turn right at the second alley and then an immediate left. And on from there until I realize that we're basically heading downhill in a slow, meandering path. Maybe the exact turnings aren't all that important. We just need to get ourselves down in a westerly direction, and preferably without running into any Taliban. Or anyone who thinks two women and a little girl out and about in the early-morning darkness are suspicious enough to report to the Taliban.

Bahar is walking as silently as possible. I'm trying, but with a pack over my shoulder, my American footfalls, and a squirming four-year-old, I'm creating far too much noise. *Please let this be normal*, I beg to the universe. *Please let no one else notice anything Western about me.*

So far, we've passed very few people. A couple men here and there, climbing back up to houses somewhere on the mountain slope. Two women walking together, holding onto each other to keep from slipping in the muck. No Taliban guards, as far as I can tell. Although several times, I've sensed someone standing back in the shadows, watching us pass. At least they haven't stopped us.

In spite of my best efforts, I'm not staying in the moment. My thoughts wander back to Fatima—lying dead in the safe house. Then to Cerelli. The two of them together. Years ago. Last night.

Stop it!

He must have loved her once. And he's got to be hurting like hell right now.

He needs me to understand. And I do understand. Whatever I can do for him, I will.

I've lost all track of time, but now the sky is lightening to a dull, slate gray. Dawn will be coming soon. And with that, the first *salah* of the day: *Fajr*. Which will mean more people charging through the alleys. That is, men will be running to the mosque for morning prayers. And the Taliban will be looking for anyone who isn't yet heading to the nearest *masjid*. I seriously do not want to run into any Taliban in these narrow alleys. It'd be way too easy for them to box us in.

Bahar has us climbing back up the slope now. And exactly what I dreaded hearing is now echoing through the alleys. The *mu'adhdhin* has begun his call, his singsong voice mesmerizing as always, a sound I usually welcome. Except today.

"*Salah!*" says Zanna. "Papa must go to pray."

Which, of course, would be very true if her father were still alive. My heart clenches as I realize that she doesn't know her papa is dead. Something Cerelli and I will have to tell her.

"*Balê,*" I whisper into her ear. Part of me wants to smile that she's said something. But the last thing we need right now is for her to start talking. God only knows what she'll say. 'My mother died in a house near here.' Or even worse, 'Bad men came to the restaurant and shot my mama.' Or maybe she doesn't know her mother has died. Maybe she thinks *Kaka* Feen is going to carry her mother to the car. At least while she's been too traumatized to say more than 'Kaka Feen,' I didn't need to worry about what might slip out of her mouth.

Bahar keeps walking—a steady pace. No faster. No slower. Never turning around. Not shushing Zanna. Doing nothing to draw any attention to us.

Then again, maybe it's odd that we're so quiet. A four-year-old would be talking, asking endless questions, maybe even whining, wouldn't she?

It's while I'm debating this thought that I hear the faintest sound. Damn, I know that sound. A safety being slipped off. And just that suddenly, the hair on the back of my neck is standing on end. Rigid. Painful.

Looking up ahead, over Bahar's shoulder, I see them.

Two men, perhaps ten yards ahead of us, stepping into our path, automatic weapons slung across their shoulders, muzzles in hand.

Taliban? Or, with any luck, men who live in Chindawul, keeping guard against the Taliban?

I allow myself one deep breath to push out my fear and calm my nerves.

A quick assessment: Sig in my waistband, loaded and ready to fire as soon as I take off the safety. After first getting Zanna out of the line of fire. MK 3 in my boot. If it comes to that, I need to plunge it into the pig just below the bottom of the rib cage as hard and as fast as I can, straight up to the heart. After I scream at Zanna to run as fast as she can, because when I pull the knife, the very next thing that'll happen is the second guard will spray me with gunfire.

In front of me, Bahar continues on her way, leading us right toward the men. Their scraggly beards now in full view, they're looking more and more like Taliban. With each step, we pull closer. It's not like we've got a choice. Retreating back the way we came would be a clear signal that we're trying to avoid them. Suspicions heightened, they'd be after us in a flash to know why. Or, more likely, they'd just shoot. Women and girls aren't exactly high-value items in the world of these militants.

Then the unexpected happens. Bahar slows and turns. "*Anaa!*" she calls to me in Dari, loud enough, I'm sure, for the men to hear. "You must be tired. Here, let me carry her!" And plucking Zanna from my arms, she whispers in my eyepiece, "Your *burqa*, it is bunched up from carrying her. They will see your boots." She's close enough that I can see the other message in her eyes. *Have your gun ready!* Smoothing out my *burqa* so it covers as much of my boots as possible, I surreptitiously snake my hand to my waistband and grab hold of the Sig. Safety off.

All accomplished in a few seconds. A young woman dutifully relieving her mother of having to carry the granddaughter. At least I hope that's how these men see it.

For once, Zanna lets Bahar carry her without complaining, without wriggling out of her arms, without reaching back to me. Thank God she's quiet. And I'm forcing myself mightily to stay in the moment. Hand wrapped tightly around the grip of the gun, wishing to hell I'd taken Cerelli up on his offer back in July to practice at the shooting range, I put one foot in front of the other.

Closer and closer to the two gun-wielding Taliban guards. Their beards tell me they're young—I'm guessing maybe in their twenties.

My index finger rests lightly against the trigger.

Eyes cast down.

My upper lip curling at the stench of their body odor.

Almost there.

One man steps back to let Bahar and Zanna pass by.

Another step, and then I'm shoulder to shoulder between the two men.

"*Estâd shaw!*" shouts the man on my left.

I look up to see him scowling, pointing to Zanna's legs. Her pants are pushed up nearly to her knees. Seriously? The morality police are questioning a four-year-old girl showing some leg? What kind of self-righteous perverts are they?

Bahar quickly sets Zanna on the ground, adjusts the pants over her legs, and carefully picks her up again. I'm ready to continue forward when the guard on my right taps my arm with the barrel of his gun. Fuck! Is he going to shoot me over Zanna's legs? *Run!* I want to shout to Bahar as I start to raise the gun, ready to shoot. But then I see his gun pointing to the ground behind me. A little girl's shiny pink shoe with black scuff marks. And a broken buckle. Zanna's shoe.

"*Tashakor!*" I try to make my voice warm and grateful as if retrieving this shoe is the most important thing of the day. Carefully shifting the Sig to my left hand, I bend down and snatch the shoe with my right. And pray that neither man focuses on *my* footwear. Then, I'm back to walking, slow and steady, never fully straightening my legs, concentrating on being invisible. *Nothing to see here, you Taliban thugs!*

Looking up ahead, I see that Bahar and Zanna are no longer in front of me. At the next turn, there they are, tucked into an alcove on the left. Neither of us says a word. Zanna reaches her arms toward me, and as soon as she's back perched on my hip, we resume plodding on, downhill now in a more direct westerly route. I'm pretty sure we both want to get the hell out of Dodge.

39

THE SUN IS RISING OVER the horizon by the time we reach the pickup point. That is, where Bahar and I think we're supposed to meet up with Ajmal. Or maybe Sawyer. After wandering the maze of alleys crisscrossing the mountain slope and taking a few more detours after we ran into those two Taliban, I'm completely turned around. Worse than that: I'm lost. And with Zanna back in my arms, I'm dead tired. Please let Bahar know where we are.

"Annie." She grabs hold of my arm through the *burqa*. "They should be here. This is where we are supposed to meet them. I am certain. You see, there is the pump."

I don't see a vehicle. But I do see girls who are doing their best to keep their *burqas* dry as they pump water into their plastic jerry cans. When they're full, each of those containers must weigh twenty pounds—at least. Wooden yokes are lying on the ground at their feet, ready to rest on shoulders as they lug water back up the slopes of Chindawul. Looking past them, I see men gathered in the shadows of houses on the far side of the pump. Some dressed in camo fatigues, others in *shalwar kameezes* and turbans, all of them Taliban—I have no doubt. They're not making a move to help the girls, even when they're struggling. Instead, they're keeping a close eye on them, making sure no *burqas* ride up too high and reveal an ankle or a calf.

And now a few of the men are watching us. Of course they are. We stand out. Why on earth would two women and a little girl be at the pump without jerry cans to fill? We should've thought to bring some. Not good.

One of the men steps out of the shadow and starts in our direction.

We need to get out of here, and fast.

Without speaking, Bahar comes to the same conclusion. But she doesn't hurry. The woman's got nerves of steel. She continues walking forward, past the pump.

I hear the footfalls behind me but dare not look around.

We also best not follow Cerelli's direction to take the first alley on the right. The last thing we should do is lead this guy to the safe house.

Bahar keeps walking straight. The second alley. The third. But she doesn't turn uphill.

He's still behind me, his footsteps louder—as though he's closing in on us.

Praying my *burqa* isn't riding up, I hug Zanna closer to me. *Don't say a word, little one! Not a single word! Please, nothing that would make the man even more suspicious.*

Finally, Bahar does turn. But not to the right, not uphill. To the left.

I hope she knows what she's doing. We absolutely cannot go to the house with the blue door and the crescent moon.

We continue down the narrow alley, our pace steady. Still the footfalls crunch behind us.

Now, finally, I feel the cold chill creeping up my spine. A sure sign that whoever's behind me is most definitely a bad guy. He's been following us for a good ten minutes. Too long. No Taliban would do this. Unless he has a really good reason. As in, he knows who we are. But how could he possibly recognize us with our *burqas* on? He couldn't. So how . . .

Zanna isn't wearing a *burqa*.

And her chin is propped on my shoulder. All the better to see the man who's walking behind us—and for him to see her. Such a beautiful child, she looks exactly like her mother. My heart sinks. The fucking Taliban behind me is still following us because he recognizes Zanna. He probably saw her at *Khosha*. There was a dining room full of Taliban the first time I went with Ajmal to pick up our food. And Zanna was most likely flitting in and out of the room with her mother.

Or maybe someone saw her the night they killed Sami.

The night they shot Fatima.

Maybe—

"Ms. Hawkins?"

Oh, fuck! I know that Cambridge accent.

Zanna stiffens in my arms. Clearly, she knows that voice, too. "The man who came to the restaurant," she whispers in Dari through the netted eyepiece.

Dari. English. It doesn't matter. This man speaks both. Fluently.

"Sweetie." I breathe the words to Zanna. "Can you run fast?"

"*Balê*," she breathes back.

"I'm going to put you down, and I want you to run as fast as you can. Tell Bahar to follow you."

For a moment, she looks like she's going to do what I say. But then she tightens her hold around my neck. "*Ne!*" She's not whispering anymore. She knows as well as I do what the Cambridge bomber is about to do. First, her parents. Now, me. And she's terrified.

Yeah, well, I'm scared, too. I'm about to die in a back alley in the slums of Kabul. A very scary prospect. But I have to get this little girl onto the ground and running to safety. Otherwise I won't be able to fight. Which means I won't stand a chance of coming out of this alive.

"Annie Hawkins." His voice is sharper now, bordering on angry. He's losing patience.

I ignore him and keep walking forward. "I'll be all right, sweetie." My voice is thick and sad, the words nearly choking me. "Please? You will run?"

She pushes back so she can look through the netting to my eyes. What I see nearly breaks my heart. This little girl shouldn't have to go through any of this. Then again, no one should. Putting her lips to the cloth below the netting, she waits for me to pucker mine, and we kiss through the *burqa*. *Please don't let this be the only kiss we share.*

Then, when we're in front of a door—blue, as it happens, with a crescent moon—I say, "Now!" And with that she kicks off and lands on her feet. A quick turn, then she's running her heart out. God, I hope her shoes stay on.

I don't see her grab Bahar's hand, but I hear a second pair of feet begin to run. Behind me, the Cambridge Bomber has stopped walking.

Spinning around, I pull the Sig from my waistband and drop into a crouch. The gun is still well hidden beneath my *burqa*. Safety off. I'm ready.

Except, I'm about to shoot this man. Without a silencer. Everyone living on this alley and the next alley, back to the Taliban gathered at the pump, will hear the shot. They'll all come running. There's no way I'll get away.

Maybe it's enough that Bahar and Zanna will live.

The Cambridge Bomber has his gun out of the holster and trained on me. No bulky *burqa* to interfere with his shot. Then, sensing my hesitation, he smiles and continues walking toward me.

Slowly.

Step by step.

Closer and closer.

Even walking slowly, the man makes a lot of noise. Too much noise.

But enough noise that he's covering the nearly silent approach of another woman coming up behind him. With my eyes locked on the Taliban militant who's intent on killing me, the movement is nothing more than a blur. Just a vague impression of a periwinkle *burqa*.

A few more steps, and the Cambridge Bomber's now close enough that he can't possibly miss me—even though I'm scrunched as small as I can be.

I've got to regain the element of surprise. Anything to take him unaware, to change up the balance of power.

I do the only thing that comes to mind: I stand up—abruptly. Probably not the smartest thing I've ever done, making myself a much larger target. But I've also switched the Sig to my left hand and slipped the knife out of my boot in my right. If I can just get him close enough, I'll gut him. Silently.

Find the bottom of the rib cage, stick in the knife as fast and as hard as you can, then straight up to the heart. Think of the tangos as pigs.

Don't humanize them. It helps. Cerelli's voice reaches me from 2015.
It probably would've helped to at least practice finding the bottom
of the rib cage.

The Cambridge Bomber's smile grows broader, but there's no
joy in it. "You're a beautiful woman. This is going to be such a waste."

Perfect, polished British accent. Cambridge all the way. But
something's slightly off with his voice. Or his accent. Or something.

One last step.

He raises his gun and sights me—right between the eyes.

And he's still a few steps too far away for me to gut him with
the knife.

So, I do the only thing I can: drop the knife and raise the Sig,
two-handing it, aiming for body mass, and praying that the woman
in the *burqa* stays where she is. I'm a pretty good shot, but even so,
if I miss this asshole, I could hit her.

Behind the Cambridge Bomber, the woman in the *burqa*
launches into action. I can't possibly shoot. My right index finger
absolutely refuses to press the trigger.

One second. That's all it takes.

Muscled arms come around from the back, immobilizing the
Cambridge Bomber. Powerful hands that don't have to search for
the bottom of the rib cage. They know exactly where to plunge the
knife. Who the hell is this woman?

It happens so fast. I'm not really sure what I'm seeing.

Around me, everything is completely silent except for one
almost inaudible grunt.

The only thing I'm certain of: the Cambridge Bomber is
crumpled on the ground in the alley, bleeding out. Dead.

I stand frozen in place, unable to move, unable even to close
my eyes.

Then the periwinkle *burqa* is dashing past him, toward me, scooping the MK 3 off the ground. "Annie." Cerelli's voice. "I need you to run. Now." He turns me around and hurries us out of the alley, out of the maze, and to the rusting white pickup that's waiting just past another water pump—this one broken, so no girls are waiting to fill their jerry cans. And no Taliban are watching to see who shows up.

I take a second look. This is the pump we were supposed to go to. Something tells me that Bahar got us pretty lost—an unintended mistake that could've cost Cerelli and me our lives.

Whipping off his *burqa*, Cerelli hands it to me along with my knife. "Wear mine. Yours has some blood on it. From the spray."

The switch complete and the knife sheathed back in my boot, we climb into the truck.

No matter that the temperature is climbing into the nineties, I'm cold. So cold. Numbingly cold. I can't feel any of my body parts.

Cerelli keys the ignition. His hands firmly on the steering wheel, he drives us out of Chindawul and away. "Needless to say, this isn't going to go down well with the Taliban leadership. Let's hope we can get the hell out of Dodge without getting caught."

Shivering, I stare at his hands. Powerful, yes. Able to break an arm in two. Even so, I've always felt so safe. But I've never seen him actually kill someone with those hands. Until now.

Stay in the moment! But no matter how hard I cling to the armrest on the door, I feel myself slipping. Out of the moment. Through the gaping glove compartment in the dashboard. Into the past. To Khakwali.

I'm Commander Finn Cerelli, U.S. Navy SEAL, and I'm going to get you out of here. Are you with me?

I nod.

Let's get the hell out of Dodge without getting caught.

Oh, God! Malalai's dead. Murphy. Lopez. All of them dead. Because we came back to Khakwali. So I could have another chance to photograph her.

Why didn't I stay away?

A hand snakes behind my neck and pushes my head down. Between my *burqa*-draped knees.

I push back, scrabbling, bucking. But no matter how hard I try, I can't sit up. The hand is too powerful. It won't let me up.

"Head down until the wave passes." Cerelli's voice. Bringing me back. To the here. And the now.

40

"YOU BACK WITH ME?" Cerelli at his kindest, gentlest, and probably most worried.

I take several deep breaths. "I think so, but . . . oh my God! Stop!"

He slams his foot on the brake.

"We can't leave. What about Bahar? Zanna? Where are they?"

Back to driving, Cerelli allows me one quick sideways glance. "No worries. They're with Sawyer and Ajmal."

"Farrakh?"

His eyes are back on the city road in front of us. "He's with them, too. We'll catch up. Never fear."

Heaving a sigh of relief, I sink back against the seat. That's all I need to know. Everyone's safe—for now. My other questions can wait until later. This op is far from over, and Cerelli needs his full powers of concentration. No distractions.

WE DRIVE FOR A LONG time without speaking. Finally, when Cerelli gets us out of the city and past the last Taliban checkpoint, he's ready to talk. "You sure you're back with me?"

I flex my fingers. No longer numb. And I'm not freezing anymore. In fact, underneath my *burqa*, I'm feeling every degree of the ninety-plus radiating down from the midmorning sun. Turning so I can see a cross-hatched version of the man, I nod. "Yeah. I'm good."

His fingers tighten on the steering wheel until the knuckles are nearly white.

"What?" My turn to be gentle.

He takes another minute. "I'm sorry you had to see that back there."

"You mean . . ."

"Yeah. It's not something I wanted you to witness."

"Remember, I'm a war photographer. It wasn't the first death I've seen. Although . . ." I start to tremble. Finally, I stretch out my hand, letting it come to rest on his thigh. *My tether.*

His hands still gripping the wheel, he waits me out.

"It's the first time I've seen you . . ."

". . . kill someone," he finishes for me.

I let out my breath. "Yeah."

"I'm sorry. But it was either him or you." He pauses. "Would it help to talk about what you saw?"

"That's just it. I didn't see much at all. And what I saw was a blur. Your arms. The knife. Him on the ground. God! I don't know why I'm reacting this way. The Cambridge Bomber was evil personified. He—"

Cerelli's hand is on top of mine. "That wasn't the Cambridge Bomber."

"Of course it was! I've seen him—up close and personal. Plus, I heard him. That voice. The man tried to kill me not once, but twice. I *know* who that was."

"I know him, too. I also know his brother, who could almost be his twin."

"His brother?"

"They're nearly identical. As far as I can tell, the only difference is the scar through the eyebrow." Cerelli lifts his hand from mine and draws his index finger through his own eyebrow. "And his English isn't quite as refined."

So that's why his voice sounded off. I close my eyes and think back to the man's face. Maybe? But I honestly can't remember. "That's pretty devious—the two of them being so similar."

"Believe me, it's helped them out of some tight spots."

"You going to elaborate?"

"Maybe later. Let's finish with the brother. I want you feeling better."

I keep my hand on his thigh—the warmth helps. "I'm sorry. I know this doesn't make sense. I mean, hell, *I* killed Ghazan six years ago."

"To save my life."

"Exactly. And I'd do it again in a heartbeat."

He puts his hand on top of mine again. The weight of it feels good. "Sometimes it's harder to watch someone else kill than to do it yourself. But I wasn't going to take you home in a body bag."

I lean over and kiss him through the cloth of my *burqa*. Not exactly romantic, but given the circumstances, it's the best I can do. "Thanks for choosing me."

"Better now?"

"Totally."

"Wonderful. Then would you mind telling me why you

suddenly stood up back there? Making yourself into a bigger target isn't part of the training."

"Maybe not your training," I mumble.

He grins. "What was that?"

"I was going for the element of surprise."

He laughs. "Well, you definitely accomplished that. Surprised the shit out of me. Probably out of him, too. Bought yourself—and me—a couple seconds. You going to tell me why?"

"Come on, Cerelli. There were Taliban all over the place. I couldn't risk shooting. They'd have been on top of me in seconds. I needed a way to take him out quietly."

"So, what were you planning to do?"

"Gut him."

He pauses for a long moment. "Smart thinking. Except a few seconds later, you dropped the knife and pointed the gun."

"I wasn't quite close enough. He was still a couple feet too far away. There's no way I could've gotten close enough without him shooting me."

"Then, Taliban notwithstanding, why the hell didn't you take the shot?"

"Seriously?" I gape.

"Seriously. Why didn't you shoot?"

I swallow hard. "I think it was pretty obvious! You got in the way. Only I didn't know it was you, of course. But still, I just couldn't risk killing an innocent person."

"You're saying you would've shot if you'd known it was me?"

He has to ask? I offer my most mysterious smile in return. "Maybe."

"Well, thanks for not shooting me." He raises my hand to his lips. "But next time, take the shot. Your life depended on it."

Next time? I almost say the words out loud, but stop myself. This is not the time to have that discussion. Later. There will be plenty of time later. Instead, I ask, "How?"

"What do you mean 'how'?" For once, the man sounds truly baffled.

I laugh. "I thought one of your superpowers was mind reading. Particularly reading *my* mind."

"Clearly, my skills are getting rusty. Clue me in."

"How were you just suddenly there? In the alley. I mean, I know you're a ghost and all that, but this was beyond. You just . . . appeared. Thank God."

"Sweetheart, I'd been following you since you left the safe house." Cerelli sounds just a little too smug for my taste, even though he did just save my life.

"Really?"

"Oh, yeah. I wanted to make sure you got down to the pickup point in one piece. And well . . ."

"What?"

"I don't want you out of my sight. At least until we're out of Afghanistan."

Now I'm confused. "But what about Fatima?"

"Sawyer carried her down."

"In a body bag?"

"Absolutely not. *That* would've attracted a lot of unwanted attention."

"Let's go back to you following me. How is that even possible? I never saw you. I never heard a thing. Damn, you really are a ghost."

Still holding my hand, he twines his fingers around mine. "All part of the training, ma'am."

41

ANOTHER HALF HOUR OF driving, and Cerelli slows the pickup. Up ahead I see an aging blue Corolla pulled to the side of the road. Two women in black *burqas* are standing on the verge.

"Do they need help?" I turn to Cerelli, not sure that I want him to stop, although that's exactly what he's doing.

"We've caught up. They picked a good spot. Far from the prying eyes of the Taliban."

I watch as Ajmal climbs out of the driver's seat, Sawyer from the front passenger seat. Then a third man, heavily bearded and wearing a *shalwar kameez*. But two women in *burqas?* "Who are those women?"

Cerelli doesn't even look. "Bahar, of course. And Farrakh. He drew the short straw." Then, with a pointed glance at me, he adds, "There's no way we would've had Ajmal wear the *burqa*. Not after what he's been through."

"And the bearded guy?"

"You don't remember Fightmaster? At Bagram in 2015?"

I dig deep and conjure up the twenty-something farm boy from Kansas with a sprinkling of freckles over his nose and cheeks. "Lieutenant Fightmaster?"

"Actually, he's Lieutenant Commander Fightmaster now."

"Why's he here?"

"Thought we might need the firepower."

God help me. Of course, we'll need all the help we can muster. There's a long way to go and probably more encounters with the Taliban before we get out of Afghanistan. This clusterfuck is getting worse by the minute.

As soon as Cerelli stops the car, Zanna peeks out from behind one of the black *burqas* and starts running—even before I can get myself out the door. Once I kneel down, she launches into my arms, hugging me for all she's worth. "Mama!"

God, no! She thinks Fatima is still alive. I can't begin to imagine the psychological ramifications once she realizes her mother really and truly won't be coming for her. For now, though, I do the only thing I can: gather her in my arms and hold her tight, planting *burqa*-filtered kisses on her cheeks.

She peers through the netting, her eyes meeting mine. I feel her body stiffen, then tremble. "Mama?" She doesn't scream. She just buries her head against my shoulder and cries.

And Cerelli does the best thing he possibly could: gathers us both in his arms. "My two girls," he says in Dari.

"*Kaka* Feen!" Her sobs subside—oh so slowly. For now.

I'M NOT SO SURE I would've recognized Lieutenant Commander Fightmaster. Looking closely, I see that yeah, he's still got freckles, but the man standing in front of me looks nothing like the younger man from years ago.

"Hey, Fightmaster!" I walk over and introduce myself.

"Ms. Hawkins, ma'am." He grins. "You haven't changed at all. I'd know you anywhere. Even with that *burqa*."

I laugh at the thought of him recognizing me under this tent of periwinkle cloth. "Well, you've changed a lot. It's a good thing Cerelli told me you're along for the ride. Otherwise I probably would've shot you."

The grin slides off his face as his eyes widen. "Oh, well . . ."

Sawyer claps him on the back. "You were lucky! Oakley's a helluva good shot. Only missed once, and that was in target practice."

Cerelli ambles over. "They're kidding, Fightmaster."

Except I'm not. I was so on edge by the time we got to the vehicle, I probably would've shot Cerelli if he hadn't said something.

"I CANNOT GO TO Wad Qol!" Bahar protests when she hears Cerelli's plan. "That is exactly where the Taliban will expect me to go. It is the first place they will look for me!"

That confounded twitch is back at the corner of Cerelli's eye. He's not used to people questioning him. Well, except for me, of course.

As it happens, I agree with Bahar. Wad Qol does seem the likeliest place for the Taliban to search for her. "Why don't we just go to the U.S. Embassy?" I try to keep my tone moderated, like I'm making a helpful suggestion, but I can't miss the scowl crossing Cerelli's face.

"Yes! The embassy." Bahar moves closer to me—*shohna ba shohna*, shoulder to shoulder—solidarity and strength. "That would be a very good idea."

"Not an option." Cerelli's voice is even quieter and more moderated than mine.

"Why not?" I ask. "It makes all the sense in the world. We go to the embassy. And they can certainly get us on a plane out. I mean after all—" The muscle next to Cerelli's eye is threatening a full-out spasm.

After a few moments of awkward silence, I switch gears. "Okay. We've got to get out of Afghanistan. And going up the Panjshir Valley seems to be the best . . ." I stop talking. All I'm doing is babbling. And further irritating Cerelli.

Sawyer draws our attention back to the rough map he's drawn in the dirt at our feet. "Once we get past the Dalan Sang checkpoint, we'll be fine. Massoud's men are in control of the valley beyond that point."

"And how are we to get past this checkpoint?" Even though she's wearing a *burqa*, I can tell that Bahar's body is stiff, unbending. "No! It is far better that we go west. To Iran."

Cerelli doesn't say a word.

Is it Iran that's the problem? Of course it is. A U.S. admiral crossing the border into the Islamic Republic of Iran? Instant hostage situation. A full-blown diplomatic fiasco between Tehran and Washington. That is, if they even take him to Tehran. More than likely, they'd execute him on the spot as a spy. The Iranians do like to accuse people of spying. Journalists. Professors. Researchers. Why not a U.S. admiral? Sawyer, too. And me.

"A lot more checkpoints in that direction. Here. Here. And here. And that's just to start." Sawyer avoids the argument by pointing out the problems even getting to the border with Iran. "From the Panjshir Valley, we've got a lot more options. Up to Tajikistan. Over to Pakistan. We stay a day or two at Wad Qol, and we can finalize the logistics."

Farrakh steps forward, kneeling at the edge of the map. "What if we go north on the Ring Road? We could go past Balkh to Shibirghan, and then into Turkmenistan. We could even take the trunk road at Balkh and go right across the border."

Cerelli shakes his head. "Balkh is a Taliban stronghold. It'd be suicide to go anywhere near there."

"Well, it will be as good as suicide to go to Wad Qol!" Steam seems to be rising from the netted eyepiece in Bahar's *burqa*. "I think perhaps it would be best for me to return to Kabul. I will go back to the safe house. From there, I will go on my own to Iran."

"Bahar?" I lean closer to her. "Why Iran? The way they treat women there is horrific. A woman was just arrested by the morality police for wearing her headscarf wrong. They killed her while she was in jail and told her family she'd had a heart attack. You must know that."

She turns her back to the men and lowers her voice so that I can barely hear her. "Yes, I heard about that. And you are right. Maybe it is better that I stay in Afghanistan and continue my work. The women here are depending on me."

My reaction is immediate. And, as all too often happens, the whispered words are out of my mouth before I think. "But they're not depending on you to die for them, Bahar! You don't need to be a martyr. It's more important for you to get out and come back when it's safer."

"Annie!" She takes a step back, as though I've slapped her. And I guess my words have done exactly that. A frontal assault.

But I'm not done. "Bahar, please, listen to me. Cerelli and Sawyer have the latest intelligence. If they say Massoud is in control of Wad Qol, then he is. You've got to trust them. I do. With my life. And with Zanna's. You know, it's not just you the Taliban are after. They want me, too. They want all of us. Even Farrakh." I stop short. She doesn't need the specifics on why the Taliban would be happy to behead each and every one of us.

She looks up at me, eyepiece to eyepiece. Such intelligence in her eyes. She's weighing my words very carefully. "You are right. Of course. I apologize for thinking only of myself. We will go together to Wad Qol. All of us." Turning around to face the men, Bahar repeats her apology. Then, she turns on her heel and heads toward the vehicles.

Baffled, Sawyer and Cerelli, Ajmal and Fightmaster look to me for an explanation, which isn't forthcoming.

"My sister," says Farrakh, his voice muffled by the *burqa*, "she is exactly like our mother." I take that to mean headstrong and enigmatic. Which I happen to think are good qualities in a woman.

THE MEN DECIDE TO continue with both the car and the pickup for as long as the fuel holds out. Zanna and I are to ride in the pickup with Cerelli. The rest will go in the Corolla with Sawyer at the wheel. We give them a few minutes head start while we tend to a whining Zanna who's finally hungry. It's been a long time since I've had to deal with a little girl. Sulking one minute, laughing the next. Still, all things considered, she's been amazing so far. Losing her mother, her father, and up till now, no complaints. Absolutely incredible.

Cerelli seems better prepared than me. He pulls a chocolate bar out of his pocket. Not quite melting in the heat, but softer than it should be. Zanna makes a grab for it.

I, on the other hand, am stepping into my role as surrogate mother. "Not the best thing for her."

He laughs as he steers the pickup off the verge and onto the road. "Always a mother, aren't you. Check behind your seat. There should be some bottles of water. Maybe some *bolani*."

That's exactly what I find. Several *nân* stuffed with *gandana* filling and others with *morgh kofta*. "Zanna. First some *bolani*. The chocolate is for dessert."

Her eyes turn thunderous, and she launches into a full-out sulk. But when I rip one of the sandwiches in half and show her the ground chicken, she actually smiles. Could Cerelli have hit on one of her favorites? She trades me her candy for the bread and munches ravenously.

I search out Cerelli's eyes. "My hero!" He grins back, and that's when I realize that this wasn't coincidental. Of course he knows what Zanna likes to eat. He's met her before. Probably many times.

As soon as she finishes her sandwich, Zanna turns begging eyes to the chocolate. Unwrapped, it disappears in a second, although a good portion of it is now smeared across her face. Using some bottled water, I clean her up as best as I can. She then curls against my chest and falls fast asleep.

Cerelli takes full advantage. "What did you say to Bahar back there to get her to back down?"

"Basically to stop being so selfish and thinking only of herself."

"You said a lot more than that."

"I embellished on the theme."

"Brilliantly."

"Why thank you, sir. I appreciate that, especially since there was a moment back there when it seemed like you were ready to go for my jugular."

It takes him a few seconds to remember. "Ah, the embassy?"

"Precisely. Why can't we go to the U.S. Embassy? They've still got a few people there shredding documents and whatever else they have to do to close down operations, don't they?"

He shrugs. "Probably. But I honestly don't know."

That stops me. How could he not know? He's a frigging admiral. He's got to be in touch with the military personnel, who are holed up either at the airport or the embassy. Unless, he's not. And why would that be?

"I'm not here with the Navy."

"A spec op?"

"Not exactly."

"A black op?"

He laughs and glances over at me. "Sweetheart, this op is so black, it's not on anyone's radar. I'm here for one reason."

"Me."

"You."

"Thank you." He's always, always there for me. "But when did you come?"

"I was already on high alert based on what you told me about your second meeting with Siraj and the Cambridge Bomber. By the time I talked with Ajmal, I was on the plane. Nic's call caught me in Pakistan."

"Yeah, Nic called me, too. And used the code word we've had for years to tell me to stay away. But other than that, I don't have a clue what's been going on."

By the time Cerelli tells me about the Taliban's 'visit' to the

TNN apartment and their demand that Nic call me, while one of them held a gun to his head, I realize how brave he was—how brave all the guys were—not to hand me over. "Nic's okay?"

"Sadim told me that Nic finally agreed to return to Washington, although he didn't want to leave without you. In fact, from what I heard, Chris had to threaten to fire him to get him to go. Another TNN crew's come in."

"Sadim and Azizullah are okay?"

"Shaken up, but still working."

That worries me. Sadim. Aziz. Ajmal. Will they join the countless other Afghans who worked for the U.S. military and the coalition forces, the Western media and NGOs, applying for visas to get out of this country? Yet another diaspora, thanks to the Taliban who want to take Afghanistan back into the Middle Ages. I stroke Zanna's lustrous dark-brown hair and can't help but think of Fatima. And Sami. Just two of so many lives lost.

"Something else you'll want to know. Mel is exceeding doctors' expectations."

"Thank God! But wait a sec . . . how did you know? I mean, Sawyer's here."

"The Pentagon is keeping me informed."

"I guess it helps to have your almost-stepfather be an admiral."

"There are some benefits."

"Any idea when Landstuhl will let her go home?"

He shakes his head. "Not yet. But I thought we'd fly back via Germany. You up for it?"

"You have to ask?" I don't know whether to laugh or cry. This man knows exactly how to play me—in a very good way.

We drive in contented silence for a few minutes until he nods toward the sleeping Zanna. "Something else we've got to talk about."

I take a deep breath, but there's no easy way to say it. "Fatima told me you promised to be her guardian. And your name is on her birth certificate." I gently cup my hand around the back of Zanna's head.

"Her *faked* birth certificate." He doesn't sound pleased. "God, I hate to think what else she said to you."

Should I tell him about that moment near the end when she said she still loved him? And, as often happens, just thinking about it is enough to let Cerelli know there's something I should let him in on.

"Tell me. Please."

I tell him.

He exhales heavily. "Let's get this straight. I love one woman. One. You."

Which is absolutely the best thing he could say. And if I didn't have a little girl curled up in my lap, I'd let him know how much I needed to hear exactly those words. "I love you for that."

He quirks his half grin and reaches for my hand. But ends up rubbing Zanna's back instead.

We ride in peaceful silence until my thoughts start to wander— to an unexpected place. Those U.S.A. passports in the bloodstained silk pouch. "You know, there's something else that's been bothering me."

"Do I want to know?"

I think about that for all of three seconds. "Yeah. No. Maybe. I think you do."

He laughs. "Go for it."

"Why were Fatima and Sami and Zanna even here? In Kabul, I mean. Why hadn't they left? For the U.S. Or somewhere, anywhere other than Afghanistan."

He's quiet for a long moment. "I told her to leave. Sawyer told her. She insisted on staying to help shut down the operation here."

Something tells me he's not finished, so I wait, giving him the time and space to tell me the rest.

"Did you look at all the papers in that pouch?" His voice is subdued.

"I thought I did."

"I take it you didn't notice the printout for the e-tickets?"

I inhale sharply. "No!"

His hands tighten around the steering wheel. "They were scheduled to fly out tomorrow."

"SO." I STROKE ZANNA'S cheek lightly. "You going to tell me what really happened back there?"

"Meaning?"

"Why did Fatima die?"

Cerelli looks out his side window, probably deciding how much I need to know. Or how much he's willing to tell me. Or even if he wants to talk about it. Six years ago, Darya's death shook him. Big-time. But Fatima? I'm sure her death is shaking him, too. Even more than Darya's. *Just be patient*, I tell myself. Finally, he says simply, flatly, "She took a bullet."

I shake my head. "In the shoulder. It shouldn't have killed her."

"I take it Farrakh didn't say anything?"

"Not much. Other than she needed to be in a hospital."

His fingers drum a tattoo across the top of the steering wheel. "She might've stood a chance if she'd gone to the hospital. But the Taliban would've made sure she didn't."

"I'm so sorry. I know this is hard. I'm glad you were there for her."

A quick glance at me, another tattoo on the steering wheel, then he tips his head. "It's never easy to say goodbye."

"You didn't—"

"If you're asking whether I helped her along, the answer is no. I held her while she died."

"I—"

"Yeah." He reaches for my hand but gives up and squeezes my shoulder instead. Then, another sideways glance, taking in both Fatima's daughter and me. Such loving, soft eyes he has. "She seems pretty attached to you."

"You think?"

He laughs quietly. "Something for us to figure out. But if we go forward with this, take her home to be ours, I have one requirement. And it's firm. No negotiations."

"Hmm?"

"No matter how attached she is to you, she's not sharing our bed."

"Deal."

42

BY THE TIME WE REACH the mouth of the gorge where the two ridges of the Hindu Kush Mountains tower high above us, Zanna is whimpering in her sleep. Curled on my chest, she's calling for her mother. Fretful, terrified cries. I can't begin to imagine her fear when she wakes up. As the days without her parents become weeks, then months.

Cerelli glances over at us. "Isn't she sleeping a lot for a four-year-old?"

"I'm pretty sure it's not normal sleeping."

"Meaning?"

"She's hiding. Life is pretty horrible for her right now."

"You think she's all right?" What he's really asking: are we ready to take this on?

"I honestly don't know. She's been through a lot. More than any kid, any adult, should have to experience. But I'm hoping she will be. Eventually." I speak softly so as not to wake her. But his raised eyebrow tells me he heard and that he's aware of how daunting our lives could become.

Above us, green trees provide some shade from the late-morning sun. Although underneath this *burqa*, I feel like I'm melting. Not to mention that my hair is sopping wet and the back of my neck is slick with sweat. Still, all the green around us at least lets me imagine I'm a little cooler. But a moment later, I'm thinking about what terrific cover this would make for armed Taliban fighters who'd like nothing better than to take out some rebellious Afghans and the Westerners helping them to escape. The perfect place. Except I'm not feeling any of my usual signs of someone watching me.

Next to us, the Panjshir River flows, but quietly. On previous visits, the river has roared past, making any conversation practically impossible. Today, though, late summer and the height of the dry season, the water is low. All the snow on the high peaks farther up the valley has already melted.

We're well into the gorge now, and the road is narrowing. Just two lanes. The sheared-off mountain forms a barrier right at the edge of our lane heading north. I could easily reach out and touch it. Cerelli's got nerves of steel, driving this close to the rock face. Me, I'd be hugging the middle of the road. Which wouldn't have been possible on my previous trips up into the valley when traffic both ways was ridiculously heavy. But now, there aren't any vehicles on the other side of the road heading southwest toward Kabul. Which feels kind of strange.

Rounding a sharp curve in the road, we see the blue Corolla stopped just ahead of us. Cerelli slows the pickup. I'm guessing he's ready to swing the truck into a U-turn if he doesn't like what he sees. But Ajmal and Sawyer are already jogging back to us.

Another glance at the fretfully sleeping Zanna and Cerelli's out the door. They'll discuss whatever out of our hearing. Except I'd really like to know what's going on, and I can't always count on him to fill me in.

He's back in the pickup a few minutes later, closing the door with barely a click. Then he relaxes in his seat, his hand resting on the back of my neck—actually the back of my *burqa*. "We'll sit here for a while."

"Much as I like having your hands on me, I'm wondering why we're not driving."

He responds with half a grin, which almost immediately slides off his face. "Taliban up ahead at the Dalan Sang checkpoint."

"That's a ways in front of us, isn't it?"

"Lucky for us, yes."

"May I ask why we're not turning around? And . . . uh . . . going someplace else?"

He leans down and directs my attention out the windshield. "Up there. Can you see?"

"Sorry, just the rock face."

"Probably just as well."

"Damn it, Cerelli! Sometimes you're just . . . maddening." My words are a bit too loud, and Zanna wiggles on my chest.

He presses an index finger to his lips.

"So, tell me!" My words are somewhere between a whisper and a hiss.

"Sawyer picked up on some action. Massoud's men outflanked the Taliban front lines. They're circling back along the ridgelines into position to clear them out from the checkpoint. Not to mention there's a drone overhead."

"And?"

"We decided it might be best to let them take care of the problem."

"That could take quite a while."

He shrugs. "Maybe. But I doubt it. There aren't that many Taliban there, and I don't think they'll put up much of a fight. After they pick them off, we'll go through. Once we reach Bazarak, we'll be fine."

Sensing his eyes on me, I turn toward him. I was right; he's studying me closely, and there's way too much worry in those brown eyes. "What?"

"You going to be okay? With the checkpoint, I mean."

"Good question." Honestly? I don't know. It's been years since Tariq and I drove this route, only to be caught in a Taliban bombing. We'd already passed the checkpoint and were okay, but scores of other people weren't. Being a physician, Tariq went back to see who he could help. I did what I could and helped birth a baby. The younger Massoud's son, as it happened. Which also gave birth to something of a legend about me. Only about ten percent of it was true. What was most definitely true about that day: the ambush further fed my PTSD.

I've passed this way one other time since then, and I was pretty much okay. It would be really good if that's how today goes. Cerelli looks dubious. Doubly so. He's not only saddled with me; now there's Zanna. I don't want to think about how she's going to react if we get caught in the middle of a firefight.

We don't have long to wait. Maybe an hour later, Sawyer is back at Cerelli's window. "They're saying we can move on through."

"Really? So fast?" I can't help sounding surprised.

Both men look quizzically at me.

"What were you expecting?" Cerelli's being extra gentle.

"I guess an explosion. Something loud. The ground trembling."

Cerelli puts his hand on my shoulder. I've never told him all the specifics of what happened here. The pressure of his hand is telling me that maybe I should.

Even though we're keeping our voices down, it's enough to wake up Zanna. A good thing. And she's hungry again, which is also good. The child needs to eat. I rustle up another *bolani*—this one with potatoes. Sawyer slaps the top of the cab, a sudden noise that makes both Zanna and me jump. Then she's back to clinging while I try to tempt her with stuffed bread that no longer seems to interest her.

BY THE TIME WE REACH the checkpoint, it's completely empty. Massoud's men must have dragged away the Taliban bodies. Not just so we don't see them, it's also a strategic move. Any other Taliban who break through the new front line won't be able to count them. So, instead of casualties, we see . . . nothing at all.

But I can smell the lingering odor of spilled blood and shattered bone. Death. I wonder how long those smells will hover over this place until they dissipate.

Ahead of us, Sawyer picks up speed, and Cerelli stays with him. With the sharp twists and turns of this narrow road, I'd be happier going slower, but the men want to get to Wad Qol by midafternoon so they'll have a better chance to reconnoiter the area, and find us someplace safe for the night. I keep my preference to myself and try to entertain Zanna with some silly songs that worked magic long ago with Mel and Seema. Even though she probably doesn't understand a whole lot of "It's Not Easy Being Green" or "I'm a Little Teapot," Zanna is completely enchanted. Cerelli, not so much.

By the tenth time through, he grabs my hand. "No more! Don't you know something else? If not, I do."

Fearing a rendition of the U.S. Navy Hymn, I quickly launch into "Here We Go Round the Mulberry Bush." All eight verses. But it's the animal sounds of "Old MacDonald Had a Farm" that finally get Zanna giggling. I unleash very authentic moos and oinks. Even Cerelli is chuckling.

WAD QOL IS NEARLY deserted. "A lot of people moved north to Tajikistan or went into Kabul even before the Taliban started their drive into the Panjshir. Any women and children who were still here, Massoud ordered them to evacuate," Cerelli explains as he drives slowly up the main street toward Gulshan and Ikrom's house.

"Just like his father did against the Soviets." Maybe I sound a little too smug with this factoid, courtesy of Tariq when he and I drove up from Kabul all those years ago.

Cerelli parks the pickup behind the Corolla in front of the Abdulin house, which doesn't look quite as forlorn as the rest of the yellow mud-brick houses we've seen so far. That gives me pause. Has everyone left Wad Qol? There were definitely people living here who were opposed to the girls' school. Especially the boys' religion teacher. I wouldn't have put it past him to be an undercover Taliban—someone who'd stay behind and welcome the invaders.

As we climb out of the truck, a burqa-less Bahar heads to the back garden. A few minutes later, she returns, her arms full of tomatoes and peppers and eggplant and spinach. Sawyer and Fightmaster emerge from the house to give the all clear, and Farrakh appears with a bowl full of eggs, proud of his find. "It would appear my mother has left us some chickens." Leave it to Gulshan to realize the coming of the Taliban would mean famine and severe hunger.

While Ajmal moves the vehicles behind the house next door, the rest of us troop inside past the familiar blue door. My heart instantly lightens at the sight of the colorful woven Afghan rugs, the floor cushions, and the stacks and stacks of books everywhere. Following Bahar into the kitchen with Zanna at my heels, I revel in the wood-fire stove, now cleaned out and cold. The planks of wood over two piles of plastic crates are exactly as I last saw them. So many delicious meals came out of this kitchen.

I turn to Bahar. "Do you cook?"

She giggles, which sets Zanna to giggling with her. "Not really. I'll never be a good Afghan wife. Can you?"

"I can make do. Nothing like your mother, though. Any idea when they left?"

"That I can answer. My mother left us a note. Well, she left it for whoever might use the house." She flourishes a piece of paper covered in writing—in both Dari and English. Gulshan is nothing if not thorough and detail-oriented. "Late last week, they went up to Anabah. My father wanted to stay in the valley to help with the wounded. They were here in this house until they feared the Taliban were getting too close."

That stops me, and I look to Sawyer. "Are there Taliban here? In Wad Qol?"

"No worries." He grins. "Massoud's men have them retreating to the west. We'll be fine for a few days."

"Good of your parents to stay in Afghanistan to help." But I'd prefer they get out alive. Gulshan's work as the director of the Wad Qol Secondary School for Girls would have her marked as someone for the Taliban to arrest. And probably imprison. Or kill. If they find out she once worked with Darya, Gulshan would definitely get a death sentence. Likely Ikrom would, too, having worked all those years with Tariq.

"I think they will return as soon as it is safe. My parents, they are both so committed to their work, they could never leave it. Or this village. Their house." Bahar sounds confident. She also seems lighter and a lot less burdened. Much more like the Bahar I remember.

"But . . ."

Bahar puts her hand on my forearm. "What?"

"I'm just thinking of the school we built a few years ago. That is, your mother built it. I just stood around taking pictures and driving people crazy."

She smiles, but so sadly. "You are wondering what will happen to the school and to all the girls who were students there."

"Exactly."

"I think that we both know." Her eyes are blazing now. "The Taliban will close all the girls' schools. They're stalling now because they want other countries to recognize them as the leaders of this country. But soon they will announce that girls and women can no longer attend school. They will try to hide behind the *Qur'an*, but you and I, we both know that the *Qur'an* says it is important for girls as well as for boys to learn. We need women doctors and lawyers and teachers. Without them, Afghan women will not have health care or be able to learn. Islam is very clear: all people must have an education."

My eyes are blazing, too. I can feel the burn. "I think the boys' school will move into the building your mother made for the girls of this part of the valley. And the girls will stay home until they are married off."

She links her arm through mine. "We can't let that happen."

43

AFTER FIRING UP THE stove, I knock myself out making a huge pan of bubbling *shakshuka* to go with the leftover *bolani*. Tomatoes and peppers and onions simmer, then I add a dozen and a half eggs to poach. Finally the spinach. The typical Afghan breakfast. No one seems to care that we're really eating a midafternoon dinner. We're all just happy to finally have some real food. And although it seemed like a lot while I was cooking, the five men devour it almost instantaneously. They're kind enough to leave portions for Bahar and Zanna and me. Wise on their part. But I notice they're all staring at what Zanna has left on her plate.

"Someone, eat it, please!" I'm not at all sure who's quickest on the steal.

I leave the men to clean up and ask Bahar to show me her mother's supply of homemade medicines and salves. "As you well remember, I got a little beaten up the last time I was here. Your mother's medicines were a godsend."

"Oh, yes. I remember the bruises on your arm from that awful man at the Bazarak market. And my mother told me about how you fell against the stove. You injured your hands, too! Are they still bothering you?"

"I'm fine." I flex my fingers as proof. "Thanks to your mother's medicines. But my daughter, Mel, was injured in the bombing at the airport."

Bahar covers her mouth with her hands. "I didn't know. She will be all right?"

"She's had several surgeries and is doing okay. I'm thinking your mother's salves will help. Not that the doctors will agree. But your mother never let them stop her, and I definitely know how well they work."

"That sounds exactly like my mother. She was always telling my father that she knew better. She would want you to take whatever you need. But she probably took most of her medicine with her to Anabah."

"Let's see if she left anything."

I follow Bahar into one of the several tiny rooms that long ago were bedrooms for Bahar and Farrakh and their sisters. Now, they house Gulshan's various projects—sewing, weaving, and medicine making. In the medicine room, there are bouquets of herbs hanging overhead to dry. Directly in front of us, there are shelves upon shelves of jars, although not nearly as well stocked as I remember. Obviously, Bahar is right. Her mother has taken a lot with her to the hospital at Anabah. I smile at the thought of her taking on not only the Afghan doctors there but the physicians from around the world who fly in to work for a few months or a year. Gulshan may be barely five feet tall, but she's a powerhouse of a woman and smarter than most people I know.

Bahar picks up a small, squat jar and hands it to me. "Do you know which medicine you need?"

I laugh. "Not a clue! Your mother always told me exactly what I needed."

"Perhaps something to reduce scars?" Sawyer, his voice uncharacteristically shy, stands right behind us, looking on.

I'm not laughing anymore. Taking a deep breath, I turn to Sawyer—the last person to see Mel. "Just how bad are the scars?"

He leans back against the wall and stares past me to the shelves of jars. For some reason, he doesn't seem able to look at me. "When I left, they were still incisions . . . with stitches. But the docs told me she'll have some permanent . . ."

Oh, God. If Sawyer's afraid to tell me, they must be terrible. I clench my hands into fists. "Where?"

"Annie, look, it would probably be better for you to talk to her doctor."

"Sawyer." I'm not cutting him any slack, even though he did fly her all the way to Germany and get her world-class medical care. "Tell me what you know."

"You better tell her." Cerelli's voice from the kitchen. "She's a pit bull."

Sawyer raises both hands in surrender. "Okay. She's got one incision on her left arm running from her shoulder almost to her wrist."

My eyes close involuntarily. And although my knees threaten to buckle, I manage to stay on my feet. "Go on."

"That's the bad one because . . . of . . . the muscle damage. She's got another on her left leg. Just below the hip down to her ankle." I have to hand it to him, he's trying very hard to be clinically objective and give me the facts. But I hear the catch in his voice.

"What do the doctors say?"

"She needs a lot of PT and meds to keep the scars from contracting and, you know, tightening her arm and leg, throwing off her gait."

I take a deep breath as my mental video of Mel dancing the *Attan* flashes in front of me. "How's she doing? I mean *really* doing?"

"It's tough going. But her head's . . . in a good place. Most of the time." Again, the catch in his voice, and I realize that this is likely hitting him as hard as it's hitting me. "She's determined to dance again."

"Then we'll do what we have to do," I say softly, the words more for me than for him. Because I'm thinking of Mel and me.

"We will." Sawyer's 'we' confirms what Cerelli has been intimating. There's most definitely something going on between this man and my daughter. And no matter that this really isn't the time or place to have this discussion, we're going to have it.

I square off in front of him. He finally lifts his eyes from the floor and meets mine. "How old are you?" I don't pull any punches.

"Forty. Does it matter?"

That's just a few years younger than me! And Mel is all of twenty-two. A huge difference. Too huge? They're from totally different generations. With wholly different life experiences. I want to tell him that. To subtly suggest that maybe he should find someone else, someone closer to his age, someone with life experience closer to . . . whatever it is he does here in Afghanistan. But I don't. Because if I've learned anything in the last month, it's that Mel isn't a child anymore. She's making her own decisions, and she doesn't want me interfering. More important, she's fully able to make up her own mind. And if things go sideways, I'll be there to help her pick up the pieces. So, I just say, "No, it doesn't matter."

Turning back to the closet, I twist lids off jars, sniffing each medicine until I find the one Gulshan gave me, the one that worked miracles on my hands. Not a scar to be seen. I take ten jars as well as a few other concoctions, including one I'm pretty sure is to reduce infections. Then, I turn back to the giant of a man standing in front of me. "Where's your backpack?"

He looks puzzled. "Why?"

"I think she'll take these better coming from you."

"You don't know that."

"Yeah, I do."

KNEELING NEXT TO THE vegetable garden in the backyard, I'm harvesting tomatoes and peppers for tomorrow's breakfast. Next to me, Zanna is weeding. More accurately, she's plucking the tops off the weeds. "Bah!" she exclaims, throwing each bit of green behind her. At least she knows the difference between spinach and weeds. Her mother taught her well.

That's when I hear the footsteps along the side of the house, trampling the remnants of dried leaves from last fall. Quickly, too quickly, I'm being sucked into the dark hole of the garden stretching out in front of me. First, the footsteps. In another few seconds, the barrel of a gun will be pressing hard against the side of my head, just above my ear. Then they'll zip-tie my wrists and ankles.

I feel my wrists cross, ready to be tied together.

No! This can't happen. Not with Zanna here. I can't let them take her. The dark earth of the garden yawns wider, pulling me toward it. This time, I fight back. No way am I getting pulled in. Not again.

"Annie? You back here?" Cerelli rounds the corner of the house and stops dead in his tracks. "You okay?"

I take a deep breath and push myself away from the hole. Not perfect. But okay. I put my head down, and the wave passes. Looking up again, I meet Cerelli's eyes. He knows. This was the place. He's worried I've had an attack.

Let the man out of his misery.

"Yeah." I point toward the stump in the middle of the yard. "I was sitting right there when I heard footsteps ... in the dry leaves."

He connects the dots. "Just like now."

I nod. "The trigger. Well, at least one of the triggers. I ... uh ... managed to fight it off. This time."

He comes to stand next to me. "You're getting better at it. That's good."

"I'm working at it."

"I am, too."

I shoot him a quizzical glance.

"Hearing them take you that morning—it was the worst moment of my life."

I push myself to my feet and gather him in my arms. "I'm so sorry. Here I've been thinking of me. Always me. And I forgot we were both here that day."

"We got through it." He presses his lips against mine. A virginal kiss by any measure. Because of Zanna, I bet. "Later," he whispers, "when little ears aren't listening." And then, "You let him off easy."

"What are you talking about?" I arch my back and work my fingers into the ache that's beginning.

"Sawyer was practically quaking in front of you."

"Get real. He can't possibly be afraid of me."

"Every man I know is afraid of you. Sometimes even I am."

I roll my eyes. "Bah!" From the corner of my eye, I see Zanna glance up and smile.

"Bah!" she says as she plucks the top off another weed.

"What did Sawyer think I was going to do?"

"Castration was uppermost on his mind."

"This is a joke, right?"

"Hardly."

"Are you saying I still have a reputation?"

"Sweetheart, you are most definitely now and forevermore a badass legend. Sawyer may come off as fierce, but you've got him beat hands down. I'll have you know, that man's got a very tender heart. I hope Mel's going to be gentle with him."

44

IT'S LATE AFTERNOON, AND we're all gathered in the front lounge, finalizing logistics for tomorrow's departure. A whole lot easier than I expected. A drive up the valley to Anabah where we'll rendezvous with a helicopter to Peshawar. I love it when a plan comes together. Except then, just to complicate things, Farrakh announces that he'll be staying in Anabah. The medical center there needs all the physicians it can get. Bahar adds that she'll be staying there, too, unless things turn dicey. Now I'm getting antsy. What if things do go sideways? Suppose the Taliban defeat Massoud's men and conduct a massive arrest and slaughter—straight up the valley?

I'm ready to argue, but when my eyes meet Cerelli's on the other side of the room, I concede defeat. Raising an eyebrow, he pushes himself to his feet, crosses the room, and lifts the sleeping Zanna from my lap. "Come with me?"

Zanna transferred to a baffled Sawyer, Cerelli pulls me up from the floor cushion.

Not knowing what he's got in mind, I grab my pack.

"You two planning a late night?" Sawyer sounds worried.

Cerelli shrugs. "Not sure."

"If you're not back by the time she wakes up, we're coming after you."

I laugh. "This will be good training for you."

Bahar looks sympathetically at Sawyer. "Oh, Annie, you have no idea. In the car this morning, she cried for you the entire time. It was heartbreaking." I notice she doesn't offer to take charge of Zanna.

Sawyer isn't giving up. "Annie, I swear to you, if she starts in again—"

Cerelli spirits me out the door, into the pickup, and we're on our way.

Where we're going, I'm not quite sure. Until he heads through the village and bears left on the road north. A few minutes later, he turns up the incline on the right to the Wad Qol Secondary School for Girls.

He holds up a large brass key with a rainbow of crocheted yarn streamers hanging from the hole. Evidently, he snagged Gulshan's key. "I thought you'd like to see it. One last time."

The perfect gift. Although I was here for the start of the construction, I've never actually seen the new school finished. I'd always imagined coming back and teaching another photography workshop to a classroom of eager, laughing girls arrayed on benches behind tables. But it never happened. My PTSD and my therapist made sure of that. Cerelli's seen it, though. He and Sawyer regularly couriered in money to support the school.

I wait impatiently on the front stoop, bouncing from one foot to the other, much like Mel did as a child, waiting for him to unlock the mosque-blue door. Once we're inside, he flicks the light switch, but nothing happens. Thanks to the sunlight streaming in through the large windows, though, we find our way down the hall to the first set of classrooms. We step through the open door on the left, and I smile. The room I once shared with Gulshan. In the old school, that is. This new room is so much bigger and brighter than in the pictures and video I've seen. The blackboard is solid—no cracks running from top to bottom. And there are the bookcases from Darya and Tariq's old house, filled to overflowing. Not just with the books we took from Seema's bedroom, but so many more. I'm pretty sure Cerelli is responsible for a lot of them. Like me, he has a thing for making sure girls get an education.

"Your classroom, ma'am."

I spin on my heel, a one-eighty, and face him. "How did you know?"

"Gulshan told me."

"It's wonderful! But . . ."

"But?"

"What's going to happen to it? The Taliban are never going to allow girls to go back to school, certainly not to high school, no matter what they're saying about consulting the *Qur'an*. I really don't want to see that dreadful religion teacher at the boys' school taking over this room."

He shakes his head. "There's nothing we can do about that. But before you write this place off, remember they'll have to contend with Gulshan. One thing I learned long ago: never underestimate a determined woman."

Cerelli shows me the rest of the school. It's a miracle, but very empty. Lifeless. How I wish I could've seen it full of girls and their teachers. Laughing. Teasing. Being brilliant. I should've come back to visit. Made more of an effort to deal with my PTSD so I could teach another workshop. And now? The Afghanistan I knew is gone.

"Come on." Cerelli grabs my hand. "There's something else."

I'm expecting another surprise in the school, but instead, he leads me out the front door and locks up. Then we're back in the pickup, cruising farther north on the dusty, unpaved road. It takes me a minute before I realize where we're going. Darya and Tariq's house. And I'm not at all sure what I think about this.

We're halfway there when I feel the old familiar chill creeping up my spine. So many times that happened when I was walking from the school back to Darya and Tariq's at the end of the day. Although there never was anyone I could see. And everyone, even Cerelli, was pretty dismissive. Paranoia. Then, I remember the puff of dust rising from the side of the road late one afternoon. No breeze. No animals trailing behind me. Nothing to explain that dust.

"You sure there aren't any Taliban in the village?" I ask as nonchalantly as I can.

"Massoud assured me they'd cleared it." He sounds confident. "Why?"

I shake my head. "Nothing. I just felt a bit of a chill. Nothing to write home about."

He studies me, then nods. "As long as you're sure."

I swipe my hand through the air.

"You don't quite have Darya's authority." He laughs.

"Excuse me? I think that was a pretty good effort."

When we pull up and stop in front of the house, I don't move. Just sit and stare. The house looks much the same as it did when I was last here, only more forlorn. Abandoned. The shutters are closed over the front windows—and boarded shut. Weeds are growing up and over the front stoop. A loud metallic creak draws my attention to the gate swinging open to the left of the house. It looks to be drooping off the hinges.

I let out my breath, along with a sigh of disappointment. "So sad."

Cerelli shoulders open the driver's door. "Let's go inside."

"Why are we here?"

"We won't be long. I just want to check a few things—make sure there's nothing here I don't mind the Taliban getting their hands on."

I seriously don't want to go inside. Nothing good can come of it. Years ago, Gulshan and I paid a visit—to see if the school could make use of any of the books Seema left behind. The interior of the house was full of ghosts. Not something I want to experience again, especially with the sun about to set. It's going to be even spookier inside.

But Cerelli isn't having it. He opens my door and takes my hand. "No ghosts. I'll be with you."

He's wrong, though. There are ghosts. Darya's.

The key turns easily in the lock, the front door squeals open, and we're inside. Cerelli's flashlight chases away all the shadows in the front lounge. Amazingly, it's still the same. The rugs and low sofas and floor cushions are all here.

"Let's check Seema's room first." Cerelli leads the way, and I follow close behind.

Her books are gone, of course. So is the bookcase. Gulshan, Ikrom, and I carted everything off to the school. Cerelli carefully checks the drawers in her dresser, running his hand underneath, and even flips up the mattress, which has me perplexed. What's he looking for? He's been here over the years. Does he really think he's going to find something new?

We skip the room I stayed in—everything in it long ago destroyed—and backtrack to Tariq's study. Nothing to find here either. Our last stop: Darya and Tariq's bedroom. He gets to work, rapping his knuckles against the walls, then studying the ceiling.

"What are we looking for?"

"Anyplace Darya could've hidden something."

"Something?"

"Probably a notebook."

"Notebook?"

He groans. "You really are a pit bull. It's a list of other operatives. I know she had it, but I've never found it. Some of those people will be staying in-country. I don't want them in even more danger because their names are on a list I can't find."

"Seriously? You think she would've kept something like that here? Why not at the school? There was a safe."

"It wasn't at the school. At least not in the safe Gulshan turned over to Sawyer."

"Tariq had a safe in his study."

"Which Awalmir managed to get into before he and Seema took off. Tariq told me he only had money and passports in there. Even he didn't know where Darya kept her notebook. I spoke to him a couple weeks ago, and he suggested the bedroom."

Directing his flashlight onto the bed, he runs his fingers along the stitching on the mattress, searching for anything that's just the slightest bit off. "Do you see anything on your side?"

"Nothing." But then my eyes fall on the cedar chest against the wall. A duplicate of mine at home in the Bay View house, only a whole lot fancier. Intricate carvings, while mine is fairly plain. "I take that back. I know where she hid the notebook." At least, I'm pretty sure.

He follows my gaze. "The chest? That's too obvious—especially for Darya. And it's not there. I've searched several times."

Slipping my pack off my shoulder and onto the bed, I offer my most mysterious smile. "Maybe not so obvious. This chest is special."

We cross the room and reach the chest together. The flashlight beam lets me see the gouge marks around the lock—as if someone tried to force it open. Awalmir. Of course. But Darya had it locked. Time was short that day. And the wood held him off.

Running my fingers along the elaborate rim, I find the key taped in place. Threading the key into the lock and turning it three times, I open the lid, then stare down at piles of beautiful clothes. *Shalwar kameezes. Tunbaans.* Headscarves. Darya had the most exquisite taste. Cerelli and I cart armloads to the bed. Farther down, we find some Western clothes, and then her wedding gown. I'm about to add that to the pile on the bed when he stops me to examine the seams and the hem. Nothing. Exactly what I expected. Reaching the bottom, I pull up the paper that years ago Darya cut to size.

"So, that's it then." Cerelli sounds discouraged. "What the hell did she do with the notebook?"

"Not quite." Inching the chest away from the wall, I feel for the button. And, finding it, press it flush to the back panel. "That should do it." Back around to the front, I carefully lift the false bottom out of the chest to reveal the *tunbaan* she wore to my wedding. Nothing in the seams of this dress either. But the heavily embroidered bodice feels just a bit too thick. Darya would never have worn anything this bulky.

"You got your knife?" I ask.

He hands it over, and sitting on the edge of Darya's bed with Cerelli by my side directing the flashlight beam, I carefully cut the stitches. So many stitches. Tiny and fine. I keep snipping until a slender notebook slips out of the pouch Darya fashioned into the dress. No, that can't be right. Darya didn't sew. And definitely not this fine stitchery. Cerelli takes the pages from me while I stare at the dress. Maybe her *Mâdar Kalân* created this sleeve. She'd have been the one to do it. That gives me pause. If her grandmother sewed this for her, did Darya know when she left the U.S. that she was coming here as an operative? She never said. Then again, she never told me anything about her secret life.

"Sweetheart, you're not only beautiful, you're brilliant. You going to tell me how you knew?"

"Simple. I've got a chest just like this at home. Back in the day, we thought it would be a good idea to have the secret compartments—just deep enough to hide something really important, but not too big that anyone would notice."

"What did you hide in yours?"

I smile. "The *tunbaan* I wore at Darya and Tariq's wedding. I wanted to keep it safe from Mel's insatiable ransacking."

He nods toward Darya's dress in my lap. "Is yours as beautiful as this one?"

"Not nearly as elaborate. In fact, mine is totally plain. Not a stitch of embroidery, but the fabric is gorgeous. Dupioni silk, shot through with threads of gold. Part of *Mâdar Kalân's* mother's dowry. Actually, it's a lot like that *shalwar kameez* you gave me. That I never got to wear . . ."

Cerelli puts a hand on my cheek and gently turns my face to his. "I never did get you another." Setting the flashlight aside, he brings his lips to mine.

One brief, sweet kiss and I ease away.

"What's wrong?"

"I've never understood . . . this." I sweep my hand through the darkness around us.

He takes a long moment before speaking—probably to figure out what I'm really asking. "It's a very long, very complicated story."

I ease back a little more. "Then let me make it simpler. How did you find Darya? Of all the women in the world. My best friend. How did that happen?"

Another long pause, then he takes a deep breath. "You gave me her name."

I wasn't expecting this. "Me?"

"During the debriefing on the *Bataan*—"

"Interrogation."

He clasps my hand, twines his fingers around mine. "You demanded your right to an attorney—Darya Faludi." His words are quiet, gentle, probably because he knows full well the volatile impact they'll have.

He's right.

Oh, God, no! I rip my hand from his. "Fuck! You mean all of this, everything that happened, Darya's dying—it's all my fault. If I hadn't—"

He finds my hand, but again I pull away. "No. None of this was your fault. This was on the Taliban. And me. And Darya—"

"Don't!" I'm on my feet, pacing back and forth through the darkness. Every muscle tightening in anger. "Don't you dare blame Darya for one iota of what happened! How could you? My best friend."

He lets me rant and pace and stomp back and forth across the room. Until, very quietly, he says, "She got to me first."

"What?"

"Will you sit with me?"

"Not yet. Tell me first, then maybe."

"During the . . . interrogation . . . you said her name. And honestly, I just filed it away . . . for future consideration. Which happened a lot sooner than I thought. A month later, Darya called me."

"Why?"

"She asked to meet. In fact, she flew down to Virginia."

I take a step closer. "I'm not following."

"She said she'd been visiting you in the hospital."

"The hospital?" But my memory is already surfacing. "Oh, yeah. A few days after I got back to the States after that lovely stay on the *Bataan*, I started feeling sick. Really sick. Todd was convinced it was some horrible disease I'd picked up in the desert and dragged me to the hospital. Many tests later, they diagnosed the flu."

"But Darya said you were there for a while."

"I was." Another step. Close enough that I can feel his body warmth. The man truly is a furnace. "I couldn't stop throwing up. So, they hooked me to an IV to get me hydrated. Stabilized. That's when Darya came to visit."

"And?"

"She wanted to know what happened . . . during the embed. And after."

He gathers me in his arms. "Which, of course, you didn't tell her because I'd warned you not to tell anyone."

"Of course!" Somehow, I manage to sound indignant.

"What did you tell her?" He starts to massage my lower back.

It's my turn to take a deep breath. "That you were a total bastard?"

His fingers don't miss a beat. "So, you're saying you told her my name?"

"Yeah, I did. So, you're saying she contacted you."

"She did."

"But why?" My knees are weakening.

"To be honest, she had this idea about returning to Afghanistan to open a school for girls. She wanted intel on a safe place—because of Seema and Tariq. Even though she was used to dangerous places because of her work with the U.N., her family wasn't. I told her about the Panjshir Valley."

I clamp my hands on his shoulders to steady myself. "A school. Spying. Still not getting the connection."

"We talked about a lot of things. She asked. I answered. Just so you know, even though I was recruiting, I wasn't recruiting *her*. But she was very convincing."

"She always was. Convincing."

"Now, I've got a question for you. Actually, two questions. Maybe three."

"Ask away."

"What are we going to do about Zanna?" His fingers have found a particularly tightly knotted muscle.

"A huge decision. Especially now that I know you were never her guardian, despite what Fatima said to me."

Cerelli exhales heavily. "It's complicated. You and I. Our jobs. It's hard to see how we'd manage. Fatima has family in Iran—"

I shake my head. "She was adamant about Zanna not going to Iran. And I have to say, I agree with her. Zanna would just be subjected to more morality police."

"True. So, if we keep her, then what? A nanny?"

"I guess that's a possibility. We'll definitely need help if we take her. But damn, Cerelli, how can we not? She's a little girl who needs us."

"She does. And it's clear she's becoming more and more attached to us by the day." He continues to dig his fingers into the muscle.

I cut to the chase. "Adoption?"

"This is going to be quite the challenge for the courts. Even with the fake birth certificate, they could well insist on a search for family in Afghanistan. And who knows what the Taliban will say. This would be a lot easier if we were married."

"Is that a question?"

He laughs. "Let me rephrase that. Don't you think it would be a lot easier if we were married?"

"Yes. I do." And I actually moan as his fingers release the knot.

"Did you just moan?" His fingers stop. I wonder if he's going to ask me to clarify the 'yes' I just said. But he doesn't. He's going to take that yes as a yes and run with it. Smart man.

"You said three questions?"

He lifts the hem of my tunic. "Would you mind terribly taking this off? Along with the rest of your clothes?"

"By my count, that makes seven questions."

"Does it now."

THE EXPLOSION IN FRONT of the house stops me from pulling off my tunic. Fuck! Someone else is here. Someone other than our people.

Gun in hand, Cerelli's on the move. I try to pull the Sig out of my waistband, but it's not there. My pack. I put the gun in my pack when we got to the Abdulin house. But where the hell did I put my pack? On the bed! Throwing aside the pile of Darya's clothes, I finally unearth the pack, and then the Sig. And flip the safety off.

By the time I reach the front lounge, gun hidden in the folds of my tunic, pack over my shoulder, I can smell the smoke. And the gasoline fumes, making their way into the house.

Someone's pounding on the door. The shuttered windows. Whoever it is, they aren't politely knocking, they're ramming their gun stocks against the wood. They know we're in here. Of course they do. The white pickup out front was a dead giveaway. This is the Taliban, and they want us.

Is there any possible way Sawyer and the others could have heard the explosion? We're a couple miles from the village, but sound travels. Right? Pulling the sat phone, I press #2.

Sawyer picks right up. "I'm on my way. Ajmal should already be there. What the hell's going on?"

"Armageddon. I think it's the Taliban. Are you okay?"

"Everyone here is good. Can you hold out?"

"I'm not sure how long."

"ETA five minutes."

"Sawyer's on his way," I relay to Cerelli.

"How very unfortunate for you that he won't be in time." The oh-so-cultured voice of the Cambridge Bomber seems to be coming from the dark hallway leading to Seema's room and the bedroom I once stayed in. And oh damn! My call to Sawyer has let him get a bead on me. I can't see shit in the dark and the smoke, but I imagine he's pointing his automatic rifle at me. Maybe he's even smiling—in that cold, detached way he has. "You should have checked the room in back. I've been waiting. And listening to your most intriguing conversation."

My stomach churns. He's been here all this time . . .

"Admiral Cerelli, I must say I am disappointed." His voice sounds a little closer now. "I had heard that you would be a formidable opponent. But that turned out not to be the case. I knew you would come for her—if I played her right. You let your emotions get in the way, and she has been your undoing." He pauses, like he's waiting for Cerelli to say something. "From what I heard just now, Admiral, I believe you have something that would interest me greatly."

The notebook.

So this is how we end.

If I know Cerelli, he'll die before he hands over that notebook. Too many other lives are at risk. He'll never give them up. But there's really no way to protect those names. He refuses to hand them over, he dies, and the Cambridge Bomber takes the list. I wait for Cerelli to say something, but he doesn't. Then, it occurs to me that the dark and the smoke are providing great cover for him. Staying silent means this executioner won't be able to see him. Unless he's wearing night vision goggles.

"Now, Admiral Cerelli, or she dies. And as you both know, I am not a patient man. I plan to be long gone by the time your friends arrive. They will find this house in flames. Just like the school all those years ago." The Cambridge Bomber continues, his voice sounding like he's moved even closer to me. "We tried once before to burn it down. This time we will succeed."

Slowly, slowly the pieces of the puzzle fall into place. "How did you know about the fire in this house?" My voice is far from measured.

"Does it matter? Let us just say I heard about it."

"Not good enough. Who told you?" Damn it, come on! Someone help me here. Cerelli, Sawyer, Fightmaster—move into position. Sawyer, get a drone or an army or something—Massoud's men—here. Now.

"It is nothing short of absurd that you are asking this question seconds before you die."

"I believe it's my choice to decide what to say before I die. Even the Taliban would grant me that." I take a deep breath and go for it. "Omar Mohaqiq told you, didn't he?"

"Omar?" he sneers. "A self-important toady. Yes, he helped us. It was easy for him to get to Pakistan. And he had no qualms about giving up that wretched woman who ran the girls' school. But he had no real power."

I ignore what he said about Darya. "Omar was in Pakistan to meet with Sirajuddin Haqqani."

The Cambridge Bomber seems surprised, but just for a moment. Then, he laughs. "I applaud you, madam. I always thought you were wasted as a photojournalist. You would have done much better as one of the admiral's operatives, not just one of his playthings. He does like to have beautiful women around him. It is too bad that you'll never know what it's like to work for him."

"That's where you're wrong." I raise my gun, but it's way too dark to sight the Cambridge Bomber. And I have no idea where Cerelli is. I'm debating whether to take the shot and risk hitting him when gunfire erupts from the other side of the room. It sounds like it's coming from down the hall, but it's impossible to tell for sure. And all I can do is stand frozen in place. I should throw myself onto the floor. Get out of the line of fire, but I absolutely can't move.

Then, at the front of the house, the incessant ramming against the door and shutters suddenly stops. A second later, another explosion blows out the heavy wooden front door and hurls me across the room, against the lounge wall, into a tangle of wooden frames from which someone has removed the portraits I made of Mel and Seema. For some reason, I find myself clutching the frames—as if they can offer me some protection. Ridiculous, but somehow, they do.

"*MORDA.*" IT SOUNDS LIKE Ajmal, but I'm not sure. My head's spinning, and my ears are ringing.

"Make sure." Cerelli's voice. Not ten seconds later, he's kneeling next to me, gathering me in his arms, against his chest. "Oh, God, I'm sorry. Please tell me you're okay."

At least I think that's what he said. "I'm okay. I think. Can we please get the hell out of here? Out of Wad Qol. Out of Dodge. Can we just go home?"

"First thing tomorrow morning. I promise. Anabah. Peshawar. Landstuhl. Home."

Despite my protest that I can walk, Cerelli carries me down the hall, past the lifeless body of a Taliban militant. He lifts me out the window of my former bedroom, over the top of the mulberry bush the Taliban must have trimmed back, and into the arms of Lieutenant Commander Fightmaster, who's most solicitous. "You all right, ma'am?"

"If you mean can I walk, the answer is yes. So could you please put me down?"

"But ma'am, the admiral—"

"The admiral is being a little overprotective."

He sets me on my feet but insists on walking with me to the pickup that will take us back to Bahar and Farrakh and Zanna. His arm is around my back, ready to support me if I stumble. Probably a wise decision because I've got to get past the fiercely burning front of the house and the truck we drove here in. Not to mention a few other bodies in camo fatigues.

A few minutes later, Cerelli's standing next to me, his arms wrapped tightly around me. "Sweetheart. God, you scared me to death."

A moment later, Sawyer joins us. "Annie, how the hell did you do that?"

"Do what?"

"Keep him talking. You bought us time to get in position. For me to blow the front door. That took a helluva lot more nerve than I've got."

"Yeah, well, I was pretty pissed off." I lean my head against Cerelli's shoulder.

45

EARLY THE NEXT MORNING, two of Massoud's men deliver a white pickup to the Abdulin house. They'll ride in the flatbed, then take the truck back to Wad Qol. We drive through the dark to Anabah, following behind the car with the rest of our crew: Ajmal, Sawyer, and Fightmaster, Farrakh and Bahar.

While Zanna sleeps in my arms, Cerelli fills me in on what happened in the final minutes at Darya's house. "Ajmal followed us to the house, then scouted the outside and found the two-by-fours missing from the bedroom shutters."

"Did he know the Cambridge Bomber was inside?"

"He wasn't sure, but he hid in the back and kept watch. When the Taliban out front blew the truck, he climbed in through the window and immediately ran into a militant in the hall. After that, Fightmaster dealt with the tangos out front, and Sawyer blew the door. I was trying to get into position to take out the Cambridge Bomber. It was Ajmal who got the shot." His hands tighten on the steering wheel.

"What?"

"How the hell did you manage to keep talking? To stall that monster?"

"To be honest . . . I don't know. I just did."

"God, I almost lost you." He reaches for my hand and holds on tight. "I should have checked that fucking room. Every room."

"May I remind you that they got there after we did. Even if you'd checked that room, it would've been empty."

"But if I'd checked, I would've seen that the window was no longer locked on the inside. Inexcusable. My sloppiness almost got you killed. Sweetheart—" He sounds absolutely wretched.

"Hey, I'm alive." I unfurl his fingers and kiss his palm. "And very thankful that you are, too."

He cups his hand behind my neck and shoots me a look that is full of promise for tonight.

Zanna stirs, pillows her head against my other shoulder, then settles into a more comfortable position. We're quiet for a few minutes. No matter that she doesn't understand much English yet, I don't want her hearing any of this. Finally, she starts to snore.

I keep my eyes on Cerelli. "There's something I don't understand. Why was Ajmal there in the first place?"

"He was following us. Well, you."

"But why?"

"He's very protective of you." Cerelli shrugs. "There's most definitely something he's not telling me."

"If you don't tell me, I'll ask him on the helicopter."

"He's not coming with us. He insists on staying in Afghanistan. To be part of the underground. Besides, his wife is here, and she's having a hard time getting a visa."

My heart clenches. "How long can he possibly last?"

"Now that the Cambridge Bomber is dead, he may have a better chance."

Something about the way Cerelli says 'Cambridge Bomber' clues me in. "Are you saying he was one of the men who bought and raped Ajmal as a teen?"

He nods. "And when Ajmal saw how interested he was in you, he appointed himself your bodyguard. He wasn't about to let anything happen to you."

"A brave man." Then, I snort a half laugh. "Although he did cut it awfully close back there."

Zanna wiggles again in my lap. Waking, she takes in Cerelli at the wheel, then leans across as if to climb onto his lap. "Papa!" Or maybe she says *kaka*. My hearing could still be a little wonky.

Smiling, Cerelli strokes her hair. "How's my princess?"

He's a total goner.

46

Northern Virginia – November 2021

STANDING ON THE BACK deck of the remodeled farmhouse Cerelli and I just moved into, I look at the sky. Heavy, steel-gray clouds. And the sharp feel of snow. Which is the last thing I need this weekend: a freak snowstorm. No one else believes it, but I'm from Wisconsin, and we know snow. No matter, I won't be deterred. I've booked a Moroccan bath at *Hammam Fatima* ten miles north of here. Snow or no snow, I'm treating myself in preparation for our wedding tomorrow. I was hoping to make it a major bonding experience with Mel and my various friends. But it's not to be. Mel's doctor wouldn't sign the release—her incisions are healed, but the scars aren't anywhere near ready for vigorous scrubbing. The only other guest to make it so far: Bonita. She drove down earlier in the week and brought Finn along. As for the bath, she made it quite clear that her skin is just fine as it is. All the other guests are flying in later today or tomorrow—if their flights aren't cancelled. This could be the smallest wedding ever. Fingers crossed that the groom makes it out here from the Arlington condo.

I wave at Sawyer pushing Zanna on the swing he hung from the giant oak tree next to the stable. Or what used to be a stable. The previous owner turned it into a guesthouse—current occupant: Mel, who's taken on the job of nanny to Zanna. For now, while she's rehabbing. Eventually, though, she'll get on with her life, which I'm virtually certain will include Sawyer.

Zanna is ours. My heart tightens as I think of what could've happened to her—with no relatives to be found, life in an orphanage and eventually on the streets selling God only knows what to survive. Or if someone had come forward, claiming to be an uncle, she could've ended up sold at a young age to some old geezer as a second, third, or fourth wife. Or had one of her kidneys sold—to raise much-needed money for her adoptive family to survive.

We ended up hiring an adoption attorney in Kabul who presented the birth certificate with Cerelli's name on it to the Afghan—now Taliban—court. Amazingly, they were okay with the daughter of an Iranian mother and an American father going to the U.S. to live. A very good thing since their militants killed her parents. But we still have to go through the adoption process in the court here anyway—so that I can be her legal mother. It will happen. I refuse to let myself think otherwise.

"Mommy!" shrieks Z-Girl when she catches sight of me. Z-Girl—Mel's name for her. "Look at me!" Then to Sawyer, "Higher!"

Finn is totally in his element, barking and running circles around the swinging dynamo. For a few minutes. Then, energy spent, he lies down and watches. Eventually, his graying muzzle comes to rest on his outstretched legs, but he's totally on guard.

The only people allowed near his little girl are family and close friends.

Seeing me, Mel limps slowly across the lawn. My heart cringes at her peculiar gait, her left calf no longer straight below her knee, her left arm half the size of her right, but I smile fiercely. She's alive.

"Hey, Mom. You off?"

"Sure you don't want to come?" Damn. I wish I could take back my words.

"Sorry. Can't." She looks warily at the sky. "When will you be back?"

"Before the snow starts. And in time for our henna appointment. Never fear!"

NAKED, I SLIP INTO THE hot water to soak. My head resting on the inflated pillow, I pick up my glass of perfectly chilled champagne and sip. How I wish Mel were here. And Seema and Bibi and Awa. And especially Dar. She would've loved this. *You're right, my friend. Cerelli and I are a good match. Sometimes a lot of rock and roll, but I know we'll make it.*

I finish off the champagne and raise my glass for another. *Oh, Mom, you should be drinking citrus water. Liquor can be dehydrating, especially when you're taking a bath!* Somewhere along the line, I got a daughter who's super health conscious. Such a drag.

I'm completely mellow by the time the masseuse comes back and helps me onto the heated marble slab. Then, she gets to work, painting on the warm, luscious clay from my neck down my back, all the way to my feet. Mud, really. Rhassoul Mud, exclusively from the Atlas Mountains in Morocco. It's been a while since my last time—

in Pakistan. A really, really deep cleansing. Almost a purification of the skin—inside and out.

Then the scrubbing begins. A full-body exfoliation. And this woman is putting her heart and soul into removing every last dead skin cell from my body. Apparently, I've got a lot of cells that need removing. Somehow, I don't remember my previous visits to *hammams* being quite this, well, invigorating.

I hear an odd whimpering sound. Not the masseuse. Me.

"You will turn over, please," the masseuse orders.

I roll myself onto my back, and she starts applying the mud to my front. Every square inch of my shoulders and chest. Until she gets to my belly.

"Oh, my! You did not say on the form."

I open my eyes. "Excuse me?"

"That you are pregnant."

My eyes widen. "I am *not* pregnant. I can't possibly be. I'm done with my period. I haven't had one in—"

"Three months." The masseuse is adamant. What is she? An obstetrician?

I count back three months. The beginning of August. Glorious, phenomenal sex with Cerelli right before he drove me to the airport—and oh, God, could I really be pregnant? I feel my cheeks heating, reddening.

"Aha! You remember. I need the permission from the boss. One minute. You wait." She opens the door and calls in Fatima herself. And no, the irony that she shares a name with Cerelli's former lover isn't wasted on me.

Fatima doesn't take more than ten seconds to make her pronouncement. "Bah! No question. Look at her breasts. They are already swelling. And see how she is poofing at her middle."

Okay, so maybe my bra has been a little tighter. But my waist definitely isn't 'poofing.' And how the fuck could I have missed all the signs?

"Tell you what," I say, tired of two sets of eyes examining all my lady parts. "Let's just finish this."

"Hmpf!" Fatima runs her eyes over my mudded shoulders and breasts, then across my belly and down my legs. "There is much work needed here."

"Go for it!" I say to the masseuse as Fatima turns on her heel and leaves the room. Meanwhile, I do my best to relax on the marble slab, wondering how I'm going to tell Cerelli about this tadpole that might or might not have taken up residence in me.

If he gets through the snow tomorrow.

IT'S A LITTLE LATER than I expected when I leave the *hammam*, and snow is most definitely falling. And sticking on the ground. Not a lot of accumulation. Yet. But the roads are going to ice up soon. I'm eager to be home.

Nevertheless, I stop at a pharmacy to buy not one, but two pregnancy tests. Which I'll have to smuggle into the house.

When I get home, I sneak into the downstairs master bathroom. Ten seconds of peeing later, a thick line stares back at me. I can't begin to imagine how I'm going to tell Cerelli. For now, I hide the stick in my vanity drawer along with the other test and pray Cerelli doesn't magically appear and decide to snoop.

Anita, the fuchsia-haired *mehndi* tattoo artist, is already here, brushes and henna supplies neatly on display in one of the second-floor guest rooms. She's already at work on Mel, under Bonita's watchful eye.

"Whaddaya think, Mom?" Mel points to her left arm, an elaborate henna vine of flowers climbing the reddish-purple mounded scar that runs from her wrist all the way up to her shoulder.

It's still startling to see the scar in all its presence. "I like it. A lot. Have you thought of another vine on your leg?"

Giggling, Zanna dances in a circle, then reaching down into her imaginary basket, she tosses imaginary rose petals high into the air. The *Attan?* Is this something she remembers from life in Kabul? Or has Mel been teaching her?

"Already done." She pulls up the leg of her baggy pants. "Too much? Do you think Sawyer will be okay with it?"

"It's henna, sweetie. It's not permanent."

Anita glances up. "You do know this drives men wild?"

A smile creeps across Mel's face. "Really? Wait till I show Sawyer. This could be a lot of fun!"

"Mel! Little ears . . ."

"Me, too!" Zanna starts to pull off her long-sleeve T-shirt.

"It is all right for the child?" Anita looks at me.

What can I say? She's a little too young. Then again, this is a special occasion. I nod. "Okay, but keep it small, please? Maybe a paisley on her wrist?"

Twenty minutes later, Anita is finishing up not one, but two tiny paisleys on Zanna's wrists.

"Hey, Z-Girl, that's really pretty!" Mel flashes her a smile from where she's leaning against the wall as her henna finishes drying.

Bonita holds Zanna's hands to keep her still—a nearly impossible task these days. "You know," she says gruffly, "I wouldn't mind having one of those on my wrist."

Before she gets to work on Bonita, Anita points me toward her pattern book, opened on the foot of the bed. "I think this one would look beautiful on you, especially since your dress is so understated." Nice of her not to say 'plain.'

I look at the picture of the elaborately hennaed hands. So many flowers and paisleys. Pretty. And before my visit to the *hammam*, I'd have agreed. But now? "I've got something else in mind. Could we talk? After you're done? Privately?"

Her smile tells me she's intrigued. "Of course!" She pats my forearm, then stops to stroke. "Did you just come from a *hammam*?"

"How did you know?"

"Your skin is beautiful! Like silk. The henna's going to soak right in. And last for weeks. Maybe months."

Downstairs, the back door slams shut. "Annie?" Cerelli's voice. A day early.

"Daddy's here!" An excited Zanna scurries down the stairs to show off her tattoos. "You should see Mommy! Her skin is beautiful."

Bonita, her single tattoo still wet, rushes to block Cerelli from starting up the stairs. "Not yet. Aren't you supposed to wait until tomorrow to see the bride?" She's become a real stickler for traditional wedding rules. Who knew?

I can just imagine his raised eyebrow.

"I'm lucky to get here at all," he protests. "They're predicting more than a foot."

"Bah! You're one groom I've never doubted. You'd have skied cross-country to get here. Have you thought of how you'll get the preacher here?"

"She's right behind me. I'm not taking any chances."

So, he's got a Navy chaplain in tow.

Still leaning against the wall, Mel is finally pronounced dry.

"Mom? You okay on your own? I'd kind of like to show off to Sawyer."

Anita stops her. "First, I'd like to take some pictures, please? For my album."

"Really?" Mel grins, then drops her baggy pants and strikes a dramatic tango pose to show off her arm and leg, cringing as her muscles and skin stretch.

"Go! And could you also start putting out food for everyone? I think I could be here for a while."

Finally, I'm alone with Anita. Only she's not looking at my hands. Her gaze is moving from my belly up to my breasts, then to my face, and back down again. She looks at me expectantly. "So, tell me about your idea."

"Well, I . . . uh . . . just found out today that I may be pregnant."

"*May* be?" She smiles. "You should know, I can sense auras, and yours is definitely pregnant. I'd say about twelve weeks." Her eyes light up. "You're thinking of a tattoo on your belly, aren't you?"

"I saw some on your website when I looked you up. See, the thing is, the groom doesn't know yet."

"Well, then I need to create a masterpiece, don't I." Grinning, she closes her pattern book. "Take off your shirt and pants and lie down."

She gets to work, painting an intricate pattern on my still somewhat flat belly. As in, not really flat at all. It's actually quite a turn-on, all these designs on my body. I hope it is for Cerelli, too.

But . . . oh, God, what if it's not? What if he takes one look at me and decides an admiral shouldn't be marrying a tattooed war photographer?

Hours later, Anita is finishing my belly image, which I can't really see yet, when there's a knock on the door. She stops, brush in midair, and looks at me. "If that's the groom," she whispers, "this isn't ready for him to see yet."

"Annie?" It's most definitely Cerelli. "You okay in there?"

"I'll be a while yet."

"Can I just give this to you?"

Anita opens the door, just a crack, takes the package from him, then brings it over to me. "You're still wet. Should I open this for you?"

I recognize the white paper and string. From Armen's *burqa* shop, I'm sure. "Thanks, but I'll wait. This is personal."

"Ah!" She grins. "Let me finish this up quick so you can dry. I can hurry things along if you'd like." She holds up the hairdryer. "I'm thinking you might like to get down to your party. Definitely down to that groom of yours. He looks . . . eager."

"That would be good."

An hour and some serious hairdryer action later, she leads me to stand in front of the cheval mirror. She's painted a rose around my navel with more flowers extending beyond. A full bouquet, each flower surrounded by crescent moons and stars. Hundreds of them.

I'm speechless. It's gorgeous. The design isn't huge, but then neither am I. Yet.

Yet? What the hell am I thinking? How can a baby possibly fit in our lives? We've already got Zanna, who takes every ounce of attention that Mel and Sawyer, Cerelli and I can muster. And then there are our jobs. And now, a baby? This is seriously not going to work.

Anita's still studying my belly. "I need to add one last crescent moon. Just stand still." A few strokes later, she smiles. "Done! Oh, and that little girl you're carrying is giving off a lot of energy. And I mean a *lot*."

"A girl?"

"Yeah, I'm pretty sure it's a girl," she says with such conviction that I think the bold line might not be a false positive after all.

AFTER ANITA LEAVES, waving off my concern about the roads, I unwrap Cerelli's gift, peeling back the white paper to reveal a gold and copper *shalwar kameez*. Not an exact duplicate of the one he bought me all those years ago, the one that Awalmir shredded, but just as beautiful. No, this one is even more beautiful. The colors so much more complex. And on the inside of the paper, he's scrawled the very first *landay* he wrote me.

May you be jasmine flowering by the side of the river.
I will quench my thirst and breathe your scent.

Making sure my henna tattoo is completely dry, I pull on the loose silk pants and tunic. Heaven next to my skin. Then I open the door.

Descending the stairs, I don't hear a thing. On the first floor, all is quiet. Making my way into the kitchen, I find the food packaged and returned to the fridge. But not a single person. Until I turn around. Cerelli is standing in the back doorway, covered in snow.

"Finally." He does sound eager.

"You're not supposed to see me until tomorrow."

"If I didn't come tonight, there was a good chance I wouldn't get here at all."

"That bad, huh?"

"It will be, although your tattooist should be okay. I dug out her Jeep for her. Four-wheel drive. She promised to text when she gets home."

"So, where is everybody?"

"You've been up there for hours. Bonita took Z-Girl up to bed. Sawyer and Mel went back to the guesthouse. The chaplain, I'm happy to say, has retired for the night."

"You mean it's just us? And me in this beautiful *shalwar kameez*." I take a spin around the kitchen. "Thank you."

"I've had it for a while now . . . saving it for tomorrow night." His delicious half grin makes me go weak in the knees. "But tonight is just as good."

I catch him looking at my henna-free hands. Is that disappointment I see flitting across his face?

"Unless you're serious about me not seeing you?" He brushes snow off his shoulders onto the floor and toes off his boots. He nods toward my gold silk *tunbaan*—the one I wore for Darya and Tariq's wedding—hanging on a coat hook by the back door in its plastic dry cleaner bag. Right next to his dress whites. Neither one of us manages to get stuff past the drop zone. "It's a beautiful dress, by the way. I guess I'm not supposed to see that till tomorrow either."

"I want to make sure Darya's here."

"She is."

I smile my best Mona Lisa smile, crook my finger, and head toward our bedroom. "I've got something else to show you."

I TAKE A MOMENT to retrieve the pregnancy test stick from the bathroom and slide it into my pants pocket. Then, standing in the doorway, I lock eyes with him sprawled across the king-size bed.

"Beautiful." He breathes the word.

I slowly cross the room. "There's something you need to see." Please let him like this.

"Is there now."

"Oh, yeah." I'm going for sexy and sultry, but what I really sound like is nervous with a big helping of scared. From the look on his face, he hears it, too.

He reaches for my hands, kisses my palms, and pulls me onto the bed with him. I know he's worried I'm having second thoughts. Maybe even third thoughts.

"Show me."

But I don't know what to say. Instead, I roll onto my back, untie the cord of my pants, and slide them down to my hips. Cerelli props himself up on his elbow and watches, eyes smiling. Maybe 'smoldering' is more accurate. But I also see the hint of wariness that's lurking. Keeping my eyes locked on his, I slowly inch the tunic up my torso, the fabric whispering against my skin.

And reveal the bouquet of flowers on my belly.

One look at his raised eyebrow tells me Cerelli knows exactly what my body has to say. "When?"

"I have no idea. April maybe? I thought I was menopausal. My last period was months ago. But the women at the *hammam* today were so sure."

"They would know."

I snort out a nervous laugh. "You have more faith than me. I stopped on the way home and bought a test kit." I dig the plastic stick out of my pocket and show it to him. Positive bold line side up.

His eyes meet mine. "Urine doesn't lie. But . . . how do you feel about this? It could change things. Not between us, but your job . . . at least for a while."

A really good question. But I don't have a definite answer. "Maybe a change is a good thing. For a while. A year or two. I could try that new therapy Sam is after me about."

"That would be good. Are you sure?"

"I'm not sure about anything. All this just landed in my lap. We need to talk it through, but I think this tadpole deserves a chance."

He's quiet for a moment, his index finger tracing one of the elaborately decorated moons on my abdomen. Then he smiles. "She's a girl, isn't she." It's not a question.

But I answer anyway with a slight roll of the eyes. "That's what Anita said, the tattoo artist. Apparently, she could see my aura and feel the energy. But *three* daughters?"

He leans over me, now tracing the outline of the entire mandala.

"Daughters born under stars and crescent moons
More precious than gold or rubies from Afghanistan."

"Oh, God, Cerelli, I love it. But by my count, there's one too many syllables."

"You got me."

Glossary

There are two official languages in Afghanistan: Dari (often referred to as Afghan Persian), spoken by 77% of Afghans in the west, north, and northeast of the country; and Pashto, spoken by 48% of the populace, mainly in the southeast. There are more than forty additional minor languages and many dialects. Dari is written in the Persian form of Arabic script; Pashto is a modified form of Arabic script. As a result, the Dari and Pashto words included in *The Rule of Thirds* are transliterated into English script based on Nicholas Awde's *Dari Dictionary & Phrasebook*, Nicholas Awde and Asmatullah Sarwan's *Pashto Dictionary & Phrasebook*, and *Dari/Pashto Phrasebook for Military Personnel*, compiled by Robert F. Powers, (Dari Editor) Edris Nawin, and (Pashto Editor) Subhan Fakhrizada. Many words have multiple variations in spelling in English. Most words and phrases are translated within the story or their meaning is made obvious in the context.

Abaya – A simple, loose overgarment, essentially a robe-like dress, caftan, or coat that covers the whole body except the head, feet, and hands. Usually worn with a *hijab*.

Adhan – The Muslim call to ritual prayer, typically made by a *mu'adhdhin* from the minaret of a mosque.

Alhamdulillah – "All praise and thanks to God."

Anaa – Grandmother

Asr – The midafternoon obligatory prayer

Assalâmu alaykum. Wa 'alaykum assalâm. – "Peace be unto you." "To you peace." This is a Muslim greeting with many variations in spelling.

Attan – Originally a Pashtun folk dance performed in times of war or at engagement announcements, now considered a national dance.

Bacha bazi (Persian) – "Dancing boys"; a slang term used for an Afghan custom of often powerful men sexually enslaving adolescent and younger boys. Although outlawed in the post-Taliban years, it is still practiced in certain regions of Afghanistan.

Balê (Dari) – Yes

Bâmân-e khodâ! (Dari) – Goodbye!, to which the response is *Khodâ hâfiz!*

Basteh (Dari) – Closed

Bolani (Dari) – Flatbread stuffed with various fillings, then pan-fried golden-brown and crisp

Borani banjân – Sliced, sautéed eggplant served with garlic yogurt sauce

Burqa – A long, loose garment covering the body from head to feet, concealing even the eyes and hands, worn by many Afghani Muslim women in public. Wearing a *burqa* is cultural and is not required by Islam. Some Muslim women see the wearing of the *burqa* as a way to show modesty. Others see it as a mandate by Taliban men to oppress women.

Dôst dâram (Dari) – I love you (in a romantic way)

Dresh! (Pashto) – Stop!

Estâd shaw! (Dari) – Stop!

Fajr (Arabic) – First prayer of the day

Gandana (Dari) – A type of leek found in Afghanistan used to stuff *bolani,* among other things

Hama (Ama) – Aunt (father's sister); in Dari, Pashto, and Arabic,
    there are different words to specify how an aunt or uncle is
    related to an individual—for example, father's sister as opposed
    to mother's sister
Hammam (Arabic, Dari) – Turkish bath; public bath
Hijab – A headcover worn in public by many Muslim women
Inshallah – "If Allah wills it."
Kabuli palaw – A lamb and rice dish for special occasions
Kaka (Dari) – Uncle
Kebabeh degee morgh (Dari) – Spiced chicken kebab
Keffiyeh – A Bedouin Arab's kerchief, worn by men as a headdress
    and popular among Western journalists and photographers in
    the Middle East
Khetayee (Dari) – Traditional cookies made during Eid celebrations
    in Afghanistan
Khodâ hâfiz – "God protect you." Literally: "May God be your
    guardian." A common way to say goodbye.
Khub astom, tashakor. (Dari) – I am well, thank you.
Kofta (Dari) – Meatballs
Kulcheh chaarmaghzi (Dari) – Fragrant and sweet crumbly cookies
    (usually made for Eid)
Landay – A two-line poem with twenty-two syllables, traditionally
    composed and sung by   Pashtun women
Lotfan (Dari) – Please
Mâdar Kalân (Dari; var. *Mâdar-bozorg*) – Grandmother
Maghrib – The sunset obligatory prayer
Mashallah – "What Allah has willed." Used to express appreciation,
    joy, praise, thankfulness.
Masjed (Arabic) – Mosque
Morda (Dari) – Dead

Morgh kofta (Dari) – Ground chicken, spiced, and used as a stuffing for *bolani*

Mu'adhdhin (var. *Muezzin*) – The Muslim official who summons the faithful to prayer five times a day

Na (Pashto) – No

Nâm-e shomâ chist? (Dari) – What is your name?

Nâm-e man Annie ast. (Dari) – My name is Annie.

Ne (Dari) – No

Nân (Dari) – Bread

Nyaw aw Badal (Pashto) – Justice and revenge (part of the Pashtunwali Code)

Pakol – Soft, round-topped cloth hat worn by Pashtun, Tajik, and Nuristani men

Piala (Dari) – Small bowl used for drinking tea

Roat (var. *roht*) (Dari) – Sweet bread

Sabzi (Dari) – Spinach

Salaateh Afghani (Dari) – Afghan salad of greens, tomato, cucumber, and radish

Salâm! Che hâl dared? (var. *Hâl-e shoma chetor ast?*) (Dari) – Hello! How are you?

Salah – Islamic mandatory prayers performed five times daily, facing the direction of Mecca

Shahada (Arabic) – An Islamic oath and creed, and one of the Five Pillars of Islam and part of the *adhan*. It reads: "I bear witness that there is no deity but God, and I bear witness that Muhammad is the Messenger of God." Written in black, this is on the Taliban's white flag.

Shalwar kameez – Traditional trouser loose at the waist and narrowing to a cuff at the ankle, worn with a long shirt or tunic by both women and men

Shohna ba shohna (Dari) – Shoulder to shoulder, as soldiers stand
    next to each other

Sobh ba khaye! (Dari) – Good morning!

Stä yur (Pashto) – Your daughter

Taqiyah (Arabic) – Muslim skullcap for men

Tashakor (Dari) – Thank you

Tunbaan – A traditional Afghan tribal dress, also known as a
    Kuchi tribal dress

Zhornâlist (Dari) – Journalist

Author's Note

On Sunday, August 15, 2021, Kabul fell to the Taliban with little to no resistance. That day, government leaders ostensibly went to lunch, but instead of eating, they boarded helicopters and fled the country. The lack of resistance was due in large measure to the many Taliban who for years had been working undercover, clean-shaven and in Western clothing, at all levels of the government, the military, and the police force as well as in civilian jobs.

The fleeing government leaders left behind a populace terrified of what life would be like under Taliban rule. Would women once again have to give up their jobs and stay home? Would girls again be prevented from attending school and university? Would women be forced to wear the *burqa*? Although the Taliban promised to be judicious in making all these decisions, the answer to each of these questions has been yes. Few unmarried women and teenage girls, however, had known to fear the "marriage markets" in which they were sold or given to Taliban militants as they swept through towns and villages across the country.

The men and women who had worked for the Afghan government and the national police, the media and in education feared for their lives. For good reason. And in the days that followed, desperate Afghans swarmed Kabul, thinking they'd find greater safety and perhaps anonymity in the city. They also camped out at the Hamid Karzai International Airport, hoping to somehow secure seats on planes leaving the country. To Qatar. To Germany.

To the U.S. Perhaps those most in need of plane tickets and visas were the many Afghans who had worked for the coalition forces and the media as translators. But for many, those exit documents didn't come.

The main characters in *The Rule of Thirds* are strictly fictional. Several secondary characters, however, are based on real people: General Mirzakwal, minister of the interior of the outgoing Afghan government and Sirajuddin (Siraj) Haqqani, deputy head of the Taliban and minister of the interior. Annie's interactions with them are based on televised interviews they gave and on my imagination.

A word about the *bacha bazi* boys: It had long been the practice in Afghanistan that adolescent and young boys often from poor families were made to dress up as "girls," rim their eyes in kohl, and dance to entertain adult men, many of whom professed their beliefs in the Taliban cause. Although homosexuality was strictly forbidden and punishable by death under the Taliban's first rule in the 1990s and early 2000s, involvement with the *bacha bazi* boys was not often prosecuted. At least, the very important people who indulged in what was nothing short of sexual abuse and often rape weren't arrested. Sometimes the boys themselves were. Although this practice was eventually outlawed in 2003, it continues in various parts of the country to this day. In *The Rule of Thirds*, Ajmal, the "fixer" of Annie's crew, was once a *bacha bazi* boy. His empowerment during the course of the story speaks to the courage and resilience of the boys, now young men, who suffered severely from this abuse.

War photographers and journalists are often the unsung heroes in armed conflicts. They put their lives on the line every single day to find the story and tell it to the rest of the world. Far too many of them end up giving their lives. To honor these brave men and women, I named the fictional Afghan members of Annie and Nic's TNN crew for three of them: Ajmal, Azizullah, and Sadim.

February 7, 2023

Photo © Agnieszka Tropiło

A former English professor at Rochester Institute of Technology, Jeannée Sacken is now a photojournalist who travels the world, documenting the lives of women and children. She also photographs wildlife and is deeply committed to the conservation of endangered species. When not traveling, she lives with her husband and three cats in Shorewood, Wisconsin, where she's hard at work on her next novel. Follow Jeannée at jeanneesacken.com.

CPSIA information can be obtained
at www.ICGtesting.com
Printed in the USA
JSHW011541090723
44419JS00003B/11